"The stakes have never been higher, and the excitement and tension are palpable in this installment of Banks' complex, sexy series."
—*Booklist*

"Duties, pain, responsibilities—what this duo does in the name of love is amazing."
—*Romantic Times BOOKreviews*

THE HUNTED

"A terrifying roller-coaster ride of a book."   —Charlaine Harris

"Hip, fresh, and fantastic."
—Sherrilyn Kenyon,
New York Times bestselling author of *Dark Side of the Moon*

THE AWAKENING

"An intriguing portrait of vampiric society, reminiscent of Anne Rice and Laurell K. Hamilton."
—*Library Journal*

"Again, Banks brilliantly combines spirituality, vampires, and demons (and hip-hop music) into a fast-paced tale that is sure to leave fans of her first novel, *Minion*, panting for more."
—*Columbus Dispatch*

MINION

"*[Minion]* literally rocks the reader into the action-packed underworld power struggle between vampire rivals with a little demon juice thrown in. Cutting-edge wit and plenty of urban heat flies from the pages of this quick read."
—*Philadelphia Sunday Sun*

"[A] tough, sexy new vampire huntress challenges the dominance of Anita Blake and Buffy . . . Damali is an appealing heroine, the concept is intriguing, and the series promising."
—Amazon.com

ALSO BY L. A. BANKS

NOVELS

The Darkness
The Cursed
The Wicked
The Damned
The Forsaken
The Forbidden
The Bitten
The Hunted
The Awakening
Minion

ANTHOLOGIES

Stroke of Midnight
Love at First Bite
My Big Fat Supernatural Wedding

BAD BLOOD

A Crimson Moon Novel

L. A. BANKS

St. Martin's Paperbacks

This is a work of fiction. All of the characters, organizations and events portrayed in this novel are either products of the author's imagination or are used fictitiously.

BAD BLOOD

Copyright © 2008 by Leslie Esdaile Banks.
Excerpt from *Bite the Bullet* copyright © 2008 by Leslie Esdaile Banks.
Excerpt from *The Shadows* copyright © 2008 by Leslie Esdaile Banks.

Cover photo of woman © Barry David Marcus. Cover photo of background image © Jupiter Images.

ISBN: 0-312-94911-1
EAN: 978-0-312-94911-2

Printed in the United States of America

St. Martin's Paperbacks edition / April 2008

St. Martin's Paperbacks are published by St. Martin's Press, 175 Fifth Avenue, New York, NY 10010.

10 9 8 7 6 5 4 3 2 1

DEDICATION

Sometimes the road less traveled, and oft times the one that leads toward truth, is paved with blood and gore . . . this is for all those who have made the ultimate sacrifice to stand against injustice, those who rally against human suffering, those who shout "Stop the violence," those who fight for freedom, those who warn us of environmental arrogance, those who actively protest that which is wrong, the ones who've taken a bullet . . . the fallen, the wounded, the unfairly incarcerated, the courageous, the protectors of the innocent . . . this story is for anyone who wittingly and unwittingly went where angels fear to tread, but who had honorable intent pulsing within them like their very heartbeat. All I can say is *thank you.*

ACKNOWLEDGMENTS

As only my editor, Monique Patterson, and my agent, Manie Barron, can do with such aplomb—those two have once again put their heads together to come up with another colossal project: Thank You! I also want to thank the St. Martin's "dream team," the folks who work behind the scenes to make everything go off without a hitch: Kia, Colleen, Harriet, Michael, and company . . . Big Philly Hug! I also want to extend my deepest thanks for the wonderful support of Walt Stone at Dream Forge Media, for yet another awesome website. Plus, where would this be without the warm and wonderful support of my sister-authors? Bless you ladies for reading multiple versions of this tale and being so generous with your blurbs! Thank you for the love. And to the VHL Street Team members, who have already preordered this book, LOL—I LOVE YOU!

PROLOGUE

Denver, Colorado . . .

"DOOR'S OPEN!" SASHA yelled without even looking up, as she clutched the confusing set of directions in her hand and stared at the mess of parts on her living room floor.

She knew it was her guys; the thudding footfalls and loud banter between them were always a dead giveaway. In a second they'd both come tumbling through the door like a pair of wolf pups—Woods with his cocky sex-machine grin and Fisher with his baby face.

When the door banged open, Sasha looked up and couldn't remain peeved even if she'd wanted to. Those two were lovable polar opposites. All she could do was smile.

Fish was a tall, lanky, Kentucky-bred blond with the bluest, kindest eyes in the whole world. She was older than him by two years and she thought of him as the younger brother she had never had. But in a fight, Fisher was fierce and played for keeps. A good man to have at your back when something otherworldly was closing in.

"I smell pizza," Woods said, heading for the kitchen without a hello. He gave Sasha a dashing smile as he passed her. "Beer, I'm oh so sure, is in the fridge, right?"

He looked over his shoulder, waggled his eyebrows, and blew her a kiss. "We've got dibs on the TV, since you're making us work during prime time."

"Save it for the ladies at the bar," Sasha said, teasing him, but secretly glad that he'd decided to hang out for the duration of a game. If Woodsy stayed that meant Fisher would stay . . . and she was sure that on a Saturday night Woods had plenty of other places he could be.

Woods was typically handsome with brown hair, dark eyes, broad shoulders, and a muscular build. He cleaned up real nice when he put on his military blues. She knew that he had had more than his share of willing females back in West Virginia. Hell, he had more than his fair share scattered all over Denver.

"Okay, so tell me again why a Marine Corps–bred, Delta One, highly trained, superintelligent chick from the PCU needs all her pack members to put together her Ikea bookshelf and entertainment center on a *Saturday night*?" Woods said as he came out of the kitchen toting two beers in one hand while chomping on a slice of pepperoni and sausage pizza with the other.

"Because I want this done before we have to move out again. I hate leaving things unfinished," she argued.

"You've got OCD, Trudeau," Woods said. "You know that, right? It's a sickness, this everything-in-its-place-before-you-deploy superstition thing you've got going on!"

"Well, if you guys can't handle the directions, that's all you had to say." Sasha jumped to her feet and headed to the kitchen to get herself a slice of pizza.

"You hear a challenge, Fish?" Woods beamed at Fisher and handed off one of the beers to him.

"The Paranormal Containment Unit not only hears but accepts the challenge," Fisher said, laughing as he saluted the lieutenant and then howled, causing Woods to join in.

"I also don't know why the pack's beta needs an assist,

but as long as there's brewskis, who's arguing?" Woods said.

A snappy comeback escaped her; so instead, she bit into a slice of pizza and rolled her eyes at Fisher to make him laugh again. In truth, she could have put the furniture together herself and carried the freaking wall unit across the room, if necessary, but that wasn't the issue. Worry nagged her gut, and before they each received a new deployment assignment, she wanted to hang out with them a little bit. Then there was the not so small reality that when it came to putting together inexpensive but fashionable furniture, misery loved company. Especially on a Saturday night. Yeah, okay, so maybe she also needed to get a life.

"Because it's a conspiracy," Sasha finally said, ignoring the jubilant banter coming from Woods and Fisher, who had long since found more beer in her fridge. "There *is no* L-wrench, and I swear they have fifteen different-sized screws that all look the same *just* to piss you off!" She looked down at the piles of nuts, bolts, screws, and washers on the floor at her feet and practically growled.

Her two pack mates smirked and clinked their bottles of beer together. Fisher had jammed so much pizza into his mouth that his cheeks bulged like a squirrel's.

Suddenly there was a low rumble of laughter and Sasha turned to see Rod Butler walking into her apartment. Their fearless leader had arrived. Rod was the pack's alpha and it was easy to see why. He was tall, at least six two, broad shouldered with a tightly corded body, and when he moved his power rolled off him, dominating everyone around him. He had startlingly green eyes and red hair that spoke of his Irish ancestry. He wasn't typically handsome, but he exuded sex appeal even when he wasn't trying.

Rod stood in the doorway chuckling low in his throat

and shook his head as he shed his bomber jacket. "Trudeau, you *know* I'm never gonna let this incident go, right? I'll be razzing you until that gorgeous black hair of yours goes stone gray."

Sasha flipped him the bird and then slapped the instructions against Rod's stone-cut chest, completely annoyed by the merry twinkle in his eyes and the way his handsome mouth offered her a lopsided grin. The backhanded compliment was slightly out of place for their normal siblinglike banter. She wanted to yank a handful of his hair as she passed him, but thought better of it.

Theirs had always been a big brother! little sister, mentor! protégée relationship but lately Rod seemed interested in something else that she wouldn't even acknowledge. It was a dangerous thing in a squad, especially within a small tactical unit like theirs. It was best to keep it light, neutral, and totally platonic. She snatched more instruction sheets off the floor, ignoring the jubilant comments coming from the other guys . . . ignoring the way Rod's eyes followed her body as she bent and remained on her ass until her face burned.

"Lemme see that," Rod said, walking over to her and grabbing the crumpled directions from her. "If you just—"

"Watch it, Cap. We just got here and she's already driving us crazy, and as you can see from the leaning tower of pizza," Woods said, guzzling a Budweiser, and then using his bottle to indicate the botched wall-unit attempt, "she might take a swing at you."

"Ohmigod. You did *not* say 'leaning tower of pizza.'" Sasha closed her eyes and slapped her forehead as Woods made a Frisbee of the huge box and sent it into Rod's grasp. "That's *Pisa,* and hey, watch the rug!"

"My bad," Fisher said, laughing and dabbing the rug with his T-shirt as the beer he'd just opened foamed over onto it. "But, hey, we don't read all that fancy stuff, like you, Trudeau. You're the diplomat—me and Woodsy just follow orders and blow shit up."

"Chivalry is dead," Woods mumbled over a mouthful of pepperoni and sausage pizza. "I think we blew that sucker up, too, on the last mission, right, Fish? Glad we've got a couple of weeks before we have to roll out again."

Fisher raised his bottle and saluted the lieutenant with a grin.

Rod opened the pizza box, wolfing down a slice as he leaned against the wall. "So you mean to tell me that between the three of you, you guys couldn't match up widget A with screw B and put together this furniture? Remind me of that when they send us out on another explosives detail."

"Oh, so now the man has jokes," Fisher said, mischief causing his blue eyes to light with the excitement of a challenge. "I can hot-wire anything. But I don't do furniture. Too domestic. C-4 and cell phones, I'm much better with. Fifty bucks says there's pieces missing." He dragged his fingers through his blond spikes and forced his wiry frame up off the floor in one fluid sit-up, beaming at Rod.

"Aw, here we go . . ." Woods moaned. True pity shimmered in his eyes.

"You always get your ass kicked in poker, Fish—when are you gonna learn? Don't bet Fearless Leader, man."

Sasha began banging her head against the wall when Rod got *the look*. Anybody who knew Captain Rod Butler knew when he got that hungry look they'd all be in for a long night of unrelenting challenge. Once Rod got hold of something, he couldn't let it go. "Please, anybody, somebody, put the frickin' wall unit and bookcase together, that's all a woman asks. I fed you. I bought you beer."

"Under control," Rod said, giving her a look that not

only sent a mild tremor through her, but that made her nervous. He'd never looked at her like that. There was nothing brotherly or platonic about it.

"Let a real professional go to work," Woods said. "Don't you just love *the alpha challenge*?"

Moonlight sent a wide swath of light through her apartment. Music blared heavy percussion through her Bose system. But every time she glanced up, Rod's line of vision hunted hers, cornered it, and made her fidget and look away. It was unnerving to have the dynamic of their relationship change so suddenly.

To avoid any catastrophic eye contact, she skirted the edge of the threesome who were now on the floor on their hands and knees sorting parts again, working as a team, and mercilessly ribbing each other. The specifics of their banter became muddied, the sound of their voices distant as she watched Rod glance at her, then look out the window at the luminous disk that seemed to mesmerize him long enough to stop time. Worry formed small beads of perspiration on her forehead. Rod needed his meds. Something was wrong. Maybe she needed hers, too.

"Trudeau is on a mission, Cap—so don't blame me," Woods said, guzzling beer. "Ask *her* why this had to be done tonight."

"Speaking of mission, I've gotten our orders."

Everyone looked to Rod.

"Woods, Fisher, and I will be shipping out to Nicaragua in two days. Gonzalez, Johnson, and Sherwin will also be a part of the team. Trudeau isn't on this deploy. Specifics about our assignment will be handed down when we report to base tomorrow at six hundred hours."

"It's going to be a full moon in two days," Sasha said, surprised. They'd always monitored them, had them hooked up to machines, testing them during a full moon. And after the tests were the hard training missions, but never too far from a base in an isolated environment. Worse yet, the team was being split up—she wasn't being given orders to move out with them. Scrambling for words, she tried to keep anxiety out of her tone. "So now they're sending us in different directions on a full moon? What gives?"

"It will be the first of many," Rod said. "I guess they finally think we can handle it." His tone sounded a little bitter. Rod had never been too cool about having his leash yanked whenever the brass felt it was necessary. "Besides," he told Sasha with a slight smile, "*you* can handle it, right?"

You're pathetic, she told herself when her face heated.

To distract herself, Sasha put her hands on her hips and replied, keeping her tone cocky to disguise her concerns. "Well, then you'd better get to work because there's no way I'm coming back from my mission to this mess."

Rod gave her another sexy smile and saluted. "You heard the lady. Let's do the damn thing, gentlemen."

The guys got down on their hands and knees and started sorting parts again.

"Anybody else want another beer?" she called out, heading back toward the kitchen.

"Make it three," Woods called out behind her.

"Roger that," Fisher said, swearing as a small nut rolled under the couch.

"Goddamn it, Fisher!" Rod boomed. Everyone froze. "That's why we can't put this fucking thing together!"

Rod was on his feet in an instant. He'd leaped back from a crouched position to a full upright stand so quickly that Sasha gaped with the refrigerator door still wide open. No one spoke; all eyes were on Butler as rage consumed him. "If you keep throwing parts under furniture, then how the hell do you expect the parts to match what's on the instruction sheets?"

Horrified, Sasha watched Rod flip her sofa over with a crashing bang to fetch the lost nut. Eerie silence filled the apartment; the blaring music was merely background noise that now seemed so very far away.

"Rod," Sasha said as calmly as she could, easing closer to him. "When's the last time you took your meds?" Her heart was slamming inside her chest. She wiped her moist palms on her back jeans pockets. Her sidearm was in the bedroom; her soul wasn't prepared for war in her own home. Her mind shrieked a prayer: *let the meds work.*

"I don't need to take my fucking meds; I need to put this goddamned wall unit together!" Rod shouted, high color now staining his ruddy cheeks.

"I have a supply in the fridge," she said in a flat statement of fact, coming to Rod slowly as Woods and Fisher slowly backed away from him. "We all have to take our meds. We've all been infected. It's policy."

"Forget about the bet, dude," Fisher said nervously. "It's cool."

"No, it's not cool!" Rod shouted, now beginning to pace. Sweat had begun to form on his brow. "We made a bet, now let's do the bullshit. Somebody open a fucking window, would ya? And to hell with a virus! I don't need meds. I'm all right."

Sasha swept up her goldfish bowl before Fred the fish became a casualty when Rod punched the wall near him. Two seconds too late and poor Fred would have been collateral damage.

"Open a window, Woods," Sasha said quickly, instructing the paralyzed lieutenant. Her nerves were drawn so taut that she moved in jerky, robotic strides for a few seconds.

As Rod rubbed the back of his neck and closed his eyes, her muscles remembered how to move and they propelled her forward to race toward the kitchen where she set Fred's bowl down on the counter hard, sloshing some of his water out of it. Trying to steady her hands, she retrieved a black medical case that had prefilled hypodermic needles in it. One eye was on the needle that she held up to the light and tapped to be sure no air bubbles were in it before she expressed some of the needle's contents into the sink, the other eye was on Woods standing dangerously close to an open window and near a man in potential transformation crisis.

Rod's olive T-shirt now had a dark V of perspiration, making it cling to the hard ridge of his back, and he held on to either side of the window frame, breathing in deeply, his eyes closed, his face bathed by moonlight.

"I'm sorry, Fish," Rod said after a moment. "You know how I hate for anything to beat me—so I owe you fifty bucks."

"Like I said, it's cool, dude," Fisher replied quietly, his eyes pained. His expression told them that he knew the last thing Rod was talking about was allowing the Ikea furniture challenge to beat him. It was the thing that they all secretly carried in their veins. The thing that bound them as a small family and made them The Wolf Pack—the virus they shared.

Sasha went to their commanding officer, their brother, the one they all looked up to, and allowed her fingers to play against Rod's elbow, warning him before she swabbed the inside of his arm with a cold, alcohol-soaked cotton ball and then quickly stabbed him with the needle. In his frame of mind he could flip into a rage, but instead he stared at her with a mixture of shame, personally directed anger, futility, and that thing they didn't speak of. She knew it had to be the moon; there was no other explanation that her mind would accept right now.

"It's never been this bad before," he admitted quietly. "Sorry about the couch . . . and the wall."

She looked down at his arm and covered the tip of the needle with cotton before extracting it, and then made him bend his arm. "It's all right. No harm, no foul."

The look again . . . It hung between them like a heavy, thick blanket.

"Moratorium on beer for one hour," Woods said, trying to find a better place to set the blame. No one wanted to talk about the virus or their own human mortality. "We'll master this, not to worry, Trudeau. Hey, how many were-wolves does it take to screw in a wall-unit shelf anyway?"

"The moon fucks me up lately . . . even when it's just waxing toward full," Rod said, shame singeing his voice as he stalked away from her toward the abandoned furniture.

Only then, once Rod Butler was farther away from her, could she breathe.

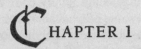

CHAPTER 1

North Korea . . . four months later

HARD, COLD GROUND bit into Sasha's torso as she lay on the ridge watching. Dirt and frost clung to her fatigues. Black grease covered her normally café au lait skin and her wavy black hair was pulled back in a severe knot secured with a rubber band.

Panting heavily, she could see her breath in the blue-black night. Adrenaline caused the hairs to stand up on her forearms and bristle at the nape of her neck. Thirty years ago the Colombian Disasters had hit, bringing human awareness to the fact that the supernatural was real.

Carnage in the rural mountainsides and then fanning out to Panama while spilling blood throughout the Amazon basin, human bodies dismembered everywhere, was not something that could happen on the streets of Chicago or New York, or anywhere else ever again for that matter. They called it drug wars and said cartels in the region had gone wild. That was so that the average human being could sleep at night.

She never got that part, why one type of monster was supposedly worse than another, but that was people for you. Admittedly, her sensibilities weren't that refined; if wrong was being done and the brass gave the order, she had no problem taking out a target. Human wrongdoing versus supernatural wrongdoing was like splitting hairs, in her mind. Thank God human technology had reached the point where they could finally codify the myths and legends and track some of what ancient cultures had tried to tell generations long ago. Tonight, however, the mission was crystal clear: *blow the sucker*.

Anticipation coiled nervous energy within her, producing a natural high. If she hadn't been infected by the werewolf virus, she might never have signed on to this insane job—and then would have missed the adventure of a lifetime.

A thin sheen of sweat coated her body and the tip of her tongue darted out to swipe at the salty substance on her upper lip. All five feet seven inches of her being was on fire. The urge to hunt made the muscles in her arms and legs tense until she almost cried out from the sudden pain—but didn't. Years of military training within the new Special Forces unit culled out of the Marine Corps's best kept her on point, on mission, focused. But there was nothing like bringing all that training to live action. This was what she and her squad *lived* for. *This* was the moment.

She lowered her night-vision goggles, no longer needing them now that the moon was full. Something powerful within her practically gnawed at her insides as she waited. She hadn't even been born twenty-five years ago when the government had learned that the paranormal was real, that things really did slither over the edges of other dimensions into our world. Ironic that her job was to beat it back to where it came from, and as a soldier, to make sure no one helped it to get out. Right now, a national adversary was trying to break a code, trying to genetically create a living weapon. Not tonight. Think again.

Narrowing her gaze, she studied the slowly moving convoy. Crazy SOBs had actually captured a live werewolf—she could smell the silver containment on the wind. Had to be lining the heavily armored truck in the center of the convoy. That part wasn't rocket science; the military truck lurched and pitched and a furious howl echoed through the valley, shredding her concentration.

Sasha licked her lips. It had been twelve hours since she'd taken her medication. Vampires were big on sleight of hand, and while gathering intelligence, vamps would swipe anything that fascinated them. Apparently her meds had intrigued Geoff. Unfortunately the shots were also a necessary evil to keep the werewolf virus from flaring in her system. But it was something her pack was used to by now. They had all contracted the virus due to a werewolf bite or scratch. Each had been found, gathered from hospital reports or police records of survivors, and brought in to be studied like lab rats.

From everything they had seen, natural-born werewolves were pure, cunning, feral, dangerous animals. They looked like wolves—on steroids—tended to be all black, and stood upright. It was their only form. They were wickedly smart and knew how to keep themselves hidden. They were also strong, fast, and tended to crave flesh.

So her small group were the lucky ones. They got the medicine. They didn't Turn.

Incessant howling from the convoy made her throat tighten as she fought not to respond to the call of the wild. Since North Korea didn't have wolves, per se, even though Asia, North America, and Northern Europe did, answering in kind would not have been a good idea.

She raked her fingers through her hair waiting for the right moment to detonate the network of explosives. Damn the moon, damn the conservative mission to just send a warning message. Rod's previous efforts in-country might have gotten a dictator's hollow apology and media photo op, but why not send a bold message that was beyond crystal clear: *start some supernatural shit, we'll finish it.*

In her mind, they had to. Rod Butler was right—it might have been a layman's logic, but it sounded right and made too much sense over a few beers out of earshot of the brass: werewolf DNA was the only DNA, thus far, that the scientists thought was capable of being fused with human DNA. The objective: to create the perfect killing machine with as much insane strength as the enemy. Humans needed to genetically evolve to fight the entities made known to man: werewolves and vampires; we could not be the weakest of those species. Made sense. She was all for it, and all about making sure that the technology didn't fall into the wrong hands. Once the werewolf virus took hold, it mutated, literally ate its way up the DNA chain until the victim of the bite or scratch flipped out and Turned. That's what had to be controlled.

Delta One, Operation Dog Star, was about containment. They kept the technology to fuse werewolf DNA with human DNA off the black market. Her squad, small, already infected, and lethal, also had to basically police the humans interested in creating more like them.

Unlike vampires, ghosts, and other demon strains, the military had thus far learned that the human body was still alive when it morphed into a werewolf. Those dead enti-ties like the run-of-the-mill vampire were not as easy to control as the living. So of all the supernatural creatures, he who managed to harness the wildness of the wolf and make it a strength within the human body would own the fiercest soldier battalions on the planet.

It was no secret that living things had an innate sense of being alive and feared the void of death, even the wildest of creatures did. What true threat could one hold over the head of something that had already been to hell? That's why vampires and demons were a crap shoot. But wolf DNA, with pack rules and familial bonds at its sub-core, was an entirely different ball game. If they could separate out the insane monster qualities of that entity and take all the positive traits, then they'd cracked the soldier-making code. It was a genetic engineering race that made the space race look like doddering old ladies in go-carts by comparison.

A man had to come up with that. Oh, yeah, her job was to blow the mother up to keep that from happening. The mission was simple: take out the cargo vehicle in the con-voy to ensure that North Korea never got a live werewolf specimen to their labs. They could not be allowed to get sample DNA.

Sasha stood, melting into the night. Speed, ridges, rocks, the darkness under a disc of silver all became one. Thin mountain air cut at the dampness that enveloped her skin and caressed her scalp as she ran toward the target breakpoint. Scaling the bridge from beneath and out of view of the approaching convoy, she strategically added more C-4 bricks and then broke away from the behemoth structure, heading back to her original location at the hold point. As she reached the top of the ridge she turned slowly and dialed the cell phone number, listening to each tone calmly before she pushed send.

The blast created a concussion of sound and vibration that knocked her off her feet. Hurling dirt and debris nearly eclipsed the bright pulse of light that flashed as the bridge fractured. Sasha lifted her head to witness the last armored vehicle plummet into the waiting ravine.

She stood calmly, threw her head back, and howled.

A bar in South Korea . . .

AN HOUR AND a half before true sunrise Sasha knew it would be tough to find her vamp contact, but the SOB had hot-fingered her meds and she was definitely going back for those. Problem was, it had taken her way too long to get across the border. That was a little unanticipated snag, yet she'd managed.

She allowed her gaze to travel past tables laden with empty glasses and patrons in near stupors who were focused on their lap dances. She briefly wondered if they knew what the gyrating women looked like or even cared at this point, pretty sure that they didn't.

Humidity was making her stolen tank top and jeans stick to her body, but that was better than waltzing into the joint looking like she'd just blown a hole in a mountainside. At least she'd been able to hit a public restroom and wash the grit and dirt off her face, albeit some of the mission crud was still under her fingernails. Dirty or not, this wasn't a tourist-attraction watering hole where a single female could simply enter and sit at the bar without a hassle. No. She was sure her contact used this as a rendezvous point just to yank her chain.

Every female in the establishment was clearly for sale, half of them on poles, the other half on laps—not that she cared, she just didn't want a case of mistaken identity to cause some poor bastard to get his lights punched out. In fact, the more she glanced around and received appreciative grins the more she knew that her somewhat dubious condition might inspire some jerk who was half in the bag to think that she *really* needed money.

Sasha sighed and blew a stray wisp of hair up off her forehead. If some horny old fart put his hands on her, she'd have to hurt him. Personal restraint just wasn't in her at the moment. Rather than kill a drunk civilian, she hoisted her pilfered sling purse over her shoulder higher, then ordered a Scotch and water, and waited. It would have been so much easier to just pack the Glock in her waistband and tote the handheld Uzi in a death grip, but why raise unwarranted suspicion. She swallowed the bitter edge of cynicism with her drink when it came, ignoring three more that were sent along with winks and business cards.

Nervous energy made her roll the short rocks glass between her palms. It had taken her a full year to get her first vampire contact, and they could say what they liked, all the training in the world never prepared one for the up-close and personal contingencies that happened in the field. She glanced around the bar again—and this was one *helluva* sleazy field. Mud and bugs under the full moon were somehow much more appealing.

"So we finally meet again," a warm, ebullient voice crooned close to her ear.

As irritated as she was, a half smile of amusement still lifted her right cheek. She took a sip of her drink, oddly enjoying the games vampires played.

"You stole my medicine," she remarked coolly, not giving her contact the courtesy of meeting his gaze.

"Just an insurance policy."

He moved beside her and sat down with such fluid grace that she strained not to look at him yet. Reflex made her glance up at the mirror behind the bar shelves and she immediately heard his soft, smug chuckle. Of course he wouldn't be there, but he was now aware just how hard she'd been trying to avoid his jewel-blue eyes. Damn.

"Insurance," Sasha said flatly, turning to now look at Geoff full on. "That's a slap in the face . . . you're saying I'm not a woman of my word."

"Never such an inference, my darling. A woman of intrigue, yes. Dishonest . . . hmmm . . . I don't think so."

"Good." Sasha sipped her drink.

He offered her a perfect, dashing smile that revealed just the slightest hint of fangs. "I made good on my end of the bargain." He appraised her slowly, taking in her slightly dirty condition. "And I take it you found your target."

Sasha raised her glass, said nothing, and then took a sip of Scotch. That was her answer, a blasé bar salute.

"Excellent," her contact crooned. "We're not so different, you and I," he added in a silky murmur, leaning closer to her. "I have, as I told you, people who are always very concerned about events that could shift world financial markets. Knowing about these unfortunate incidents in advance helps my superiors to, how shall we say, hedge against investment losses by tactfully and discreetly moving them to safe havens before your human military blows things up."

He eyed her profile and inclined his head closer to her neck. "I think we make a perfect match, don't you? I have insight about where these beasts roam, you know where your government is going to lob a preemptive strike—I move my clients' investments; you blow a bridge, and no one but the raging beasts suffer."

She gave him a tight, sarcastic smile. "A match made in heaven. Insider trading on the supernatural Dow Jones."

He chuckled softly and arched a sexy eyebrow. "Isn't everything about what's on the inside, Sasha? Human power bases are secured the same way."

Yeah, yeah, yeah, and everybody from local cops to the CIA had moles, but having one with fangs was new, even for the military.

"My good faith effort was that you found your werewolf . . . all I asked for in return was to have some assurance that the information you feed me is accurate to the best of your knowledge. I'm sure you can appreciate how inconvenient it would be if I moved my clients' portfolios to a location that suffered a man-made disaster . . . millions of dollars could be—"

Sasha held up her hand. "I know. You've already coached me on the finer points of global markets. I said I would come back and give you what you wanted—you didn't have to steal my meds."

"Borrow," he countered with a sexy smile. "And, at the time of our earlier negotiations, we didn't know each other this well, true? I don't think you would have even allowed me to sit this close to you, then." He shrugged, still grinning, and leaned on the bar on his elbows, lacing his graceful fingers together. "I vaguely recall your having a hallowed earth grenade in one hand as we discussed terms."

Sasha couldn't contain her smile. It slid out and lifted her cheek, encouraging another brilliant smile from him. What he'd said was true; the first time he'd rolled up on her looking to form an alliance she'd held a silver-shell-loaded Glock nine-millimeter on him. The next meeting devolved the moment she'd noticed his fangs cresting; she'd threatened to pull the pin on a grenade, and had meant it.

Much as she hated to admit it, his good faith effort made a small difference. Besides, she'd learned that her reflexes were almost as fast as his and he didn't unnerve her any longer. Sasha took a liberal sip of her drink, releasing a sigh before she set her glass down with precision.

Alas, a deal was a deal and she'd have to make good on it since Geoff's intel was solid.

She watched merriment shimmer in his big blue irises that were a color so intense it made one feel as if they were being swallowed by the sea. He was handsome to a flaw, she had to admit that much. He had a full, lush mouth and his strong chin was marred only by a tiny cleft that added character to his stunning profile. Silken brunette waves created an onyx fall over his shoulders.

Even in his relaxed black linen tourist suit with a collarless shirt to match, his bearing still had Old World Europe firmly stamped on it. There was no getting away from his nobleman heritage. But the more she stared at him the more his smile faded, giving way to a more intense expression of raw desire.

Without making her ask for her meds he produced them from his breast pocket and slid them beside her hand on the bar. "Not to rush, milady, but dawn approaches."

It was her turn to smile wider when she saw a hint of fangs begin to crest again in his mouth. Sasha was certainly having an interesting effect on him. She picked up her small black medical kit and dropped it into her purse and then knocked back the rest of her drink.

"You're right," she murmured, watching his Adam's apple bob as he swallowed hard.

"I promise you'll enjoy it."

She released a little laugh but declined comment. Sometimes, it was so much easier blowing things up than doing this covert shit. Not to mention how being told in training that this entity could read surface thoughts was one thing, but to have it done in one's face was . . . strange.

"Okay," she said after a moment. "How does this work? We just do it right here in public?"

"Is there any other way?" he murmured, now caressing her cheek with the pad of his thumb.

Somewhat unnerved by the proposition, she studied his face again, burning it into her memory. If something foul went down, she wanted to be sure she remembered every detail of her potential attacker. Never stare into their eyes, another training axiom, but she felt no compulsion from him.

"You guys are so kinky," she finally forced herself to say, using humor as a cover.

He simply smiled. "You have no idea."

"All right. Do it."

He looked dismayed. "Madame . . . there is a certain . . . flair, style, protocol to a mind blending."

Not sure what he meant, for a second she stood before him bewildered. "Okay . . . well . . . then what? You gave me intel, now I'm supposed to let you go into my brain to better understand that we're not really after vamps, and to find out what we consider hot spots to possibly move on—you know this is classified data, but a deal is a deal."

For a moment he didn't speak and just simply placed both palms against her cheeks, softly caressing them. "Don't you feel anything?"

Her mouth had gone dry. "Yeah, but it's not an information exchange."

"That's how we do it," he said, so quietly she had to strain to hear him. "Gentle, erotic, and unforgettable. Let me go in . . ."

Then just as suddenly as he'd spoken, he took her mouth and took it hard, the impact of the kiss blotting out all sound from the club around them. What began as a slow, sensual meeting of mouths and parting of lips soon became a passionate struggle of tongues twining, long, graceful fingers threaded through her hair, her body melting against his to feel every hard contour he owned. She had gone from uninterested and slightly creeped out to combustible in less than five seconds. Patrons and bartenders became a blur; showgirls were simply flesh-toned smears as she held on to him while fighting vertigo.

He broke the kiss, panting. Sound returned. Sasha stumbled forward and kissed him again before she could stop herself. The second she did that, took the lead, something unexpected entered her with the shudder he'd released: information.

This guy was *a baron*? A really old, powerful money-changer . . . not a lower-level messenger? Whoa . . . a freakin' *Vampire Cartel financial industry baron*? Sasha stepped back, breathing hard. The experience of siphoning information with such clarity was disorienting. Sure, she'd had gut hunches as a kid, but this was an entirely different level of understanding that really put the term "giving head" into perspective.

"My place?" His gaze searched hers. "I know that wasn't part of the bargain . . . but . . ."

"But damn." She dragged her fingers through her tousled hair.

It had to be going so long without her meds that was making her feel so primal, but she was not about to shoot up in front of a vamp or people in a club. Even if she went into the ladies' room, there was the other not so little problem; the old bait and switch. How the hell did she know if he'd tampered with her vials or not? For all she knew, he could have switched them and given her something to really make her want to spend a week locked away with a vampire.

"Sasha . . ." he murmured. "Aren't you curious, just a little?"

She took a deep breath and told herself to pull it together. She had to remind herself that she really wasn't attracted to the vampire. That he actually reminded her of those privileged pricks who had made her life a living hell when she was in high school. God bless Doc for finding her and taking in an orphan, and even giving her the best education money could buy—but Geoff was one of *them* . . . the *in* crowd. Soul tormentors. One of the beautiful people, alive or dead, it didn't matter; there was a human caste system and she wasn't anywhere near the top rungs of it. She'd been here before, desired by one of them and then humiliated, and was never going there again. Ever. So she would have to watch herself around him from now on. She was a fool for allowing herself to get cocky in the first place.

She opened her mouth to tell him that it wasn't going to happen when Geoff let out a low snarl, jerking her attention up to his face. His gaze narrowed and he stepped in front of her in a blatant display of possession.

"Shogun," he said between his teeth.

Sasha slipped her gun out of her purse and moved several quick steps away from the vampire, keeping it down by her side so as not to draw the attention of the humans in the bar. Her senses on guard, hair on her neck bristling, she held his arm. "Geoff, what is it?" She watched his mouth fill with fully presented fangs, obviously not caring if drunken patrons and high pole dancers saw. "Shit!" she muttered.

"Werewolf," Geoff practically growled.

Sasha's heart immediately began to pound. A werewolf? Here? Among all these people? And why hadn't she smelled it approaching? Her senses were never off, so that little mind-mating thing with her handsome contact must have seriously messed her up. No way would she be doing that again. She scented the air. Why was a werewolf here of all places? They liked to hunt, but in dark, quiet places. "Look, Geoff," she said, continuing to carefully glance around the club, "we can't have a gunfight or a supernatural species brawl in a bar full of innocent humans. I'll shoot you both, first."

"Listen to the lady," a voice said, and Sasha swung in its direction. A dark figure was now sitting at the far end of the bar. "She's loaded with silver. But since your nose has been so far up your own ass tonight, I guess you didn't notice. And for the record, the only reason you might have persuaded her to go home with one of you undeads is, you got to her under a full moon."

Fury burned in the stranger's dark eyes as he slung a shot glass across the polished wood so hard and with such precision that not a drop spilled until it collided with Geoff's hand. "I forgot," the stranger added in a low rumble as Geoff shook off the whiskey and then cleaned his hand with a handkerchief he'd produced from thin air. "Wrong vintage," he said, referring to the fact that it wasn't blood.

Then the dark stranger stood and stepped out of the shadows. At first glance, he was half a head taller than Geoff, oddly making her vampire contact's six-foot-one-inch frame appear short by comparison. His shoulders were massive and strong, his arms nicely muscular, and he had a six—possibly an eight—pack under his olive T-shirt. His narrow waist drew the eye down to his powerful thighs and legs and back up again. He had flat features, dark, intense, almond-shaped eyes, and his skin had been turned a burnished bronze by the sun.

Sasha's mind was scrambling to catch up to what her eyes were telling her. *This* was a werewolf? *This* was one of the monsters she and her pack had hunted down over the years? But it . . . couldn't be. Werewolves were like a cross between the Tasmanian devil and Cujo. This man was . . . well, too human and too damn pretty to be one of those out-of-control animals.

Okay, she needed to stay calm and find out just what the hell was going on here.

Both males eyed each other, saying nothing, as they sized each other up. She gripped her Glock tighter, ready to shoot if this went beyond posturing, civilians or no civilians. The newcomer gave the impression of a casual stance, but from her training, she knew it to be a relaxed martial arts pose that could turn into deadly force within seconds. Shogun, huh . . . ?

The strength of his being was implicit. His raw grace nothing short of majestic. As they stood in diametric opposition to each other, she found it hard not to look at both males from two different species and see the exquisite beauty each possessed, predators or not.

She wondered if Shogun was his real name, or if Geoff was just needling him. It would not be beneath the vamp to go there, even if he knew better, given what she'd learned about him thus far. Then again, it could have been his name or title. He didn't necessarily have to hail from South Korea just because he'd shown up here. In fact, he probably wasn't from here, if he was a werewolf (which she still couldn't wrap her mind around), and could have aegis over a wider Asian territory that had indigenous wolf populations. The endless possibilities made her brain hurt.

He appraised the vampire before dismissing him in favor of her. Sasha tensed when he turned that penetrating gaze on her.

Of all the remarkable things about him, she immediately noticed that his scalp was clean-shaven and that gave her pause . . . a werewolf, under a full moon, with not even a five o'clock shadow? He had to have some kind of serious personal restraint or Geoff was simply hurling a species slur at another vamp. But there was no mistake that this stranger was what Geoff claimed. It was all in his earthy scent and the slight amber flicker around the edges of his irises, something that she *just knew* despite everything she had seen and had been told. It also allowed her to scent the others who had come in with him. There were about five of them. She had picked up on them when Shogun had stepped into the light, though she still couldn't see them. They weren't moving, but she had been aware of them all this time.

"You're in my territory, vampire," the stranger said after a long, threatening pause. His eyes said it all, even though he'd spoken quietly, calmly, but with a lethal tone that was not to be ignored.

"We were just leaving," Geoff sneered, gaze narrowed.

"Really?" Shogun looked at Sasha with a challenging half smile. Then he said, "Stay and have breakfast with me. He can't do the sun and I'm sure what he ingests would turn your stomach."

"Now *you* are poaching, wolf," Geoff said, pointing at his competitor. But no sooner had he uttered the words, than he wisely drew back his hand and arm.

"Me? I'm poaching by protecting this lovely lady from the likes of your blood-sucking ways?" Shogun said with a snarl, beginning to circle Geoff with his palm flattened against his stone-cut chest. "You, who have lied? Your kind, which has openly hunted my kind without finding out which of us was demon-infected or not, have the nerve to now hunt in my territory and expect me not to drag your foul, dead carcass up to the highest rooftop to fry when the sun comes up?"

"Don't you *dare* threaten me, you flea-ridden, rabid—"

"Hold it, boys," Sasha said quickly, coming between the would-be combatants. "Not in here, not around all these humans." She stared at the one called Shogun and watched righteous indignation flickering in his eyes. "I don't understand—did you say *demon-infected*?"

Shogun sighed and crossed his arms. "There's a lot your so-called vampire contact neglected to explain. For instance, before you ever let another one of them violate your mind, demand an even exchange. If you request it, they must give it—but if you don't, they'll cheat you every time. Send him packing and I'll further discuss it with you over a cup of coffee under *the sun*."

Sasha was deeply torn. Clearly the military had so much more to learn, and bringing home strategic information was as vital to missions as blowing things up. It might even go a long way in helping her do the least favorite part of the gig, namely, supernatural diplomacy and negotiations. Just observing this Shogun character and the way he spooked a very old, powerful vamp made her need to know a *lot* more than she obviously did. Her biggest challenge at the moment was absorbing all these species nuances for which there was no intel. This was learning on the fly if ever she'd seen it!

And perhaps it was all a trap . . . Damn it, she would just have to take the chance and be very, very careful.

The offer of knowledge was just too titillating to pass up, and the vampire seemed to know it.

"Seduction with information . . . I guess you wolves have finally learned something from us after all," Geoff nearly hissed, and then glanced at the blue-gray horizon and was gone.

Sasha looked at the retreating vapor and then saw a couple of liquor-bleary patrons yawn, squint, and then rub their eyes as though they were confused.

"He thinks you stole his kill out from under him," she said.

"That's why we're called wolves," Shogun said in a deep rumble. He gave a swift nod to several corners of the room and patrons that had seemed out of it were suddenly very alert. "We always hunt in packs."

Sasha now saw the others, standing in various positions throughout the club. Clearly they were now allowing themselves to be seen. She understood why Geoff thought better of standing his ground. It would have been a lost cause, anyway. She kept her eyes on Shogun, but now also held his men in her peripheral vision. This was definitely going to get interesting.

Shogun didn't say another word, just turned on his heel and began to walk out of the strip joint, head held high, back straight, exuding unfailing confidence that she'd follow. While that irked her, there was little else she could do. She *had* to find out what he was talking about. Sasha tucked her Glock into her waistband, grabbed her purse, and trailed after him.

Following him through a series of small streets and alleys, she was hyperaware of her gun pressed against her spine and hung back just far enough to keep up with him, but with space enough to fight—or run—if there was an ambush. The fact that he had an alert, attack-ready pack at his beck and call was not lost on her in the least.

Finally he made an abrupt turn and took a steep flight of apartment steps in three swift lunges. Sasha stopped. Two things immediately hit her: one, this guy had an incredible ass; two, it would be very foolish to go into a closed-in space behind a potential threat in a South Korean ghetto. There had been five of them at the bar, probably more of his pack.

"What's wrong?" He stopped walking and turned to look at her, then folded his thick arms over his chest.

"I don't know you."

He shrugged. "You're armed, packing silver. I don't know you, either—and?"

"I don't do closed-in spaces."

He sighed and sat down hard on the crumbling concrete. "No restaurants are serving yet at this hour. I don't know about you but after a full moon, I need a strong cup of green tea, at the very least. My assumption is that you're Western-born and take coffee. I have some in the apartment."

Sasha pulled out her Glock, studied the clip, and leaned against a building. "I'll wait." What the hell did "at the very least" mean? She stared up at him.

"Wish I had met you last night," he said quietly, and then stood and turned and slipped into the building.

"No, you don't," she muttered, thinking about loading C-4 under a bridge. She still had some on her, if he wanted to get technical or crazy.

About the only thing worse than watching water boil was waiting for it outside on a desolate foreign street. If the guy didn't come back soon, she'd go out of her mind with the questions that were rattling around in her skull. A significant part of her was ready to run up the steps in the direction he'd gone just to go investigate, overriding common sense, combat training, and her gut, when he appeared with a glass coffeepot in hand.

"How do you want it?"

She looked him up and down, trying not to read too much into the sexy tone of his voice or his loaded question. He had the nerve to come to the door with a deep V of sweat now making the shirt cling even more to his torso.

First Geoff and now this one, she thought with a sigh. *It must be the full moon.* "Real sweet, with cream. Thanks."

He nodded. "Don't have milk, but can make it real sweet."

She didn't say a word; he didn't move off the top step. Just stared. For a second she wasn't sure she was breathing. Was he about to attack?

"Hey, I'm sorry. Full moon aftermath," he finally said, and disappeared into the building again and then reappeared with her coffee mug in one hand, his green-tea-filled mug in another. "Last night, the whole pack had to respond to a call to arms." He set her cup down on the steps and backed away so she could pick it up. When she just stared at it, he let out a weary breath. "Well, if you think I drugged it, then why would you let me go to all the trouble of making it?"

"I didn't think about that until just now. Sorry."

She glanced at the mug and allowed it to remain where he'd left it and just continued to lean against the wall. What did he and his pack having to respond to a call to arms have to do with her? He was speaking to her as if she knew what he was talking about. Having another entity within the same hour messing with her head annoyed her no end. Beyond that, the fact that werewolves were organized into packs and not lone rogues who occasionally ventured out to snack on a human was blowing her mind. Dangerous or not, she needed to gather more data from him.

He picked up her mug and took a sip from it and then put it where he'd left it, then bounded up the steps to sit yogi style on the landing. "I guess now you don't want it because I have werewolf germs, huh?" He took a slow sip of his green tea, eyeing her over the rim of his mug.

What could she say? Werewolf cooties were on her list of things she didn't need in her life; besides, that's why she was taking meds—she already had them.

"I just don't get it," she said, ignoring this comment. "You say you're a werewolf, but you're—"

"Not slobbering on myself and pulling out people's entrails?" He shook his head. "Don't ever believe vampires. Snobs, the lot of them."

"All I know is, thirty years ago a war between supernaturals broke out in rural Colombia—"

"Those were demon-infected werewolves that your military encountered," he said sharply, cutting her off. "The vampires try to act like their kind hasn't had rogues . . . What the hell was Jack the Ripper other than one of them gone insane?"

Sasha felt as if a boulder had fallen on her head. She blinked furiously and said, "*What?*"

He just stared at her for a moment, incredulous. "You really don't know, do you? You don't know the politics behind the war, either, do you?"

She shook her head, dazed. "Uh, no."

"The demon betrayal is a long story, one that children are told growing up. Your parents never explained?"

Sasha shook her head again. "I never knew them," she said. "They died when I was young."

Compassion filled his serene gaze and she prayed it wasn't pity. She had grown up during the second half of her childhood with Doc's housekeeper as the closest thing to a mother, though the woman was dear and loving. But she hadn't felt that vacancy in her soul in years and wondered why looking into Shogun's understanding gaze made her feel it again as if it were yesterday.

"I'm sorry," he finally said in his low-key, dignified manner.

Sasha shrugged. "I got a good deal, raised by the man who found me . . . He was pretty well-off, even had a housekeeper who watched out for me."

"Then I really am sorry," Shogun said, his voice now nearly a murmur as his gaze coated her with empathy. "To be raised by humans . . ." He shook his head and looked down into his tea for a moment and then released a long sigh. "The pack is everything, family is everything. To be raised without one's history and native language is incomprehensible." When his gaze captured hers again, she was rendered temporarily mute.

"I did okay," she said after a while.

"But we teach our children the history of the packs from as far back as—"

"Hold it." She pushed off the wall. "Kids?"

He smiled as he took a liberal sip of tea and she could feel him baiting her mind, but she didn't care.

"Yes, Sasha . . . I heard the fanged one call you that. May I?"

"Yeah, sure, but get back to the kids part."

"We're alive, Sasha. The vampires aren't. We reproduce like any other species; they don't. They build their numbers through the bite and death. That's why we despise them, and they're viciously jealous of us."

"That's . . . *wild*." She moved closer to the steps but still wasn't ready to take a sip of coffee after he'd drunk from the mug, even though it smelled divine. "But I've seen the real McCoy—full-blown werewolves. You can't be a werewolf!"

A wry smile overtook his face as his gaze hunted hers.

"Oh . . . Sasha, you have no concept how wrong you are."

His five o'clock shadow began to spread across his square jaw as he closed his eyes for a moment and inhaled slowly through his nose. Sasha quickly backed up, drew her Glock, and pointed when jet-black bristle began to emerge from his scalp in hard spikes, to finally give way to a long, lustrous, blue-black silky curtain of tresses that framed his body to his elbows.

He opened his golden-amber eyes. The mug of tea he held trembled between his palms, but she was certain that it wasn't from fear. His gaze was steady, like her aim.

"Thousands of years ago, the territory wars began. The vampires blame the genesis of it on us, but if they hadn't fed so outrageously, the scenario would have never played out to tragic conclusions." He spoke in a low, controlled, modulated voice, intermittently sipping his tea and closing his eyes, seeming completely unfazed that she held a weapon on him.

"Our side was suffering heavy casualties, and a militant

faction decided to go against clan policies to strike a strengthening bargain with demons. Those that went into that ill-fated alliance soon learned why the International Federation of Clans had banished such practices. The demons' pact created bad blood, literally within the veins of the recipients. Those werewolves were strengthened, but at a devastating cost. We began to fight among ourselves while also warring with the vampires. Neither side of the internal civil struggle is particularly proud of its part in this disturbing history, but it is what it is. As all demons are known for duplicity, there was a catch of course. What was spawned from the strengthening through a demon alliance created human flesh-eaters within our species—not all of us are infected, but those that are . . . Tragic."

He sighed and set his tea mug down very precisely on the edge of the concrete wall near him.

"Because we are living beings that can breed, we sometimes pass on the demon infection through a recessive gene. Not all of us have it and, like I said, it is a recessive trait. But it did get into our gene pool. The werewolves that humans know about are those that have this viral defect. We have quarantined many, but some escape from time to time. Hence, the strongest voting bloc on the United Council of Entities, the Vampires Cartel, called for an open-season hunt thirty years ago that erupted into a civil war that humans should never have seen. The Werewolf Federation of Clans couldn't stop it. None of the other entities took a stand beyond lip service. The damned Fae Parliament is ruled by factions that couldn't come together, and the mythics, like the Order of the Dragon, are still disorganized and feudal . . . not even the phantom realms could stop their contentious debates to form a voting bloc from their lodge halls that would go against the vampires, because half of them, like the succubi and incubi, are heavily embedded in the vampires' cartel enterprises."

Shogun stood in one lithe move and paced on the landing. His posture was regal and the sunlight glistened on his silky black hair that now hung down his back.

As she watched him pace while he struggled to find the right words to continue, she knew in her soul she wouldn't tell the brass. At least not right away. They kept things on a need-to-know basis and she was always blind to the big picture. She hated that. But as soon as she got back and could get Doc to a secure location, she would drop this on him. He, if anybody in the world, needed to know how wide and deep this went. He'd know how to play this politically; that was his forte, not hers.

"So, uh, all supernatural politics aside, real bad werewolves began eating people in the Colombian hills and it took the human U.S. Government in coordination with—"

"It is still up for debate whether your nuclear tests weakened the demon doors that caused that environmental hazmat or vampires somehow let out ten infected wolves so that they could begin the war that they already wanted to wage," he shot back, cutting her off. "We reasoned that the escapes should have happened near where there was heavy testing. Colombia didn't fit. The vampires, of course, claimed that it weakened the overall dimensional fabric, and the escapees chose to exit where they could easily blend into the dense foliage but eat very well near populations that were not heavily protected."

Stunned by his revelations, Sasha stared at him without blinking as he railed on.

"However, our federation was fully prepared to contain the problem without human intervention. We had militias readied. We could also have brought in Fae peacekeeping forces on the ground to scour the mountains—a terrain they prefer—and teamed with members from the Order of the Dragon for an aerial assault!"

"All right, I admit it," Sasha said, raking her fingers through her hair. "This is real, real new."

"Well, then, be advised," he said, seeming vindicated and somewhat mollified that someone, a human, was truly hearing his side of the story. "That was the argument presented at the UCE, but without evidence, it was considered unsubstantiated rhetoric. However, the one thing that wasn't just rhetorical werewolf opinion was the fact that the vampires finally transgressed the ultimate rule among all supernaturals, considered sacrilege at the council— they made humans aware of us with hard, cold evidence of our existence and are willing to help exterminate us." He pointed at her angrily. "That's a fact, and the only reason your military can find us now!"

The whole thing was incomprehensible . . . supernaturals had something akin to her human U.N.? *Get the hell out of here*. Federations, parliaments . . . wha? It was crazy enough that they knew vampires had certain business connections and were embedded in what seemed like normal human enterprises. Now the cartel thing she'd picked up from Geoff made sense—so did the animosity between him and the guy pacing on the landing of an apartment building. But she didn't know what to tell that very upset being.

"Our brothers, the ones that can shift at will, have long since separated themselves from us," he said, drawing back his arm but his voice still booming with rage. "Even they have cast out those of us beholden to release our wolf only under the full moon . . . afraid that we could pollute their bloodlines. None of the others, not the Faeries, or Yeti, or Phantoms, or even castes as old as the Dragons— none of them would stand with us. We are the only ones strong enough to go against the vampires, but none of the others wanted to incur their wrath. So, an edict issued thousands of years ago, which allows them to hunt our rogues rather than letting us contain and remove our own, was established to combat the virus . . . and the crafty senior vampires dusted off their ancient scrolls and reminded the UCE of this thirty years ago when several rogues got out of their quarantine zones."

"Okay, okay, hold it," Sasha said, placing one hand on her head while she gestured with the gun, forgetting it was in her grip. "Councils, multiple entities—"

"Yes! Anything written in legend and mythology has a basis. Humans just don't have all the facts! All of these ancient beings have coexisted with humans for eons, and until there was the war between the preternatural superpowers that got visibly out of hand, all was well. We had our own checks and balances, and humans hadn't so polluted the planet or crowded the open spaces that we had to come into constant contact with them. The biggest problem we have now is that humankind has evolved to the point where its technology can eviscerate the planet. Dragons need not worry about dragon slayers, you have F16 fighter jets, nukes—anything living is in peril . . . but vampires do have the advantage of already being dead."

"Okay, okay, I hear you—just give me a second to take it all in," she said, trying to regain her mental equilibrium. If what he said was true, the old man with the yappy, annoying little dog who lived down the block from her might well be the gnome he resembled, or the short, rolypoly little lady who made pies for the local church could be a brownie? Her known world was deconstructing in milliseconds. "So there's good werewolves and bad werewolves, good vampires and—"

"Of course. No different than humans that are a varied lot. The supernatural is all around you, Sasha. I'm amazed, given your heritage, you can't see it. But the second part of your statement regarding vampires is a subject for debate, although I admit bias." He gave her his magnificent back to consider and took several deep, cleansing breaths. "Stop waving the gun at me. Please. Brandishing a weapon if you don't intend to use it . . . is . . . aggressive foreplay right after an unfulfilled full moon."

She looked at him and then looked at the gun, put the safety back on it, and then quickly tucked it in her waistband again. "Sorry."

He spun on her. "You came after a full moon, and we haven't fed or anything else, but I'm trying to make you understand. Thank you for destroying the threat that got smuggled to North Korea. That's the only reason we're having a conversation. Normally, for obvious reasons, we don't allow those outside our packs and clans to see us. But since you're in the elite corps of humans who already know we exist but might have a skewed view of who we all are, I wanted to give you the other side of the picture. Not all of us deserve to have a target on our foreheads and we despise the profiling propaganda campaign that the vampires so effectively launched after that recent war. But regardless of how we've been depicted, we're not all monsters. Besides, what you'll need to worry about is the rumor that *your kind* is trying to get their hands on lab-created demon-infected toxin, so they can introduce it to a wider audience."

What? And what did he mean by "your kind"? Did he mean people infected with the virus? The military? Oh, shit . . .

Shogun walked away and punched a huge section of brick out of the wall. "We got the other demon-infected werewolf that escaped here, in the southlands. But I'd swear on my mother the vampires had a hand in releasing the threat years ago, as they might have now. I cannot prove it, but my gut tells me this is so. It gives them an open hunting license against us each time a demon-infected is spotted. And, as you can imagine, more than the one or two escaped, infected werewolves get assassinated. It's the vampires' shrewd way of controlling our numbers, culling our packs, and reducing our ranks with full multientity sanction—and *that's* why outright war broke out decades ago."

She didn't know if there was any way to get her trusted source inside the military, Doc, to absorb all this, nor was she sure it was accurate. There'd have to be more proof, even though it was one hell of a story. She needed something more to go on before they draped this on the brass and asked the entire Black Ops mission to stand down . . . something beyond Shogun's mere word. But the fact that he'd transformed from clean shaven to not, right before her eyes, but hadn't flipped into a nightmare, gave her some trust. Still, in the preternatural world, just like the human one, nobody did anything without a damned good reason. The key thing she needed to know now, after he'd shared all this significant intel, was what was in it for him.

"What do you want from me?" she said, her tone earnest.

He stopped pacing and stared at her. "Short term or long term?"

"Both."

"Come inside," he said. His voice was raw and quiet. "The building is deceptive . . . there's beautiful caverns beneath it, furnished by thousands of years of Silk Road caravans. Be my guest for as long as you'd like . . . whatever you'd like to eat can be procured."

There was no way in the freakin' world. "Long term," she said.

"An alliance," he murmured, clearly disappointed.

Sasha said nothing.

Shogun sighed. "I wish you would trust me for just a

few hours, then, Sasha," he said in a quiet rumble. His intense gaze raked her in a hot sweep that lingered on her mouth for a moment and then captured her eyes. He started down the steps. "You cannot tell me you do not feel the moon's fullness still pent up within you demanding release. Last night other matters prevailed for both of us . . . we hunted but did not conclude the beauty of the moon's promise. I can feel your wolf struggling . . . her breaths so shallow. Do not give that vampire bastard credit for what is natural among our kind."

So he thought she was a natural-born werewolf. Interesting that he couldn't sense otherwise.

Shogun reached the bottom of the stairs. He reached out and brushed the pad of his thumb over her mouth.

Sasha stepped back. "Now, wait a min—"

Suddenly he closed the gap between them, pulling her tight against him. He nuzzled her hair as his hands slid down her shoulders and then lower and lower.

Sasha was just about to flip him when a cold dash of water from somewhere above solved her dilemma. She jumped back with a yelp, dripping water. Also soaked, Shogun spun around and took one lunge and leapt up to the landing, furious. A female was hanging out one of the upper windows gesturing violently and shouting in Korean. Sasha didn't need to understand her to know that she was cursing Shogun and his two-timing ways. Shogun shouted back at her in Korean then turned to look down at her.

"Don't leave," he said, breathing in short bursts between his words. "It's not what you think."

Sasha nodded. "It never is," she muttered, and then simply waited for him to go inside to address his household issues before folding away into the neighborhood fabric and disappearing.

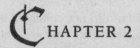

CHAPTER 2

Somewhere along the border of Afghanistan . . .

NOTHING IN ALL his twenty-two years of living had pre-pared Woods for what he was witnessing. There weren't enough simulations in the world to emotionally steel him for this. Cold sweat drenched his body despite the insufferable heat as he stood amid the elaborate network of caves with his small strike force squad, clutching the alternate clip in his fist. Fear had a stranglehold on him. Not one of their own. Not Rod. He told himself that it was the constantly blowing sand and grit that made hot moisture form in his eyes.

Temporarily paralyzed like the others, he waited as seconds clicked away, eating up the training that was supposed to prepare him for this moment. All they could do was stare in horror.

Rod had gone into a violent seizure. Phase one. Doc Holland's voice echoed through his mind as a distant memory. Give the man a shot. He did. It didn't work. Step back—way back, out of lunge range. He did that. God knew, he did that. Slam in your clip of silver shells if any team member's eyes changed. They had. Motion should be fluid and precise. Lizard brain. Don't think about it, just do it. A new clip was supposed to go in. His mind told him to yell to his men to switch to what they only thought was hollow-point ammo. But his clip was still in his hand, frozen. His vocal cords were frozen, too.

Cap's eyes glowed gold, his pupils pitch-black orbs of never-ending darkness. His normal shock of red hair had lengthened and gone midnight black right before their very eyes and covered his face, his jaw . . . a jaw that became distended and filled with glistening, saliva-slicked fangs. Bones and ligaments ripped and snapped, the sound causing nausea as the leader of their squad cried out in sheer agony. Clothes tore away from his body as he shivered on the ground growing larger, and larger, becoming less human . . . and—

"Hollow-point clips in!"

Survival instinct immediately took over the second whatever was on the ground swung its huge head in his direction and snarled. The clip was in, weapon leveled, a gaping maw opened, and the thing went airborne. He yelled to his men to take cover and squeezed off rounds falling backward; the other men, in a frenzy, fired, began running, chaos. Chunks of flesh and gore fell from the beastly body; warm wetness splattered his face and fatigues. Nausea made his stomach pitch. A huge creature was still coming toward him, and only a split-second roll away kept it off him. When it hit the ground it didn't move. The bullet-riddled carcass lay limp on the rocky terrain for a second, then was up and gone in a blur.

Jumping up quickly, Woods ran to find cover with the other men. Johnson held out a sat phone to him with a shaking hand. Four other pairs of wide eyes looked at him for direction.

"Oh, shit . . ." Johnson finally whispered. His huge dark frame was covered in sweat and he just kept shaking his head, backing farther and farther away from the group.

"Mother of God," Gonzalez croaked, crossing himself. "I don't fucking believe it."

"I'm out. Fuck all this, man," Sherwin said, hoisting up his weapon. His blue eyes darted between where the carcass had been on the ground and the lieutenant. "Shoot me in the head now, if you gotta. I didn't sign up for this shit, Woods. Uh-uh. They never told us this was possible!" His voice broke and he raked his brunet hair with stiff fingers. "Did you know? Huh! Did you fucking know! I didn't sign up for this!"

Sherwin, Gonzalez, and Johnson were the select human soldiers who served as backup for them, depending on the nature of the mission. They knew about the pack and their infection, but what had just happened was a whole other ball game.

"If something like this showed up on your mother and sister's back porch, would you give a shit then, Sherwin?" Lieutenant Woods said between his teeth. "Pull yourself together! This is a domestic threat." He looked around at the men on his squad. "Be clear. I will shoot all deserters point-blank range. And what we just saw here is exactly why you're part of Delta One."

Hard gazes looked away from Woods and sought the horizon. Fisher turned away and puked, his lanky body shaking uncontrollably. Sweat had turned his blond hair dark. Blood splatter and hunks of animal meat dropped from his face and uniform.

Sherwin and the others lowered their weapons toward Fisher and Lieutenant Woods, unsure. Both were covered in what had been Rod Butler's blood. Both obviously carried possible contagion, in their minds.

"Everybody stay calm. I'm calling for an extraction.

They gave me a code. Just like they gave us the special bullets to take one of these things down. You can't catch the virus like that—you have to be bitten."

"It wasn't a thing a few minutes ago," Johnson argued. "It was Rod, man. *Captain Butler.* How'd this happen, man? What, are there more of them in the caves? They think some of it got loose in the States? What the hell!"

Sherwin nodded, backing away with Johnson. "Yeah. Had us searching through this endless cave network with him. Anything could have happened in the caves. Something ain't right. Why'd they send us with Butler, if they knew this was possible?"

"Because he was the best man for the job," Woods argued, holding firm on his orders to keep as much of Operation Dog Star under wraps as possible. "He had a sixth sense about—"

"First off, that wasn't no fucking man, *hombre,*" Gonzalez argued and then spat on the ground. "Second off, is that the bullshit they told you to get you to go along with this loco shit? You got that in you, is that why you're so cool?"

The threat of mutiny left a thick residue of distrust in the air. It was not above his own men to frag him on the spot, fear was running that rampant.

"I don't have anything in me but red, American blood. What we just saw was on a need-to-know basis, and I followed my orders. We're looking for underground virus labs that could breed something like this. Period. We didn't find any before we had an incident . . . Butler might have gotten infected on a previous mission. The way he was wounded he probably won't last much longer. God rest his soul in peace." The lieutenant punched in the number, his hands still shaking from adrenaline and heartbreak. The moment the call connected, he spoke rapidly into the mobile unit. "This is Delta One. We need a Black Hawk *now*. Pull us out! Man down; transformation in full phase."

"Roger that, Delta One. Give us your coordinates."

Quickly rattling off their location, the lieutenant kept his eyes on his squad. They were all jumpy enough to frag each other if anyone blinked wrong. His listened carefully to the directions that gave him a pickup point and then disconnected the call.

"We just have to make it over that ridge," he said, beginning to jog toward salvation.

"Oh, sweet Jesus," Sherwin said in an awed tone, causing the others to turn and stare at the dark cave openings that surrounded them. "What if he's not dead? What if he comes back . . . He could be anywhere hiding and waiting for us."

"Let's get out of here!" Woods shouted as the familiar thud of chopper blades beat the air in the distance. Leading the charge, he hustled a dazed Fisher along with him and began waving wildly for the Black Hawk to put down.

But as they crested the ridge he noticed that something was wrong. The pilot conferred with the copilot, and in that instant, Woods looked at his bloodied condition and then glanced quickly at Fisher's. An uneasy feeling made the hairs stand up on the back of his neck and he slowed his gait. The Black Hawk wasn't lowering for a pickup now; it was angling at a rocket-launch pitch to purge possible contagion. Seconds elongated into eternity as he yanked the closest man to him into a cave while screaming for the others to take cover. Blood-slicked fatigues were in his fist as he and Fisher began falling. From his peripheral vision he saw Gonzalez turn with Johnson. Sherwin had disappeared over the ridge, running toward what he thought was safety.

Then came the impact, searing heat, and blinding light.
Everything went dark.

SATCOM . . . location undisclosed

"SHE'S GETTING WORSE," the general said quietly, looking up at Dr. Holland. Concern creased his weathered
brow more than age did.

The doctor paced around the long mahogany briefing
table in the war room with his hands clenched behind his
back. Each lanky step forward was punctuated by worry.
Sasha was more than an experiment; she was like a
daughter to him. "I know," he finally said, hating to con-
cede it. "We should never have sent her out on a mission
under the full moon—"

"That's the damned point!" the general snapped, running his thick fingers through his silver-gray hair. "We
have to know that they won't break under pressure, will
follow orders to the letter, that their medication works
and will hold the beast within them at bay—otherwise,
what damned good are they? This whole paranormal in-
festation of the planet is out of control."

"Sir, there is no actual *control,* only containment of
certain species—"

"Don't tell me that crap after we've invested over a bil-
lion dollars in life sciences to make the Young Wolves
even possible. Goddamned arrogant vampires cannot be
trusted and are a walking hazmat, just like demons, and
ghosts, and whatever else is slithering around out there. I
swear to you, it feels like we've all landed on an alien
planet. Who knew?"

Xavier Holland contained a sardonic smile. "Ancient
cultures knew about them and drew them on the walls of
caves, told of them in legends, and painted them on

scrolls. We're just now coming to terms with what's been around all along. Thirty years of knowing, through new technologies never before available, is a drop in the bucket of time compared to mankind's stories over millennia. Our nuclear blasts opened the gateways even more between worlds, just like all of our electromagnetic interference did. We trespassed on the supernatural turf with our technology, now they're in our world in larger numbers than ever before. In the past only a few at a time ever slipped through the—"

The general held up his hand. "Spare me the history lesson. What's done is done. My main concern is that the general public never knows what's actually out there and that our wolves are controllable. Stable. They have got to help contain what keeps breaching our dimension borders and wriggling out from the other side. Imagine if the general public knew—do you have any idea the level of chaos and panic that would cause . . . not to mention what could happen on the black market? What do you think would have happened if the general public truly understood what was behind the Colombian Disaster?"

"I'm well aware—"

"Are you?" The general looked at Xavier Holland hard, cutting him off again. "If thugs and terrorists were to become able to call up these preternatural species, kiss our civilization as we know it goodbye." He let out a long, weary breath. "That's why you've been given an almost inexhaustible budget to study the phenomena, develop a containment strategy, and monitor anywhere they might be breeding."

While it was impossible to argue the general's point about the potential dangers, they were at polar opposites when it came to methods of handling the situation. Rather than add gasoline to the already roiling flame between them, the doctor opted to remain silent for the sake of diplomacy. He had a full team to consider. More importantly, Sasha and Rod were the eldest and at risk. Darien Woods and Jim Fisher had a few years, but he didn't trust the general not to take matters into his own hands.

Xavier Holland carefully studied the general's body language during the brief standoff. Something was very wrong. The team's psychic monitors and tech support shaman had whispered that truth in his ear. Winters had thrown the bones. Clarissa had cut the cards. None of the other geneticists or dimensional code breakers trusted the brass. The general was delusional—life as they knew it had already changed. There would be no going back to the old way ever again. Control was impossible; coexistence was the only chance of survival. The older, indigenous cultures knew how to combat the scourges of the supernatural realms and live with the more harmonious elements within it. Supernatural species couldn't be weaponized to fight human battles; the concept was insane! But the doctor kept his expression serene as he listened to the general take a deep breath and then resume his hawkish diatribe.

From the very beginning, he'd tried to warn them. Injured soldiers that had been medivaced out of the hot zone were viewed as living repositories of scientific breakthrough. It was fast and sloppy work—as soon as the human body died, so did the active werewolf virus within it. The core medical team thought those shredded men were turning into werewolves, and they were. Despite the chaos, scientists on the Sirius Project were ecstatic. The answer to their scientific questions had practically fallen into their laps. The perfect sample to bond with human DNA was right before their very eyes.

However, what the general could never seem to grasp was that the werewolf virus proved tricky.

Xavier Holland swallowed down the acid burning his

esophagus. As the general railed on, Holland reflected that the instability of the virus was the very foundation concept that a man of war and a man of science would probably never see eye to eye on. Defeat and fury raced through Holland's body, elevating his blood pressure. It had been impossible to get the chain of command to understand that, once the werewolf virus was introduced to a human, it mutated, literally ate its way up the DNA chain until the human went mad and Turned. In the end, they'd lost all of the soldiers to a Turn.

Unfortunately, rather than taking it as the warning it was—to leave that species alone—project scientists guided by military pressure weren't allowed to give up. In fact the brass believed that they had a breakthrough on the medication that would suppress the Turn and that would be enough. It wasn't.

The more Xavier Holland remembered, the farther and farther away the general's voice became. Panic at the top echelons had forced a genetics engineering race that expanded the search for others who had been bitten or scratched by a werewolf. Soon, hospital and police records were discreetly searched for wolflike attacks. Black Ops was out of control, with no checks and balances. A new paranormal unit was formed under the secrecy of the Patriot Act in the name of Homeland Security. Anyone who questioned authority was considered a traitor, so compliant silence became the watchword.

Feeling mired in politics, some members of the team thought looking for domestic victims was a futile search, because if others had been bitten then there would have been reports of humans turning into ravenous beasts. And then there were those who thought that the paranormals were very good at cleaning up after themselves, and had probably done much to keep their existence a secret over the many thousands of years. The researchers just needed to know what to look for. And slowly they began to find what they had been seeking: subjects who had been bitten and infected with the werewolf virus. That had been the beginning of the end. The vampires had stepped forward and given them tips on how to find the few living subjects they'd needed . . . all for a price, of course. What was bartered away in the unholy alliance, even he didn't fully know.

Xavier Holland smoothed his palm over his thinning hair, ignoring the general's droning voice. It was always the same litany, anyway. No one had been thinking about the future ethical or legal potential for disaster then. The legal ramifications alone were beyond comprehension. He couldn't even begin to fathom the spiral of ethical or moral considerations. No one was rational when it came to this supernatural dilemma, and it couldn't be openly debated on the world forum. Secrecy was a dark cloak of insanity over the entire project. Madmen.

Infected subjects had been brought in and studied like lab rats. Eventually, the medication developed by the Sirius Project scientists appeared to keep the virus from flaring in the test subjects' systems without suppressing their superior strength, agility, speed, and sense of smell. It was a triumph. Or so it seemed. But he knew better then, just as he knew better now. That triumph had become a time bomb, one set to detonate at a werewolf's first alpha spike—at twenty-five human years.

The entire human world had lost its collective mind. The United States' allies asked that the U.S. team share its findings; rumors always crawled out on the battlefield. Death and combat had a way of erasing lines of national demarcation in foxholes and while under attack. Other nations knew the U.S. had taken home some of their badly injured men alive. Claiming sovereignty over their findings and razing all dead human bodies, the U.S. refused, stating that it would not be in their best interests to give any nation what amounted to the schematics to one of their most dangerous weapons in this new fight. The rest of the world was on its own. Politics became so strained that alliances were near total disintegration.

In the meantime, the Americans who survived the testing and responded to the meds jumped at the chance to join the newly created Paranormal Containment Unit. It was a chance to put what most of them viewed as their curse to good use. Those who didn't respond to the meds were put down. All those over twenty-five immediately Turned within the next full moon phase and had to be put down. It was a fate that hung over all of their heads. Although the squad members were never told about the twenty-five-year time bomb they carried within them.

They'd been infected and were now on meds—that was as much of the story as the PCU squads were allowed to have, and why those soldiers stuck together. Keep it simple. What the young ones never knew was, not one man or woman had survived that Colombian Disaster. There were newer meds now, the experiments refined, but what had entered those badly mauled soldiers' systems a little over three decades ago, there was no cure for. The new squads were told that they were found from survivors of civilian attacks. It was the only part of the truth that team psychiatrists and behavioral scientists had introduced to ensure cohesiveness and what made the squads a family—because who else could understand them, but each other?

The brass, feeling smug and self-congratulatory, had dubbed them the Wolf Pack because of their lethality. But Sasha had told him proudly that she and the guys had taken possession of the name because they'd truly become a pack. The memory made him nauseous.

The doctor simply stared at the general for a moment,

needing a fraction of time for his thoughts to return to the war room.

"Xavier, for the amount we've invested in these wolves, getting only a few short years before they Turn is an unacceptable risk factor. The Sirius Project can't lose another one. Fix this." The general stared at the doctor over the tops of his glasses, stood slowly to thrust out his barrel chest, and then leaned on the polished wood to make a menacing point.

"We are working on it," Dr. Holland said, his too calm tone belying his inner rage. "But do remember, I was opposed to this aspect of the project from the beginning. We didn't know enough about the way the virus mutated, but we were instructed to push forward before another nation made a breakthrough. So, I'm well aware of the risks."

"Oh," the general scoffed, glossing over and ignoring the most critical part of the doctor's statement. "You're well aware of the risks? I don't think so. This is beyond budgets—I'm talking intangible costs. If you can't fix this, you know the protocol. Once they start showing signs of a Turn we burn 'em out on mission after mission so we can recoup as much of our investment as possible before we terminate. So either fix it or terminate each wolf, that's the bottom line. The cold war days are over, and truthfully, so are worries about nuclear or pandemic biowarfare. *This* is the new warfare. *This* is our problem now."

Xavier Holland couldn't hear over the sound of his blood rushing in his veins. Fury made his tongue thick and he fought to keep a calm, professional demeanor when responding. Terminating Sasha and the others was out of the question. If he had only gotten to Rod first . . .

"I know that since the discovery of paranormal dimensions the nuclear capacity of any nation is no longer our major concern," Holland coolly retorted, humoring the general. "In fact, that's just a cover intended for the general public now. I'm also well aware that the supernatural represents humanity's greatest threat. Therefore, those dimensional rips have to be monitored—"

"Correct! Dimensions we cannot control that have every damned thing that goes bump in the night potentially allying with nations outside the Alliance must have gatekeepers who follow orders without fail."

Both men stared at each other for a moment.

"Which is why, I'm sure, Sasha instinctively sent North Korea's preternatural convoy a strong message not to piss in our yard," Dr. Holland said, his voice straining with the effort to remain calm. "That convoy had genetic cargo that, if safely couriered to the labs, might have been their first breakthrough in genetic fusion technology to develop—"

The general waved his hand to stop any further discussion. "How long do we have with her?"

A pair of cold gray eyes met a pair of intense dark brown ones without blinking.

"All the subjects have proven stable until at least twenty-five years of—"

"She's twenty-four and already slipping," the general said, cutting off the doctor's explanation and pointing with a hard snap. His arm extended toward the three-dimensional map screen that was now blurred with orange and red hues over a remote section of North Korea. "Has she turned into one of those things yet, Xavier? Has she?"

"No," the doctor said. A silent plea entered his soul: *not Sasha*. Losing Rod was bad enough.

"A *whole team* saw Rod Butler Turn. Don't you think questions will be asked? You didn't have a damage control strategy for that, did you?" When Dr. Holland didn't say more, the general pressed on. "Did you see that heat signature she left from what was to be a quiet, unobtrusive message? Sending her there was a test to see if she could go in under tempting conditions against a known territorial enemy and follow orders under a goddamned full moon. She failed."

The general smoothed a thick palm over his hair and released a weary sigh. "I know you've grown attached to her over the years, more than the others, especially since you raised her. We're all aware of who her parents were to you, Xavier. It was a tragic loss. Shame the way Catherine and Bill died. Nevertheless, do not let your emotions cloud the issue or your loyalty."

"Then let me fix it," Xavier Holland said in a tight, angry tone.

"Fine," the general said, lifting his chin in a way that shook his jowls. "But, ultimately, you're going to have to face the fact that she might be a candidate for extermination before she hits twenty-five if we totally lose control of her. You owe that to Bill and Catherine, as much as anything else."

The doctor's expression didn't change. "I'll fix this. We're working on new dosage levels now and time-released distribution systems that can be embedded under the skin in the event the subject gets separated from his or her supply during battle conditions. We'll rectify the problem immediately."

"You'd better."

"*I said* I would fix this," the doctor repeated, coming dangerously close in tone to insubordination.

"Raise her on sat phone, Xavier. I wanna know what the hell happened out there—what damage control strategies we have to put in place."

A stalemate almost made the air in the room crackle with tension.

"It could compromise her position. She knows to call in when she's clear."

The general's gaze narrowed on Dr. Holland, his assessment raking every line in the doctor's gaunt brown face. "Then I want to be here personally for the debriefing this time."

Three days later: Cheyenne Mountain, Denver
North American Aerospace Defense Command (NORAD) . . .

CLOSED AWAY BEHIND twenty-five-ton steel doors in a windowless world beneath two thousand feet of granite, Sasha instinctively knew she had to pay the band now that the dance was over—but it had been one helluva party. Doc X's body language said as much, too, no matter how calm he tried to keep his voice. His eyes begged her to be on her best behavior. And she had so much to tell him. That little-girl part of her wanted to slip her hand within his big, comforting one. But the independent female within her squared her shoulders and straightened her spine as she tipped her chin up in unspoken defiance. The general could kiss her ass.

As the general dressed her down Sasha held herself back from snarling, but was unable to keep the look of disdain out of her expression. What were they gonna do, court-martial her for blowing up a potential fusion operation in a hostile country that went against every international treaty? *My bad.* The flippant response was on the tip of her tongue, but she held it back.

The part that was frightening was that she almost didn't care. The more she noticed the armed MPs standing at attention near the exits, the more defiance bubbled within her. As she watched the general and saw him warily regard her, the scent of his fear spiked something animalistic inside of her. More animalistic than usual. Sasha gave herself a little mental shake, like a dog shedding water, and wondered where Rod was. And the rest of the pack? She needed to escape these underground steel walls, surface, and breathe fresh mountain air.

"Are we clear, Trudeau?" the general bellowed.

Startled back into the conversation, she met his eyes quickly. "It won't happen again, sir." From the corner of her eye she saw Doc Holland nearly sigh with relief that she'd given the correct response.

"Good. Make sure it doesn't."

She watched the general spin on his heel and stride out the war room doors. She kept her salute rigid until the doors closed behind him and his escort. For a moment neither she nor Doc spoke.

"This time was serious, Sasha," he said in a quiet tone.

Although she felt bad about putting her adopted father in such a tough position, she tried to dismiss the unsettled feeling she had with a wisecrack. "He'll get over it, once he sees that nothing with four legs is going to come out of their labs for a long time."

"That's not the point," Doc snapped. "They were testing you to see if you could follow a direct command under a full moon, and you went extreme—just like they'd predicted."

"Okay, okay," she argued, growing agitated and walking away as she spoke. "Maybe I went a little over the top. I got separated from my kit, was off meds for twelve hours. So, yeah, I was a little antsy. But I saw an opportunity and took it."

Sasha lifted her chin and hoped Holland wouldn't start asking about her sources. He'd wig right now if he found out that a double-dealing vampire had swiped her personal effects for fun. The intel she'd gotten from Shogun would definitely cause apoplexy. And God help them all if the general got wind of it before the facts had been double-checked and sanitized; the man would have a heart attack right after he birthed a cow. Timing was everything, and now obviously wasn't the time. She'd let Doc calm down and would tell him all she'd learned later, in a place where the walls didn't have ears. Waiting was tough, though. Now she knew how he must have felt all those years ago—waiting to tell a fourteen-year-old that she was infected.

Sasha jettisoned the painful memory. She had to stay focused.

What the guys in the war room could never understand was, what happened on the ground was waaay different than all the crap they simulated on cool 3-D monitors and in the sim rooms. And while they trained her in diplomacy, they still distrusted the information coming out of the paranormal communities. However, if you wanted to find a supernatural, you had to go to one. Despite the general's fears and prejudices, the supernatural species was here to stay—wasn't that why they had shamans and psychics on the intel squad monitoring breaches?

Doc Holland began pacing while eyeing her. He didn't need to worry. Vampires didn't seem inclined to attack her, simply because they were revolted by the werewolf virus tainting her blood. Killing her served no purpose. They were in no hurry to see werewolves proliferate on the planet, so it was in their best interest to help . . . as long as it wasn't too inconvenient, aristocrats that they were.

They loved a good sparring match and they played every side against the middle anyway, without allegiance to anything but themselves. It meant they were always good for info, if you could make it worth their while. The ultimate freelancers.

What had happened in North Korea stayed in North Korea. What had happened in the strip bar *definitely* stayed there in South Korea . . . Yeah, later, once in a less hostile environment, she'd debrief Doc on what she'd learned about werewolves. What she needed to tell him would go down better with a beer.

But right now, Holland was slowly pacing, something he did only when very upset. Whatever ration of shit the general had given him, it was clear Holland didn't appreciate it. The muscle in his jaw pulsed and the poor man seemed like he might spontaneously combust where he stood. His usually easygoing manner had been replaced by tight, choppy motions that strangely resembled those of a tin soldier. He seemed to be drowning in thoughts, searching for words as though his mind had stripped a gear. Needing to get out of the steel underground, Sasha tried to mollify the man. Anything to get out.

"Okay. I said I may have gone over the top. You can stop the silent treatment. I'm sorry. It won't happen again."

"Over the top . . . you blew up a bridge, half a mountainside, and an entire convoy. Hitting those targets *were not* your orders," Holland finally shouted as he reached the far side of the room and whirled on her.

The strain in his voice made her bristle. There was something almost desperate in the quality of his tone. Fear wafted off him so strongly that it put tears in her eyes and she turned away. Of all the people in the world, he'd never feared her. Screw the argument about the mission, it hurt like hell to sense such fear coming from her surrogate father. She blinked back the moisture in her eyes and swallowed hard, unable to speak for a moment.

"Sasha," he said more calmly, going to her. "You have to do what these people tell you."

For a moment she just looked at him as he hugged her, now better understanding. He was afraid *for* her, not *of* her.

"They're not the boss of me," she said quietly, trying to make a joke and lessen his worry.

"Yes, Sasha, they are," he said firmly, hugging her tighter.

"You really think they'll actually court-martial me next time, don't you?"

The tall, lean man who held her kissed the top of her head and nodded sadly. "Just do what they say, keep your nose out of trouble . . . and take your meds. All right?"

A CORONA AND some male companionship were calling her name. Stress had kicked her butt all the way down the icy mountainside for eighty miles past Peterson Air Force Base in Colorado Springs, until she could finally pull her red Dodge Nitro up to her apartment.

Being home had never felt so good. Sasha cut the ignition and stared at the door of her walk-up duplex for a moment, getting her bearings. She just hoped Mrs. Baker hadn't overfed Fred. The woman thought all creatures needed far more food than was necessary. It would be just her luck that she'd find him floating belly-up when she opened the door.

On cue, Mrs. Baker appeared at the door of her apartment in neon rollers that were partially hidden beneath a sheer white scarf and clutching her pink and gray plaid flannel robe over her ample breasts. The elderly matron waved and smiled widely. Sasha got out of the car and waved back.

"Good to have you home again, sweetie," Mrs. Baker said. "I took good care of Fred and all your mail."

"Thanks so much. It's so good to be home. Now you let me know if you need anything from the store. Roads are bad," Sasha said with a warm smile. A sense of belonging wafted through her as the older woman's breath caught on the night air in frosty puffs. After what Shogun had told her, she was starting to believe in fairy godmothers.

"I will, I will. It's just nice to have young folk around . . . makes it not so lonely in the building."

Sasha nodded as Mrs. Baker waved good night. She knew exactly what her neighbor meant. There was comfort in numbers, a feeling of security in a pack.

With a sigh Sasha depressed the lock button and alarm on her key ring, causing a little beep-beep to sound, and then mounted the stairs taking two at a time. It wasn't fair; they were supposed to give her two weeks off after a mission like the one she'd just been on, but instead she only got forty-eight hours after today. Saturday and Sunday. Monday she had to report in. She understood it as the punishment Doc explained it to be, but resentment still made her want to growl. However, resentment was a waste; the general could probably give a rat's raw behind about what she thought or how she felt. Asshole.

Shake it off, she told herself, and simply kept moving.

Once she opened the door to her place she could see that Mrs. Baker had dutifully taken in her mail and neatly stacked it on the coffee table. The woman had also tidied up, leaving every surface of her Ikea-created home glistening with lemon-scented furniture polish. If she didn't know better, she'd swear that Mrs. Baker was ex-military, based on the way the woman had cleaned.

"Aw . . . Mom Baker . . ."

Sasha's eyes scanned the meticulous living room and dining area. She'd throw in a pie, too, when she went to the market for her elderly neighbor. Growing up in foster care early on, until Doc had claimed her, had made Sasha appreciate even the smallest maternal gesture. A good old-fashioned hug was in order, too. Next time she saw Mrs. Baker, she'd claim one of her meaty-armed bear hugs.

Oblivious to her arrival, Fred was making endless circles in his bowl while she took a moment to sense her environment before entering it. Out of habit, Sasha scanned the apartment for signs of anything being out of the norm, and finding nothing, she relaxed and shut the door behind her.

"Did you miss me?" she called out to Fred while shedding her chocolate-brown leather bomber jacket and tossing it on the sofa. "You eat today?" Sasha smiled and tapped her finger against the glass bowl, watching a pair of bulbous eyes and a gaping mouth try to peck at what probably seemed to be a huge worm. Leaving a tiny pinch of food for Fred to chase on the water's surface, she went to the telephone to check her voice-mail messages. There were none, so the guys weren't back from their mission.

Crossing the room with purpose, she opened the fridge and stood before it with her arms folded. "Everything smells like a science project," she muttered. Sasha glanced over at the fish. "So, Fred, wanna order Chinese?"

Disgusted, she whipped out a kitchen trash bag from under the sink and began to dump. The routine was always the same, but it still annoyed her. Order takeout because you never know when you might have to stop, drop, and roll.

But she really couldn't complain. Her dishes were all done, neatly washed and dried and left stacked on the side counter. Mrs. Baker clearly respected her unspoken boundaries by not going inside any cabinets, drawers, or even the fridge while she was gone. Theirs was an implicit truce where an invisible line of demarcation existed.

"C'mon, guys . . . get your assignment done and get home . . ." Sasha muttered to herself, becoming forlorn as she walked through the apartment with an overstuffed bag of garbage. She willed herself not to start doing some crazy thing like calling around to the rest of the pack. They'd be in touch as soon as they were Stateside. She flushed thinking about the signals Rod had been sending the last time they had all been together.

She stepped outside with her trash and chilly November wind slapped at her face and cut at any exposed skin not covered by her gray cable-knit sweater, hurrying her steps. A stray cat arched and hissed and then bolted away from the cans in the driveway. Cats did not like her, but God bless Mrs. Baker, who took in every stray that would lap milk at her front door.

Sasha ran back up the steps and closed the door behind her.

A disturbing thought followed her into her apartment. What if Rod fell in love with a pure human woman one day? One who could cope with what he was? After all, women were always more flexible about weirdness than men. What if, once Rod found his soul mate, things changed? She would miss him for sure.

Sasha shook her head. If Rod fell in love with someone else, she would still be his beta. Nothing could change that except a challenge to her authority within the pack. And what was wrong with her anyway? She sounded pathetic even to her own self. Geeze!

It was time to get out of the apartment. Time to go find people and get out of her own head. A hot shower, a change of clothes, and a visit to the Hawg was in order.

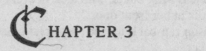

CHAPTER 3

FAMILIAR SCENTS, HARD-DRIVING music, and a blast of heat washed over Sasha as she opened the door to Ronnie's Road Hog Tavern, which everyone also affectionately called the Hawg. It was hard to stay in a bad mood in a joint like this. There was just too much revelry all around.

Ronnie was a local legend in his own right, claiming to have seen a Sasquatch up close and personal, and he maintained a neutral position about all things supernatural. In a way, his bar was the preternatural's equivalent of Switzerland, and a comfortable place for her and the guys to hang out. It was haunted, too, they said. Something about a shoot-out and gold miners, but that was ancient history. However, not everything supernatural passed through Ronnie's doors. Vampires seemed to shun the low-brow life of beef and beer, snobs that they were—and her pack would have to do them, anyway, if they witnessed a civvy being bitten. Regardless, it meant Ronnie's joint was always the place to be, sawdust on the floor notwithstanding.

Werewolves . . . other than the few attempts at black-

market experiments, they didn't see much of them anywhere lately, and definitely not here. But now she had to
reevaluate everything she knew about them.

Sasha scanned the establishment as she walked through
it. Werewolves infected by the demon virus were possibly
the easiest to hunt, because one had a window to track
them, namely during a full moon, so their attacks on civilians were limited. Now that the security forces knew what
they were looking for, they knew the questions to ask,
how to monitor incident reports, how to zero in and test
human blood.

But, again, Shogun had added a whole new layer of
complexity to the thing. For the military, it was black-
and-white—other species meant bad and she was supposed to kill them or negotiate best terms with them. Now
she'd have to reevaluate her entire approach and thought
processes, regardless of what the brass said. It was the
only right thing to do. As soon as Doc got free, they
needed to talk. Plus, this Shogun guy might have the key
to help Doc combat the bad infection she and Rod and the
others had contracted. Maybe.

There was even a partial antidote now, for crissake.
Well, until all this new info got sorted out, at least there
were meds that somewhat controlled the virus, if one was
infected. And Doc was refining the cocktail daily.

Sasha shook her head and ruffled the hair up from her
neck. Why wouldn't her brain simply turn off about this
crap? As it was, she was still pissed that she had to go right
back into the line of fire in two days. The least she could do
was give her own mind a break. Besides, the Hawg served
the best steak and fries in portions that were ridiculous.
The burgers were awesome, too.

As she waded through the crowd toward the bar, an
ice-cold Corona on her mind, Sasha nodded at the regu-
lars and unzipped her bomber jacket, prepared to stay a

while. The bartender spotted her and held up a Corona and she smiled, giving him the thumbs-up.

He slid it across the wood with deft accuracy and she caught the frosty bottle that had a lime wedged in the top with a quick hand and blew him a kiss as a joke. In their ongoing ritual he jerked his head back as though the air-kiss had knocked him out, and then he laughed.

"I'll run you a tab, babe."

"Cool, Bruno," she shouted over the din. "Thanks."

Now to find someplace to sit down and eat alone. Everything in the primary bar area was already taken. In the billiards area, tables were temporarily abandoned by players but were already claimed with pitchers of beer and buffalo wings marking territory. There wasn't even a tiny table available by the back wall on the way to the ladies' room. Fine. Takeout could work.

She let out a defeated breath but took one last survey of the joint. A couple of guys gave her a bold once-over but she ignored their silent offers. Bikers and truckers. She wasn't in the mood. If she was going home with any-one tonight, for once she just wished it could be with a guy that she didn't have to explain things to—things like medications, having to be sure not to get too rough and break his skin, or to worry about a virus ruining his life.

However, she didn't want to leave as if she'd been chased out, either.

She would admit, though, that the more crowded the establishment was, the lonelier it felt.

And who the hell was watching her so hard that it was raising the hair on her arms?

Sasha pushed the lime into her beer with her index fin-ger, raised the slim bottle up to her lips, took a few swal-lows, and then glanced around. Definitely no sign of the guys.

Moving through the crowd as if she had a specific

destination in mind, Sasha enjoyed flowing through the tangle of bodies to the beat of the music. Warmth, sweat, scents, the thrum of pulsing melodies . . . blood, heart-beats all merged as her spine became fluid, her footfalls beyond graceful. Her stomach rumbled as her nose keened to the charbroiled beef wafting from the kitchen and she made a game out of separating scents, sounds, and voices, keying in on bits of conversation as she now loped through the large dance floor headed for the second bar where takeout orders could be placed.

Mid-step she stopped, tilted her head, and gazed into the darkened corridor beyond the bar. A cool breeze had brought in a scent from somewhere, a scent she'd never picked up in her life.

Sasha turned her beer up and polished it off, then continued to head toward the second bar, her eyes fastened on the dark corridor. She could smell multiple male scents. The men's room? A back room? An exit? A closed section of the tavern? Curiosity stole over her as she slid the empty bottle onto the edge of the bar. She quickly placed her order, trying to forestall the insanity, but her gaze continually wandered past the server toward the back of the establishment.

The scent came to her again, raising her hackles. Suddenly out of nowhere, she rounded the bar and stepped into the semidarkness. Fortunately, the server's attention was diverted with the next order. That scent . . . that wonderfully unsettling male scent. All others evaporated, but that one lingered. Dominant. Who the hell was it? Moreover, *what* the hell was it? It wasn't human—at least not wholly so, she could tell. Yet there wasn't the rancid, fecund smell of wet, filthy animal that came with infected werewolf sightings. This was . . . *wonderful* and all wolf, but somehow different from Shogun. Plus . . .

Insides on fire, hair bristling, Sasha slipped deeper into

the employees-only area undetected and passed through the long corridor scenting locked doors . . . Faster, moving like a blur, following the scent that led to a cool breeze. Her hand slammed against an exit panic bar, and suddenly she was outside in the back employees' parking area. Her gaze quickly took in the huge Ford F-150s and Dodge Rams that haphazardly littered the small back lot amid the overflowing Dumpsters.

Still now, she listened to her own breath, her own heartbeat, keening her hearing to the very slightest movement against the icy ground. There was no sound, but the scent was moving, circling her, producing a delirious combination of adrenaline and something she wasn't prepared to admit.

Moving with the scent, she crouched, lowering her body's center of gravity, arms readied, muscles tensing, turning in a slow circle. A back floodlight instantly blew out, leaving her in total darkness, save for the blue-white wash of the moon. She smiled. He had no idea . . .

He smiled and cocked his head to the side, fascinated that she could not readily detect him. This time she was alone. And this time she was no less exquisite than any other time before. Too bad it was impossible to stay downwind from her this go-round.

Her smoky gray eyes had become almost a translucent crystalline, like that of a husky . . . pupils open so wide they nearly eclipsed her irises. Her stare intense, her honey-kissed skin awash with maddening moonlight, waves of velvet barely kissing her shoulders and yet slowly lengthening as her beast flared right before his eyes. Her beautiful jawline was set hard, her voluptuous curves sculpted beneath a wisp of gray mohair sweater partially hidden by her bomber jacket, her throat so gloriously exposed for a submission bite . . . if she would accept. His gaze raked her lean hips that tapered into seemingly endless legs all the way down to deep brown hand-tooled leather cowboy boots. Damn . . .

He briefly closed his eyes and inhaled deeply, taking in her scent, wanting her more deeply, needing her more intensely than his pride had allowed until now. She was of his clan, his pack—a shadow wolf.

But he had an assassination to pull off. On each previous encounter she'd been with an abomination of their breed. He'd been sickened, scenting the predator on her, especially when his mission was to hunt down the demon-infected werewolves. That was her job, too, but she seemed ignorant of the task. Then again, he hadn't seen the predator in approximately a month. Perhaps she'd done her job and killed him already?

Slightly distracted, he moved again but a footfall broke through the shadows. She immediately spun and lunged at the nothingness, no fear in her eyes, but she missed. He stepped out of the shadows. Her response was a hard snarl as she quickly picked up an empty beer bottle and broke it on the edge of a Dumpster, gripping it like a weapon.

"That's not necessary," he said in a low rumble.

"Fuck that I-come-in-peace line. You were invisible a second ago."

"Yeah, and?" Perplexed, he simply stared at the disoriented beauty before him. Didn't all shadow wolves remain unseen until advisable?

"I hate you goddamned vampires, ya know." She flung the bottle away. "So what do you want?"

He was so offended that he folded his arms over his chest. "I've been called a lot of things in my time, sis, but *a vampire*? Never."

She cocked her head to the side and sniffed the air, but the confusion was clear on her face.

What the hell was he—a new species? Something that moved between shadows and didn't make a sound.

Smelled all wolf, all male. The rumble of his voice bottomed out in the pit of her stomach. Still left a flutter in its wake. Accent was strange, had French-Canadian and also West-Indian tones embedded in it. His ethnicity was hard to judge. He was a nightmare and a fantasy all rolled into one, wearing a deerskin suede jacket, a charcoal sweater, ripped, rough-rider jeans, and well-worn cowboy boots. Had accosted her in the back lot. She rolled her shoulders and began snapping closed the brass buttons on her jacket.

"Whatever. You were following me, staring at me while I was trying to get my dinner and mind my business. I didn't appreciate it."

Complete disappointment singed her voice as she yanked the bottom of her jacket down hard and warily turned away to round the building to reenter the bar. The sound of her voice reverberated through him and lingered on the night air, with her fabulous feminine trail thickening his groin. Yet he sensed no fraud; she really didn't seem to know what to make of him.

Her piercing gray eyes haunted him as she disappeared around the edge of the huge building. He watched her ass move beneath the leather, kneading muscle and sinew in an almost soundless stride. But he also had to find out what had happened to the huge predator she'd been with a month ago, if there had been more infected by him. She wasn't at risk; like him, her shadow wolf blood was impervious to the scourges of other species. Their bodies were even uninhabitable by ghosts and possession demons—the wolf kept them at bay. But if she didn't eviscerate the infected alpha werewolf and track the others he'd probably infected, a deadly demon wolf pack could form. Why wasn't she hunting the threat?

He shook off the question and decided to follow her back inside.

Sasha boxed the cold away from her arms, realizing

that the shiver that had overtaken her wasn't from the frigid temperatures outside. She was getting that burger and a six-pack to go, and that was all there was to it. She kept walking toward the back bar, unceremoniously parting the crowd now with sheer shoulder-blocking force and without apologies. She *needed* to eat.

The man was an unbelievable specimen. He was massive. Six foot four or five and coulda probably ripped her throat out, but had not. That was some sexy shit, even if he was possibly a vampire messing with her mind. But the scent wasn't of the undead. His sweat held life, vitality, and ungodly testosterone. It was a scent that combined the earth and deep, sensual musk. Geoff had gotten to her with mind games, Shogun she could appreciate visually, but her reaction to this man was different. More . . . real somehow.

She allowed a shudder to pass through her, and hailed the bartender. "I'm the monster burger with the works. To go, with a six of Corona," she shouted, determined to shake off the experience.

But as she waited and kept her gaze roving the establishment, she remembered feeling him before, although never seeing him and definitely never scenting him like this. Now she knew his signature and she had an incredibly rugged, too ridiculously handsome face to place with the impressions. His heartbeat was a slow, long thud. Hue . . . unflawed darkness, making his actual age impossible to judge. Skin like rich, semi-sweet chocolate that made one's hand ache to touch it, just to feel the texture. Sasha licked her lips, unwilling to admit that she also wanted to taste it.

Features—strong, nose owned a slight bend in the bridge . . . Native American. Mouth, thick, lush, so sensual a feature that she was mesmerized by it. African. Hair, thick tendrils of dark velvet pulled back into a leather strap with Blackfoot tribal markings on it. Glistening white teeth . . . a warning held in check; a square jaw covered by a dark spread of evening shadow. Eyes, an intense midnight engulfed by shimmering amber. So strange, as though backlit by some inner light.

Amber and silver—the necklace he wore told her he couldn't be werewolf. Rod broke out in hives just from a pair of earrings she'd worn once; couldn't tolerate it anywhere near him. It gave him nausea, vomiting, burns, the works. A piece the size she'd just seen would have landed Butler in ER, code blue. Probably the only reason she could stand it was the virus hadn't advanced in her system as quickly, yet. But she wasn't gonna chance it.

So how could this mystery man, who was definitely something supernatural, have on a thick rope of silver chain with a huge hunk of rare, etched amber dangling from his neck like a talisman . . . in fact, even vampires weren't big on silver, come to think of it. Shaman? Warlock? What else was out there that they didn't have catalogued?

But the way the guy moved . . . like the night itself, like a thief cloaked within the very folds of every shadow. An assassin's stealth, but owning what had to be anywhere between two hundred and two hundred and twenty pounds of pure sinew. Massive shoulder width; arms and legs lean, muscular, moving as though every joint were a well-greased ball bearing. Sexy as hell, if she did say so herself.

How did he do it, though? Not even vampires had been able to catch her unawares: their absence of scent, the very stillness as they repressed their absence of life, was always, literally, a dead giveaway, as was the oppressive feel of their power touching the edges of her aura. Ghosts, same thing. The temperature dropped and they moved through the atmosphere like a reverse heat wave or like the clear ripple on a lake's surface before they materialized.

Demons made her gag with the foul scent of rotting flesh, and their eyes were red orbs of insanity. Nah. If he wasn't any of the above—then what was he?

Curiosity and a looming presence thickened with a now familiar scent made her jerk her attention toward the entrance. He nodded coolly and parted the crowd with a fluid ease that was unnerving. For a moment, all she could do was watch him walk.

XAVIER HOLLAND SLOWLY stirred his cocoa and added more brandy to it under the soft, golden night-light in the kitchen of his home. His conscience dueled with his logic as he brought the thick mug up to his mouth and allowed the aromatic steam to warm his face. Dear God, what had they done? What had he done? How was he to break it to Sasha that Rod was dead?

Blood was as much on his hands as it was on those of his beloved mentor, Dr. Lou Zang Chen. But they hadn't known, hadn't thought things would ever escalate this far!

Xavier closed his eyes and fought the building moisture. Sasha . . . run, pretty baby. Run, if they come for you in ignorance. Three decades devoted to science and now they were asking him to be a murderer. Chen had already given his life in the line of duty—with the very first of the infected. That had been the beginning. That was how they found out that the virus affected an already adult male subject in horrible ways.

Vivid memories poured into the doctor's mind in a gruesome flashback and held him enthralled. His hand shook so hard that he had to lower the mug to the counter as he stared out the bay windows at the moon.

Instead of the frosted glass that led out to his deck, he saw the lab separation glass from all those years ago. The last surviving soldier, Subject 004, had been strapped down to the table while they ran some routine tests. This subject had lasted the longest, so much of their hope had been pinned on him. But in that last month, he had begun demonstrating the familiar signs of a Turn. All of a sudden, he had begun to convulse and then change, turning into a beast. He had torn free of his bonds. He'd leaped across the room, pinning Chen down before he tore open the doctor's throat and chest. A monster was on the loose.

Blood and gore splattered lab windows as he ate the man. A brilliant mind lost. Pandemonium. MPs firing ineffective rounds. The lab floor a wading pool of crimson. Glowing eyes meeting his, then a lunge and crashing glass. The beast racing forward, scientists screaming, diving beneath equipment. More death. And then one silver bullet fired from his Glock nine-millimeter that he had always kept nearby. Dead aim. Survival a matter of seconds, a matter of inches. The beast fell and he'd lived.

Doc Holland brought the cup up to his lips calmly and took a steadier sip. The general had not been in the lab that day. He took another even sip. The entire lab had almost been lost. Then what? Fingering the small amber and sterling piece he always wore beneath his shirt, Holland allowed his thoughts to stray.

There was so much he'd learned since those early days. But they had experienced the true horror of a demon-infected werewolf that day. Oh, yes, he had known about demon-infected werewolves. He had fatefully met a Blackfoot shaman named Silver Hawk, a few years before. Silver Hawk had opened his eyes to a great many things that he had not dared share with anyone else. The general, in his insanity, couldn't know . . . he'd start a global war by sending in troops against a part of the species that had no culpability for those hit with the deadly virus. However, he knew in his heart the military made no such distinction. But from the very beginning, anyone who had known what to look for when studying Rod's blood would have known that he had been demon-infected. And now Sasha and the others faced extermination, too. What he had managed to keep completely secret for all these years was that Sasha, Woods, and Fisher were very different from Rod.

Tears streamed down the doctor's face. "God forgive me," he whispered. "Rod, forgive me, son." He clutched his fist to his side and looked up toward the ceiling, a sob choking him as tears glistened on his dark, weathered face. "What was I to do!"

Feeling quite old, Holland rubbed a weary palm over his thinning, kinky hair and let out a shuddering breath. His personal cell phone ringing in the distance snatched his attention away from the past. He set down his mug quickly and began running through the spacious Tudor to his second-floor bedroom. He'd gone to great lengths to hide this cell phone from all brass. Only Sasha and the team had the number.

Breathless, he picked up on the sixth ring before it went to voice mail. Not even looking at the number, he took the call as sweat broke out all over his body.

"Doc, oh shit, they fired on us! The whole squad was hit—by our own!"

"Easy. I'm listening." Doc Holland's eyes scanned the room, knowing that his home was probably bugged.

Snatching off his robe that could easily harbor a listening device, he headed back down the hallway like the house was on fire, down the steps toward the back deck, and flung open the doors. As Woods's hysterical voice battered his senses, he frantically shed his leather slippers, then stripped naked, running, shivering, into the backyard with the phone that never left his possession. He pressed the cell phone to his face as a panicked voice continued to fill his ear.

"What the fuck is going on! We weren't bitten again . . . Sherwin, Gonzalez, Johnson didn't even have the virus, Doc . . . but they're all dead—with . . . with Rod! The chopper fired on us—*us*."

"Have you called Sasha?"

"No, I called you—"

"Don't call her," the doctor warned. "You could put her at risk. Make me your only contact."

"Okay, okay," Woods said in bursts. "I understand."

"Are you safe?" Ice and snow sent stabs of freezing pain into the doctor's feet. The bitter cold and wind made him double over in agony as he covered his genitals and hunched his body.

"Yeah, yeah, for now—but—"

"Listen to me, son," Dr. Holland said, his voice a low, urgent hiss. "You have to disappear if you want to live. I'm so sorry, that's all I can tell you right now. It's not your fault. None of this is your fault."

"Where are me and Fisher gonna go? We have no money, we're *Americans*. We didn't do anything wrong! We followed orders!"

"I know, I know . . . I need to talk to some people, find a way to safely bring you in. But right now they'll shoot you on sight." Thoughts of the general's damage-control strategy carved at the doctor's soul as he tried to talk Woods down. Young men had died to keep a secret; they had seen Rod Butler transform, knew what they could possibly become, and the general feared they'd go AWOL—their bodies living contraband on the open black market for anyone who learned what they were. "I'll have to find a way to get assets to you—but right now you can't call me. They could track the call. We've already been on the phone too long." His mind was whirring as he spoke. He had to get to them, or they'd be hunted down and incinerated.

"But what about our meds, man? Doc, you can't leave us out here like this with no meds! We saw what happened to Butler without 'em in his system too long!"

Xavier Holland closed his eyes as a young man's voice broke into a splintered plea.

"Oh, dear God, Doc—don't leave us to turn into one of those things. It wasn't our fault me and Fish were bitten when we were kids. I swear to God we'll take the medicine, me and Fisher will . . . Jesus Christ, don't leave us like this!"

The doctor swallowed hard. "Listen to me. You won't Turn like Rod. You have to trust me on that. I'll get medicine to you and money—I swear on my life, son. Just shut down the call and get away from wherever you called me. If they picked this up on satellite and triangulate . . . need I say more?"

He clicked off the call abruptly and stood in the darkness letting the wind lacerate him. But it was the hollow chill within his soul that caused him to shiver.

"DID YOU KILL him? Is that why he's not here with you tonight?"

Sasha blinked twice at the mystery man who was now before her, not sure that she'd heard right. Her gaze narrowed. "What did you say?"

He leaned in and she jerked her head back. He straightened.

"I said, did you kill him? The werewolf you were always in here with—the big redhead."

The question was asked in a low enough timbre that only one with superior hearing ability would have been able to make out what the man had said, but Sasha's hands balled into fists in outrage.

"And what are you?" she asked, her eyes hard as she

hurled her newly acquired information at the intruder. "Some kind of warlock on a vigilante trip?" She'd delivered her warning with a low growl through her teeth, also keeping her voice low enough that the average human wouldn't have heard the comment over the din.

It annoyed her no end that he just cocked his head to the side and stared at her. It also deeply concerned her that one of her team had been made, in fact, possibly all of them, and now there was a hostile force asking very dangerous questions.

Sasha turned, paid for her meal, then set the bags down hard on the bar for a moment, and turned back around. She looked him in the eye. "I'll tell you this much. You're yanking with the U.S. military, pal, and if the big redhead goes missing, you'll have an M-16 shoved so far up your ass you'll choke on it. Believe that."

"You do not understand—"

"No, correction—*you* don't understand," she said, pointing toward his massive chest. "You got a problem with one of my pack brothers, then you've got a problem with me. And trust me; you *do not* wanna have a problem with me."

"You've picked the wrong pack to defend," he said quietly. "Pity. Soon you will have to choose and step into your destiny. You are of our clan."

Sasha turned briefly to collect her food and six-pack, fury making it almost impossible to speak. But when she whirled around with a hot comeback line, he was gone.

An eerie calm came over her. She knew her guys could handle any potential threat that came to their door, but there was no way she was going to allow her brothers to get ambushed by a nutcase. And it hadn't escaped her notice that he hadn't asked about the rest of the pack. Could that mean he had already gotten to Woods and Fisher and was now going after Rod? Her heart was pounding hard and fast. Maybe that was why she hadn't heard from any of them. Well, now it was time to blow up cell phones, ask questions about the guys' whereabouts, and use keys she swore she'd never use. If there was some huge psycho stalking Rod because he'd somehow picked up on the virus in him, then all privacy bets were off. Sasha stood still for a moment, her instinctive distrust of the general blossoming. What if they'd sent an exterminator from another branch of Special Forces? This guy knew too much about them for it to be strictly coincidence. If that was the case, then this was an emergency. A 911 in full effect.

As she dashed through the crowd, her heart was in her mouth. She had to get more info on this guy, zero in on his angle. The only way to beat a threat was to understand how it thought, follow its modus operandi. But she'd been so angry at the affront that she'd chased him away rather than luring critical intel out of his sick, twisted brain.

"Damn!" she muttered, as she scanned the parking lot, knowing before she looked that she'd never spot him that way. She couldn't even smell him any longer; the only scent cloying at her was her burger.

She stalked over to her vehicle, depressed the alarm locks, and opened the door, checking the back seat both visually and with her nose. The moment she hopped in, she locked the doors, tossed the burger and the six-pack onto the passenger seat, opened the glove compartment, and withdrew a nine-millimeter. She placed the nine-millimeter on the passenger seat as well and extracted her cell phone from her bomber jacket and shoved it into the hands-free unit.

Adrenaline still pumping through her, she gunned the motor and tore out of the space, hitting Rod's number on the contact speed dial first. Ripping into the packages, and driving with one hand, she balanced the burger, took a bite, listening to and counting rings with despair.

"Damn! Pick up, Rod," she yelled at the phone in order to be heard. "Got a serious situation. Watch your six, got a lunatic looking for you. Call me."

Repeating basically the same message for Woods and Fisher, she groaned in frustration, the sound coming out more more like a growl.

"Hate it, hate it, hate it! I *hate* voice mail," she finally yelled, now crazy enough to be driving with her knee at eighty miles per hour on Colorado's ice-slicked roads as she held her oversized burger with one hand and slapped the dashboard with each word with the other when her next call even rolled over to Doc Holland's message center.

When the Nitro swerved, she grabbed the wheel, resigned to finish her burger later and go door to door with her quest.

CHAPTER 4

PANIC BECAME A monster of its own as Sasha skidded the Nitro to a stop in front of Fisher's building and leaped out. Jim's apartment was the closest along the way.

The only person's keys she had were Rod's—keys he'd oddly given her without explanation before they'd all left on their most recent assignments—and Jim's fourth-floor apartment presented a challenge. Sasha tucked the nine-millimeter into the back waistband of her pants beneath her jacket and then leaned on the buzzer, feeling her heart slamming against her breastbone. The rational part of her brain kept asking the primal, irrational side of it what was wrong as she rang Jim's bell like a lunatic. Common sense dictated that if they were on assignment, just like she had been, there'd be no answer. They did this all the time, so what was her problem?

That was the problem: the fact that she felt like something was wrong and her gut never failed her.

She shoved away from the building, disgusted. The other problem was that this time they had been separated without warning, had been told not to inform the others on the team of their whereabouts. A tight-knit group that was forced to keep secrets within it. Her gut was on fire, as though some unseen warning was making every hair follicle on her body stand and shout an alarm. And all that had happened after she'd met the big predator who seemed like he was on the hunt for her guys.

Screw it, she was going in.

Rounding the building to find the back alleyway, she scanned the possibilities. A huge Dumpster was twenty feet from the fire escape, but could give her a leg up to hit the iron ladder that was two stories up.

Without mentally debating the plan, she hurried over to the Dumpster, dragged it under the fire escape, scaled it, and reached up. An entire story still separated her from the last ladder rung. If she went into that apartment and found Jim murdered . . .

Her eyes focused on the single rung as she crouched low. Then she leaped. She grabbed the rung with sure hands and held on while her body swung awkwardly. She began to push her lower body back and forth until she got enough momentum to swing her body up into a handstand before hooking her feet into a higher rung. From there, it was a piece of cake.

She made fast work of getting to the fourth floor, but the steel door was locked. Damn! But what else had she expected? Windows for adjacent apartments were too far from the fire escape to reach, and she wasn't big on scaring some innocent person half to death, or getting shot.

Sasha raked her fingers through her hair and judged the ledge to the windows. Too narrow to even think about walking it . . . but then again, she was sure she had enough upper body strength to make it to the first window. That still didn't solve the issue of people being home. Alternative—she looked up. Go in from the roof.

Climbing fast and hard, she got to the top floor quickly, but still had another floor between where she stood and the roof, with no iron ladder to make it easy. Frustration cascaded through her muscles and she jumped as high as she could and grabbed the gutter rails, then half dragged, half pulled herself over the edge.

Sweating, breathing hard, she rested for a second before scrambling to her feet, and then rushed toward the roof door only to be disappointed. Just like the fire escape, it was steel, opening from the inside only, and was locked. Steam vents were too small, there was no skylight, just an endless square of blacktop that made her pace, kept a growl rumbling in her throat. And then something completely insane tore through her. Rage.

Running full throttle toward the door, she let out an attack sound, and slammed against it. She collided hard enough to make her see stars and to bounce her body off the structure and onto her side. "Ow . . ."

She got up with care, checked her weapon, and then studied the door while rubbing her shoulder. To her complete surprise a part of the frame had given way—at least enough to expose the tiny blue emergency light inside. Her hands suddenly became tools, pulling at the metal, digging at the weakened brick, until the compromised barrier pulled away from its anchors enough to allow her to squeeze through it.

Inside. Yes!

Again, running, this time with direction, following, following, knowing Jim's scent, corridors a blur, his door no true barrier. The heel of her hand at the knob and a hard shoulder where the dead bolt would be was an easy way to take out the frame. She just hoped his partying neighbors weren't home, and that a dear old lady like Mrs. Baker wasn't the local Town Watch committee chairman.

She was in Jim Fisher's apartment in a flash and gently closed the door behind her. Sasha's eyes tore around his place. General male clutter. Sneakers in a corner, things definitely rotting in the fridge. She lifted her nose. God, the bathroom needed a good swabbing down. But there was nothing registering alarm.

Still wary, she moved through Jim's place with calm stealth, listening, looking, searching. But on the whole it just appeared like the man had rolled out as per usual and would be back. Feeling foolish now as she stared at his broken door, her shoulders sagged as she let out a hard breath and blew her hair up off her forehead.

Raking her fingers through it, she nosed around his place, checking out his bulletin board in search of the super's number. That was the least she could do—alert the late-night maintenance dude that someone had tried the door and it needed to be fixed. Jim was gonna be soooo pissed.

Business cards, porn Web site postcards, old party fly-ers, and a couple of numbers on napkins, as well as several group shots of the team were stuck under thumbtacks on the wall corkboard behind his computer chair. Even though she knew it was a violation of Fisher's privacy, she couldn't help smiling and reaching out to touch the photos that held such fond memories. And then panic washed through her again.

Either she was crazy, or something was definitely wrong.

She sat down, moving with purpose, and clicked on Jim's computer. Screw it, she had her reasons.

Her eyes narrowed at his desktop wallpaper while she waited for all the icons to settle down. It was a blonde in the most *open* doggie-style position she could imagine with a pair of the biggest breasts she'd ever seen on a woman that tiny. It was definitely TMI about Jim's preferences.

Feeling no guilt or regret, she made an Internet con-nection, got the secure NORAD screens, and then began playing with combinations of Jim's birthday, favorite color, zodiac sign, and favorite sports team numbers until she got into his official e-mail. She had to shake her head at herself as Shogun's words again pierced her brain: what if there really were such things as computer gremlins? "A little assist," she muttered, still working password combinations. Then bingo.

"Afghanistan . . . they went right from the deployment to Nicaragua to Afghanistan? No wonder," she said, now truly feeling foolish as she booted down the system and stood. But her prayers had been answered. At least Fisher's file said "still active," which meant he and the other guys were not only alive, but that they also weren't home to deal with a lunatic yet.

Without many options left, she went to the kitchen wall phone to call 911, when she spotted the super's number written on the wall in pen. Such a guy thing. She released her breath hard, got into her best airhead persona, and calmly dialed the super.

"Well, I know this is all illegal," she said, walking back and forth as she spoke. "But like, he and I were going out for like a week and he had my toothbrush and my CD, so he wouldn't call me back—but, like—I don't want the guy to get robbed or anything . . . and I'll know you were the one who took anything if you do, 'cause I'm also calling the police, so if you don't fix it—"

Sasha smiled as the very grumpy man on the other end of the line cut off her statement and called her a bitch. "Loser," she murmured as she fled the apartment and left the building in a much more traditional way than she'd come in. At least Jim's door would be repaired. But what a fiasco.

Woods, thank God, had a town house. Something still gnawing her gut made her hell-bent on checking up on all her guys, just to be on the safe side. When she pulled her SUV up into his driveway, she knew it would be easy to walk around the periphery, find a window or something, and get in. If he had an alarm, oh, well . . . she just needed a few moments to establish that he hadn't been home in a while and was on a mission.

It was easy, too easy, to get in through a back window. She would have to tell Woods that when he got home. A quick jab with an elbow against glass, a small breaking sound that was not loud enough to rouse neighbors, and she was up, over, and in.

His place was much neater than Jim's by far, but her nose told her that he, too, hadn't been home in a while. It was still a bachelor's pad, mainly comprised of sound system technology, televisions, music, and a Bowflex.

She made a quick reconnaissance through the small town house and sighed a breath of relief as she made her way through the house to leave, then remembered the window. Grudgingly she stopped and looked around for something to help secure it.

"Damn, Sasha . . . you are just cuttin' one helluva swath through this town tonight, aren't ya, girl?"

Unfortunately, if she was going to secure Darien's house, she'd have to go to his basement, find a board, cover it, and then nail it shut from the outside; all this assuming he had said implements in his basement and that she could do all this without alerting neighbors. A royal pain in the ass. There had to be an easier way.

She went to the basement door and opened it, but an eerie feeling of being watched made her hesitate at the top of the steps. Unfounded wariness made her slowly close the door again and move away from it.

Going back out the window quickly, she strolled around to the front of the house and went to the nearest neighbor's home that had a car in the driveway. As pleasantly as possible she leaned on a bell until lights came on, and then looked at the disheveled occupants who opened their door as though she were selling Girl Scout cookies at high noon.

"Hi, I'm Sasha, a friend of your neighbor Darien Woods." She motioned to Darien's town house and kept a pleasant expression for the middle-aged couple. "While he goes out of town sometimes, he always asks me to just cruise by to be sure everything's okay at his house, and I noticed his back window was smashed. Did you guys hear anything?"

The man wearing a blue flannel robe stepped forward and peered down the street as his wife leaned forward, craning her neck to get a better look.

"No," he said, squinting. "Honey, maybe we should call the cops."

"Yeah," Sasha said. "Good idea. I have to go to work, you know, four A.M. shift, but uh, I'd hate to have another prowler get in his place once the cops give the all clear."

"Bud, maybe you could put a board up over the break and nail his window shut," his wife said, clutching her robe against the elements. "I mean, that's the least we could do as neighbors—since that poor man's home might have been burglarized while he was away in the military and all."

"Yeah, yeah, call the cops, and I'll put on my clothes. Once they say it's clear, I'll do that." The husband turned to Sasha. "Thanks, miss. Good thing ole Woodsy's got good friends keeping a lookout. Can't be too sure these days, either, no matter how nice the neighborhood; crime is everywhere."

"Yep, I hear you," Sasha said, feeling slightly guilty for the necessary ruse, but very relieved.

At least she had a key to Rod's place and could avoid the melodrama.

HE HADN'T PLANNED on driving up the mountain in the rental car until morning. Knew well before Woods and

Fisher had called that he would make the drive that was long overdue. Knew it the moment the general had threatened Sasha and he'd heard about Rod's loss that he was going to see an old friend. Knew that going to see that friend would necessarily mean that he couldn't take a vehicle that was tracked, like the government-issued one he normally drove.

Knew that he'd have to put on brand-new clothes and put his money in a brand-new wallet . . . would have to get rid of everything they could have bugged before he left. Knew that since he'd been home with his rental car tucked inside his garage the whole time . . . several hours during his watching, listening, with new alarm codes set on the keypad . . . he was certain the vehicle was clean. Knew that he had forty-eight hours to return so he could be in place when Sasha received her new orders.

Paranoia had been his watchword for more than thirty years and it served him well now.

Dr. Xavier Holland cleared his windshield with his sleeve as the mountain air became more frigid and biting, his vehicle headed for the small, privately owned Ute tribal outpost just over the ridge three hours away in the Uncompahgre National Forest. This was something he had to do.

BY MID-STEP ON Rod's town house landing, she could literally smell that something was terribly wrong. Not caring if anyone saw her now at three-thirty in the morning, she drew her nine-millimeter and carefully opened his front door with a key.

The stench was so acrid that she immediately covered her nose with her forearm and breathed against her leather jacket sleeve. Her eyes watered as her horrified gaze took it all in. Flies fled toward the porch light, despite the frigid temps. Carcasses littered the floors. A chant took over her mind: *Oh. God. Oh, God. Please, not Rod.*

Remnants of a dog with tags still dangling from the collar around its neck lay at her feet. Sasha shut her eyes and swallowed hard and then opened them again as she stood in the dark about to dry-heave. Half of a cat. Her eyes followed the scattered entrails to discover the other half of it on the sofa. Her line of vision tracked a wide smear of dried blood across what had once been gleaming hardwood floors and a Turkish rug to the stairs that led to Rod's bedroom. At the top of the landing her stricken gaze stopped at a well-eaten deer carcass and everything that was wriggling on it.

Trembling with revulsion, she briefly lowered her arm away from her face and did the unthinkable—she took in a substantial inhale through her nose and began to separate the scents. She had to know if there might be a human body inside this town-house-turned-tomb. She no longer feared that Rod's would be among any human remains she might find. Her sole objective was to know in advance where she might find such carnage before she tripped over it and freaked out. But the scent scan only revealed Rod's unmistakable signature and that of animal remains.

Deeper worries claimed her, however. They'd all been sent to Afghanistan together, and if Rod had flipped out like this . . . Perhaps the least of her worries was the strange wolf.

Sasha kept walking, patrolling, not even sure of what she was searching for, because Rod was obviously not there.

Rivulets of sweat coursed down her back now, the death vibrations were so intense in the confined space. Every fiber of her was poised to bolt and run toward fresh air. She wanted to feel the cleansing power of the night and wind on her skin to peel off the wretched scents that clung to her hair and clothes.

Her sweater and pants stuck to her as she eased deeper into the apartment, her gun in a lethal grip, her chest rising and falling in short agonized bursts. Foul-scent taste covered her tongue as she sipped the decay-thickened air. She headed for the refrigerator to see if his vials were still there. Her cowboy boot crunched something that she hoped was plastic.

She stooped down and picked up a crushed needle and then gazed at the kitchen floor strewn with his entire month's supply of them. Frantic, she began picking each one up and inspecting it in the dim moonlight that filtered through the windows. Each had serum residue in it. The cabinets down low were shredded with huge claw marks, as were the tiles.

Mentally reconstructing, she looked at the abused condition of what had once been new appliances. It seemed as though he'd gone to the refrigerator, gotten his meds . . . panicked . . . got more . . . and more . . . nearly overdosing to stop something from happening. She swallowed hard, knowing now what that something was. She squatted low and touched a cabinet with trembling fingertips and allowed them to follow the deep gashes in the wood. He'd fallen, convulsed, and Turned. She drew her hand back quickly as though it had been burned, and stood.

"Oh, Rod . . ." she whispered into the emptiness around her. "One of us should have been here with you." For a moment the room became blurry. "I should have been here with you." But if she had been, what could she have done?

"I wish you had been," a low, gravelly voice said.

Sasha jerked her attention toward the voice, muscles coiled, heart beating in near arrhythmia as she spied Rod in the hall shadows. From his silhouette she could see that he was naked and his hair tousled. But his eyes . . . God in heaven, they glowed in the darkness. Instinct made her level her weapon at him.

"Missed you, babe," he said with chilling amusement in his voice. "I got fucked up in Afghanistan, had to come home to heal."

She could barely speak, but slowly moved out of the kitchen where she felt boxed in. Trapped. "What happened over there, Rod?" she whispered.

He let out a long exhale as though bored. "The pack turned on me, babe. Fucking losers." He stepped forward and she noticed that he favored his left side. "But I ate, and I feel so much better now. Did I mention that I missed you?"

"You've gotta get to a hospital . . . to Doc Holland on the base. He's the only one that knows how—"

"No," Rod said with a menacing snarl. "It's gone too far for that. I finally figured out how to heal on my own. Sasha, it is *so* good."

All she could do was stare at him, blood draining from her knuckles as she gripped her nine and he slowly walked forward. Doc had told them how bad it could get. That they could actually become what they'd hunted.

"Don't move!" she shouted, backing up into the kitchen again as he stepped into a shard of moonlight. His once handsome mouth was distended by a set of upper and lower canine teeth. Nearly hyperventilating, she supported her right hand with her left.

"Open the fridge," he said in a too-calm voice. "You'll see that I've finally beaten this thing."

Sasha froze in the middle of the kitchen floor, half afraid to open the refrigerator, not sure what she'd find. Dried, blackened blood covered the counters and cabinets. Every surface was scarred. Sweat was beginning to bead on her brow. She was so close to vomiting that it was hard to breathe. The stench of death in the air revolted her as she opened the fridge with two fingers.

Soft appliance light from the refrigerator illuminated the darkened kitchen. She practically gagged at the mixture of spoiled food scents and rotting animal flesh in the room, but was thankful that there wasn't anything weird in there to further claw at her heart. She shut the door and fell against the appliance and then wiped her brow with her forearm, mentally spent, but kept her weapon and eyes on the potential threat.

A low rumbling chuckle filled the kitchen. "See. No meds left, and I'm fine," Rod said, moving closer. "The first time you change is the worst. After that, you can go back, once you eat. That's all we have to do, baby, is eat once the wolf hits." He stopped advancing as she took a wide-legged stance, nine-millimeter at the ready. "You don't have to be afraid of me, Sasha. All those nights we used to have fun together with the pack . . . now we can take it to another level. We've both thought about it. C'mon, why would I hurt you, babe?" He glanced down his body and chuckled. "Does it look like I wanna hurt you?"

Tears had made her vision blurry as she looked at the man who'd once been her mentor. Something horrible filled his green eyes; his hair seemed to be getting longer and shaggier as she stared at him. His shoulders were now roped with layers of sinew that he'd never owned and his fists were gnarled and huge. That he was standing before her with a dripping erection amid the carnage in his home revolted her. She blinked away the tears and swallowed hard. "Rod, back up," she said in a near whisper. "Don't make me kill you."

He didn't back up, but didn't advance, either. He tilted his head as his gaze narrowed. "What did you say?"

The two stared at each other for what felt like forever.

"Not you," he snarled. "You've turned on me, too!"

Her gaze ricocheted around the small enclosure for a way out. He was blocking the entrance, but the pass-through was a slim option. And that's when she glimpsed it: a severed, naked female foot just behind the wrecked entertainment center.

It all happened in what felt like slow motion. Rod's gaze followed and trapped hers; in a blur of transition the sound of bones cracking and form changing filled the room. Sweat was flung off her brow as she instantly pivoted, lined up her shot with his chest, and squeezed. Something huge and dark and incomprehensible was airborne and coming her way. She stooped and kept firing into the barrel chest, momentum causing the creature to continue hurtling forward. It collided with the wall; she was up and had backed far away from the crumpled form in seconds, weapon still trained on it while she gasped for air.

What had been a beast was slowly transforming into the naked body of a man—the man she knew as Captain Rod Butler. The man she'd known as her mentor and potential lover. Glassy green eyes stared up at her, and a destroyed chest and torso lay open and gutted. Every now and then the body twitched, making her start. She swallowed hard and covered her mouth with one hand, but kept her right arm extended with her gun on the beast.

"This is what I had come to warn you of," a deep male voice said in the shadows.

Sasha spun, fired several shots not caring, her ears tuned to the movement that was agilely sweeping past furniture and rounding the living room. In flashes she could see a huge outline as she caught glimpses between shadows, her body turning three hundred and sixty degrees to follow it as she ran into the living room, splintering wall units, shattering windows, sending shells into brick and drywall—then suddenly she was pinned from behind, both arms held tightly to her sides by incredible pressure and strength.

A fierce, angry growl tore from her throat at the same second her cowboy boot heel came down hard on an instep and her body lurched the massive weight over her. For a second the image sprawled on the floor, and she fired at it two-handed, but in another second it was gone.

"Stop shooting, you'll kill an innocent!" a deep, rough voice commanded.

"Fuck you!" she yelled back, trying to get a bead on his location from his voice.

"The drywall," the voice said, winded but continuing to move, making her circle with it. "Nines go through that and brick and windows—kids, mothers, regular people live here, Sasha, stop fucking shooting! I came to be sure he didn't attack you!"

She couldn't catch her breath, but could hear sirens in the distance. His words made her stop for a split second and think beyond the survival panic. Her mind latched on to the image of Jim's innocent neighbors as her line of vision caught sight of some family's dead golden retriever in the middle of Rod's living room floor. Her mind quickly brought up memories of being at his home during football games, and seeing children sledding. The front bay window had been blown out. Sirens were getting closer. Dogs were barking. An unseen threat was in the room with her. Moonlight and freedom was calling her name. Rod's dead body was in the kitchen. The authorities wouldn't understand.

"Your boots, your car, your jacket, your phone, everything on you is being tracked by someone, Sasha!" the voice said in a low, urgent whisper. But it hadn't moved from the last location, wasn't circling her as though hunting her, and spoke at a level only one with superior hearing could detect. "Listen to the tone of the tracking devices—can't you hear them? The high-pitched whine? Stop taking their medicine and you'll be able to call your wolf!"

Two lunges and she'd reached the spoiled sofa, hit the back of it, and propelled herself in a flip roll through the front window. She landed on the hood of her Nitro on all fours. He knew her name. He'd been following her all night, of that she was now sure. He'd been in Darien's basement—that had to be what she'd sensed. She was inside her car within seconds, engine started, wheels screeching and eating up asphalt as she careened out of the driveway.

Where to go, where to go! Her mind was ablaze. She couldn't lead this thing back to her apartment where she might have to engage it in a firefight to kill it. God forbid stray shells might pierce a wall to harm Mrs. Baker. But she had to draw it to where she could even the odds. Ronnie's lot, now that the place was closed. There wasn't another building for miles and the lot was wide open and surrounded by a thicket of mature trees.

Sasha slid into the exit on two wheels, dangerously close to a rollover, but kept going. Yeah. She had all sorts of ammo in her trunk—of the automatic variety. Something was tracking her, someone was hunting her. Rod had Turned. Woods and Fisher, her best friends in the whole world, were missing, too. Doc was unreachable. Yet the stranger spoke levels of truth. Her bullets could have killed someone.

She said a quick prayer that Butter's neighbors had been in bed; that her wild shots had passed over sleeping heads but hadn't struck anyone.

Driving like a maniac, she reached down and yanked off her left cowboy boot heel, ripping the slanted wood block from the leather in one tear and then looked at it hard. Nothing.

"Bullshit!" she shouted, but still crossed her left shin beneath her right calf to trade feet on the gas and removed the heel from her right boot.

For a moment all she could do was stare at the tiny transistor that was mounted in a small cavity within the heel. Unnerved, she pitched it out of the window and then jammed her free hand in her pocket to find her cell phone. Quickly unhooking the casing, she yanked out the battery housing, and glimpsed the thin transistor chip that was glued to the back of it.

Flicking it off and out of the window with her thumbnail, she dialed Doc Holland's private number as a new wave of panic overtook her.

"What's going on?" she said, the moment the call picked up.

"Say nothing," Holland's urgent voice replied. "Do not say my name. Your clothes, your car, all monitored. We have fifty-five seconds left to speak. Are you safe?"

"Yes. Rod—"

"I know. Later, I'll explain. Get a prepaid phone and do not call until you do. Search all surfaces and clothes. Your car is low-jacked. Rent one, get new clothes. I will give you a meeting point when you call back. Sweet pea, I'm sorry."

The call disconnected. Tears ran down her face. Doc had used the pet name he'd given her as a child. He was like her only dad, and she could tell he was on the run. He knew about Rod. Her free hand covered her mouth as a sob threatened to rip through her. What was happening to her world? The stranger had warned her. He hadn't lied. She was being monitored, even Doc knew. The man of the shadows said he'd come to protect her from what Rod had become.

She swerved her car into the vacant lot, spinning and sliding on the ice and then finally lurching it to a complete stop. She got out quickly as a gleaming, black Ford F-150 slowly pulled in and came to a controlled stop. Hobbling on destroyed boot soles, she rounded her red Nitro like greased lightning, opened the back hatch, and came around the front of her vehicle toting a pump shotgun loaded with silver shells.

"Talk to me and say it from a distance!" she called out.

She watched the figure she'd come to associate with dread get out of his truck, hands raised and motions steady as he approached. Inside her gut she knew that he'd only taken that position to calm her; it wasn't working. The fact that he was so sure of his ability to outrun her gunfire kept every cell in her vibrating with fight-or-flight hormone.

"That's close enough!"

He stopped walking.

"The lining of your jacket," he said, inclining his head. "Somewhere in the hem toward the collar. Listen. It's whining."

Shit. That was her favorite jacket.

Warily she shrugged out of her bomber jacket and flung it onto the hood of her SUV.

A slow half-smile appeared on his face as his gaze traveled down her body to land on her feet. "I see you found what was in your boot."

Her gaze narrowed. She refused to dignify the comment and bristled against the shiver that his hot, visual assessment of her had caused. To her horror, all she could do was watch his gaze slide down her body again to this time stop at her belly button, causing her stomach to clench. None of what was happening made sense. She'd just killed Rod!

"I hate to tell you, but those beautiful leather pants are—"

"You must be crazy or think that I am. Say what you

gotta say!" She raised the gun and cocked back the hammer, entirely willing to blow his head off.

"In the waistband," he said calmly, unmoved by her outburst. He closed his eyes and tilted his head from side to side and spoke in a breeze-soft murmur that ran all through her. "On the left hip, in the seam. Run your nail along the edge and you'll feel it . . . right where the tag is, probably so that you wouldn't notice it."

Sasha hesitated, but then finally removed one hand from her weapon, hating that he'd been right so far. She kept her eyes on him and smoothed her left hand down her hip against the seam, blindly searching, allowing her nail to score the butter-soft leather. It didn't help that she'd seen his breath hitch, or that his eyes held a dark hunger that clearly had nothing to do with killing her tonight.

"I can find it for you," he said in a husky rasp.

Her nail hit a metal object and she blindly scrabbled with something that felt like the size of a pencil lead while still staring at him. "Thanks, anyway, I got it," she said with a half-snarl, and then glanced at the bit of technology that fit under her nail.

Flicking away the offending device, she lowered her weapon. "Why are you following me and my pack?"

"Because one of your pack was demon-infected and it was soon going to overtake him . . . and you were at risk. I think you saw that. I'm sorry you had to."

"So how is that your business?" she said with an edge in her voice, not willing to allow a complete stranger to see how thoroughly broken up she was. Rod, demon-infected. She could hardly believe it.

Howling winds separated them as liquid silver moonlight bathed them together.

"You're of my clan. You are my business."

Taken aback by his plainly spoken statement, she fell mute for a moment.

"A little while ago, though, you were talking about murdering my pack brothers," she finally retorted. "How do I know you're not some wacko vigilante or serial killer? How do I know you won't try to kill me, just in case—since like you said, I was with Rod before?"

He shook his head and his eyes grew sad. "Even you don't believe that, Sasha," he said quietly. "Listen to your inner wolf."

"How do you know my name?" she said, her tone deadly.

"I followed you and heard you say it to the couple outside the town house. But don't worry. You can't get what your alpha had," he said, the low rumble of his voice making her insides quake. "Your blood is different. You are shadow wolf. Werewolf virus cannot co-opt that." He sighed and slowly lowered his arms to his sides, obviously no longer fearing that she might shoot. "But the two younger pups . . . the ones named Woods and Fisher, are only wolf. Familiars. But we do not understand how they were made. Their paternity is unclear; they are not like our other Familiars. I don't know why, but they only smell of wolf, not shadow, not demon wolf. That part has intrigued me since I began tracking the new predator in the area. But you needn't worry about Rod again. He was badly injured before, but they never got him in the heart. You hit him point-blank. That hunt is over now."

Her head felt like someone was taking a sledgehammer to it. "How long were you following us?"

"Six full moons," he stated plainly. "I had to be sure he was Turning, had been infected, and I wouldn't have moved against him if the medicine I saw him taking had worked. I, like you, hoped the scientists had come up with a cure." He looked off toward the horizon, his voice mellow and somber. "I want to be out of a job, unemployed one day . . . I would welcome no longer hunting the beasts."

Sasha lowered her weapon to her side slowly, completely, the pure shock dazing her. Everything was on her now. She had to lead the pack. That had always been Rod's role. The weight of the reality felt like a gut punch. "You work for *the project*?"

The unnamed man before her shook his head and returned his endless gaze to hers. "I work for an ancient clan that has kept the balance in the Great Spirit's land for centuries. The military is playing with fire, and will get burned."

The look he gave her scorched all the saliva out of her mouth. There were too many questions and too few answers competing with way too many emotions.

"I don't understand this shadow wolf, or how Woods and Fisher are just . . . natural wolves from their attacks. Familiars, as you called them?"

"You will have to ask those who know, for I do not."

"But you seem to know more than me! Who gave you orders to track him, and hunt him? He was . . . my friend, my family. Who told you to assassinate him? What gives you that right!"

"Did you love him?"

She blinked and remained very still for several seconds. "He was my alpha, my brother. Pack member. Of course I loved him . . . just like I love Woods and Fisher—maybe a little more." She looked away at the dark stand of trees when her voice hitched. The last thing she was about to discuss with a complete stranger was her relationship with Rod.

"Then, when you saw him, you did the right thing by putting him out of his misery quickly. Now just pray his spirit onward to better hunting grounds. I am glad that you loved him but were not in love with him. Later, as time wears on, you will find that this will make what you had to do easier. I am so sorry, and would have done it for you, if you had let me. If any other of your family Turns, next time call me on the howl of the wind."

The horrifying offer was made with such honesty, even what one could sense as integrity, that for a moment she was speechless.

"It is our way as hunters to spare each other the pain." The man before her released a weary breath as though hunting Rod were the last thing he'd wanted to do in the world, but was resolved to complete the brutal task. She could relate, had been on many a mission of said nature, but hated it now that she was in a deadlock with someone on a mission against her own. However, that also told her several things in an instant; he hadn't found Woods or Fisher yet, hadn't assassinated them yet, therefore there was still time. With time, if she could get the guys back to the labs, back to Doc Holland, there was still hope.

She eyed the dark stranger who stood seeming to wait for her decision. Keep your friends close and your enemies closer—she'd heard that before. Now she understood the axiom completely.

"Understand that they cannot reverse what is done," the unnamed man finally said, pressing his point when she didn't respond. "Your Rod was too far gone. He finally took human flesh and would have taken yours, while the moon had him, especially while sustaining a gut wound. He needed human blood and flesh to knit, heal. It would not have been personal, Sasha, but a matter of his survival. You or him. Just as you chose yourself over him in an instant back at his town house. That is why I came to you; to protect both your life and your conscience. You had to do what you did. Clear your conscience now, tonight. Purge it."

He stared at her until she looked away. "Could you

have been able to live with yourself if you'd let him go, knowing he'd taken a human life and knowing that a beast dwelled within him? What would you have done if you'd tripped over a child's body in that house of horrors? How many feedings do you think occurred between when he was hurt overseas and tonight—how many did he have to eat in order to properly heal enough to be strong again? You saw it in his eyes! There was no shame. The beast reveled in the carnage—that is the demon! They grow to love the killing and kill more than they could possibly consume or would ever need!"

She shook her head and hot tears rose in her eyes. The unnamed man before her had finally pushed the right buttons. "Who sent you?" she said, her voice a shaky rasp of emotion.

"The elders."

"Fuck the brass!"

He shook his head no. "Tribal councils. Not your hierarchy."

"There has to be a cure, a containment strategy, first. I'll find Woods and Fisher, my way—*I'll* get them off the streets. Not you!" Her voice fractured and she clenched her jaw, breathing hard. She knew this man was right, his concern sound. She'd seen evidence of Rod's deteriorating condition with her own eyes. But it still carved her up. Then it came to her in a jolt. Shogun had said that her kind was trying to take demon-infected werewolf blood and introduce it to a wider audience. Was it the military and could they have been using Rod as a guinea pig? Testing the demon infection on him? Did it have anything to do with why they had been sending him on one mission after the other? It would definitely explain his growing edginess over the last four to five months. Could Doc have known about it and allowed it to happen? Could he have been the one who had given it to Rod? No, she couldn't believe he would do such a thing. Doc was the only one who looked out for them. But she could believe that he may have been forced to keep his silence about it. They might have even hung her life over his head. From their all-too-brief conversation, it was clear that Doc was still trying to protect her.

"Sasha," the stranger said, bringing her back to her current problem. "I will respect your territory, so long as you hunt with purpose and keep the innocent safe. But I will be your shadow . . . until you learn to be your own wolf. That is as much of a compromise as I'm willing to offer. Purge the guilt, Sasha. Do it now, before it consumes you. Grieve for the man, but do not grieve for having to do what you had to do."

She let the wind howl between them for what seemed like a long, cold while.

"Would you take my coat?" he asked quietly, truly wanting peace between them. "Perhaps we can drive to a diner, so we can talk? You can see my goal is not to harm you, and I believe you are capable of defending yourself, even if that was my intention."

"I'll follow you in my car." She backed up, still wary, her heart heavy.

"I thought we'd established that you were being tracked." He waited, his voice calm, flat, matter-of-fact. "I am no liar."

She glanced over her shoulder at her Nitro, knowing that it could take her the rest of the night—until dawn broke—to find a minuscule transistor embedded within it. Doc Holland's words tumbled around in her brain. She had to get a new vehicle, had to get new clothes, had to get an untraced cell phone. Had to call Doc again. If she was going to find Woods and Fisher and protect them for their own good, as well as protect the general public, she had to learn more. But the fact that Doc now knew how far gone Rod had been made her worry less about Woods's and Fisher's safety. If Doc knew, surely he wouldn't have allowed the brass to ship them off together. He was possibly working on a cure even as she thought about it. If anything, they might already have the guys contained . . . if they were dead or about to be killed, Doc would have told her, right?

Caution still made her back up to her Nitro. Her gaze un-blinking on the mystery man before her, she opened the passenger's side door, and traded her pump shotgun for her nine, wedging it into her now loose waistband, and gathered a fresh clip and a Bowie knife from her glove compartment. For a moment her hand slid over her medical case, and after fingering it, she decided to leave it, no longer sure of what she'd been injecting herself with for years.

Stripping her wallet, she jammed loose cash, her ID, and credit cards into her back pants pocket and tossed the potential bug carrier onto the car floor, and then slammed the door and locked it.

"Try anything funny, and I slaughter you," she said, her voice matter-of-fact and her gaze steady. "I don't care if you're driving at a hundred miles per hour—yes, I'm just that crazy, will blow your head off just for grins, and will take my chances with an airbag. We clear?"

"Very," he said with no strain in his tone.

For some odd reason, she felt a lump form in her throat as he cautiously slid his deerskin coat off his body, ex-posing wide shoulders, a massive, stone-cut chest, and bi-ceps that flexed as he moved like liquid night. Feeling surreally drawn to him, despite what had just happened, seemed so bizarre. She didn't understand it, and could only chalk it up to postbattle trauma. Perhaps it was the need to connect and forget, simply blot the horror out of her mind with something primal, something raw and feral. She wasn't sure.

But it was impossible not to be mesmerized as she watched his muscles move beneath his dark sweater and skin. He tossed the coat to her and she caught it with one hand. His scent spilled over her, making her hesitate to cloak herself within it.

He understood exactly where she was. Distrust was in her eyes, as well as deep heartache. More than anything else, there was a loneliness of spirit that drew him. He'd been there too many times to count.

"Before, when I followed you to the back of the bar and outside, there were a lot of you." She glanced around to be sure there was no ambush coming.

"A gift of the shadows—taking the scents from the shadows that you step into in order to throw a hunter off your trail . . . the same way you would stand upwind of a doe, or hide in a blind covered by the scents of the woods. I will show you the shadows . . . your wolf that they have never explained . . . as well as the nobility of your clan . . . if you just have coffee with me."

He watched her dissect the subtle plea in his voice, knowing that the nonthreatening resonance of it made her tilt her head and study him harder, unsure of why he'd taken that tack, knowing that she had to be wondering if it was all a part of his game to lure her. It wasn't.

"I truly mean you no harm. You can leave at will. But even if you don't trust me, there are things that you should know if you're ever to survive an attack by the ones you have befriended."

That was as much as he could give her while standing outside in the bitter cold. It was the bitter truth. She had to do the rest. Only she had the power to take the first step to gain knowledge and to shed her blindness. Now it was a waiting game to see if she would accept or reject what he'd told her.

Quiet relief washed through him as she grudgingly

hoisted his coat over her shoulders. Remaining statue still, he watched her move toward him with the wariness of a she-wolf cornered by a potential trap. Her lovely nose was raised, scenting everything around her for a trick along the way, each step a careful footfall closer to him.

Just watching her approach, he fought to remain still, almost not breathing. She had no idea how gorgeous she was under the waning light of the moon, her eyes brimming with tears. He knew that no one had ever shown her the glory of her wolf, how it wasn't a monster like the aberration of the demon-infected.

His own loneliness suddenly pressed down on him, making him want to howl. He wondered if one day, once the pain of her loss ebbed, she could ever feel that pull to one's own like he did now.

She touched the side of his truck as though sensing, her shadow abilities beginning to awaken even though unbeknownst to her. The touch was more like a caress and she studied it, then studied him. He nodded as she carefully got in the vehicle and then pressed her body against the still partially open door, ready to bolt. He got in the truck slowly and slid into the seat, keeping his motions easy, fluid, and his hands visibly on the key and wheel at all times.

"You have to close the door all the way," he said, keeping his eyes on the windshield.

"Nick's Diner isn't that far—ten minutes, tops, at this hour with no traffic. Drive with me holding the door ajar," she said, keeping her gun trained on him.

"If I hit a bump—"

"Either you'll get shot or I'll fall out, so I suggest you drive with care."

He drove with care.

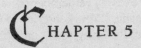

CHAPTER 5

TRUE TO FORM, and even truer to what she was, she'd held on to his truck door, keeping it ajar and her gun leveled at him all the way to Nick's Diner while he pushed seventy-five miles an hour on pure, open highway. Half of him wanted to smile; the other half was ready to snarl when she'd insisted that he walk in front of her, given the heavy crowd of eighteen-wheeler rigs in the lot.

She was tough, something he really liked about her but that he also decidedly hated. He found the most remote booth in the place, the one farthest from prying eyes, and watched her slide into it across from him, sitting only after he'd settled in. Weary, he let out an exhale of frustration and rubbed both palms down his face. Only the waitress's tired footfalls and the distant clatter of silverware punctuated the silence at their table.

"What can I get y'all folks this morning?" the waitress drawled with a fatigued smile that still reached her wan blue eyes despite how exhausted she seemed to be.

He gazed up at the deep lines in her face and the dark roots of her hair that ended in blond, almost absorbing the ache in her swollen ankles, and then looked over to Sasha.

"Just coffee," Sasha finally said, giving him a warning glare.

"Steak, really rare, and eggs with a side of bacon and sausage," he said. "Keep the coffee coming, too. Thanks."

"You got it, hon," the waitress replied, merriment slowly filling her eyes. "I remember them partying days." She winked at Sasha. "You keep 'im in line, and if you change your mind, I'll bring you a breakfast, too, okay?"

"Thanks," Sasha said with a tight smile. "I appreciate that."

They both watched the waitress shuffle off and dispense her Florence Nightingale–style attention on weary truckers who sat like lone soldiers hunched over plates and steaming mugs. A few late-night party people reclined within the dull, tan plastic booths in small clusters of humanity trying to sober up or service a case of the munchies, but at the near dawn hour—transition time—the diner was fairly empty.

"Okay, you can knock off the guilt thing," Sasha said, once she was sure the waitress was out of earshot.

He shrugged. "I don't know what you're talking about."

"Yeah, you do. Okay, so these people . . . or people like them, shouldn't have their lives snuffed out by . . . by a situation beyond their control."

He leaned forward quickly, not caring that she had a Glock nine pointed at his groin beneath the table. Fatigue was eroding his patience.

"Call it what it is," he said between his teeth, feeling his upper and lower canines beginning to crest but willing them back. "None of these people in here should have their lives suddenly taken in the most horrible way you can describe, namely being eaten to death, savaged, by a demon wolf." His gaze held hers captive and he watched her eyes begin to change as she struggled unsuccessfully to disengage from him. "It's better to always call it what it is than to play games with yourself. That way you never forget your true calling, or your ancestry. *This* is your job."

"First of all," she said, a low, warning growl layered beneath her words. "Who the hell are you? That's what you need to answer before you start telling me about whatever."

He rolled his shoulders and leaned in closer, his gaze hard and steady on her. "The name is Hunter."

"You're being funny, right?"

A long silence sat at the table with them, taking over the booth.

"Max Hunter," he said, thoroughly offended.

She pushed back and smiled a slight smile as the waitress returned with two steaming cups of strong coffee. "Okay." But she glimpsed from him to the waitress's back to the coffee like he might have poisoned it.

He remained silent until the waitress left before resuming the conversation. "What does 'okay' mean, and why is my name a problem? And you're acting like I drugged your coffee or something, when you saw for yourself that the woman brought it out from the back and poured it from the same pot she's serving everyone else from!"

"Sounds like an alias." Sasha sat without looking at him. She focused on adding lots of cream and lots of sugar to her coffee, thinking about the same line of conversation she'd had with Shogun. "And you could have accomplices."

"Right. The bleached blonde is my contact," he said sarcastically in a near growl, then took a slurp from her cup and then his. "Satisfied—or now do you want your own fresh cup?"

She swallowed a smile. "This is fine."

"Too sweet. The levels of refined sugar in it are lethal enough."

"So he makes jokes." She dismissed him with a wave of her hand. "I like my coffee this way."

He noted that she'd finally stashed the weapon in the pocket of his jacket that she was still wearing. He sat back to add a little cream and sugar to his coffee, and tried not to think about how much he liked seeing her wrapped in his coat. "Well, it's not."

"Not what?"

"An alias," he shot back, thoroughly annoyed.

"Who are your people?" She didn't stutter, didn't blink, just hit him with the question right between the eyes.

He met her smoky-gray gaze. "My father was Blackfoot and French Canadian of the Haitian variety, up near the Canadian border. My mother was full Ute, what we call Noochee, 'the people,' from here." He brought the cup up to his mouth as she brought hers up to meet her lips. "Trudeau . . . that's French. So—"

"Hunter isn't. Where did the name come from if your—"

"My mother's last name."

"Oh." She sat back and cradled the cup in her palms and then looked down into it, seeming a little embarrassed for making assumptions. "Trudeau is Creole, by way of Louisiana. New Orleans." But when she glanced up at him again, her gaze had hardened just that quickly. "But I figured since you'd been skulking around my apartment, you would know that by now."

"I never went into your apartment or violated your personal space."

"Yeah, right," she scoffed, taking a liberal sip of coffee.

"I told you once before, I am no liar. I won't say it again. My second point is this," he said, setting his cup down with angry precision. "My goal was to be sure you weren't savaged. My other goal was to find the infected one. 'Skulking,' as you call it, wasn't necessary. Going through your personal effects wasn't necessary to do that—so I didn't."

"All right, my bad. But given all these circumstances, I have every right to think the way I do."

He couldn't argue the point, especially not while sitting so close to her and absorbing her dancing shadows. They played across the table as she moved, touching his hand, grazing his skin, teasing the wolf within him. He watched her move the table flatware nimbly between her fingers in an absent gesture, not sure if it was a warning or just something she did when nervous. Then he realized what he'd said and why she perhaps seemed to mellow by slow degrees: he'd said his first task was to protect her, then the community at large, and not the other way around as it should have been. The tribe first, the pack first, with individual concerns *always* second. Whoa . . .

"Okay," she said more quietly. "Let's say I believe that you haven't gone into my apartment, how'd you get my last name?"

"Your brothers in arms called you that at the bar a lot more than they called you 'Sasha.' "

She nodded and peered at him over the rim of her cup. He was practically lost in her smoky eyes until she lowered her gaze from his.

"Right . . . at Ronnie's Road Hog Tavern . . . where you were spying on us for months."

"Gathering intelligence, much like I'm sure you do on your missions. That doesn't make me a bad person, just informed. I needed to be sure, not just act on a whim."

"That's valid," she said quietly after a moment. "So, the tribal councils, plural, are Blackfoot and Ute, then?"

He nodded, his voice temporarily failing him as her hackles lowered and her tone lost its strident edge. "And more . . . each tribe has a legend of the honorable wolf as old as the tribes themselves," he murmured. "There's also a larger Federation of Clans."

"In your culture, they're good—wolves in general?"

She looked up at him, her eyes seeking. This had to be the truth; he'd confirmed what she'd heard in South Korea.

Again for a moment his only response was a nod.

"Then . . . tell me where the bad ones come from. What happened?" Her gaze searched his face, her eyes furtive and drinking from his. She wanted to hear his version of the story.

"We have a saying that there is a good wolf and a bad wolf in each man or woman. That's the shadow wolf, a different species than the other."

She shook her head. Did he mean good werewolves were shadow wolves or was there a completely new entity he was describing? Rather than tip her hand about how much she knew, she threw out a question as bait.

"I hear you, Max . . . but how does one know which one will win, which one will be the one that comes out?" Her voice had become so quiet that he could barely hear her. She'd meant to bait him, but found a partial confession in her statement. Battle fatigue was wearing on her; it had to be the phase of the moon. "My parents were good people. Military, they tell me. Dad from New Orleans Cajun folks, my mom was African American from Alabama. They died in the line of duty in Rwanda. But Mom was attacked here, Stateside, before all that. Guess back then they were just learning about it all." She let out a resigned breath. "Anyway, short story is, she got the virus while carrying me and unwittingly passed it on. Does that make me a bad wolf, or a good one?"

"I'm sorry, Sasha. For the loss."

"Yeah, well, I only did the early years in foster care, until Doc was able to rearrange his life to take me in. I survived." She looked at him hard, hating that her eyes were probably sad and the pain within them deep. But somehow just saying what she had seemed to ease the burden of her recent loss. "That's why I hate to give up on anybody I care about . . . what if they'd given up on me? I just want to know which wolf it is and how to control it."

He fought not to place his hand over hers. There was so much to tell her, and so much, still, that he didn't know. But he accepted her confession as the peace offering it seemed to be. It was more than that, it was a sacred trust given. A supreme gift when she had no reason at all to trust him. She'd also finally warmed enough to his presence to say his name.

Didn't she know that also sharing his scent by wearing his jacket, as well as sharing a meal that he'd provided . . . following him to a feeding place . . . meant *everything* among the wolf clans? Yet he had to remember that she knew nothing of these customs and that these instinctive mating rituals probably had no meaning for her.

Still, so much of him wanted to make healing-touch contact with her soft, café au lait skin. He knew the pain of feeling isolated and alone, the mourning howl of loss that clawed at one's soul. But he knew better than to spook her by offering her his touch too soon.

Rather than touch her, he made a tent with his fingers in front of his mouth to occupy his hands for a few seconds before he spoke.

"When I was a boy, I asked my grandfather the same question," he admitted after a long pause. "And rather than tell me directly, he told me a story about another boy and his grandfather. He said that he wasn't sure who first told the story, but as things go in the oral tradition, sayings and stories transform as they are passed along. So, he said, 'There was a boy who asked his grandfather, "Which wolf inside me will win one day—the good one or the bad one?" The grandfather simply replied, "The one you feed."' That's as much as I can say about it, for that's all I know."

"You are speaking of the shadow wolf now, right?" Her gaze slid from his to the window. "The other one . . . it can't be helped, can it? There's only destruction."

"Yes," he murmured, and chanced touching her hand, then covered it. "Sasha, if I knew any other way . . . But you aren't what you fear. That is not what attacked your mother—your scent would be different, if it were."

"Promise me." She closed her eyes for a moment as she finally allowed someone she didn't even know to quietly understand her deepest fear.

"I swear it. Scent me. You know I am different from the one named Butler."

She breathed him in, almost afraid to open her eyes, and nodded. Until now, without the comparison, she hadn't known, couldn't tell. Oddly, his scent was also different from Shogun's, but she knew instinctively not to mention the werewolf.

Slowly opening her eyes, she stared at the man sitting across from her for the truth. The heat of his rough-hewn hand soaked into her bones, practically melting them. His hand was massive compared to hers, his fingers long and thick but with a graceful quality to them. Yet the searing warmth brought such comfort that she had to fight the urge to allow her fingertips to trace the contours of his hand. There was so much honesty transmitted in his touch, something like being home, something that she was sorry the waitress interrupted when she brought his huge plate and multiple side orders.

"Enjoy, hon," the waitress said. "But, um . . . you sure I can't bring you just a little something to eat, too?"

Sasha had recovered her hand but hardly her composure. She glanced at the mouthwatering meal on Max's side of the table and then glanced up at the waitress. "You know . . . come to think of it, a steak, rare, with a stack of pancakes, and some corned beef hash could work."

The waitress grinned. "I'll put that right in—but I'm gonna whisper it, because every other woman in here will want a piece of your hide for having a figure like yours and eating like that. It just ain't right."

Sasha laughed as the waitress walked away, keeping up her good-natured banter, but noticed that Max's expression was stone serious.

"What?" she said, tilting her head to closely study him.

He briefly shut his eyes. "I was just surprised that you would eat with me."

She smiled and swiped a piece of his bacon. "What can I say, your steak looks good."

He immediately cut a piece of it off for her and stabbed it with his fork, and then offered her the flatware. She noticed that his hand trembled ever so slightly as their fingers touched. Then she watched him watch her as the natural juices leaked from the meat onto her chin as she bit into it. He was so still that she was sure he'd stopped breathing.

"I'm sorry, thanks—here," she said, licking as far down on her chin with her tongue as she could and handing him her clean fork. "Good choice, the steak." She didn't know what else to say; the hunger in his eyes was disorienting.

He took the fork from her, allowing a caress to briefly unite their hands, but held her gaze, cutting his steak without looking at it, and then brought a large, dripping piece of meat up to his mouth, still holding her gaze.

As embarrassed as she was by her own response, she couldn't help staring at his mouth. It took all of her willpower not to lean across the table and run the full width of her tongue across his lush, sensual lips as she watched steak blood wet it . . . wet her, awaken parts of her anatomy that were supposed to be off limits for a potential foe. What the hell was wrong with her? She was practically panting, just watching the man eat, and she was so glad that his huge jacket hid her nipples that now felt like tight little stinging pebbles.

But when he opened his mouth, she nearly gasped. His eye teeth had lengthened, as had the bottom canines. She was almost up and out of the booth—forget the Glock, she was about to be gone in sixty seconds. However, an instantaneous tight grip held her wrist, accompanied by a low, nearly inaudible growl. And the man never stopped eating, just looked up at her.

"Your teeth," she murmured in a choked gasp.

He nodded nonchalantly, but didn't remove his hand from her wrist. "Run your tongue over yours."

She did it and nicked her tongue. "Shit . . ."

"You need to eat, that's all." He shoveled huge forkfuls of eggs, bacon, sausage, and hash browns into his mouth as though they'd been discussing the weather.

"Shit!" She knew she was repeating herself as she quietly freaked out, but couldn't help it.

"Remain calm, and have some more of my steak until yours comes." Max Hunter kept eating and also kept his hold on her firm.

She didn't wait for him to cut her a piece, but leaned over and stabbed one of his few remaining sausages with her fork. He released her hand and suddenly didn't seem to fear that she would bolt, shoot him, or otherwise try to stab him with the dull dinner knife that was on her side of the table. The moment both her hands were free, she cut a section of his steak off and retreated to her side of the table, putting it into her mouth and moaning as she closed her eyes.

The sound of him shoving his plate toward her made her open her eyes. He didn't say a word, but began cutting sections for her and handing them to her from his fork.

"What happened?" she said through a mouthful, suddenly ravenous.

"How long have you been without your medication?" His breaths were coming in short bursts.

She stopped chewing for a moment, her jaw filled with meat. Her gaze narrowed. "Hey, I thought you said you didn't go into my apartment. How would you—"

"I never said I didn't go into his," Max replied, no apology in his tone. "And I think you'd have to agree, I had reason."

She began chewing again. He resumed cutting meat. She kept accepting it.

"I've been off now, like, twelve . . . thirteen hours. I don't understand the teeth," she whispered, leaning in. "Do they go away?"

"After you've satisfied the wolf, yes."

"How do I do that?" she whispered urgently, leaning in, still eating, her eyes wild.

"You tell me," he breathed.

She stared at him as he closed his eyes and tilted his head, and then pulled in a deep inhale through his nose, scenting her. When he opened his eyes, they'd gone amber at the edges, his pupils now depths of eternity. He dropped the fork and picked up a piece of cut steak and brought it to her mouth. To her horror, she took it from his fingers, laving them with her tongue. The only thing that kept her from going over the table toward him was the arrival of the waitress with another plate for them to consume.

But rather than set it on Sasha's side of the table, the waitress timidly set it down in the center between them. Flushed, she tore off their bill from her pad and slid it onto the table, then quickly left, her voice wistful. "I'll leave you two alone . . . don't think I'm ignoring you— but just call me if you need anything else."

They didn't even look up at the woman, but kept their mouths closed and eyes averted until she was gone. Sasha immediately picked up her steak knife and the fork closest to her, cut off a large piece of meat from her plate, and then reached out to give it to him.

Almost as though the interruption of their feeding had been painful, Max wove his legs together with hers, capturing one of her thighs between his beneath the table, leaned forward, and took the offered steak. But before she could catch her breath, he'd slid the fork out of her hand and licked the full palm of her hand . . . then down her wrist and back up again to suck the residual juice from his feeding off her fingers. He then captured her damp hand within his as he began chewing what she'd given him; her thighs locked his between hers and she couldn't have stopped the rhythmic pulse of muscles within them if her life depended on it—and perhaps it did.

His hand went to her hair and the low sound that he released as he touched it bottomed out in the pit of her stomach. The new plate of food that separated them was abandoned. Something insane made her want to cut her palm with her steak knife and offer it to him to lick instead. Before she'd finished the thought, he'd allowed her hand to fall away from his so that he could pick up the knife. Without taking his eyes from her, he scored the heel of his hand and offered it to her. Unable to resist, she cradled his hand, trembling with need, and luxuriated in the scent of his blood before giving in to the pull of it by lavishing the wound with her tongue.

His nails scored the underside of the table in a slow, agonized rake as she tended his wound, nearly lifting him out of his seat as he fought an arch. She knew others couldn't hear the timbre of sound that he'd released, but she could feel it run wild and feral through her insides.

As though swallowing liquid, salty heat, a slow, pleasure-filled burn covered her tongue, making it yearn for his, making her writhe in her seat to lean in closer to him as it coated her throat, lit the inside of her chest behind her breastbone, and then lay awake in her belly causing her insides to shudder.

He was breathing through his mouth now. Colors formed behind her lids as she squeezed her eyes shut and his massive thighs became a pulsing vise around hers. His other hand fisted her hair until she was done laving his wound. The moment she looked up, his eyes met hers, and within the span of a blink, he'd found her mouth, consuming it mercilessly, allowing his tongue to roam over her trembling lips, then plunge deeper to hunt her tongue and chase hers with his own.

Were they not in a diner . . . but that reality was becoming cloudy at best as his massive hand covered her throat and she released a low moan into his mouth. That sound and the way she'd tilted her head back slightly to expose more of her vulnerability to him seemed to be the very last of his undoing. If she had any modesty left, any shred of nonwolf in her, she knew she had to pull out of the kiss before he came across the table and created a scene.

They both parted, panting. The burn he'd left between her thighs almost made her whimper. Her body was so hot that she nearly ripped off his jacket, but his scent that clung to it made her slowly stroke the arms of it with flat, trembling palms instead. He simply closed his eyes for a moment and began breathing very slowly through his nose. Watching the way his chest rose and fell, the way his nostrils flared slightly on each inhale, the way his Adam's apple bobbed in his throat as he tried to compose himself, was almost more than she could bear.

She watched his wound heal, his skin knit closed as though it had never been cut. Inhaling deeply, she snuggled into his jacket, not taking her eyes off him.

"You smell familiar," she murmured, her voice low and husky with want.

He nodded. "I am familiar. I am your shadow." His voice was raw, just like his gaze. "You've just healed your shadow."

"Teach me about my shadow. I don't understand it." Her voice was a blend of plea and demand. She didn't care. She'd never encountered anything like this in her life.

"You need to come with me up into the mountains, then." His body was in constant contact with hers. His hands fondled hers both roughly and gently. His legs burned against hers, capturing them in complete possession. But his gaze literally ate her alive.

"I can't," she said, hyperventilating, and unashamed that she was. She closed her eyes and leaned forward, finally touching his hair, pulling the band from it, and allowing the lush texture to spill through her fingers. "Oh . . . God . . ."

He gently slipped the band into his inner jacket pocket that she was wearing, allowing his fingers to graze her left breast. "Why not . . . before dawn, before the moon finally—"

"I have to report to base in forty-eight hours . . . less than that . . . and if I don't show up on Monday morning at nine hundred hours, they'll send MPs."

He took her mouth. She nearly crawled across the table to him.

"They'll never find my den."

"I can't—plus, it isn't prudent to disappear with a man who might want to kill me at some point." She stopped kissing him for a moment, and swallowed hard, still breathing hard. Her inner woman was in a death struggle with her inner wolf, and it felt like hand-to-hand combat, her with a mental Bowie and the wolf with all the advantages. "Because I *am* changing. I can feel it in me . . . If I transform, then what?"

"Do I seem like I have killing you on my mind?" His fingers sought her hair as his smoldering gaze trapped hers.

"Yes. I think you'd probably try to fuck me to death right about now."

He stared at her for long seconds without smiling. "Lesson number one—never deny the wolf. That only makes it hungrier."

"Was I wrong about *how* you'd try to kill me?" A half-smile appeared on her face.

"No. I will most assuredly try to do that, if given half the chance." He nuzzled her neck roughly. "Sasha . . . let your wolf come out to play."

"It's a long drive up the mountain . . . and I have to go to Wal-Mart . . . then gotta call Doc," she whispered roughly, kissing him between words, finding his deep, musky scent delicious, and now able to smell her own wetness, knowing it was driving him crazy.

"Wal-Mart? You're not serious, are you?" He traced her cheek with a finger and then cupped it, his mouth on her collarbone as he breathed her in.

"Yeah . . . I need to buy clothes. I have to call Doc . . . sometime later today. Gotta rent a car, for reasons you've shown me. The bugs. Gotta buy clothes, again for—"

"Go later today. I'll take you there. Use my truck." His gaze became furtive. "If you have only forty-eight hours before they ship you off again . . ."

"I have others to consider . . . I—"

Another feral kiss stole the words right out of her mouth. She'd lifted up and half out of her seat, he'd caused her breasts to ache so badly; his mouth had been so close to them, his knee was pressed tightly against the swollen, pounding flesh between her thighs. Right now every one of her arguments seemed so distant . . . as long as he kept touching her, pulling her wolf up and out of her. She needed to be with him so badly now that tears stung her eyes. Her skin hungered for his, creating a need to rub the length of it, all of it against him. She bit her lip not to cry out and sensed a strangled howl trapped in his throat.

"Don't make me go against my people. I can't walk away just like that. I need answers." She was begging him, sure now that if he demanded it she might agree to his terms.

Her fingers splayed in his hair and then she slid her palms lower until she touched the wondrous shadow on his face . . . it was like a covering of black velvet and growing longer by the moment, making the very centers of her palms ache. He quickly turned his face into one of her hands and pressed a deep kiss there as he held the nape of her neck firm.

"I understand you not wanting to abandon your pack," he said on a breathless murmur, pulling back enough to briefly look into her eyes. "But I am now your totem to call upon whenever you need me. I've willingly given you my blood. You've willingly healed my wound."

She nodded and stood, somehow understanding the connection. "Pay the lady."

THE BLARING OF the telephone made him reach blindly toward his nightstand. Through bleary eyes he saw the clock and a surge of worry cleared his mind.

"General, sir, sorry to wake you at this hour, but there's been a significant disturbance at Captain Butler's home." The voice on the line hesitated, sounding extremely stressed. "There was gun report that brought local police . . . they found carcasses . . . and his body."

The general sat up and closed his eyes. "Jesus H. Christ—clean this up, man."

His wife stirred and her worried gaze asked if everything was all right. He nodded to her absently as the major on the line filled him in with the details.

Up and out of bed now, the general pulled on his robe and walked into the hallway toward his office for privacy. He closed the bedroom door behind him as he clutched the cordless telephone receiver to his ear. Dorothy didn't need to hear this, never needed to hear anything related to what he did to keep her and their family living in safe, secure comfort.

"Send in a team with FBI badges to spin a cover-up that there was a crazed stalker who used the apartments of deployed military—something," he said as soon as he closed the heavy walnut doors to his personal sanctuary. "Make this go away as an unsolved but pending case and then drag in some known serial killer within the next two weeks and close the books. *And find her*. You tracked her Nitro to the homes of every man on her team; there was a police report at each one. She's armed, might be in some kind of state of transition. Get Holland on the line and ask him if we need to put her down yet."

"Yes, sir, General, sir . . . but—"

"But what! Speak, man!" The general rounded his desk.

"We can't find her, sir."

The general closed his eyes. *"You can't find her?"*

"We've located her car, and it seems as though she's gotten rid of her clothes, sir. The vehicle went first to each squad member's home as stated, as though she were trying to bond with her pack. Then, as I told you, sir, her location culminated at Captain Butler's, where it was clear that she was in some level of distress. The recordings register . . . her talking to him, then growls, snarls, animal sounds, and shooting as though she panicked when she saw him in his transitional state within the apartment.

What she found might have sent her over the edge. Then her vehicle went north to where it had been earlier that evening, sir. An establishment called Ronnie's Road Hog Tavern. We sent in a capture-and-recovery unit there because her movement seemed to be stabilizing and we feared she was injured, sir . . . might have, considering what she saw, put her own gun to her head. We drew that as a possible conclusion because she hadn't moved in so long. But what we found was shreds of her clothes, her empty wallet, weapons, unspent ammo—"

"Raise Holland, stat!"

"We're only getting voice mail, sir. He says in his message that he will be on vacation this weekend and returning to the office Monday morning at nine."

"I want a full manhunt. She might have Turned. I want her back in our possession before she does any more damage or before she's abducted by a black market cell."

"Sir, do we shoot to kill, or bring her in alive?"

"If she's in a human body, bring her in so we can study her further—she's the last one we've got. Wasn't scheduled for extermination for another six months at least. But if she's too far gone, you know what to do."

•

CHAPTER 6

BARELY MAKING IT out of the diner to Hunter's truck, down the road a half mile to the pay-by-the-hour motel, she suddenly found herself somewhere she'd sworn she would never go in her life. But the moon was dipping below the mountains and the sun was trying to fight its way across the slate-blue darkness. Like the horizon, she was in transition. Her entire life as she'd known it was in chaotic transformation.

Sasha forced herself to stay within the steamed-up F-150 while Hunter handled the necessary transaction to get them a room.

It was a good thing that she could barely see out of the windows. Watching him jump down from the truck and lope toward the office had almost made her flee the vehicle to tackle him in the parking lot. Oh, yeah, it was a good thing that a tiny shred of her nonwolf mind remained. It was absolutely terrifying to be this out of control.

She never heard him or saw him round her side of the truck. The door simply opened and she was abruptly gathered into his arms. Under any other circumstances it would have been a fight to the death. But instead she anchored her arms around his neck and sought his mouth with hers in a primal hunger.

Somewhere in the back of her mind she heard the truck door slam, felt him reach behind her to close it, but that was all so distant as she climbed up his body, her nails raking his back. Right now the only thing she could hear was his ragged breaths as he walked a short distance holding her, then a thud against their room door, a key turning in a flimsy lock. A slam. Additional warmth. They were inside. Another slam. A flash of sensation. Belly against belly that would soon be skin against skin. He'd dropped to his knees. Her back and skull hit something solid—the floor. He'd put her down hard and covered her with muscular heat.

"I'm sorry. I didn't trust the bed to hold—"

His apology went ignored, eaten from his mouth as she rolled him over onto his back and blanketed him. He stripped her sweater up over her head and she pushed up, straddling his waist, breathing hard while staring at him. His eyes and the strange amber amulet he wore were both softly glowing.

The last shred of sanity she had left was spent on a single, halting statement. "I don't want to curse a child with what we have," she whispered, "because I'm not prepared, but I want you."

He nodded in the semidarkness and leaned up slowly to kiss her abdomen, making her gasp when his lips pressed against her skin. The slow, suckling caress from his mouth left a deep burn of pleasure in its wake and his tongue became a patient, licking reminder not to deny the wolf.

As though quietly debating the dilemma she'd presented, his hands glided over her hips, molding to them through her ruined leather pants. He didn't say a word but kept moving forward until he was fully facing her and she slid back to straddle his lap. She had to close her eyes for a moment. Feeling the rock-hard length of him straining against his jeans, straining to get inside her, the muscle it owned causing it to pulse against her swollen slit, crushed the last of her will.

"Look at me," he said quietly, his voice a low, calm rumble as his hands swept heat up her back to unhook her black lace bra. "I told you I'm no liar."

She could only nod as she gripped his thick biceps. The sheer force of his unblinking gaze was like an entity unto itself, something that was part of him, but also something with its own aura that called her out and made her look at him.

Drowning in that deep, endless gaze was so possible. Touching his skin, letting her fingers tangle in the onyx spill of hair that washed his shoulders, scenting him, trembling in his arms, all of it was necessary, every bit of it impossible to avoid.

The moment he stripped off his sweater her hands slid over the sculpted bricks of his chest. She held his gaze as his eyes demanded, even as his hard, coffee-bean nipples bit into her palms and his breath hitched. Surprisingly, the amber piece that he still wore glowed brighter as she caressed it with her thumb and traced the oddly cool silver chain. Watching his eyelids become heavier with desire as she studied his expression made her suddenly need to rub her skin against his.

But he kept his chest a fraction of an inch from hers, close enough for her to feel the heat rise off his skin to lick hers, but not soothe it. Ever so slowly he peeled her bra away from her body as though taking off a wound dressing, and as the last of it came away from her skin, she literally cried out from the sensation of being freed. The urge to drop her head back and close her eyes was so fierce that a shudder devoured her. She needed him to touch her but he seemed intent on communicating something with his gaze that she couldn't fathom.

"I am your totem," he whispered. "Your wolf . . . You cannot conceive from me unless you're in heat."

She nodded, not knowing what the hell he meant but sure that she was experiencing heat.

"No, it's much worse than this," he murmured against her throat, while not allowing her breasts to press against his chest. "This morning we are shadow dancing."

"What is shadow dancing?" she whispered into his mouth, not really caring as long as he kept making her feel like this.

"Look," he murmured as he pulled away from the kiss gently. Holding his body farther away from her, he nudged her jaw with his so that she could peer at the long shadows created on the wall in the semidarkness.

Mesmerized, she watched his shadow touch hers even though he wasn't moving. What's more, *she felt it* . . . felt his arms encircle her, felt his mouth rain kisses over the swell of her breasts until she cried out—and the man hadn't moved!

"How?" she asked on a pleasure-strangled gasp.

"Would you like to keep dancing . . . or do you want me to stop and explain?"

Again she could only nod, but had to close her eyes.

"Yes, you want to keep dancing?" he asked in a quiet, raw tone. "Or, yes, stop and explain?"

"Keep dancing," she finally managed to say.

His hands swept a new wave of heat up her arms as their nestled groins slowly rubbed back and forth, causing a light friction sound to whisper between them. Her pores ached, she wanted him inside her so badly. His gentle trace of her eyebrows with the pads of his thumbs made her eyelashes hurt with need. Gooseflesh pebbled her arms as his fingers slid through her hair, singeing her scalp, and he finally cradled her skull to return her gaze to his.

"Please hear me," he said in a rumble that entered her body everywhere they were joined. "You cannot catch disease from me, because we do not contract them—our blood heals itself."

That made her open her eyes. He gently kissed her shoulder and then the edge of her jaw and pulled back.

"You've never been sick as a child, have you? Never gotten any of the childhood diseases."

She touched his mouth with trembling fingers, her eyes now drinking from his directly as her mind thirsted for knowledge. "No. But how could you know that?"

"Every cut healed within a day, within a cycle of the moon, and barring mortal injury, you'll live for a very long time. If you were a demon wolf, you'd seek human flesh and then the injury would instantly heal. You're not that, Sasha. Neither am I. We are of the Great Spirit."

"But—"

He kissed the question out of her mouth. "A human male can get you pregnant, per the human rhythm of your cycle . . . and they are disease carriers that can make you temporarily sick, can compromise your immune system. But you'd eventually shake it off. However, shadow wolves, unlike werewolves, are not disease carriers, and cannot make you sick."

"What are you saying?" She'd asked the question on a gasp as he kissed the cleft in her neck.

His response was a wolfish half-smile just as he lowered his face to her breasts. Having waited for his real touch there for so long, she realized the sensation ripped her voice from her throat in the form of a low, resonant moan. Velvet-soft texture from his upward nuzzle competed with a prickly, teasing sensation as his jawline moved down and grazed her overly sensitive skin. She arched against his mouth; the slow lick of his tongue just beyond her nipples made her thrust. His hands splayed against her shoulder blades and then she was suddenly braced at her back by his knees, anchored by his arms around her waist, and framed by the V of his body.

Slow French kisses against each taut nipple drove her nails into his arms. Frantic for release, she bore down against his groin until she found the head, could distinguish the ridge of his crown, and made him pump hard. It was clear that she had to tell the man something, had to let him know if she trusted him not to be a liar.

But speaking was impossible as his mouth greedily sought hers. Thinking was impossible as he rolled them out of the V to sprawl her on the floor. Objecting was futile as he knelt before her, stripped off her destroyed cowboy boots, and peeled away her leather pants and black thong.

Cheap carpet nap was under her nails, that velvet covering along his jaw teased her inner thighs. Heat from his nearness to what hurt so badly, what craved his touch so desperately, made her lift her body off the floor to meet his kiss. Tears leaked down the sides of her face as he gripped the lobes of her ass and spread her wide. Delirium seized her while his tongue hunted her for pleasure . . . stalked it . . . cornered it, played with it, and then finally devoured it.

The wail she released was so primal that he shuddered and lifted his head from her body panting, then slowly took off the amber charm and dropped it on the floor beside her with precision. She was sure she'd lost her mind as another orgasm crested within her so fast and so furiously that for a moment his shadow against the wall changed from human to wolf and back again.

Something very fragile within her snapped. The urge

to permanently unite raged at frightening levels, but to stop was impossible.

In one fluid lunge she tossed him onto his back again and took his mouth while ripping open his jeans. She moaned, unashamed, as she tasted herself in his kiss, breathed in her own scent from his damp face. She had to have him inside her, be joined to him in a mating dance . . . was so tired of being alone in the world, being stronger, the hunter, the one able to do it all . . . having to fend for herself—finding an equal was a gift. She tore open his jeans as though they were made of wrapping paper at the mercy of a child on Christmas Day.

Eager, he tried to help, almost foiling her attempts to free him from denim hell and to get him out of his boots. The moment every barrier was gone, she sat back on her haunches and simply stared at his dark majesty. He was absolutely gorgeous, like dark, polished mahogany. Every inch of him was sculpted into smooth perfection.

Her line of vision traveled from his smoldering, amber gaze and thick black lashes down the bridge of his regal nose, then flowed over his mouth and down his throat, not missing the breadth of his naked shoulders and chest, or the way his jet-black hair spilled against his skin. Dragging her gaze down his abdomen brick by sexy brick, she just shook her head. His limbs were tight, lean, muscular . . . his thighs, incredible.

Even his cock was beautiful. The hues along his member went from the smoothest, darkest ebony near the base to a ruddy walnut tone along his shaft. His skin, there, was stretched to shining where it had obviously expanded to capacity over an elaborate network of veins. Sasha ran the pad of her thumb along the slick groove in the wide bell crown that was dark like his base, fascinated as it jumped under her light caress. He was barely breathing, each inhale a shallow sip of air as his lids lowered to half-mast.

Awed, she explored him more slowly, using the side of her face to caress his chest, his trembling stomach, and that wonderfully soft onyx down trail that began just below his navel. Before he could recover she turned her mouth on him, spilling hot licks over his swollen sac as she gripped him tightly at his base and watched thick, shimmering need leak like his member was weeping. He arched hard, his groan reverberating through the room and contracting her canal, and she looked up as he reached for her.

"You are no liar?"

He squeezed his eyes shut and shook his head no. She followed the dense, bulbous network of veins in his shaft with her tongue and suckled the place just under the ridge of the head, making him cry out.

"Seriously, I'm not in heat?" She allowed her breath to coat his glistening skin and watched his desire leak over her fist as she slowly began to stroke him. "Because it damn sure feels like it."

"I swear . . ." His words trailed off in a strangled growl as he closed his eyes again.

"*I swear* I'll hunt you down like a dog in the swamps and slaughter you if you're lying," she murmured against his distended skin and then quickly, suddenly, her motions became a shock to his system, pulling him into her mouth hard and fast.

"Oh, God, Sasha . . . trust me!"

He sat up and nearly convulsed on a gasp as he fisted her hair, thrusting hard. Her mouth hunted his sanity, trapped it, her swirling tongue now torture . . . just like her velvety hair and satin-smooth skin . . . and sweet, feminine musk—her taste intoxicating. She was definitely the promised prophecy. More than that. Her graceful fingers, her hands pleasure predators, finding agony along every inch of him they claimed . . . her fleshy breasts and the swell of her hips, the taut length of her thighs, all of it had cornered him and he needed to mount her. He could still taste her on his tongue, smell her fresh on his face; the fast, hard pull of her mouth was causing his eyes to roll toward the back of his skull.

She held him with both hands now as she moved with him. But he couldn't drag enough air into his lungs fast enough when she suddenly released him and bit him inside his thigh.

He lost it, flipped her, pinned her on all fours, and entered her so forcefully that he literally saw stars. In the same moment she convulsed beneath him, her voice a gash to his will, her hard, erratic jerks dredging his sac, making him thrust like a madman. No control left, he was cuming so intensely that each return to her body causcd a call-and-response holler to thunder from his throat.

She'd marked him, broken the skin. His mind was on fire, his scrotum seizing hard enough to almost draw up into his body. *Oh, God, it feels so good* . . . pleasure and pain, spasms in his shaft so wicked that they knotted muscles in his calves. His face was burning up, sweat dripping, every snap jerk of her spine sending shards of insane ecstasy through him. Needing to stop, but *oh, damn, don't stop*!

Her wolf had marked his. Her shadow-self had emerged to dance with his in the darkened room, seducing him all over again. His body was no longer under his influence— she owned it, she kept it hard, she made his cock jump and his muscles twitch. His wolf was her totem. His hands couldn't touch enough of her creamy skin. If the moon had been full, he would have completely lost his mind.

She turned her face into his left bicep and nipped him there hard before releasing a low, feminine, growl. "Mine."

He slid his hands up her sweat-slicked body and captured her ear with his teeth, sending rough confirmation into it. "Yours."

"Yeah . . ." she said possessively, licking the place where she'd nipped him.

Didn't she know what a mark like hers meant? He filled his palms with her breasts and kissed her nape, breathing in her hair. Had she any idea how long he'd waited to feel like this, to experience a shadow dance?

She pushed against the floor, flat-palming the hard surface, her limbs trembling beneath him as he anchored a forearm around her waist tighter and bit into her shoulder without warning.

"Mine," he said roughly, his voice a near growl.

The taste of her made him throw his head back and howl. But the sound of her voice ripping up her vocal cords to blend with his call, to fuse with it, put tears in his eyes.

She reached for him blindly, backward, trying to touch him. "Hunter!"

He knew what she needed and released her quickly then turned her over to lie on her back. "I'm right here, baby."

She took his mouth as she wrapped her legs around his waist, tears streaming from her gorgeous eyes while he gently sank into her again.

"Yours," she said on a high-pitched gasp and gave him her exposed throat.

His hands sought her hair as his hair became a curtain over his face. Never in his life had he expected this from her so soon. Gingerly, reverently, he opened his mouth and covered her windpipe with his canines, moving against her until she arched. "Mine," he whispered, briefly pulling back to witness her pleasure.

She clutched his shoulders, so near completion that he could feel the cresting orgasm contracting her womb. Urging him, her hands slid down his wet back and gripped his ass, pulling him into her with forceful tugs. When he covered her throat again with his mouth, she dissolved into a sobbing climax that simply pushed him over the edge of his own.

They lay sprawled out on the floor, joined, breathing in halting jags, holding each other, fingers tracing skin, palms caressing tousled hair. Soon he could begin to feel the icy tendrils of Colorado air violating their den, trying to invade their peace through a draft beneath the door.

Carefully he withdrew from her body while gently taking her mouth.

"Don't," she murmured, reaching for him.

"I'm not leaving," he said quietly as he positioned himself to lift her. "Let's get into bed . . . it's too drafty down on the floor."

She looked up at him with complete trust and he cradled her cheek in the palm of his hand for a moment before gathering her into his arms. Once he laid her on the rickety queen-sized bed, she snuggled into him with her eyes closed and curled into a loose ball. Beyond exhausted, he drew her even closer, kissed her shoulder, and pulled the comforter and blankets around them.

"I'm not going anywhere, I promise," he said quietly, as he drifted off to sleep.

EARLY AFTERNOON SUN stabbed at the edges of the drawn drapes. Highway traffic in the distance and the occasional car rolling over ice, salt, and driveway gravel finally pierced her senses. A heavy warmth surrounded her, making her lethargic as she dozed in and out of consciousness, completely relaxed. A slightly callused hand made a lazy trail up and over the swell of her hip and down again, nearly hypnotizing her back to sleep. Then came clarity.

Rod was dead. She had killed him. What was she doing screwing some man she didn't even know?

Sasha's body tensed. "I have to go to Wal-Mart," she said, her eyes still closed. He was warming her again, making her body respond and come alive when it shouldn't, given the circumstances and the time pressure she was under.

"I know," he said after a moment on a soft exhale, brushing her shoulder with a kiss. "So do I."

Sasha hesitated, trying to keep herself from bolting. Rod was dead.

"For what?" she said, as Hunter pulled her in closer, stabbing her bottom with a ramrod-stiff erection. She fought not to cringe. Anxiety was making her breaths short. She shouldn't feel this way or be doing this, her mind screamed, in opposition to her body.

"Pants," he whispered, nipping her earlobe.

She was out of bed like a shot.

"Pants? Right," she said, now staring out the window.

"Mine are ruined. You ripped them so badly I'll have to go shadow into the store to get them."

She squeezed her eyes shut as she remembered. "Sorry."

"Yeah . . . so, since there's been a wardrobe malfunction—"

"No, no, no, I've gotta get back on track here, Hunter."

He watched her spine and could see the tension slide into it just the way it had tainted her voice. Slowly pulling his body to the edge of the bed, he eased beyond the warmth of the covers and went to her. There was no healing misplaced guilt, and he knew only time could heal the trauma of a loss . . . but he would damn sure try. "It's going to be all right," he murmured, allowing the warmth of his palms to slide down her arms.

"I'll be fine," she said quietly. "I just never thought . . ." Her voice trailed off in a thick whisper. "What's done is done. It was better that way. I'm okay."

He splayed his hand across her belly, making it quiver as he dragged his tongue over a shoulder blade. "You sure?"

For a moment she didn't answer . . . couldn't answer. "Yeah. Doc is worried, I know he has to be."

He could feel her battling for emotional distance and respectfully backed off for the moment. "You're right," he said quietly and then kissed her shoulder, unable to completely abandon her to gloom. "Would you like the shower first?"

"Thanks," she said softly, hugging herself as she slipped around him.

Hunter didn't move. He simply listened for the bathroom door to close, but was somewhat mollified that Sasha hadn't flipped the lock. Still, he would respect her space, wouldn't push past the new barrier she'd erected between them. A tragedy had occurred; one of her pack had Turned and she'd been the one who had to put him out of his misery.

Melancholy settled into his bones as he stared out of the window. A beautiful woman like Sasha shouldn't have had to do a pack kill—but the virus was no respecter of gender. He closed his eyes and dragged his fingers through his hair, hoping that what they'd shared in the early morning before dawn wasn't just posttrauma sex. True, it had been, but for him it was so much more. He understood where she was at, though . . . probably washing those same questions through her mind as she washed her hair.

He turned slightly to stare at the bathroom door, listening to the shower spray. He would have gladly washed her gorgeous hair and allowed the soap lather to run though his fingers as his hands slid over her skin.

Damn. How did a man heal a heart that wasn't even his, that was damaged before he'd even been given a chance? Then again, maybe he wasn't supposed to. Maybe it wasn't his job. Hunter turned back to the window and squinted at the sun. The best he could do would be to maybe make her smile by teaching her something new, but in his current morose state, even that was doubtful.

SLIGHTLY DAZED FROM the stark sunlight that she'd been staring at, and oddly disappointed that Hunter hadn't pursued the conversation, for a moment she tried to play it off, not knowing exactly what there really was to say. In frustration, she began washing her hair, wishing he'd let her do his, or at the very least, had done hers.

Yet it was so insane, this place where she was at—and it disturbed her more than a little. It was as though there were some eerie connection between her and Hunter that had no rational basis. She should have been in deep grieving, but wasn't. The pain came in unexpected waves and then mellowed, only to rise within her again at a most inopportune time. But even thinking that was freaking her out. What was opportune about mourning? A good man was down; her own brass had her under surveillance. The rest of her pack could be at risk or could, for all she knew, be captured, or worse.

Sasha cringed and washed the thick suds out of her hair, allowing the water to drown out the horrifying thoughts. She'd spent the night in a cheap motel with some mysterious male who actually had shown signs of going wolf, after she'd put half a clip of silver shells in her captain's chest. Panic brought her hands to her face to feel along the edge of her jaw. What if she was Turning and just didn't know it? What if she was just like Rod, delusional, slowly slipping into mental collapse before the full transformation, and what if another one had sought her out? Was that why Shogun had come to her?

Who the hell was Max Hunter?

The question was so terrifying that she could feel her heart slamming against her breastbone. Her mind raked over every detail about him, trying to put her insane behavior into rational context. But all she could imagine was what his hands would have felt like, soapy, massaging her scalp while her wet body was pressed against every brick-hard ridge of his under the spray.

Flight was the only rational answer her mind could scavenge, and she jumped out of the tub, left the water running, and headed out of the bathroom with a towel loosely draped around her.

"Hey, hey, hey, whoa," he said, watching her rush around the room and gather her ripped, soiled clothing.

"I'm out," she announced, struggling to pull the fabric over her damp skin.

"You're panicking, and will catch your death of cold out there," he said calmly, staring at her.

"Better to catch it out there than in here."

The verbal snipe cut deep, but he tried to shrug it off, telling himself that the wounded always lashed out.

"I'm not a threat to you, Sasha . . . and you aren't one to me."

She found her nine that had been in his jacket pocket. "Oh, no?"

He shook his head. "You don't wanna do that," he said with no judgment in his tone as he headed for the bathroom.

"Yeah? Why not?" she called out behind him.

"Because I'm going to show you the best part of the day," he said, jumping into the tub, and then ducking into the shower spray, while leaving the curtain open and making a complete mess of water on the floor.

Strange curiosity drew her to the bathroom entrance. "What's the best part of the day?"

He ignored her and kept washing his body, then finally glanced at her with a half-smile. "You still plan to shoot me for just breathing this morning?"

"Okay. I'm sorry. I just feel . . . really . . ."

"Out of control." He looked at her and trapped her gaze. "It's the meds, or the lack thereof, Sasha. Think of how long you've been on them, and how this is perhaps the longest stretch you've gone off them."

"I hate that you might have a point." She briefly closed her eyes as water from her wet hair dripped onto her shoulders. "I've taken that crap for as far back as I can remember, and this is the longest stretch without it." She didn't explain that she was also panicking about the Rod thing and her own possible contagion. Hunter didn't need to know all that. But maybe the man had a point; her emotions were all over the place. It had to be the med withdrawal.

"Then can you not shoot me, at least not when I haven't done anything?" His eyes were merry but his voice was patient. The combination did something to her.

She grudgingly slid the gun onto the dresser as she watched him towel off, half expecting him to just shake the water from him, her gaze hunting every delicious line of his body. Deep wood tones against stark-white, very small towels. Oh, yeah . . . Onyx waves of thick hair sent water streaming down his back, chest, and over his shoulders, adding to the glistening beauty of his sculpted frame.

This was outrageous; her own body was betraying her again. Had to be the heavy med withdrawal. He lifted a foot and rested it on the edge of the tub, toweling off his leg, and all she could do was stand there watching the muscles work beneath his dark skin. Then with one majestic shake, he sent water everywhere from his dripping wet hair, spraying her face—then winked at her and quickly strode out of the room with a taunt in his eyes.

Oooohhh, she was gonna get him!

On him in a flash, she dashed to tackle him from behind as bizarre playfulness thrummed within her and he quickly sidestepped her and then jumped on the bed. Suddenly they were laughing, nipping, and making quick snatches toward each other, each missing, reversing the hunt as whim dictated. First she chased him, and then he would fake left or right and go after her.

"We need to do this outside," he said, panting, after missing her again.

"Revenge is a bitch—I will prevail," she said, laughing and sidestepping him.

"Not during the best part of the day." He grinned a wolfish grin. "You don't know how to do it yet."

"Ha!" she said, hands on hips and breathing hard, chuckling. "Do what?"

"Wanna see?" He had the excited expression of a little kid on his face. "The long shadows are the best part of the day, Sasha . . . c'mon!"

Too curious to even fake a refusal, she gathered up her torn boots. His smile widened, and he quickly picked up his amber and silver amulet off the floor, looped the long silver chain over his head, and began pulling on his clothes as best he could.

She laughed hard when the front of his jeans flapped open, destroyed.

"Not a problem," he said, lifting his chin in mock indignation. "I have bungee cords in my trunk, thank you very much, mademoiselle."

"But you don't have on any underwear!" she shrieked, covering her mouth and doubling over. "Oh, no, Hunter— I am not walking into Wal-Mart with you like that!"

"They won't see. I move fast. And you should talk—you're still half wet and your pants are half hanging off you, so I'll be fine shopping au naturel."

"Oh, no. Not."

"How much you want to bet? I'll even make you a wager."

"No. End of story. Plus, you are not going to steal stuff out of Wal-Mart. You just aren't."

"I won't steal it. I have money. You give them the tag and tell them I decided to wear my selection out of the store."

"Oh, my God . . ."

"Come outside and play, Sasha. The shadows are amazing in the afternoon."

Grudgingly, she followed him out to the parking lot and squinted at the bright contrast of sun versus dark motel room. Pure embarrassment kept her looking anywhere but at him as he boldly strode to his truck holding the front of his pants closed with one fist and then fumbling under the seats for the infamous bungee cords.

"This is beyond tacky, Hunter. Why don't you just stay in the truck, tell me your size, and let me get the jeans?"

"Because I might see something else in there I want. And I'm hungry."

She rolled her eyes. Clearly this man was just trying to push her buttons. His antics were so outrageous that a smile continued to break free of her restraint.

There was nothing to do but laugh as he yanked out a tangle of stretchy cords in varying lengths and made a huge production of finding the shortest one to thread around his waist through his belt loops. Hooking the ends together, he gave her a triumphant snort.

"Voilà!"

She took off his jacket that she'd draped around her, despite the bitter temperatures, and casually handed it to him. He tilted his head in a question. She couldn't hold it in any longer and burst out laughing again.

"Put the jacket on, please," she said, shaking her head.

He grabbed it from her good-naturedly and looked down and shrugged. "What can I say?"

But the moment he slid the jacket on, he reached for her hand, clasped it, and began running. Stumbling, laughing, and having the time of her life, soon she could give fleet-footed chase as he dashed toward the densely wooded area that sat back from the roadside motel.

The whole thing was surreal—highway at their backs and nothing but thickets and trees looming before them. Being with him was a live-in-the-moment flash of intensity. Something about this man eclipsed the past and the future, making the present the only slice of time there was.

Her heart beat in a hard, joyful rhythm as she tried to catch up to Hunter, who scaled fallen logs and came down with stupefying grace. She slowed her chase to better watch him plunder the woods, her muscles contracting and releasing in anticipation of motion that her mind overrode. Fear of breaking an ankle, stepping wrong, being stabbed by a jagged branch or rock made her wary. She'd never been in this terrain before, never on this stretch of land.

Sensing her nervousness, he turned and stared at her, his eyes sad as she slowed her gait.

"Don't tell me you're going chickenshit on me, Trudeau," he said, baiting her by calling to her like one of the guys she'd trained with.

Her gaze narrowed a bit. A challenge was something that she found hard to ignore. But she also had common sense and a mission to fulfill; apparently he had neither.

"Uh, the store?" she said with a hint of sarcasm, even though she'd smiled. Sasha turned her wrist over as though she had on a watch and tapped the back of it with her forefinger. Plus, it was so cold outside she could see their breaths! Now that they'd stopped running, her wet hair and top was beginning to make her teeth chatter.

"They stay open all night—we've got time. But check this out," he said, running, leaping, and then he disappeared.

Sasha stood very, very still, her hackles up, senses keen. Then out of a shadow ten feet away, he landed in full view.

"What a rush!" he said, smiling widely. "It'll warm you up, too."

She backed away slowly, the hair on the nape of her neck bristling. "What the hell was that?"

"Dance with me, baby—come on, it's sooo cool."

She looked him up and down. "Explain."

He let out a weary sigh. "You're taking all the fun out of it, Trudeau." When she didn't move but folded her arms over her chest, he relented. "Oh, all right."

Walking past the endless stand of trees, he stretched out his arm and touched their long, eerily narrow shadows. "Like jumping railroad ties," he said plainly. "This is easy, the shadows are close together. It gets challenging when they're far apart. But this is the best part of the daytime hours, while the shadows are long and stretch far." He stopped walking and turned to smile at her with a dashing smile. "Want to try it?"

"I . . . wait—how do you do it?"

He threw up his hands and rolled his eyes. "How do you do it? That's like asking how you have sex."

"Well, the uninformed need directions the first time out." She reinforced her stance and folded her arms over her chest again.

"Yeah, yeah, one can tell you the technical basics, but to really do it, you've got to follow an experienced teacher, if you ask me," he muttered, growing peevish. "It's all about trust. Just one man's opinion."

"How do you—"

"All right, all right!" He stalked up to her and looked her in the eyes, and then laid his hands on her shoulders. "You have to get to a place in your mind that's still, and call the wolf. When she comes, you'll feel this incredible surge of energy . . . heat . . . like your body's burning up. It makes you want to shed your clothes, run, feel the wind on your face, ripping through your hair . . . this heat is so intense . . . so erotic a pull that it steals your breath until you almost cannot breathe."

"Like last night," she said quietly.

He nodded, and for what seemed like a long while, neither of them spoke.

"Then," he murmured, "you reach out and touch a shadow. It will feel cool to the touch, will stop the burn, and the next thing you know, the only thing that keeps the agony in check is moving faster and faster through the shadows. You're running, dancing, ripping from one to another, gaining momentum, energy, prowess, and when you come out of it, for a brief while you can sustain whatever the properties were of the object that cast the shadow."

"Whoa . . ." she whispered, awestruck. "Like the multiple scents you cloaked yourself with before?"

His intense stare began to slightly glow and the hunger it suddenly exuded made her swallow hard. "Yes," he murmured. "If you step into a stone shadow, the spirit of the stone will lend you its strength. If you're being hunted, find metal or stone shadows, or that of a tree, and the blow you lob when you come out of it will literally crush a man's jaw." He smiled a wicked half-smile. "Buildings work like that, too."

"You have *got* to be kidding me," she said in a faraway voice.

"If you need speed, catch and jump into the shadow of a car moving quickly. You can ride that shadow doing sixty, seventy, eighty—whatever the vehicle is doing." He laughed and shook his head. "But a couple of times, trying it as a kid and chasing rigs along the side of the highway at night, I was almost road pizza."

She just stared at the man, wide-eyed.

"Hold my hand and run with me after you call your wolf . . . and don't let go. I'll take you through the trees, run you back to the clearing, and let you feel the shadow dance outside." He waited for her response like an excited child. Unable to withstand her hesitation, he pressed his point, cupping her cheek with his warm palm. "It's not a curse, Sasha. It's an extraordinary gift from the Great Spirit. It's not from the demon realms . . . it's Mother Nature sharing all her children's gifts with each other through the shadows."

While she didn't claim to understand, the gentle plea in his voice and the honesty she saw in his eyes made her step forward. She fingered his amulet and he closed his eyes.

"Yes . . . I admit, there are dangers."

Bingo. Her gut was never wrong.

"There are shadows made from nature, then those not of the Great Spirit." He looked down at his chest and then removed the amber and silver he wore, and looped the chain over her neck. "Sometimes when running or in hot pursuit, things are a blur, the shadows so dense . . . things are whirring by so quickly that you cannot make out one from the other. Normally the unnatural darkness is colder, like the most severe absence of warmth, not refreshing coolness. It will make the hairs on your neck stand up. This," he added, tracing where it lay against her breasts, "will keep you from falling into a demon door."

"Shit, then forget shadow dancing." She began to take the chain from her neck, but he placed a calm hand over her chest.

"When we go to my people up in the mountains, I'll have them make you a ward . . . until then, keep mine. I've been doing this for a long time."

The soft timbre of his voice and the gentle promise in his eyes stilled her. Never had someone so completely given of themselves to her. She touched the amber while looking at him.

"This looks so old and sacred . . . it's too important to who you are . . . I—"

"Please," he said quietly, his eyes searching her face. "Wear it and dance with me unafraid."

Not waiting for her answer, he took her mouth. Soon the unbearable heat that he seemed to summon from her just by his touch began to consume her. His tongue writhed with hers in a sultry dance, one that promised so much, and his arms surrounded her, pulling her into their exquisite warmth. Her hands sought his back, her chest straining to create a friction bond with his. Her pelvis locked with his and his ruined jeans soon provided him no protection. It was insane how much she wanted this man.

"Let her out to play, Sasha. She's not a monster . . ."

"I'm afraid to . . . I've never been this long without my meds, never—"

"What color is she?" he panted against her neck.

"Black?"

"No." He kissed her hard and fast and then pulled back.

"Yes, yes she is," Sasha argued, squeezing her eyes shut tightly. "She's huge . . . stands like three feet at the shoulders . . ."

"That's *my* wolf," he said in a low, sensual rumble. "I can't believe you saw it within your own wolf's shadow land."

"The silver one, then . . . she's me?"

He nodded as his breath hitched.

All she could do was stare at him for a second. He had a
look on his face that held such blatant arousal, she wasn't
sure if she should make love to him on the spot or run.

"Run . . ." he whispered, reading her eyes, if he hadn't
read her mind.

A flash of glowing amber lit his gaze with unmistakable desire. Instinct kicked in and she turned on her heels
and became a blur though the trees. Within seconds she
could feel his nearness, his hot pursuit, the burn of something within her reveling in newfound freedom. Her
strides became longer, more fluid, and obstacles to sail
over in graceful hurdles were now sought-after things.
She could hear Hunter's deft footfalls, his breath. Sweat
coated her body and the pleasure now bordered on agony.

A burning hand suddenly clasped hers, and the next
thing she knew she was sailing. Each footfall hit a cool
dark place. The rich, earthy scent of the forest clipped by
snow filled not just her nose, but her lungs, her soul. She
came out of the shadows into a clearing, her eyes wild,
her hair static charged, her body on fire. And then he
grabbed her again, this time pulling her so she almost fell.

"Sasha!" he yelled, excited, his voice deep and commanding. "Look up—birds!"

She wasn't sure which direction to look. In the air or
on the ground, but clear as day she could see the fast-
moving shadows of a flock of Canadian geese.

"Oh, God, wait until you feel this, Sasha!"

She didn't have time to even respond. In two long
strides she'd been pulled into the shapes flitting across the
ground. Weightlessness, sailing, climbing, her stomach
rising up in the cool, soundless space, feeling like she'd
dropped in a roller coaster . . . the ground was beneath
her, and then she landed on all fours on the other side of
the highway in another stand of trees.

A gleeful shriek tore from her throat and she began

running with her arms open and leaping into nothingness, running the length of tall pines. She saw Hunter loping beside her, a smile on his face, his form only visible in broken frames as he passed from a tree into dappling sunlight and into another tree. Happiness filled her as his laughter echoed like a sonic bomb, making her feel it as well as hear it. She wanted to dance, twirl, make shadow angels in this glorious between-worlds place. Then he reached out and grabbed her hand again, this time veering off sharply toward the highway.

She began screaming before he did it. The eighteen-wheelers were moving at ninety miles per hour! Jerked into a flash of sunlight, he jumped, made them both hit the shadow, and the next thing she knew she was running at a speed her mind couldn't comprehend. Then like skipping stones, he jumped into the shadow of an SUV, and another, and a car, crossing the highway, reversing their steps, and returned them back to the motel pull-off in a tumble to the ground within a tree shadow.

He kept her pinned beneath him for a moment, both of them breathing hard and laughing.

"We're invisible, you know . . . even right out here—as long as the shadow of this tree doesn't move."

"That was incredible!" She was laughing, crying, panting, and holding him tightly. "Hunter, it was—"

"The sexiest thing a woman has ever done with me in my entire life," he said, and then kissed her hard. "Wait until we're in the mountains . . . the hawk shadows, the eagles—breathtaking. The streams, shadows of fish in the lakes . . . you can feel the spirit of moving water . . . the towering strength of the great cliffs. Oh . . . baby . . . you just don't know . . ."

He'd kissed her hard while tugging at her sweater. She felt the hard press of his erection and felt a fire ignite within her.

She lifted her head when a car careened into the driveway. "We have to get up, this is so—"

"They can't see us, Sasha," he murmured against her throat, practically dry-humping her in the snow.

She looked at him, looked at the highway, looked at the cars in the lot.

"They really can't," he said, his nuzzles growing in aggression.

He leaned in for another kiss, but she flat-palmed him with a smile.

"I guess I believe you, but as long as I can see them, then that's a problem."

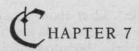

CHAPTER 7

"SHE NEVER CALLED," Xavier Holland said, coming into the oblong-shaped room of the cabin and sitting down on the dirt floor next to his friend. He gathered the Indian blankets tighter around his nude form as the thick, stone-heated air weighed on his skin and oppressed his lungs.

"We will sweat and come to an answer sent by the Great Spirit and the ancestors. She is learning about the other realms that exist and about the way of the wolf in her own time. Do not worry."

Familiar with the sweat lodge divination process, Xavier Holland waited. Firelight danced, sending leaping shadows against the mural-decorated, mud-packed walls. Medicine wheels and dream catchers adorned with eagle feathers framed them. The dim interior light cast a golden-red glow to their skins as they sat around the center fire waiting for a vision.

His dear friend knew what was at stake, understood what was happening . . . had predicted this outcome even before Rod had been born. Smoldering sage, regret, and tobacco smoke caused Xavier's eyes to water as his friend of over a quarter century scooped up sacred water from a wide-mouthed urn using a polished turtle's shell, and splashed the glowing rocks that were heated by burning logs. Instantly a sizzling, sputtering sound like the hissing of an angry rattlesnake echoed through the small, private sweat lodge. Smoke billowed up through a conical opening in the roof.

"She will come." Silver Hawk's gaze searched the doctor's face. The sureness of his tone made both men stare at the circle that had been drawn in the middle of the floor.

"You had a vision?"

The elder Ute shaman nodded. "She will come home to herself. That which we had hoped for as old men will come to pass. The time is near . . . very, very near. Soon she will learn the politics of the Federation of Clans and the other ruling bodies that make up the grand Council. You will not have to teach her this. She is with my grandson. Two wolves are at play; one midnight, one silver—this is your Sasha. My grandson's eyes are different. I must make her an amber ward. Of all the females, she is the only one blind to his blood taint and would shadow dance with him."

"She was not natural born. The others might not accept her." Xavier's gaze searched the shaman's.

Old fear seized him. Xavier tried to keep a calm exterior before his serene, meditative friend, but his insides roiled with the rise of harsh memories. In his mind, Sasha was still that young, angry adolescent who had been abused in the one place he thought might be her haven: school. He had gotten a phone call that no parent wanted to get. "Dr. Holland, we need you to come to the school. We're afraid there's been an incident." He had rushed down to the school, his heart in his throat. When he had stepped into the infirmary, he saw Sasha sitting on one of the beds, a soft gray blanket draped over her hunched shoulders, her face dirty, scraped, and her lip bloody. She had other bruises and scrapes on her arms and legs, and her blue, white, and gray uniform had been dirty and torn. She had been drugged by some girls as part of a vicious prank and left to be molested under the bleachers by members of the lacrosse team who'd been complicit with the scheme. He had stared into her huge, questioning, tear-filled gray eyes and had felt fury . . . and fear.

What did one tell a child who had been hurt by the world, simply because they'd sensed her difference? How did one create a place of safety and teach that child right from wrong when the most privileged had so horribly broken the rules? What would he tell her now as an adult? Her top commanders, men of privilege and power, had again broken the rules and destroyed their once-firm covenant of honor. What in God's name would he tell his Sasha?

Trying to quell the demons in his mind, his only comfort then, like now, was when Sasha had told him she'd prevailed. The athletes who had attempted to rape her under the bleachers had been sent to the hospital. Wherever she was now, albeit on the run, she would survive. He had to hold on to that hope and he clung to that as though it were a mental life raft—Sasha was a survivor.

The only reason she hadn't killed anyone in the group that had attacked her as a kid was because there'd been the date rape drug in her system that had made her sluggish. Even with that, she was too strong for them to hold her down and have their way. But once she finally backed the arrogant young aggressors up and found out that one of their girlfriends had slipped something into her drink at lunch, there was no stopping her. The main culprit behind the scheme, a senator's daughter, required reconstructive dental surgery—but given the circumstances the authorities didn't expel Sasha. Doing so would have opened a whole can of worms. Instead they ostracized her and that had been another kind of hell for her.

It just wore on his soul that, even in the shadow wolf clans, his Sasha would again be the newcomer . . . considered different, just like before . . . and he'd have to put his arms around her and explain how and why she'd become that way.

The thing that chilled him was that this time, he'd finally have to tell her the truth. The full truth.

"My grandson has broader understanding than the others. This is why he leads. His difference has taught him much humility for those considered outcasts. In that regard, he is like Chief Ouray, who, as you know, spoke many tribal languages of our people, and also your English and Spanish. The Great Chief could cross boundaries and bring bands and tribes together. Hunter will do this with the shadow clans."

Xavier Holland looked into the fire. He didn't want to show disrespect by reminding his friend that Chief Ouray's wife had almost been lynched by settlers who wanted revenge on him, and that, ultimately, the treaties the U.S. Government made with him were betrayed.

"Diplomacy will prevail." Silver Hawk lifted a long, tobacco-stuffed pipe and drew on it slowly, causing the eagle feathers attached to it to sway. He'd spoken as though listening to the doctor's innermost thoughts, and yet his composure remained serene. "We must reveal the truth soon, before the children come to believe less of us."

Xavier nodded, but his thoughts were far away. "You have not told Hunter how his father died yet, then?"

There was a long pause, a stillness in the room that made the smoke's movement seem that of an uncoiling serpent.

"Have you told Sasha how her parents truly died?"

Xavier's friend asked, no hint of judgment in his tone, just a question.

"No," Xavier Holland said after another long pause. "And there's another complication. I have two additional men to bring in. Right now, they're at risk."

Again the elder shaman nodded. "We have shadow wolf clans in Europe, Asia, and North America keeping the demon doors guarded. We can send messengers to assist your stranded men with money, identification, food . . . to bring them through the old route home."

"The old Native American passages, across the Bering Strait?"

"Yes, my friend. The route that bonded us to where my people are your people. We have all walked from the mother continent where the father sky made mother earth conceive humankind."

Intense heat combined with stress made the doctor rub his palms down his face. "I have to get word to Woods and Fisher so they don't attack those you send to help them, don't think they're being set up. Right now, they could be anywhere over there."

"Our wolf clans are excellent trackers and will find your men. They cannot overpower the wolves that will find them, and in due time, through demonstration, your stranded men will come to trust their guides."

"Across Asia, through Russia, in Siberian temperatures, across to Alaska?"

"The oldest walking route. Our wolves know this well and will cover much ground. We have dog-sled teams and nomads who live off the land as in times of old. But my advice is to keep them in Canada, Yukon Territory, and let it seem as though they'd died during their last mission. This would be the fox's advice. Let them remain as ghosts for those who have tried to kill them."

Both men sat quietly for a long while, their aged, nude bodies sweat-slicked beneath elaborately woven blankets.

"You should prepare those who seek Sasha's return. A fox's wisdom is needed there as well. It is in her nature to gnaw off her own paw if trapped, rather than submit to being domesticated. Thus, give her the shadow wolf's mission so that she does not feel trapped; bring a wise treaty between what your world wants her to do and what our world needs her to do . . . and what her inner wolf will ultimately demand that she do."

The doctor nodded, sweat running off the bridge of his nose as he looked at his serene friend. In his world, however, treaties were always violated. Yet, just like in the past, he had few alternatives but to strike a deal with the general and hope that it held. Sitting next to his old friend and counselor, he reflected knowing that the Ute people, like so many others, had been in this position, too, with dire results. Sadly, history was repeating itself.

Currently, it was a matter of blind faith. That was all either of them had to lean on. Silver Hawk had led him right thus far. So had his quiet entreaties to heaven above.

Staring at Silver Hawk's long, snow-white braids that were wrapped in silver and leather bands and the way his ruddy, lined face seemed as ancient as the mountains, Xavier Holland marveled at the spiritual gifts that modern science still couldn't fully comprehend. Despite the abuse, the theft of fifteen million acres of Ute lands in Colorado alone, and a violent relocation to Utah for most of that tribe under a history of pure slaughter, genocide, the people still had a serenity that went beyond what anyone could fathom. He wondered what was more evil—men who stole land and broke treaties, wiping out entire groups of people, or the demon species they now hunted?

Like him, his long-dead friend Dr. Zang Chen had understood the blend of mystical, spiritual, to the scientific . . . just as his bayou people understood roots and the other side long before computers and scientific instrumentation could measure alpha and beta brain waves. Respect for the environment, and respect for what was naturally occurring in nature—that was the bedrock of all original peoples. Harmony, coexistence, not conquest and conquer. How would they survive going up against the resources of the general?

The general didn't understand. There were different dimensions of reality, places where different intelligences existed, places yet to be explored. Then there were demon doors . . . places that every human culture since the dawn of time instinctively, rightfully, had set up barriers against. All of it, and the choice about what to explore and what to leave as one found it, was a matter of respect.

Xavier Holland studied his friend. Silver Hawk's head was held high, his dark, liquid brown eyes gazing at a point beyond his sight into the vast unfathomable realm where seers go. Xavier Holland conferred the utmost respect to the process of divining the truth.

It was said that it took an honest man to draw an honest answer from the cast bones. If that were so, and he believed it to be, then going to the one person as vested in the outcome of Sasha's well-being as he was, was the only way he could seek the truth.

Xavier Holland stood after a long, silent while. More than an hour had passed though it seemed like just a few minutes.

"She will come home before the storm does. The storm is a good omen from the Great Spirit. It will slow down men who do not understand the Great Sky."

Xavier Holland nodded and quietly withdrew from the

sacred circle, leaving the heavy-lidded Silver Hawk in private contemplation. But first a preemptive strike was in order. Something that would make the general need Sasha.

Thoughts crowded the doctor's mind as he walked the length of his friend's small home, and entered his room. He picked his unmarked cell phone up off the dresser, sat down on a hard chair in the sparsely furnished, utilitarian room, and stared at the second hand on his watch.

With his thumb he punched in the code-red emergency number that would put him through to the general. It would also ensure he'd be traced. That part wasn't important. He wouldn't be on the telephone long enough for that.

"This is Xavier," he said the moment the call connected with the general's command post. Not giving them time to respond, he talked quickly, firmly, and without any waver or hesitancy in his voice. "Please let the general know that after Butler, I needed a break, had to clear my mind over the weekend. I'm on vacation in the mountains but there's a storm approaching. I'm coming home before the weather gets bad. Oh, and I forgot my damned phone and had to buy a cheap one on the road. And the signals up here are weak. You're dropping out as we speak."

"Doctor, sir, please stay on the line and give us your location. The general—"

"Hello? You're breaking up. Hello? Listen, I've been in communication with Lieutenant Sasha Trudeau. She's all right, no sign of a Turn. The lieutenant simply went on leave to clear her head and grieve the loss of her friends, her unit. She's running scared, however, based on what she recently saw at Captain Butler's, and has taken off to pursue a hot lead, Stateside. She's on to a trail, here, in North America—Rocky Mountain area. Monday, when she reports in, we need her data . . . Hello? . . . Hello? I'm losing you . . . Hello? Listen, she was on to something big."

He ended the call, then simply sat and looked out at the majestic mountains.

SASHA PULLED INTO a parking spot in the Wal-Mart lot, turned off the car, and looked at Hunter.

Part of her wanted to throttle him just to get the amused expression off his face, another part of her wanted to climb across the seat and straddle him. He made her crazy, plain and simple. His clothes were half ripped, his pants hanging dangerously askew. The bungee cord that was threaded through his belt loops would keep them up, but there was no keeping his erection behind the shredded flaps of fabric.

"Okay, here's the plan," she said, fighting laughter. "I go in, you stay put. I bring you some jeans and some grub, then we motor."

"I'll be bored," he said like a disgruntled child. "I'm good, Sasha. They won't see me."

"Put your wolf back in the cave and then I'd consider it, but not while you're saluting me in the freaking parking lot!"

He leaned his head on the steering wheel and breathed deeply. "I just need a moment."

"Stay," she said, laughing, then jumped out of the truck.

Truthfully, she needed a little space, a little normalcy—and what better place to find it than in Wal-Mart?

Being a shadow wolf was not normal.

Chasing werewolves for the government was not normal.

Meeting a man who made you wet from leaping into the shadow of an eighteen-wheeler was *not* normal!

God bless the elderly man who'd just said, "Welcome to Wal-Mart."

That was normal.

Tears stung Sasha's eyes for some unknown reason. She was sure that she was losing her mind. Out of nowhere a pang of loneliness stabbed her in the chest. What had happened to her guys? Why did Rod have to turn into a beast? Why was she running from her home and career with some unknown shadow wolf guy she'd just slept with? Had she freakin' gone insane? Had she had a psychotic break with reality?

She grabbed a cart. She needed to find Doc, figure out what had happened. This shadow wolf thing was creepy, very weird, too seductive . . . what if it was all part of the going-werewolf stage?

Mentally focusing on the task at hand, she shoved every question to the back of her mind. Survival training kicked in. Right now she and Max needed the essentials. Right now in Delta, Colorado, snow hadn't hit the ground yet, but as they climbed up into the Uncompahgre area, which was two hundred and fifty-three miles past Delta, there would be drastic weather change. They needed down coats, gloves, hats, long johns, jeans, sweaters, underwear, socks, prepaid cell phones, hiking boots, blankets . . . rope, matches, dried foodstuff, flashlights, bottled water. In ten minutes her cart was full. Damn, what size was the man? Extra large.

She stared at the men's jeans for a second and then rubbed her palms down her face. From the corner of her eye she glimpsed the men's dressing room and then shook her head. Thoroughly embarrassed, she stalked over to a shadowy area and folded her arms over her chest.

"Fluorescent light is a real bitch," a deep male voice rumbled.

"I thought we agreed—"

"I wanted something to eat . . . they have hot dogs and—"

"Oh, my God! What size do you wear? You make me crazy!"

"Thirty-four, but check the inseams, get the longest ones they have."

She walked away from the shadows without comment. How was it that the night before she'd entered a bar happily single and now she was buying jeans for a man whose dick, literally, wouldn't stay in his pants? Something was so wrong about this.

After a moment she found several pairs and stalked back to where he'd last been. "Here," she said, holding out the pile to him.

She'd expected to watch them disappear, but hadn't expected him to pull her into a shadow with him. Eyes wide, she glanced around as he took off his pants. "I . . . you . . . my wolf body-heat wasn't even—"

"It didn't have to be, because it's finally nightfall and the moon is up." He looked at her like she was dinner. "A couple of these dressing rooms have really great shadows in them . . . would you like to see?"

"Put your pants on, man."

He grudgingly obliged but the half-smile never left his face.

"Do we, uh, get a little crazy during the full moon, too?" She raked her hair, feeling very much like a lost Alice in Wonderland.

He broke the alarm off the black jeans he'd selected and zipped them with a loud rip, then handed her the tag off them so she could pay for them at the register. "What do you think?" he asked in a low, sexy rumble, and then walked into the light.

THERE WAS SO much to ponder that talking simply hurt her brain. Sasha watched the scenery pass as a muscle pulsed in Hunter's jaw. He'd just have to get over it. Mrs. Baker was a doll, and she'd made a mental promise long before she'd met him that she would see to it the woman had groceries the next day no matter what. Plus with a storm on the way within the week, and her future whereabouts being a very unsure thing, she *had* to be sure Mrs. Baker was taken care of.

Men. They didn't get it. And all that bull about having a bad feeling about going to her house. Fact was, Hunter probably just didn't want to deal with an old lady. But enough weirdness had already overtaken her life. Doing for an elderly neighbor was normal. She needed many more normal things to surround her.

Hunter pulled the truck up to the end of Sasha's block and glanced around. She hated to admit it but her gut was jumping again.

"I'll say this one last time, do as you like . . . but someone with serious authority and technology has had you under surveillance—even your contact, Doc, said so. You hit three residences where police activity followed. I'm sure that showing yourself is foolhardy. The police, or whoever bugged your home, car, and clothes, could have a sharpshooter out there with orders to shoot to kill. They don't understand that you aren't a demon wolf."

Her shoulders sagged; she hated that he was probably right. But pride made her look out the passenger's side window and consider her chances. "There's plenty of shadows."

He studied her hard and then his gaze softened. The pull to her was immediate as he caressed her forlorn cheek with the back of his hand. "Let me leave the bag on her step . . . you call her by cell phone . . . we'll watch her collect it to be sure she's safe. But be careful to disconnect the call before it can be traced, just in case they also tapped her phones, since she's your closest neighbor and she goes in and out of your apartment. We'll have to pick you up another prepaid phone at a 7–11 after that, too, because they'll have your new number on her caller ID."

The compromise was acceptable. Sasha nodded, wondering how she and Hunter had become a veritable shadow wolf Bonnie and Clyde.

"All right," Sasha finally conceded and handed Hunter the bag. She had to admit that she liked watching him negotiate the night, blend into the darkness. There was something so seductive about it, something that she knew she had to learn to do quickly and efficiently very, very soon.

Unsurprisingly, the car door opened and closed without a sound. Sasha counted to thirty beats, and then as though her eyes were playing tricks on her, there was a bag suddenly leaning against the door on Mrs. Baker's top step under the porch light. Another thirty-second count and the door to the truck quietly opened again, the seat depressed, and a familiar scent and warmth neared her. A kiss pulled her face into the light and she could then see him.

"You have *got* to show me your kung fu in the moonlight, Hunter," she murmured against his mouth, truly impressed.

"Any time, any night," he said, tracing her cheek with his finger. "There's so much to show you but so little time . . ."

She clasped her cell phone in one hand, kissed him slowly, and pulled back to allow her thumb to glide over the seam of his lips. "I know."

"I DON'T KNOW when she came, sir," Mrs. Baker said nervously into the telephone. "She kept the call to twenty seconds and claimed her signal broke up and that she'd call me back. But I don't think a werewolf would have left a bag of food for an elderly woman." The senior agent checked the magazine on her weapon and peered out the front window.

"Could have been bait," a stern voice on the other end of the line argued. "Eleanor, don't go soft just because the target has a pretty face."

"I've been doing this a lot of years, sir, and everything in me says the girl is running scared after what she saw in Butler's place. If she was at Wal-Mart, then she's local, rational, able to function like a normal person . . . thinking about things, maybe even trying to piece together clues about what happened to Butler and where her team is. If she doesn't show up on Monday, then we worry, sir, is my assessment."

"Well, you'd better pray that you're right."

SO MANY QUESTIONS hammered through her mind that a tension headache made her temples throb. Oddly, Hunter had taken her hand into his and threaded his fingers through hers, while driving with one hand. Oddly, she thought, because it was such a natural gesture, so tender, so unlike anything she'd experienced. This man knew how to make the simplest gesture feel intimate. And although she couldn't deny the chemical attraction to him, there was something else, something deeper. Friendship, yes, but that didn't wholly define it.

In an extremely shortly space of time, she'd seen the man angry, laughing, annoyed, patient, teasing, fun, on guard . . . passionate, joyous—naked. She knew practically nothing about him, but felt like she knew everything about him, which made no sense. And how could she know him when she hardly knew herself?

Sasha toyed with the amber piece about her neck, al-

lowing her thumb to rub over the elaborate Ute etchings
as she glimpsed Hunter from the corner of her eye, then
returned her attention to the blue-black horizon beyond
the passenger's window.

"Thanks for stopping before we left," she finally said
as the quiet of the cab wore on her.

"She is an elder . . . you had made a promise. That I do
understand, you know."

Silence enveloped them again, only their breathing
and heartbeats and muffled exterior sounds from the road
could be heard. She wondered what kind of music he listened to, what his childhood was like . . . whether he had
siblings, where he grew up—on Native American lands
or in a city. And while it made sense to get away from the
surveillance to learn more, was she going with the right
person? Doc hadn't answered her calls. Still, there was so
much about this shadow thing she needed to learn. Then,
again, she had to admit that spending a couple of days
with this Hunter guy sure beat spending forty-eight hours
freaked out, going down blind alleys and following leads
to nowhere. If anybody could help, it was most likely
him. Why she thought that was yet another unanswered
question; she wasn't sure.

"If you don't mind me saying, all of a sudden you
seem like you're about to jump out of your skin." Hunter's
delivery was calm; he spoke matter-of-factly.

Even though what he'd said was somewhat of an affront, she had nothing to hide, really, and shrugged, opting for directness.

"Yeah. I'm pretty freaked out." Sasha let her breath out
hard. "Lemme see. In the last twenty-four hours, I find
out that my alpha and pack brother went full-blown demon wolf. I can't find the rest of my guys. *Then* I find out
that I'm this new species, a shadow wolf . . . or have it in
me, whatever. Then I find out all my gear and whatever is

under surveillance, not sure by who, but can guess it's the same people who gave me and Rod and the squad meds."

She sat back against the seat for a moment and squeezed her eyes shut. "I'm military, Special Forces . . . if the project team bugged my apartment and Rod's . . . oh." She covered her face with her hands and slid her palms down it, then sent her gaze out the window. "We talked about everything—he was like my brother." She closed her mouth, pursing her lips. It wasn't appropriate and was no longer relevant how much they'd confided over the years. Yeah . . . her relationship with Rod had been on a collision course with intimacy. Sasha finished her sentence with care, opting for the neutral. "But if I ever hear those recordings of me and Rod before he got sick on playback over a loudspeaker . . ." She closed her eyes again as the reality of the violation swept through her.

"Once you learn to use your shadow, you can go in and find the recordings and remove them . . . at least the sensitive data."

Sasha glimpsed Hunter's profile, wishing she hadn't. The smile he fought just made it worse, even though what he'd said had definite merit. Hunter didn't understand, and she didn't feel like explaining, that they weren't sex tapes, just stuff on there that was too private to blast in a war room before generals.

"Then, the one person I trust in the whole wide world doesn't call me back, but confirms I've been low-jacked," she said, skipping Hunter's comment and venting out loud. She had to, her mind couldn't hold the outrage. "Meanwhile, I meet this guy who seems on the up and up . . . and it gets a little out of control. I sleep with him, *unprotected*, on some shadow *wolf* theory. And then he takes me bungee jumping in the shadows from Canadian geese to semis on the highway. God, am I crazy?"

"I didn't lie to you, though," Hunter said, unable to conceal his good humor.

"And now I'm driving up into God's country where people get lost until spring thaw with somebody who can disappear in the dark."

She looked at him straight on, growing peevish as he tried to swallow another smile. "Yes. I am officially freaked out."

"You still have a gun and a Bowie knife," he said, gently teasing her.

"Yes, and that is the only thing keeping me from leaping from this moving truck and running screaming into the night. A person can only take so much, you know."

He nodded, his mood pleasant. "That's very true. I can relate."

She released a sarcastic snort. His lopsided smile lengthened.

"Hmmm . . . let me see," he said, removing his hand from hers and rubbing his jaw. "I guess I had no cause for worry while I was tracking the accomplice of, and possible paramour to, a known werewolf—one that went into a full transition in my backyard. My job is to keep demon doors closed, protect the general public, but this lady is all shadow wolf and my mission gets a little hazy. Now, after she fires on me with a Glock nine-millimeter then calls me out, Western-movie style, wielding a pump shotgun with silver shells in a vacant parking lot, I finally get her to calm down enough to talk."

Hunter glanced at her from the corner of his eye and smiled. "Did I mention she is Special Forces and has enough strength and training to kill the average man in hand-to-hand combat? But I digress." He drove a little while, saying nothing, allowing the silence to speak. "Oh, yeah, where was I?" he added after a long pause. "Somehow, my libido gets more than a little out of control while on an information-gathering mission . . . and, what the hell, I lose focus, started shadow dancing, and next thing you know I'm in Wal-Mart like a damned Joe regular buying sweaters and jeans. Freaked out?" He looked at Sasha without a smile now, as though the sudden reality was slowly entering his mind for the first time. "You have no idea."

Again, silence filled the cab of the truck as their gazes sought refuge in the blacktop and white lines of the highway whirring past.

"Okay," Sasha said after a moment. "We're even."

"You think?" Hunter said, his line of vision now affixed to the road. "I'm bringing you up into the mountains to my people and exposing them to someone who could lead a demon into the pack."

He swerved the truck to a skidding stop on the emergency shoulder, turned quickly as the carriage bounced and lurched, and looked at her hard.

Sasha stared at him in surprise. Then she frowned. "If you tell me to get out of here I will—!"

Hunter rubbed his palms down his face. "You see what freaking out can do? It can make you act ridiculous!"

"Oh, well, then stop freaking out," she said sarcastically.

"No, you stop freaking out! Stop acting like you're the only one with something to lose!" He punched the dashboard, denting it.

She folded her arms over her chest and stared out the window. "Okay," she said more evenly. "So we both have something to lose."

"Yes, we do, don't we?" he said, way too calmly for her liking.

She whirled on him. "You just did that to—"

"Show you what it felt like," he said. "Stop doubting, turn on your shadow wolf instincts and *feel me*. Period."

She had to avert her gaze from his intense stare.

"If you do that, you'll stay in control, Sasha, will trust the right people, will know which questions to ask, or which ones you already have the answers for."

"Is that what you do with me?" she asked quietly, her gaze still on the horizon, not ready to meet his.

"Kind of."

She looked at him and that lopsided smile was back. "Kind of?"

"I admit my gut wasn't fully engaged . . . when I, uh, took certain risks."

"I'll bet I know what was engaged," she muttered. "Risks . . ."

"Yes, Sasha, risks."

"Like what? You said I wasn't contagious, so . . . ?" She shook her head.

What was on the tip of his tongue slid back down his throat. Suddenly, being right, winning his point in the argument, was unimportant. It was clear she didn't know . . . and telling her would be like a slap in the face, a hurtful and unnecessary thing. How could she understand that the natural-born shadow wolves would be hard-pressed to accept her? They didn't give half-breeds with weak silver shadow auras respect. One without a silver aura at all would likely be shunned. He and his grandfather had discussed this issue at length . . . and this was why he *had* to bring her home to make an alpha declaration that she was to be granted safe harbor, if she ever had to run from the treaty-breakers.

Her luminous gray eyes held him captive. Hunter allowed his finger to trace her satin-smooth cheek. She'd spoken of a mother and father, but it was clear to his senses that she'd been genetically made . . . it was in her aura, or the lack thereof. And as such, it wasn't until he'd joined his body to hers that he'd learned that she might even be susceptible to the werewolf virus. His blood was supposed to reject it, but did a lab-made shadow wolf have immunity? He didn't know.

"Risk that you might shoot me," he finally said after the long pause needed to gather his words. "Risk that I might just fall in love with you and forget some of what I'm destined to do."

He allowed his palm to drop away from her face, and he gripped the steering wheel with both hands. She looked away slowly as though dazed. Good. He'd hoped what he'd said would turn the course of the conversation.

The thing that scared him shitless was that it was the truth.

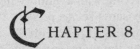

CHAPTER 8

THEY RODE THE rest of the way in silence.

She watched Hunter turn off the primary forest road to an unpaved, gravel-pitted one covered by ice and snow that soon gave way to true four-by-four territory. After what seemed like forever, he brought the truck to a desolate area within a stand of tall trees next to a tiny cabin. He said nothing as he studied the area for a moment and then drove slowly to what seemed like snow-covered underbrush, opened the door, and jumped down out of the truck. Thoroughly intrigued, she watched him uncover a blind large enough to hide the truck and then slowly return to drive them into the dark enclosure.

"You've done this before, I take it?" she said, getting out as he unloaded their backpacked supplies onto a snowmobile with a small carrier rack attached to it.

He didn't respond, just continued to conceal the truck.

"Should I be worried?"

"Not if it snows good and hard before morning," he said, bringing the snowmobile out to the bumpy road area.

"Why are we hiding?" She wrapped her arms around herself and waited.

"Why were you under surveillance?" He stared at her without blinking.

"I don't know," she finally said. "Maybe they think I've got what Rod has . . . had."

"Then I don't know why we're hiding. But right now it feels like I'm traveling with a military fugitive. So taking precautionary measures seems prudent. Aren't those the guys that have missiles, if pissed off?"

Unable to argue the point, she unfolded her arms and walked forward, climbing into the snowmobile beside him.

"I just have one question. How is this whole shadow group or whatever you call it funded?"

He placed his hand on the ignition key, but didn't turn it, and glared at her. "The tribal casinos have a secret, off-the-books fund for this. Call it investment protection of their territories."

"Oh." She looked off into the woods.

"Any more questions?"

"Not right now," she said, lifting her chin. "Just wanted to be sure that drugs or something like the illegal sale of arms or technology to other nations wasn't funding this." She turned to issue him a pointed look.

"Shouldn't we be working together instead of fighting each other? We're not that different, and our objectives are the same."

"Oh . . . we're different."

"How?" he demanded, clearly losing patience with her. "Because you work for the government?" He shook his head. "Try this concept on for size. We're secretly funded and I bet your project is not an obvious line item in the national budget, probably buried under layers of bullshit, Sasha. And if you've ever heard of the Iran-Contra scandal, that had something to do with drugs and guns being illegally converted to cash to support secret government projects, or did I read the newspapers wrong?"

He leaned in closer when she turned away again. "We're small, your group is small. We're underground, your group is underground. We use a network of shamans, you probably use a network of surveillance since your technology replaces what our people with gifted perception do naturally. And if you stop and think about it, we have fewer resources than you, but we're more effective because we're closer to the situation . . . we're frontline, not holed up in some technology-riddled war room."

She refused to look at him as he ranted and his voice escalated. She'd pushed his buttons and now he was pushing hers.

"But if you could get off your high horse for a moment, you'd realize that with the resources you have at your disposal by working on the inside, and the ones I have at mine on the outside, an alliance could make our teams virtually unstoppable against this thing we're up against."

Now he had her attention.

"An alliance," she said coolly, flatly.

"Yes." His gaze burned into her.

"I'm already in enough trouble, most likely, and I'm to propose—"

"Tell me you never work with outside sources . . . ones that have no interest in coming inside to be lab rats."

Her gaze narrowed. Those damned vampires were such gossips. She also wondered if word had crossed borders, wolf pack to wolf pack—even though, according to Shogun, there was bad blood between werewolves and shadow wolves. Sasha turned her head. Hunter's proposal had merit, one that would allow her the best of both worlds, but one she'd have to get past the general. The biggest hurdle would be keeping knowledge of the species called shadow wolves on the down low. Even though she wasn't sure she completely trusted Hunter, she was certain that she didn't trust the general not to try

to wipe out something new that he didn't understand . . .
or to try to capture it and dissect it in a lab.

"I'll consider it. Working together against a common
enemy is better than working at odds against each other."

He looked away, the muscle in his jaw pulsing as
though he needed time to deescalate from the argument.
Then, suddenly, he turned the key in the ignition and
changed the subject, lurching the snowmobile forward.
"We'll go as far as we can, and then we may have to hike
some of the way."

She raised an eyebrow at him.

"You're military. I assume you've done that before."

"The man has jokes."

"The wolf will keep you warm."

"I'll bet."

A half-smile tugged at his cheek. "The heat from
yours, not mine. Call it while we're hiking and we'll get
where we're going a whole lot faster, too."

"Don't worry about me," she said. She could handle
the hike.

Sasha listened to the dull hum of the snowmobile and
watched the shadows go by under the blue-white wash of
the silvery moon. It was gorgeous outside. The snow, the
scent of the forest, the scent of where deer and rabbits
had passed, all of it was breathtaking. His distinctive
scent—divine. The forlorn hoot of a hunting owl made
her want to throw her head back and send a call into the
echo-barren wild.

At a fallen tree, he stopped the snowmobile. "From
here, I guess it's on foot."

"We came the long way, didn't we?"

"Yes, we came the long way, true . . . but this is more
scenic." He chuckled as he hoisted up the backpack of supplies and glanced at her over his shoulder with a challenge

in his eyes. "I heard your wolf . . . she wanted to howl. Let her."

Before she could respond with a snappy comeback, he began running. At first it was an easy jog, and she prayed that where they had to go wouldn't be too far away. But as she scaled snow-covered rocks and frozen underbrush, her lungs began to normalize . . . her body warmed . . . her muscles stretched and worked in pleasurable rhythm beneath her skin. Her eyesight and hearing keened, as did her sense of smell. She wanted to get out of her coat, out of her socks and long johns and boots. She wanted her hair to be free and her scalp to feel the bite of winter. Her hands felt trapped within gloves. She was burning up. Gasping, not from the run but the need to strip.

"Seek the shadows," he called out, dodging into them only to emerge yards away in the full glory of the moonlight.

Almost blind with heat exhaustion she fell into a shadow, twirled in it, spun her body in spirals of delight and relief, and then leaped as far as she could to the next one.

Sasha laughed out loud as they came upon a clearing and she spun around with open arms, her face lifted to the night sky. An urge so natural, so deeply embedded in the pit of her stomach, bubbled up her throat and came out on the night song of the wolf.

Hunter stopped, turned to witness her poised silhouette in the moonlight. She was so absolutely stunning that for a moment he couldn't move. She'd ripped the knitted cap from her hair and jammed it into her pocket. Her gloves were gone, jammed in the other pocket, as she raked her hair, head thrown back, a look of ecstasy overtaking her beautiful face . . . His call met hers, exploding from his chest up to his larynx and out to follow the wind.

Instantly other calls came in response, sobering him. He hadn't meant to alert the pack. They had to keep moving before a welcome party convened—and he definitely had other plans.

Hunter released a series of short barks to ward off a group meeting in the woods, which snapped Sasha's attention toward him. He'd rendezvous with his pack brothers later . . .

Trying to recapture the shattered moment, he held out his hand to Sasha. "Run with me. We'll get there sooner."

She reached for his hand, her eyes ablaze with desire. "It's so beautiful out here, though."

He knew what she meant, what she wanted—the same thing had definitely occurred to him. But border sentries were on the way. It would not be how he wanted to introduce her to the pack—naked, sprawled out in the snow, gasping.

"I know . . . but the other howls mean—"

"There's wolves," she said in a deep, husky tone that ran all through him. She closed her eyes. "Hunter, I don't know what's the matter with me, but . . ."

He watched painfully as she began to unsnap her down coat. "Baby, listen, you'll get frostbite out here. Seriously."

It was a lie; he knew she'd caught it from the half-smile of disbelief she offered as her answer.

"Then can we hunt?" She closed her eyes and breathed in. "Something big?"

He swallowed hard. "Five-mile run and we're at my cabin." He stood before her trying to stay calm, trying to catch his breath, listening for shadow steps. Quickly, before he changed his mind and gave in to her erotic pull, he held out his hand. "Run with me," he whispered. "You trust me?"

She nodded and took his hand. "I probably shouldn't, but I do."

Her sultry statement and the way she gazed at him with those large, luminous gray eyes of hers suddenly made him not trust himself. A second of hesitation carved away rational thought, but knowing his curious band of brothers were on the move broke his temporary trance.

Pivoting his body in a fluid turn, he pulled her through a patchwork of shadows that morphed into a line of trees, speed escalating. Power flowed through them. Each shadow sending a shiver of want through him, through her, the moonlight showering them with a blast of silver warmth. And then he heard it. Heard their breaths sync up along with their footfalls and heartbeats—her hand squeezing his.

They sailed over a downed log bathed in moonlight and when they hit the next series of shadows, she moaned with such abandon that he almost turned to fell her in the snow. Running, breathless, hair lifting from their shoulders, hands clasped, sensations joined, scattered howls in the distance—his brothers picking up on his hunt, scenting female in the air—chaos . . . glorious, glorious chaos, and it wasn't even a full moon.

Leaping through moonlight and shadows keeping the wolf within his skin was becoming painful now. Pleasure had reached its zenith and now had nowhere to go, like a prolonged orgasm left hovering on the edge of the crest. He could see her swooning from the unspent agony, the feral look in her eyes as she tried to keep up with him. Pressure was building in his groin. And his amulet was around her neck.

Hunter closed his eyes, running blind, biting his lip till it bled. The wolf could not come out, not like this, not before talking to her, not before she was ready to deal with that part of herself.

They hit the porch of his cabin at the same time, landing hard on their boots, making the wood reverberate. In two seconds she had him by the lapels of his deerskin jacket, shoved him against his own front door, and took his mouth, moaning into the kiss, climbing up his body, tangling her hands in his hair. Multiple sets of watching wolf eyes glowed in the underbrush, but he didn't care, couldn't stop kissing her as the silent sentries disappeared one by one.

"Why does releasing my wolf make me feel like this?" she gasped, devouring his mouth and not giving him a chance to respond. "I can't act like this all the time. Can't go on missions like this," she choked out between kisses. "I have to be able to control it. Right now, it's controlling me."

He had no words of wisdom for her; right now his wolf was controlling him, too. All patience gone, he couldn't fidget with keys, and simply lifted his elbow and brought it back hard, opening the door by ramming the dead bolt off the hinges.

The scent of fresh-split pine filled his nose as the door gave way and he walked backward, blind, her warmth, her mind-eroding kisses all he could focus on. She was stripping the heavy backpack from him, and he had to make a decision—let her down to get her out of her clothes or prolong the mutual torture.

He dropped her with a deep groan that synced up with the whimper she'd released. The sudden loss of her body heat and friction against him was agonizing.

Colorado wind had blown the door open, sending blasts of freezing air in along with snow flurries. As he worked on her coat, his thoughts fractured and he put his boot against the sofa and shoved. In the back of his mind he heard a loud bang, something that sounded like wood breaking, but he couldn't be sure. All he knew was that the wind had stopped its invasion. All he knew was that Sasha was burning up in his arms. All he was sure of now was, come the full moon, there'd be no holding back the wolf, if she were around.

Tears coursed down her cheeks as she clawed at his clothes and they both fought with layers of fabric. This time he was mindful that he had to present her to the pack, to the elders, and he covered her hands, guiding her, helping her fight the urge to rip the offending materials from her overheated skin.

Writhing in his arms, she was practically twisting out of her own skin. He could feel the she-wolf within demanding release as he kissed down Sasha's throat, her freed breasts lifted to his mouth. Her voice was broken to a low, urgent moan, breaths becoming staccato. It was exhilarating, terrifying, and so different from the previous time. A night run had changed everything, her first moon dance in the shadows. The first glimpse of brand-new female shadow wolf coming into her own, mirroring his wolf . . . hunting by his side, hunting his passion . . . chasing it down to the thick, hand-loomed rug.

His control teetering on the very edge of his humanity, he kissed the amulet between her breasts and said a quiet prayer that his form would hold as his hot, wet skin slid against hers.

Delirium. Burning satin thighs gripped his waist, his shaft so hard it felt like the skin would split. Agony. Hard plunge, hilt deep, his voice rent the air, head thrown back, her nails scoring his ass and hips, the sound of her voice maddening. Lost. Abandoned to the fluid run, every muscle connected to locomotion. Pleasure. Her breath, his breath, her lunge meeting his in perfect sync. Oh, God. Breathless. Spasms convulsing his sac, pleasure sucking his balls up into his abdomen. Sheath pulsing wetness bringing tears, bringing sweat-lodge visions. Fist-pounding ecstasy, cries that sounded like murder.

Shivering beneath him, she clung to his body as a pool

of moonlight bathed them. Ragged breaths torn raw by
ecstasy haunted the room, fled the shadows, till the next
shudder joined them. He dropped his head into the crook
of her shoulder; she made fists at his back and began to
sob. All he could do was stroke her hair with a trembling
hand. He had no explanation for this; one couldn't explain the wolf, one had to experience it.

Slowly, as the tremors abated, he was able to gather
her in his arms and shift his weight to pull her on top of
him without leaving her body. He kept a possessive hold
around her waist with his arm, his other hand gently
cradling the back of her skull. His chest was so filled
with emotion that he could hardly breathe. Her cheek
against his breastbone felt like it would burn right though
to blister his heart. He couldn't open his eyes. Could
only experience the night with his other senses . . . his
skin belonged to her. Sasha's breaths were all that he
heard beyond the thud behind his breastbone. Her skin
was all that he could feel. His chest was so tight, like a
creek overrun at spring thaw.

When she weakly lifted her head to find his mouth, the
cool air kissed the vacancy she'd left, making him know
that a part of him had been ripped away. They shared a
soft whimper, their tongues circling it and chasing it
down their throats.

"Don't move," he whispered against her cheek as her
weight shifted so that she could touch his hair. "Not yet."

She pressed her body against his tighter, making him
release a low, rumbling groan.

"Hunter . . . what just happened?" she murmured, pet-
ting his shoulders with a soft, rhythmic caress.

"First run, first shadow dance under the moon," he said
with his eyes closed. "We mirrored."

She had fallen silent but he could feel a question brimming just below the surface. Exhausted, dozing, he waited,

breathing slowly, stroking along her supple spine, over the meaty rise of her behind, and back again.

"Will it always feel like this . . . after we moon dance? Be mirrors?"

He leaned up enough to find her mouth and kissed her slowly. "As long as you're my mate."

She tensed. "Mate?"

He nuzzled her hair. "When you mate-marked me last night." His voice was a balmy, satisfied murmur.

"Ohmigod, Hunter . . . I didn't mean—what I'm saying is, that sounds permanent . . . isn't it?"

He sighed. "It is and it feels fabulous. It's supposed to feel like this."

Panic seized her. "How do you know?"

"Because my grandfather told me," he murmured, and brushed her lips with another kiss.

She traced his left nipple with her index finger. "Have you ever . . . no. Unfair question."

"No, to answer the unfair question," he said, leaning back against the rug and closing his eyes. He shook his head. "I've never had a mate."

"But—"

"Women, but not a mate." He gently brought her head back to his chest. "That's different . . . they were different from this."

This was bad. *Real* bad. The man had gone to the next level and she was still idling in the garage. She was most definitely not going to *mate* with anyone. Yet she wasn't ready to hurt him, either. "I've never experienced anything like this in my life, Hunter," she murmured against his chest, trying to find the right words.

Pure contentment entered his spirit and pure exhaustion made him groggy. "Good," he murmured, beginning to doze.

"But . . . this is like agreeing to get married based on a

one-night stand," she said quietly, firmly, and waited until
his gaze met hers. "It's too soon." Her palm cupped his
cheek. "A lot has happened and it's just . . . too soon."

The disappointment in his eyes matched the tension in
his body and she hated that she'd been the genesis of
both. But just as he'd told her he was no liar, neither was
she. His reaction was no less than she'd expected of a
man with integrity, which pained her all the more. He
simply lifted his chin, allowed his eyes to slide shut, and
gave her a one-word answer that may have been the first
lie he'd told her.

"Understood."

SOMETIME IN THE middle of the night she felt herself
gently lifted and delivered to soft goose down and covered in mounds of blankets. Familiar, comforting skin
heat soaked into her back, arms, and thighs as it spooned
her, cradling her entire body in quiet protection. She felt
his heartbeat against her back and took comfort in its
consistent rhythm and the warmth of his breath against
the nape of her neck, letting it lull her to a place of peace
she'd never experienced.

So the absence of that warmth and deeply comforting
scent was enough to wake her, even though Hunter moved
in complete silence across the room.

She watched his nude back, staring at him in the semidarkness without a sound. Moonlight added a blue sheen
to his jet-black hair that cascaded over his dark shoulders
like an onyx waterfall. His breathing was measured,
heavy; she could feel something troubling his soul. She
wondered if her reluctance to be his life-mate was the
cause, or if it was something deeper.

New snow was falling, a gentle whisper against the
heavy-limbed trees and crystal-white ground. Waning

moonlight made each flake sparkle as it passed the large window and she wondered what was falling down in his world. He didn't turn but she knew he'd finally sensed that she was awake. It was all in the minute tension that crept into his posture. Then again, maybe it was something else, a deeper knowing that she didn't understand but simply felt.

"I didn't mean to wake you," he murmured, his back still to her. "The end of the moonlight is just so beautiful."

"I missed your warmth," she admitted quietly. "But I didn't mean to intrude on your peace. I know sometimes you need that. Space to just be still."

While what she said was true, he couldn't gather the words to describe the breadth and depth of what he was feeling. Never before had he been so completely taken over . . . never so accepted for what he was. There would be no going back—once he'd experienced Sasha there was no past. Yet there were so many things that could make her leave, with valid cause. And his pack . . . how would he explain their probable icy reaction to her? Although they wouldn't dare challenge her in his presence, they wouldn't bring her into the fold as a welcomed part of it. She'd be *tolerated*. Perhaps she'd instinctively known this and therefore refused to claim him as her permanent mate. Maybe her inner wolf knew more than his did.

Hunter closed his eyes, feeling the heat of her gaze boring into his back, feeling the weight of her silence seeking an explanation. But how could he explain her lack of silver aura without destroying her sense of self? He knew what that felt like, had suffered being different, a mixed breed, not even a half-breed. He dropped his forehead to the cool window and closed his eyes, releasing a weary breath.

"Come back to bed," she said quietly, "and tell me."

Hunter stood where he was for a moment and then

slowly pushed away from the window. He turned and looked at her and her gentle gaze drank him into her. The expression of concern, compassion in her eyes, nearly seized his heart. For what seemed like eternity, he couldn't move, and then she simply held out her hand and he could move forward.

The warmth of her hand when he clasped it radiated up his arm, and he slipped beneath the sheets into a private den that smelled like her, felt like her, was her as she gathered him into her arms. The sense of rightness, of being home, was so complete that his eyes slid shut. Velvet hair brushed his face in a dark curtain, her soft lips soothing the ache within him as she took his mouth and then laid her hand against his chest.

"If there's someone who might not understand this," she said quietly, "I can go."

He exhaled tightly. There was no other woman. She didn't understand. "It's not like that," he murmured, stroking her arm.

She didn't respond but her body had tightened slightly.

"There are things about the shadow life that are difficult to explain," he said, choosing his words carefully, and dismayed when she tightened even more. "Nothing illegal. This is all about customs and culture, all right?"

He felt her immediately relax in his arms, and continued to caress her as her creamy skin melted against his.

"Sasha . . . we can see each other in the shadows by the silver in our auras. That's also like a protective shield. The stronger it is the more protected one is from demon attacks." He fell quiet for a moment to allow her to process what he'd said and then kissed the crown of her head. "No shadow hunter wants to flank a wolf with a weak aura. It imperils the hunt, puts the wolf flanking you at risk. We separated from werewolves long ago because they never acquired the silver, cannot shift at will . . . there is long-standing prejudice that I find hard to explain."

He felt her nod slowly.

"Same thing where I'm from. Nobody wants to be in a firefight with a weak link, somebody not prepared. Good way to get your head blown off."

He nodded slowly, sadly. "No one wants to permanently bond with another of us that has a weak aura, because that means the child will suffer the same defect. It will be vulnerable. It might even be full human."

She kissed his chest and he closed his eyes. Pain scored the place where her tender kiss landed.

"I don't have an aura, do I?"

He swallowed hard. "A human one, yes . . . every living thing has one."

"But not the shadow silver."

"No," he said quietly, after a long pause.

She pulled away. "Then I guess I understand why the leader of a shadow wolf pack wouldn't want to tarnish his future with me as his lover. Like I said, all of this happened too fast. Too soon." There was no anger in her tone, just sad acceptance as she moved to leave the bed.

He sat up and held her wrist before she could flee. "No, that's not what I was saying. Hear me out."

Her gaze trapped his. Heartbreak and the need to understand shone in her luminous gray irises, but she didn't say a word or try to escape his hold. It was as though she were hanging on everything he might tell her, waiting to breathe.

"Sasha, I had to fight, literally, for number one alpha position in the pack—"

She snatched her arm away. "Like I said, I'm not trying to bring you down or create—"

"Listen to me," he said in a deep, booming command.

"My aura is not as it should be." He slapped the center of his chest. "Due to the circumstances of my birth."

He leaped from the bed and walked to the window. In all his life he'd never said that to another living soul, much less a potential mate in his bed. None before would have him . . . they'd seen the schism and refused to even mate. Old pain resurfaced with such a vengeance that he found himself dragging in hard breaths, feeling cornered. His gaze sought the moon for answers. Suddenly he wanted to be outside, dash into the arms of nature, escape the conversation . . . get away from her.

Only a pair of soft palms gliding over his shoulders calmed the wounded beast within him. A satiny cheek soon lay against his back, and the warmth of naked skin slowly pressed against the length of his body.

"Tell me what happened, Hunter. No judgment . . . I won't pull away again . . . I'll let you tell me without trying to second-guess what you're about to say." A kiss planted at the nape of his neck made him close his eyes. "Trust me . . . I am no liar," she whispered.

He braced his hands on the window frame and soaked in her warmth, soaked in her promise. "My mother was almost due to deliver," he said in a low rumble filled with shame. "My father had been hunting the beasts . . . his pack brothers had tracked two, but they lost the trail. Werewolves are like us in that regard, part human, part wolf, and very intelligent. This pair were infected. They circled around, the hunted became the hunters, and they found the shadow dens. On the full moon, they attacked. That's when they are at their strongest, as are we. My mother was savaged before my grandfather could get off a shot. My father died in the battle. Several of his pack were severely wounded and had to be put to their deaths for mercy."

Arms enfolded him as he spoke in a low, raw rumble.

Touch made him believe in soul-healing from the mere laying on of hands.

"My mother was so badly mauled that she died in her father's arms. I was trapped inside her body . . . the virus spreading through her, to me, an unborn infant not fully immune yet to the werewolf toxin."

"Oh, God, Hunter . . ." Sasha came around him when he stiffened and she held him tightly. "It wasn't your fault." Her head sought his shoulder; her voice was a warm, balmy caress.

"There was a doctor," he said quietly, fatigue weighting his words. "A man who'd once been a World War II military trauma surgeon but had become interested in genetics late in life. He was here in the national forest . . . investigating . . . had been asking questions about the wolves. He was testing some kind of antivirus; humans had just discovered the existence of some supernatural species."

He watched her eyes carefully as she looked up, slow recognition dawning in them. But there was no distrust, no narrow judgment, so he continued in a quiet, far-off voice, staring out the window.

"My grandfather was so bereft that he couldn't bring himself to put me to death once he'd freed me from my mother's womb, and he didn't know if I'd make it without additional medical care. Her entire insides had been gutted, entrails everywhere, with me trapped, smothering and struggling, inside her womb that lay in the snow. I was convulsing from the werewolf toxin and had also been severely scratched. They couldn't cut the umbilical cord fast enough. My mother was on the forest floor, slaughtered, her father's hands covered in her blood. The human authorities wouldn't have understood. The pack was howling in mourning. So he had the pack, those still standing, fetch the doctor, unconcerned what he might learn. Then, Grandfather was the alpha and they did as he commanded."

"Oh, dear Jesus," she whispered, hugging him tighter. "You remember this?"

"I was told, but our shadow memories are different than humans' . . . I see impressions like fast snapshots from a camera. The mental pictures fit into my grandfather's words."

"The doctor . . ."

"Tall, brown, worried eyes, gentle."

Sasha covered her mouth with her hand. "Holland?"

Hunter simply nodded. "Grandfather said the doctor did as much as he could, and then asked him if he wanted him to try an injection . . . a new drug."

"Oh . . . God . . . it explains everything . . . Doc's obsession with the vaccines, with werewolves, with finding a cure for the virus-fatal bites. He could give a damn about military maneuvers, but he does want the infected beasts exterminated like you and I do. His primary goal, Hunter, has been helping infected people not to transition. It's his life's work."

"If he hadn't been working on a cure, if he hadn't brought some antidote along for his own protection while tracking the phenomenon, I wouldn't be telling you this story today." Hunter looked at Sasha briefly then sought the safety of the dark horizon again. "It was an experiment, giving me the antidote—I was an infant, they didn't even know if it worked, it had never been tested on a living subject before . . . but it was also a last resort."

Feeling exposed, he pulled back and became silent. Telling her his story was one thing, unveiling hers was quite another and not for him to do.

"But it worked," she said, pressing both hands against his chest.

He nodded and looked away from her, his gaze seeking

the shadows again for confirmation. "My grandfather was nearly insane from the loss and agreed. I was as good as dead, anyway. His visions confirmed what my paternal grandmother had warned her son—my father. An infected child would be born, a line lost, if he married my mother. My father's mother was her pack's shaman, a revered shadow-woman seer, even though of mixed breed. The pack was circling, snarling, ready to do what a grief-stricken shaman could not, if it didn't work. The only friend my grandfather had in that moment was the doctor, and the only thin line between the doctor and his certain death from stumbling upon shadow clan secrets was my grandfather."

Hunter pushed away from the window, needing space from Sasha's intense gaze. He walked to the far side of the room and stood in the dark, also needing the shadows. "I was a mixed blood like they'd never seen. The convulsions stopped, but my aura was fused with that of the demon that had killed my parents and had slaughtered half of my father's pack. Silver laced with a black line of death. Infected werewolves are demons, Sasha. Every year I grew stronger, my wolf grew even stronger than the others. No female in the shadow clans would ever *dare* be my mate."

Sudden bitterness claimed him as he moved from shadow to shadow, keeping himself invisible from Sasha now. "Mixed bloods with humans are bad enough, in our world. They are considered human, never taught the ways of the wolf, unless they have a special gift like my Haitian grandmother did. The union between my mother and father wasn't even recognized by the clan; not a strong alpha female, daughter of the pack's leader, with a mixed-breed mate—my father."

"That is such bullshit." Sasha's hands went to her hips, her indignation on his behalf glittering in her gorgeous eyes.

"Yeah, well . . . Half-breeds are only *tolerated*, never fully included. They're isolated from the clan packs, but they have the human family and are never the wiser . . . unless your grandmother is a seer. But, given my mother's lineage, I was supposed to be of pure-blood parents—a solid silver line that went back to the beginning of our kind—and shadow wolf parents drew their children away from me, fearing that if I played with their offspring, one bite could pollute. Females . . ." He chuckled harshly, the sound brittle. "All human. So, you needn't worry. You were my first shadow dance."

He lifted his chin, his posture proud and angry before he disappeared into another shadow. "Now do you understand why I am conflicted about presenting you to my people? I don't know how I'll react if they snub you . . . I don't think the outcome will be good."

Her gaze scanned the room and she found a very quiet center within herself. Right now, for her own reasons, she wasn't ready to commit to a permanent bond with any man. At some point she had to make him know that she hadn't made that decision for the same reasons all the others in his life had. This was her own shit, not his. But clarifying that at the moment was impossible. She had to remain still; his wounds were so deep that instinct told her he'd probably lash out at the closest thing to him— which was her. She'd done that herself on a number of occasions, lashing out, and knew where he was. Any sign that he was being pitied and he was out. It was a delicate dance, but she knew the steps very well.

"Then I'm glad I was your first," she said after a moment, folding her arms and lifting her chin as she stared at the shadows. "Fuck 'em. Their loss. I'm used to being the oddball wherever I go, so whatever. Take your pick, schools, in the service, in a damned club. *The pack* can kiss my no-aura-having ass. Anyway, you became the pack's alpha, right? So what's your problem?"

"I only became the alpha by default," he shot back, moving into another shadow.

"Define default." She followed his voice, circling as he paced and moved around her.

"I grew larger than the others," he said with disgust. "When my wolf is out . . . it's more . . . ferocious. Harder to control under a full moon. Not like shadow wolves—a fucking birth defect left over from the werewolf virus latent in me. But it has more power."

He found another shadow, not wanting her to see him or have her gawk at his oddness now that she knew. "That's why I have to wear a damned amulet; the others don't," he said in a near growl. "The infected werewolves sometimes can't tell me from their kind because the black line in my aura overlaps when my rage goes beyond the normal darkness. I can go in and out of the demon doors more easily than the others. I don't burn, and my grandfather fears one day I'll go in and won't come back out—at least not the way he knew me. The pack fears it, too . . . they fear to even battle with me for dominance because none of them wants to risk getting bitten or slashed. *That's* the only reason I became the alpha. From pure fear and this defect. Not from the normal ways of our kind . . . And I lead mateless. Solo! In a culture where clan is everything, the pack is your identity, and one's life-mate is the bedrock of all that! It's not like with the werewolves, who do not necessarily mate for life—we do!"

He spun on her, a snarl of frustration released beneath his words. "Until I met you, there was no hope of having that—and I'll be damned if they chase you away. I just need to know where you stand before I bring you to them."

Sasha's expression was not what he'd expected. Not what he'd ever witnessed in the eyes of a she-shadow. There was infinite patience, but no pity, and then the patience quickly transformed into outright indignation.

"Okay. Now I understand why you hate werewolves, infected or not." She folded her arms over her lovely breasts and set her jaw hard for a moment. "But have you ever heard the phrase 'by any means necessary'? Who cares *how* you got to be alpha, as long as it wasn't by criminal means. Birthright is overrated. So are genetics. I'm the only female in the pack and the others thought I couldn't hang at first—until they saw that I could strategize my way out of almost anything when they couldn't. So, yeah, I like position by merit, myself. It's more respectable, if you ask me. The point being, you *are* the leader of an elite fighting force that addresses the same problem that I do. Demon-infected werewolves."

She went to the bed and flopped down on it hard. "I fail to see the problem. If anything, it seems like you got a whole lot of extras from being a mixed-breed . . . double seer capacity from grandma and grandpa, plus a little werewolf superstrength and stealth ability—if the enemy can't tell you're not one of them until you're right up on 'em, whoa. Package that up in a body like yours, and I can only shake my head." She shrugged and sighed with an easy smile. "So, let those other bitches pass. I'm in."

"What does that mean?" he asked through his teeth.

She paused, not sure how to define it yet, but knowing that her statement needed definition. "We have a relationship and I've got your back." That's as far as she'd go, as much as she could commit.

"Like my *maîtresse-imposeur*?" He released a hard chuckle and turned away.

"Clarify?" She folded her arms over her chest but her tone was gentle.

"My alpha-enforcer paramour." He released a hard sigh. "I want you so badly, Sasha, that it's pathetic."

"I want to be with you so badly," she said in a quiet tone, "but without the pressure of making a permanent decision about us, till it's pathetic." She waited until he glimpsed her over his shoulder, wanting him and an alliance with him more than she'd realized until this moment.

He just looked at her "Then be my alpha female—the clan's alpha female—for now. I don't want to lose you. Can you live with that?"

A nod and a kiss was her best answer.

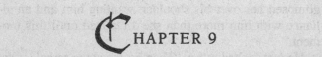

CHAPTER 9

SHE WAITED, WATCHING without directly looking at him, and saw him slip from a shadow in the corner of the room. Although she wanted to hold him, she knew it would cut at his personal dignity until he came to her. To be different, shunned, considered an abomination all his life . . . she almost cringed under the pain she knew that reality had brought him. He'd said he'd been rendered mateless, and after witnessing the pure ecstasy of a shadow dance, that, more than anything else, stabbed her heart.

"I never remembered a thing about my parents," she offered quietly, staring down at her hands. She purposely kept her gaze averted, allowing him to circle her and decide when he'd sit down. "I only have a few photos. They were both orphans, I have no clan, no grandparents living, no one to care for me. They were slaughtered, too, in a bad situation that went down in Rwanda, I'm told. They were diplomats. Mom was bitten Stateside, carried the disease, it passed to me, I was born, she and Dad were murdered in a coup. Doc was their best friend. That's the only reason I know as much as I do."

Telling Hunter her story, as much as hearing his, felt like peeling back years of hurt and releasing it to run free. She didn't look up, just kept talking, hoping that her truth could help him see that she really did understand isolation.

"But when they both died so suddenly, there was trouble getting me out of that country," she said, her throat tightening with emotion as she revealed her innermost truth. "At the time Doc was on a special mission . . . studying all this paranormal stuff . . . and the military wouldn't allow him to adopt me. I went to foster care for a few years. Lemme tell you, that was no day at the beach. Talk about outcast . . . damn."

She kept talking, her voice casual, her body relaxed. "I was this long-legged tomboy who could and would fight anyone who messed with me. Let's say I had anger management issues, and not even a clue about why I'd get real aggressive at certain times of the month. Of course, I hadn't made the connection that it was always during the full moon."

"They should have told you at least that much," Hunter said quietly.

"Yeah, well, we all know how that goes—somebody dropped the ball in that department. Family secrets are a bitch. So I went around fighting and acting out, not knowing why, taking injections for the periodic convulsions . . . thinking they were giving me Ritalin or something because I was fighting all the time . . . couldn't sit still in class long enough to learn, needed to run. They said I had ADHD. And . . . kids can be cruel. Hell, they'll pull the wings off a fly just to get a laugh. What chance did a bucktoothed, wild-haired, knock-kneed orphan have in public school? Then Doc called, saving me from the horrors of public ed when he finally got me. Trust me, an elite private school was worse. Those kids . . ."

Sasha let her breath out hard and stared at the floor.

Just talking about it brought the tight feeling back to her body, to her chest, memories so painful that she had to find that special place of calm Doc had shown her in order to finish.

"Before Doc, I didn't have a momma or dad, just folks who got money for *tolerating* me. Once he claimed me, the rich kids acted like I was either invisible or a blemish that needed to be erased. Yeah, I know what it is to be tolerated." She let out another long, weary breath. "Still, Doc found me and was finally able to take me in. That had been his mission all along, his own private mission, to get to a point in his research where he could appease the authorities enough to convince them to let him have me. But by then, I was an unruly adolescent who hated authority. And poor Doc." Sasha closed her eyes. "That man took me into his home not even knowing if I was contagious or not . . . and put up with all my shit. I owe him. Can't just up and walk out of the project."

"I owe him, too," Hunter said quietly. "The man saved my life and even gave me my name."

Sasha didn't open her eyes as a depression weighted the bed and a familiar warmth next to her once again heated her skin. "Tell me," she said as gently as possible. "We share the same people . . . we've already shared our bodies, and some real old wounds."

"True," he said in a thought-filled tone that sounded very far away, even while he sat beside her. "My grandfather wouldn't name me until he knew I'd live. Then the clan wouldn't accept me owning my father's last name for some reason and especially not my mother's . . . given that I was something so apart from all of them. But the doctor had put me in my grandfather's arms, relieved when the convulsions stopped, and had said, 'Maximus Hunter . . . this baby boy is gonna be fine.' It stuck. Grandfather said it was the sign of a new clan. At least that was his explanation to make me as a child feel less isolated. I suppose that is also why I took such exception to you thinking it was an alias . . . and at that point, we hadn't . . . bonded yet. There was no trust."

"Oh . . . Hunter," she whispered, wanting to reach out to him so badly, but ever so careful not to allow pity of any measure to be confused for genuine compassion. "I wish I had known, and wish we had . . ." She simply let her words trail off.

"There are a lot of things I wish, Sasha . . . like not having this bad blood within me."

"You're not contagious. Neither am I, right?"

A pair of hands clasped hers and a gentle kiss brushed her knuckles.

"I don't know, honestly," he said, drawing her into a hug. "But I am no liar. I wouldn't have put you at risk. I knew enough to know that you couldn't catch what I already had in my system, because I could see a little of it threaded in yours . . . and I knew you couldn't give it back to me—I already had it."

"Why didn't you tell me when we . . ."

His finger touched her lips and his eyes held so much pain as he spoke. "Do you remember the state we were both in that early dawn?"

She closed her eyes as the heat of the memory washed over her.

"I'd never been with my own kind. I was losing my mind for you. If you had bolted, had gotten that look of disgust in your eyes that the others not human held . . . I don't know if I could have . . ."

"You wouldn't have hurt me." Her palm slid against his jawline until he opened his eyes.

"No," he said flatly, "I would have shredded my pride and gotten down on my knees to beg you . . . but hurt you, no."

"I don't know what they see with their shadow wolf eyes, but they are so blind," she whispered. "I don't know how they passed on you." She shook her head. "How they could have withstood your hunt . . . but I'm glad they did. Werewolf taint and all."

He rested his cheek against the crown of her head and hugged her closer to him. "Every time I fight one of them, go hand-to-hand combat with one, their bite seems to strengthen my immunity . . . but I can't kill enough of them to bring my parents back."

She nodded and lifted her head to seek his mouth. "Hunter . . . you are *not* a birth defect. Neither am I. At least the only people who ever cared about us are good friends. I'm also not such a wimp that if I go somewhere and people snub me, I'll cave."

He remained very still as she took off the amulet he'd given her and looped it over his head. It was such a sensual gesture, the way she allowed her fingertips to glide over his hair, his ears, and then down his neck as her eyes searched his. With her lids heavy, her soft palms cradled his face, her moist lips parted as though she could barely sip enough air. Gooseflesh slowly rose to her arms as her palms slid over his shoulders, seeming to chase away hurt and pain in their heated wake. He felt his nipples tighten and watched hers draw into hard, dark pebbles that dried his mouth as his hands rested on her hips.

"I've never been anyone's chosen mate before," she murmured. "I'm honored, even though I'm not quite ready for the title. No one ever picked me and I don't take that lightly. I don't wanna mess this up—but I need time to figure it all out. I was never even chosen as a lover beyond a brief, well . . . you know, before this."

"Nor I . . . Until I met you, I thought that might never happen . . . and I was okay with that, if I couldn't feel this." He let out a weary breath. "I'll give you time—I'm

just not ready to go back to the way I was living before. I
want to see where this can go."

"Me, too," she said just above a whisper. "And I was
okay with that, never deluded myself in relationships.
I've been a sex buddy, a booty call, a friend, a decent
lay . . . but never chosen to be brought home to a family.
No one ever thought I was worth the sacrifice and I knew
that."

His palms caressed the soft flesh beneath them, desire
awakening in a slow smolder within his groin as he stared
into her eyes. "They were foolish . . . blind. Second sight
didn't need to tell me about your heart. Human eyes
should have been able to see who you were inside."

"I was always different, Hunter. No one's pick of the
litter." She threaded her fingers through his hair as she
kissed him deeply and straddled his lap. "Just for once in
my life I want to feel what that's like, even if it's a temporary thing . . . Love me like I'm yours, like there'll be nobody else. We can sort all the commitment stuff out later."

How could he make her comprehend, how could he
make her know? His voice was an inadequate instrument.
Communication through touch, through pleasure shivers,
was all he could offer as they fell back into endless blankets and goose down. Didn't she understand? His skin
burned for her, his wolf was unleashed by her. Never in
his life had he made love in a shadow dance.

Heat swept up his back following the sweet trail of her
hands as they rolled, twining together. The shudder she'd
released was marrow deep, just like his secrets had been.
His every inner shadow had been chased to the surface. It
was as though the Great Spirit had made her just for
him . . . their pasts matched, their family circumstances
were similar, their missions parallel, their beliefs were in
harmony. Her body made him lose his mind.

But it was her heart that she offered, had sacrificed; he

could feel it woven into the trust that ruined him, even if she wouldn't verbally commit. She'd unlocked the steel cage around her faith in him, brought pure sterling truth out of its hiding place, and trusted him not to consume her without care.

"For me, this isn't temporary," he breathed against her lips before taking her mouth again. "Shadow wolves take a mate for life. You don't have to—for now I'll accept what you've offered. Hope."

He felt her grip tighten in his hair as she arched. Two large tears escaped the corners of her eyes and rolled down the sides of her face as she swallowed hard.

"Choose me, please, baby," he said harshly against her ear. "You have the power as female to accept or reject . . . I so want to be yours. If not as a life-mate, then as your lover."

He pulled back and looked at her, waiting. Her eyes said she didn't understand the shadow ways. Her trembling fingers explored his face as though she were reading Braille.

"I have the choice?"

"I'll hunt for you," he said, overwhelmed. His kiss stole her breath as his body slowly moved against hers and his impassioned words gained momentum. "I'll fight for you," he said in a rush, spilling hot kisses against her throat. "Will protect you, defend our den. Whatever you need, whatever you ask." He could feel himself separating from the plane of waning moonlight, pulling her with him into their shadow selves. "Mine is a permanent condition—one day you must ask, is yours? But for now, just this is enough . . ."

"Yes!"

He slid into her wet, pulsing sheath, eliciting her cry. The sensation of being inside her silky grip made his back arch and her name formed inside his chest. Part growl, part words, part breath, all passion. "Sasha . . ." He couldn't stop moving against her sweet lunges, couldn't fill his hands enough with her sweet ass as it lifted, her pelvis undulating beneath him, rolling his eyes back in their sockets, destroying all his plans for slow technique . . . only once the burn stopped, only once what they shared cooled, would he be able to take his time and tease her. Calling the wolf was foreplay; the run was hot, sweaty sex. Being inside her was beyond *la petite mort*—it was something akin to a grand mal seizure that might leave him foaming at the mouth.

With no warning to prepare him, she gripped the lobes of his ass as her eyes opened wide, her whole body craned forward, and convulsed. The pleasure spasm that attacked his groin came so hard and swift that his mouth opened, his larynx froze, and no sound exited. Wave after torturous wave of ecstasy sucked his sac dry, spiraling heat up his shaft so quickly that his entire body heaved in rhythm with hers. When he finally could draw a breath, he sucked in a huge gulp of air with a gasp, shuddering.

"For now, I choose you," she said, burying her face in the crook of his neck.

That was all that he needed to hear.

"I'LL BE BACK," he said while calmly dressing. "Not more than a half hour." He watched her watching him as she toweled her freshly shampooed hair dry.

"I don't care what they think, you know," she said, her gaze searching his. "You don't have to do this, if now isn't the right time."

"I'll make it the right time. Tomorrow morning, you have to be back at your post . . . who knows where they'll send you, how long you'll be gone. Or if you'll need a safe house. I want you to have that in our network."

She nodded and said, "All right."

TEN MILES AWAY, in a flat-out dash, his grandfather's outside home was in sight. Covering the ground was easy; most natural wolves covered twenty or more miles a day at a five-mile-per-hour trot, and could do forty-five miles per hour at top speeds in a hunt. Those were normal wolves. Shadows were more than that.

The safe house on the outer perimeter of the shadow lands where Sasha waited wasn't part of the inner core of the mountainous den network, and he knew that with his scent there, none of the pack would dare challenge her. But as he neared his grandfather's cabin, the scent of a familiar human slowed his gait. The doctor was here? His hackles instantly rose. No one was taking Sasha away.

Max shook his head, clearing the wolf mind. Holland was a friend. If anything, he'd come out of concern for her safety. Max had to find his balance. He'd been so prepared for confrontation that he was becoming slightly irrational. Then again, he had just cause for the condition: Sasha.

Scenting for the others, he walked up his grandfather's wooden porch steps. Every member of his pack had been here, yet strangely, none of the she-shadows had visited with their mates. Only the males. That was not a good sign. The first snub had begun. He knew the pack dealt in absolutes—us or them. There was rarely a middle ground.

Max hesitated at the door, trying to quiet his rage. First they'd come to his grandfather's outer dwelling, as though Sasha were a mere human and barred from the labyrinth of sacred caves. Then they'd hide themselves from her as though she weren't good enough to see them, keeping her from the company of her shadow sisters. It was an outrage.

Why couldn't any of them understand that when his people in general were hunted to near extinction during the colonization of indigenous peoples' lands, the shadow clans were almost wiped out? Being the first to step up to a challenge to their way of life, the first to address the threat, the shadow wolves died first against technology-caused mortal wounds.

Hunter raked his fingers through his hair. It was global genocide, every land mass experienced the wipeout . . . now, just like before, technology and weapons were in the hands of men who had no respect for the land or the Great Spirit. Fighting among themselves about bloodlines and heritage was so foolish and such a waste of time.

Out of respect, Max knocked on his grandfather's door, gaining impressions as he waited for the elderly man to respond.

Crow Shadow, small, with ravenlike features and jet-black hair, had come and gone first with Bear Shadow, a big, brown, barrel-chested pack member. Fox Shadow, named for his cunning mind, auburn hair, and lanky build, was still around, along with the sandy-hued, lightning-quick Rabbit Shadow.

Oddly, it seemed as though Hawk Shadow and Mountain Shadow had left long before the others had. Of them all, he wished those two had not left. Hawk was like a brother, and although slight of build, he was the fiercest fighter and stood steadfast by Hunter's side. Mountain was a large, looming shadow presence, who said little, but didn't have to. Those two, plus himself, kept the pack balanced, the roles clear and defined. He just hoped his brothers wouldn't force a choice between them and Sasha.

"I knew you would come when it was time," Hunter's

grandfather said as he opened the door and warmly embraced him. "Come in, Wolf Shadow. We have a guest. He has already been introduced to Fox Shadow and Rabbit Shadow."

"I know this guest, Silver Shadow. He is a pack friend and friend of our clan." Hunter sent his gaze around the room to settle on Dr. Holland. "It's good to see you, sir."

The fact that his grandfather used his pack name, not his given name, put him on guard. Once his grandfather was no longer pack alpha, he'd gone back to his Native American name. But out of sheer respect, he would call the old man Silver Shadow until the end of time. To bristle his pack brothers, he'd quietly reminded them of the old man's previous dominance over their fathers and grandfathers. Hunter left the door open. No need in damaging property if the challenge had to go outside.

Tension residue still hung in the air as Dr. Holland stood and nodded.

"Long time no see, Wolf Shadow," the doctor said, picking up on the unspoken vibes in the room.

Fox Shadow and Rabbit Shadow flanked the older man slowly, and simply stood with a nod.

"Can we take this outside, *Hunter*?" Fox Shadow said after a moment.

Hunter's eyes narrowed. Using his given name while the others were referred to by their pack names was a clear affront.

"Yeah," Rabbit said through his teeth. "Some pack business doesn't need to be discussed in front of outside guests."

"Sure, *Gerald*," Max said in a low rumble. "Let's go." He turned and strode out the door, taking the battle away from the house.

Apparently the scent of Sasha in the air, along with the presence of the doctor, was making Fox bold and stupid. Maybe he even thought that without Hawk and Mountain there, or others to break it up, his constant bid for dominance might somehow work this time.

"What's your problem?" Max said circling, beginning to snarl.

His grandfather was on the porch with Dr. Holland, silently watching. Just like in times of old, an elder had to witness the challenge of power and communicate it through the region. Rabbit Shadow was on the ground as referee, also a necessary part of the match to make it official, and not be considered murder if things went too far. This had been a setup.

"My problem is," Fox Shadow said through his teeth, warily circling, "that you're taking sloppy seconds behind a damned demon wolf that she used to deal with and you've brought her to—"

He was on Fox's chest before he'd finished the sentence. The impact knocked the wind out of the man. Hunter had gone from human to wolf with barely any transition time. He'd shifted as he sailed from the shadow he'd been standing in into the light, clothes left behind him in a jumbled pile. The only identifier was his amulet. His wolf had never been as strong, the urge to kill never as fierce as it was now.

"End match! Submit, Fox, submit!" Rabbit yelled out to a paralyzed Fox Shadow, as he backed up. He had never seen anything like Max's transformation. "Call your grandson off, Silver Shadow. He'll rip his throat out!"

Snapping, snarling, saliva-slicked jaws growled a warning as two-hundred-plus pounds of furious wolf bore down on Fox Shadow. Massive claws slowly dug into his chest through his coat and T-shirt, causing blood to rise in seeping pools around the depression of each digit.

A whimper finally escaped Fox Shadow's strained larynx. The sound only seemed to make Hunter crazier and he released a series of fast, vicious barks close to the offender's face, slinging saliva. Only when Fox closed his eyes did Hunter pull back. Not a sound could be heard except that of the snarling, pacing wolf as it circled the challenger three times. Fox curled into a fetal ball as Hunter loped toward his pile of clothes in the snow, circled them, and shifted back.

He snatched up his boots and clothes, breathing hard as he stood in the clearing in front of his grandfather's log cabin.

"If you *ever* fucking call her sloppy anything, I promise you I'll rip out your throat!" Hunter was still pacing, naked, face burning, eyes wild. "You want a challenge to the death over who holds this pack? Any day, any night, Fox Shadow. But until then, if she gets anything less than VIP treatment, it's your ass!"

He took the porch steps in two bounds and slammed the door behind him. The doctor looked at his old shaman friend as Fox Shadow slowly stood and loped off with Rabbit Shadow not far behind.

"I think that settles the question of your Sasha's safety," Silver Hawk replied in a deadpan tone. "Yes?"

Too stunned to reply verbally, the doctor simply nodded.

SASHA WAS PACING on the porch when Hunter returned. He needed to get her back to his grandfather's but was glad she didn't have a full handle on the nuances of shadow culture. He had the hopeful thought that she'd miss the slights.

"How'd it go?" she asked, following him into the cabin as he gathered their weapons and supplies into the backpack.

"Everything went well. C'mon." His nerves were wire-taut. He knew she'd be able to smell the lie.

She hesitated. "Something's wrong."

"The doctor is there. He was in a sweat with my grand-father when you were calling before. There's things he needs to tell you . . . Please, we need to hurry."

SHE BEGAN RUNNING, but this time she didn't require that he hold her hand. Doc was up here, of all places. Had something important to tell her. Her lopes were outpacing Hunter's and the only reason she slowed down was be-cause she wasn't wholly sure of the way. But as they got closer, the scent of wolf blood and Doc made her practi-cally strip a gear as she rushed forward and landed on her hands and knees on a cabin porch.

"Safe," Hunter said, slightly panting.

Sasha stood quickly and walked in a circle, trying to calm down.

Hunter clasped her hand and opened the door. Two el-derly men stood. Sasha barreled into the doctor's arms.

"I'm all right, it's all right," Doc said, rubbing her back as she pressed her face to his neck. "There's so much I have to tell you. Oh, Sasha . . ."

"I have to tell you about Rod," she said, swallowing hard. She held him away from her. "It was too late."

Holland nodded and briefly shut his eyes.

"What about the others?" Her gaze searched the weary, aged eyes before her. "Woods, Fisher . . . they left with a whole squad."

"Crow Shadow and Bear Shadow have been sent to collect them," a voice she didn't know said.

Sasha's gaze jumped to the elderly man with white hair plaited in long braids that hung down his chest. "I'm sorry, I—"

"My grandfather, Silver Hawk, once Silver Shadow," Hunter said. "Just as to the pack I am Wolf Shadow."

"No apologies needed," the older man said, coming to

Sasha. "We all understand the heart is full, the losses deep."

Dr. Holland nodded. "He is a dear friend . . . Sasha, there's so much that's happened, but now more than ever before, you have to trust me. The general doesn't understand what he's doing . . . the project went haywire, none of this was ever supposed to occur. The only ones left from the pack are you, Woods, and Fisher."

Confusion tore at her; she could feel things pulling at her that didn't make sense. Hunter's gaze held hers for a moment and slid away, and then he left the room.

"What's happened?" She watched in fear as the old man named Silver Hawk placed a supportive hand on Doc's shoulder and also left. "Doc?"

"Sasha . . . the others—"

"What happened to all those men?" she whispered, covering her mouth and closing her eyes. Her hand fell away, but she didn't open her eyes. "Did they . . . hurt anyone?"

"No," Doc said carefully, so carefully that it made her open her eyes.

"They're dead."

Holland nodded. She turned away.

"Rod Turned on the team . . . the evac helicopter was given orders to eliminate all contagion, if there appeared to be a clear and present threat of the virus spreading. Only Woods and Fisher escaped. They're now on the run and in hiding."

"Oh, God . . ." Tears filled her eyes and she let them fall. "Those men should at least have been given the chance for medical treatment." She whirled on the doctor, his image blurry through her tears. She wiped them away and shook her head. "Were Woods and Fisher bitten? Where are they?"

Dr. Holland crossed the room slowly. "I want you to

listen to me very carefully, Sasha, hear every word I say. It is imperative, if at no other time in your life, that you hear me."

He waited. She held her breath and nodded.

"Rod's DNA was compromised by something different than what you, Woods, and Fisher have in yours." He rubbed his palms down his face. "But the general didn't know that, doesn't know that. Only I do, and for good cause." He stared at her hard and then looked away. "They knew that poor young man was in crisis. For the last six months the serum was less and less effective." He turned to face Sasha. "*I* sent him to Afghanistan right after Nicaragua without a break in between! It was I who convinced the general to send him into vacant caves . . . when I knew the inevitable was about to happen. I wanted him far away from the others, far away from any civilians . . . someplace where he couldn't harm himself or others, a place too far to traverse in one night . . . a place uninhabited due to the bombings from before. Daisy cutters had razed the area. Then, we could pick him up and I would have another month to help him."

"Doc, why . . . why wouldn't you lock him up in a lab and—"

"I wanted him away from you!" Holland shouted. "Sasha, you're like a daughter to me, and you'd never seen a Turn, have you? Have you!" He walked up to her quickly when she turned away. "Not someone you know, not someone who was like your brother—you haven't seen it. And if I had had Butler in a lab and he got out like the one before him, he'd go straight for *you*. You've got shadow wolf female in you, Sasha. You're a natural enemy but also a very natural draw for that particular beast. I couldn't chance it! I refused to chance it, not my baby girl."

"I saw it," she said quietly, tears filling her eyes. "I put a full clip in his chest in his apartment."

"Then you know why I didn't want to chance it."

She looked away and swallowed hard, unable to argue against the truth.

Tears coursed down the doctor's face and his words were thick and garbled by mucus as he spoke. "Oh, God, Sasha, I hate this damned project. The general wanted to protect his investment and see what would happen under live conditions—so he sent those boys with Rod . . . Woods, Fisher, to see if Rod's Turn would spike one in them. He sent them in as bait, lab rats, as well as the others. Every man was under thirty—just kids! Johnson, Gonzalez, Sherwin, they never made it."

He covered his face with his hands and spoke to her, broken. "Woods and Fisher had quicker reflexes and unloaded an entire clip of silver shells, but they just maimed him, they were so spooked they didn't get him in the heart . . . then they called for an extraction, called what was supposed to be the cavalry, and a Black Hawk, one of ours, fired on them—the general's orders. Shoot to kill if there's any blood on uniforms."

"No . . ." The horror of it chilled her, shock sent shivers through her limbs until they shook. Nausea roiled in her stomach.

"Here's the pity of it," the doctor said, collapsing against the back of a living room chair. "If they think you know, for the sake of secrecy, they'll eliminate you."

"Not if I get to the bastard first."

"Do you know how high up in the food chain this goes?" the doctor asked calmly, obviously trying to get her past the emotion into a strategic state of mind. "I didn't, at first . . . I can't even imagine now. The money, the power, it's beyond presidential levels. The general is following orders from someone, and then that someone is following orders . . . why do you think I've stayed around so long?"

Fury and frustration were making new tears rise in her eyes. "Why?"

"I owed it to your mother," he rasped. "Owed it to her and William."

"Doc, you're scaring me," Sasha whispered.

"I'm scaring myself, honey. I'm scaring myself."

Quiet tension fell between them for what seemed like a long time. Finally Sasha pushed off the wall and looked at the man who'd been like a father to her.

"They didn't die in Rwanda, did they?"

Xavier Holland shook his head. "They were Black Ops, Paranormal Unit . . . and part of the requirement was to donate reproductive cells, in case there was an accident. Twenty-five years ago, those cells were the baseline for individual antidotes, a serum that bonds to the specific DNA structure of the infected host. I was working on a vaccine with Dr. Lou Zang Chen . . . and he was close to a breakthrough, when there was an accident in the lab."

The doctor pushed away from the living room chair and began to slowly pace with his hands behind his back, speaking to the floor as though dictating into a microphone before a student lecture. "About four soldiers came back from the Colombian Disasters infected from demon wolves. The first two Turned within months of returning, the other two seemed to respond beautifully to the treatments. Then a year later the third soldier Turned. A year after that the fourth soldier Turned. But when that last one Turned . . ." The doctor shook his head and ran his palm across his thinning gray hair.

Standing very still, Sasha reached out to his pain with a quiet question. "Doc, what happened in the lab?"

He stopped pacing and looked up to meet her gaze. "Everyone was slaughtered except me." Never taking his eyes from her he slowly reached beneath his ivory cable-knit sweater and extracted a silver necklace with an amber amulet she recognized. "Two seconds of hesitation from the beast allowed me to lift my arm and squeeze a trigger. None of my colleagues had that chance." His voice became a hard whisper as new tears rose to fill his eyes. "Your mother and father were on the wrong side of the glass."

"But you saved me," Sasha said, a sob so close to spilling out that she placed her hand over her heart. "You couldn't save them, but you saved me."

He turned away from her. "I did what I could, child . . . pulled you out of the grip of madmen."

"They were going to kill me, weren't they? Just like Hunter's clan would have put him to death as a baby, were it not for you."

Xavier Holland shook his head. "They were going to do something so much worse than kill you, baby . . . I couldn't let them."

Something dark slithered into her psyche, keeping her rooted to the floor where she stood. Then she was pure motion and had crossed the room in milliseconds to grab her adopted father by both arms. She had to see his eyes, had to see his face.

"What happened?" she demanded, hysteria bubbling within her and spilling into the small space between them. "What did they make you do to me? When you took me from her dead body, what was I?"

"I didn't take you from her body. She wasn't even pregnant, then," he whispered, tears coursing down his weathered brown face. "I took you out of the freezer before they did . . . and bought you a chance."

She dropped his arms and backed away, stumbling over furniture, and then dry-heaved.

"Before the accident, five embryos had been created from the demon-infected soldiers," the doctor said, his voice clinical, detached, sharp enough to make her really hear him. "The fourth soldier had been responding well to the adjustments in his medication and the brass wanted to move ahead with its ultimate goal: the creation of their own genetically engineered soldiers. But when the accident happened the lab had almost been destroyed and all the embryos had as well. Except one. That was Rod. And they wanted to create more, despite our failures at keeping the subjects from Turning. But zygotes were on hand, already cleared, legal waivers signed, which meant military participants, their samples were fair game. I smuggled your mother's out and destroyed your father's . . . no child of my dear friends would be tampered with—it was heresy."

As he began to pace, her eyes followed him. "I am a scientist, but this went beyond the realm of science. Yet, I knew if I balked, if I went against the grain, they'd shut me up and shut me down and would get someone else to do it. For twenty-five years I watched Rod Butler grow up, waiting for what was in him to take him over . . . I just couldn't see that happening to you, baby. No."

Xavier Holland stood by the window, looking older and more haggard than she'd ever seen. But what he was saying was so horrific that she couldn't even form questions in her mind.

"So I came here," he said plainly. "I had spared the life of a friend's grandson . . . I asked that he help me spare the life of a child that would be made one way or another. If all the cells were destroyed, they would suspect foul play. I'd disappear, but the project would go on . . . with available donors in prison, the military, unsuspecting donors in fertility clinics . . . you have no idea the lengths."

"They gave you shadow clan DNA," she said flatly, her voice distant, her mind numb.

"It's so close to the werewolf strain, it bonds to the genetic spiral just like the toxic demon virus . . . but as you've probably learned, it's so different."

He paused and stared at her, regret and love brimming in his eyes. "I wanted you to have a chance. They gave me a sample from a male who shares no bloodline with Max, Sasha. You're of his pack, same clan, but not a relative. I gave you your mother's maiden name—Trudeau . . . She was from New Orleans, not Alabama, like Bill. It was the other way around. I never wanted you to find out. Not like this."

He paused and let out a long exhale that sounded as though he'd exhaled the weight of the world. "The shadow DNA came from a fallen clan warrior, one who gave his life that fateful night protecting Max's mother's body, keeping a predator from eating her remains. Wolf Shadow—that's why Hunter's grandfather passed him that name, in his honor. He fought the monster for the struggling, suffocating, living thing in the snow—Hunter."

"The others, the rest of the pack . . . you said you didn't let anyone else get the demon wolf virus added to their test tube." She didn't care that his eyes looked pained. It was what it was.

"I wish you wouldn't refer to the start of your life that way." He released another tired breath and briefly closed his eyes. "Woods and Fisher are diluted strains—shaman familiars, natural wolf. As I perfected the tests, I could mask you kids from the insanity. Rod was the first, though. All eyes were watching and there was nothing I could do."

She punched the wall, taking out a chunk of it. "But I don't understand! Why did they keep this a secret? Why didn't you just tell us?"

"Because it was all about control, Sasha . . . and covering their own asses. The psychologists," he said sneeringly, "thought that your loyalty to the government would be suspect if you actually knew you had been created solely to be a supersoldier. That thinking of yourselves merely as experiments would work against us as opposed to for us. Feeling like you're part of the human race was invaluable. They also didn't know how you children were going to turn out, and if something went horribly wrong, they didn't want the responsibility of your existence to be traced back to them." He shook his head. "All those years and all those lies. And I couldn't say anything or I would be taken out! And then who would look after all of you?"

A sob racked Sasha's body so hard that she hugged herself to hold another one in. "They played God, Doc! What gave them the right to play God? They put me in a position to have to exterminate Butler like he was a disease after they'd watched him like a culture under a microscope—he was my friend! They grew me out of a goddamned petri dish, Xavier! Yes, I heard you! They put me in foster care, because I had no mother and father!" She paced back and forth as though trapped, tears streaming, mind on fire. "I know why I was there," she said, sputtering. "In foster care."

The doctor had mentally retreated to a still place and his voice was so calm that it made her shiver.

"You're right, your hunches are accurate, Sasha. You need to know so you can beat them. They wanted to break your affiliation to any group but the military. On the project then, just as now, there were behavioral scientists, psychologists, psychiatrists, and they wanted to create the ultimate fighting machine—a person with no sense of family or past, who only received a sense of community from the squad, which was designed like a pack so your natural instincts would be subject to the rules of the pack. But after years of debate I asked them to give me one subject as a control to the test . . . to see what would happen if that subject had a deep bond with someone in authority on the project. I begged them for you, because my heart was breaking."

She simply stared at him. "All those people in my life worked for the project?"

He nodded.

"Even my neighbor . . . Mrs. Baker?"

"Special Agent Baker."

"And Max knew." She stared at the only person she'd ever trusted, watching her world turn to demon dust.

"No, not all of it . . . don't lay this at his feet. He's only three years older than you. This was the business of sick men while you both were babies."

"But he knew some of it." She looked out of the window at the snowcapped mountains and blue, blue sky. The urge to run made her muscles twitch.

"Some. So very little it's negligible."

"I'm not going back, except to rip the general's throat out."

"Two things," Xavier Holland said carefully. "We have a leak in the department. I don't know who, but we do. Someone has always stayed one step ahead of me after I did the sample switch. If they ever truly found out that your DNA is different, I'd tell them that it was the natural absorption and mutation process. That you had adapted to naturally heal yourself, just like sickle cell was a natural defense against malaria . . . Your blood changed. But be clear, if you go directly after the general, they'll hunt you down like an animal. I didn't love you this hard and go through all these machinations to let them have you."

He let out a slow breath when she didn't answer. "So, if we have a leak and this thing goes higher than the general, that also means the technology to do this type of science is being brokered on the black market. You can escape, but how many genetic mistakes will they make and lives

will they ruin before they achieve the goal of creating the
ultimate killing machines? And what will that do to the
natural hunters of this demon plague if the virus prolifer-
ates? That's my second question. Shadow wolves are
nearly extinct. Let a lab screw up, Sasha, or some terrorist
release a biohazard on a populace not caring about the results, and what do you think will happen?"

"So what am I supposed to do? Sit around like some
pawn and let them continue to control my life?" Incredulous, she headed for the door.

"No. You're supposed to get to the root of this poison in
our system, bring all of the bastards down, and blow this
operation up—from the inside out. You're supposed to
work with every source, resource, and natural advantage
you have at your disposal. You're supposed to play them,
like they played you, gathering data, thwarting them without them knowing you did it, recording their conversations
like they did yours—building an ironclad internal affairs
case, while fighting this scourge on the outside. You're supposed to let Max work the outside while you work the inside, sharing resources and stopping this shit from
spreading. Something was creating infected werewolves in
record numbers on this side of the demon dimensions, as
well as brokering the technology we foolishly developed in
a lab, and then all of a sudden it went underground like it's
waiting for something—why, who, we don't know."

Xavier Holland talked with his hands, and all calm
evaporated from him as his pained gaze sought her for-
giveness and understanding. "Sasha, you're supposed to
keep Woods and Fisher hidden and working to feed you
leads. The brass doesn't know they're not dead. Right
now, for all intents and purposes, they're ghosts."

"And I'm supposed to just keep on going like a machine, forget how my whole life has been manipulated? Is
that it? I'm supposed to be okay with all of this?"

"No. You're not supposed to forget," he said, his voice becoming gentle. "You're supposed to be outraged and hurt and angry, but not to be stupid and give up, baby. No. That, you're not supposed to do. You're supposed to get mad, but damn sure even. I'm an old man—soon new scientists will take my place . . . and they'll keep coming, updating the work, and screwing over lives until you can core the apple."

Winded from his impassioned speech, he walked over to the door and flung it open. "You can hate me for my part in this until the end of time. I can't blame you. But if you give up on yourself and let them take you down easy, that, above all things, would kill me, because I love you."

CHAPTER 10

SHE'D BEGUN RUNNING to escape, running to clear her head, running to feel clean, running to get the muck and mire of filthy politics and dirty deals off her. Running to release Rod's soul from her heart, running to keep the sobs at bay. No matter what, the man hadn't deserved to die like that. No matter what, her parents shouldn't have been slaughtered by a botched experiment. No matter what, Woods and Fisher shouldn't be stranded and exiled. No matter what, she should never have been born.

Shadows chased her, taunted her, eluded her, until she found a lonely plateau to sink down upon and sob. There was no lie in Doc's eyes, no fraud in his tone. She understood why he'd done what he did ... but, damn, who were these people? What gave them the right? She cried so hard that she began to dry-heave.

She lay in the snow, breathing hard, slowly calming, and closed her eyes. For a long while she allowed the passing clouds to blanket her with shadows, thinking of all the laughs she had had with Rod and the guys over pitchers of beer, playing video games, training ... and more private moments that seemed so far away now.

Childhood memories, good and bad, slipped through her mind, made hazy and color-muted by time and selective memory.

Now the only thing that was real was any time spent with Holland. She wondered how people like the general slept at night. What might she have been if she were a regular kid, not just an experiment? What if she'd been raised in a real family . . . But then again, what was that? A real family.

She thought about Woodsy and Fisher. Out there somewhere, alone. They had watched the Butler they all knew die, had watched their own government blow the whole squad away. She was all they had left and, damn it, they were still a pack. She had to find her men. They were the only family, save Doc and Hunter, that she had now.

Sasha sat up and wiped her nose with the back of her hand, face numb. Just as importantly, she had to find out who was pulling the strings. She looked off in the distance toward the mountains and thought of Max's proposal to join forces. There was no going back to the way things were before, now that she knew. Walking away from the challenge also wasn't an option—she'd never be able to let it go.

This horror couldn't be allowed to get out of a lab.

"SHE'LL COME BACK, son," Silver Hawk said quietly, gathering a blanket around him as he sat on the ground beside Max.

They both stared at the sky while sharing the snow-covered plateau.

"Maybe I should go find her—storm's coming."

Silver Hawk shook his head. "No. This pain is deep. This pain is personal. Let it purge on its own . . . like snake bite, she has to draw the poison out. The storm will not come for several days."

"I should have told her what little bit I knew . . . maybe—"

"It was not your secret to tell."

Silver Hawk lit his pipe and drew a long drag off it, releasing the smoke with his eyes closed. "I will say this, however. I'm glad we had these years to be close."

"What are you saying?" Max could feel his pulse kick up a notch.

Silver Hawk took another labored drag from his pipe. "I am saying that the Great Spirit has both blessed me with a grandson I can be proud of, and after all these years, has given him a beautiful life-mate who lights his eyes, makes him pure wolf . . . this girl who is family of my good doctor friend. I can die in peace save for one thing."

"Pop, cut it out," Max said, teasing him with the private pet name that he'd used for him as a kid, heart racing. He didn't have it in him to admit that Sasha hadn't committed yet to be his life-mate. The thought still stung. "You're not dying. You're already over a hundred and fifty and still going strong."

"True, but I grow weary of this plane . . . I want to go to the shadow caves where the wall drawings dance at night. I miss your grandmother, my mate. I see her in visions and remember her beauty. There's not much left for me to do now. You are a gifted seer, one day the truth visions will come to you, if they haven't already. The clan is going to dust; the ways of the wolf are no more. New things replace what we've done for centuries in the old way. I must rest."

"You're talking in riddles to avoid talking to me straight." Max forced himself to smile, but it slid away from his face as his grandfather's composure remained somber. "It's bad, isn't it?"

Silver Hawk closed his eyes and released a stream of smoke into the pristine mountain air. "It's human, weak, I would have said years ago. But now my friend Xavier has shown me frightening strength. To expose one's throat is to accept death, to expose one's heart is to accept annihilation at the hands of another."

"Whatever you have to tell me, you'll still be my grandfather."

Strained silence made the whipping winds seem to howl a forlorn call. The vastness of the Uncompahgre, where each leaf and twig it contained was as carefully created and individual as a fingerprint, proved to Max that the Great Spirit cared for everything woven into the intricate design of life—even him. His grandfather had taught him that. Everything was part of the tapestry, part of the grand design. He wasn't sure what was troubling the old man, but he knew his grandfather spoke profound truth when he talked of exposing one's heart as the closest thing to annihilation one could get. Sasha had made him know that to be true; he'd never felt so vulnerable in his life.

"When I look at Sasha, I think of your grandmother, how she made me feel," Silver Hawk said after a long while. "Thinking of her makes me think of your mother. I should have understood how she felt about your father, and never begrudged her that happiness."

"Because he wasn't full shadow," Max said quietly, understanding how deep-seated the old clan prejudices were. "But that was a long time ago, and you never held it against me . . . you defended me, in fact. We grow."

"Yes, even in old age, we grow. But I was younger and angrier, then. I hadn't had a child in my arms to make me know complete selflessness. Your mother, I never raised. I was a warrior, protecting our lands and our ways . . . your grandmother's duty was to raise her and protect her, and to initiate her in the ways of the female shadows. I doted on your mother, but I missed all the joys and nuances of actually raising my daughter. That was a time when we didn't know better—we were male. Don't make that mistake."

Relief wafted through Max. If his grandfather was going to give him a lesson about being a good mate, then that was all the old man had to say. The theatrical buildup was completely unnerving, especially all the talk about getting old and dying.

"I'll be a part of my kids' lives, if I'm blessed to have any," Max said with a half-smile. "Is that what all of this is about—you want me to hurry up and make you some great-grandchildren before you supposedly die?" Max chuckled when his grandfather puffed his pipe harder.

"Would that be so much to ask?" Silver Hawk looked at him with a sideways glance, his expression peevish.

Max stared at the horizon and tried to suppress a grin.

His grandfather looked at him straight on and set his pipe down slowly. "Her scent will change, son."

"I know, I know, yeah, all right."

"You've—"

"We don't have to talk about this. Doc seemed real upset, maybe we should—"

"You need to know," his grandfather said flatly. "She will feel like the consistency of honey—thick. Not slippery."

Max looked away at the horizon, jaw pulsing. "We really don't have to have this conversation, Pop. In fact, I don't even know *why* we are. I just met her."

"She will not be able to hold back her wolf . . . it will show in her mouth . . . her teeth. Her eyes . . . her hair will lengthen through your fingers. But her scent will drag you across the mountains."

"Okay, okay, I get it."

"Did that happen?"

"No." Max stood and paced.

His grandfather looked up at him. "By next full moon. She's close . . . because Fox Shadow became foolish and jealous of you in her presence and your wolf was uncontrollable. I am glad she makes you happy . . . last night your howl bounced off the mountains and I was glad. If you are not ready for a family, you should take forest medicine. I have remedies." The old man chuckled softly and drew on his pipe as Max looked away. "It has been a long time since I have gone to the forest for such herbs and berries, but some things a man always remembers. Forget the sheep bellies . . . or now it is man-made plastic—I don't know—latex . . . what is it called? Condoms." He shook his head. "They don't work on a full moon. You will not be in your right mind. *This I know*."

Max walked away from his grandfather. "Can we change the subject?"

"I will also make her an amulet from our clan. The other she-shadows shunned her in complete offense because she is new, not purebred, and so near her time . . . and yet, she has completely stolen your attention."

"Yeah, even though they never wanted me." Max shook his head and chuckled, peering over the edge of the plateau. "Women."

"Not true, they wanted you more than you know . . . but were afraid, had been told stories by well-meaning parents. I was like them once. Those parents."

"No you weren't, Pop. You were never like them."

"I was, and your father died because of it," Silver Hawk said, standing. He walked to the edge of the place where they'd rested, and stared down the steep plateau wall into a ravine. "I have lived a long time and I am ready to release the stone from my heart. Maybe that is why I chose to avoid this part of our talk by thinking of your future with the new she-shadow. This deep shadow of my soul I never wanted to think on again."

"You're back to scaring me, Pop," Max said, gently drawing the old man away from the edge of the plateau. He looked over the side of the endless drop. There wasn't a shadow for a thousand feet, and Silver Hawk wasn't a young pup.

"I was proud back then," his grandfather admitted, lifting his chin, his profile regal. "We come from a line of great hunters. Our exploits have been told in legends and painted on the rocks around the world. And my daughter, my heart, the replica of my life-mate . . . she chose a lover who was a beta male, mixed blood." He closed his eyes and let the wind lacerate his face. "What I never told you was that when I saw her left in the snow, pregnant, savaged, her body torn limb from limb because she fought valiantly . . . and he couldn't defend her but was alive and cowering in the shadows . . ."

Silver Hawk walked off a bit. "It should have been his body ripped to shreds. You should have been born without worry of the taint. You should have never experienced the life of hardship you did. My heart was left buried in that snow. My heart was torn out each time they shunned my grandson. My heart breaks now as I tell you that the human side of me, the side that is weak, picked up the shotgun and shot your father at point-blank range—and I refused to let you take his name. The clan didn't impose that sanction, *I did*. You deserved more than that—you are better than that. But I had no right. Let me go to the hunting grounds of the ancestors . . . you will leave me, so there is no more reason to live."

Stunned, Max held his grandfather's sleeve, knowing that in this fragile moment the old man was not above pitching himself over the edge of the cliff. Wetness stung his face in freezing streams, but his face burned, his ears burned. His grandfather's image was blurry . . . his life's story was blurry. All this time he'd been told that his father had died heroically trying to protect his mother, and was mauled to death. There had been two beasts hunting and pillaging in tandem. One slaughtered his parents, the other took off, and the pack gave chase and many more died.

His grandfather had shot his dad at point-blank range on the battlefield?

Being the son of a coward was worse than being tainted by a werewolf. Max began walking, pulling his grandfather away from the plateau's edge, his eyes distant and blind. He could feel the elderly man struggling to be turned loose, but that wasn't something he was willing to do until they were far away from the edge.

"This is my choice!" his grandfather shouted.

Max just stared at him for a moment. "And I don't get a choice this time around, either?" He released his grandfather's arm and watched the old man huff a bit before settling down. "I'm not leaving you, Pop."

"How can you forgive me? We are warriors. I stole from you and betrayed your trust."

Max shook his head and swallowed hard. "You reacted in battle . . . if it were my daughter . . ." He looked away as images of his mother's desecrated body stabbed into his mind and made him shut his eyes. "If it were Sasha . . . I'd kill the man who was supposed to be guarding her, but didn't. If he hid and allowed her to be ripped to shreds while carrying my baby, I would kill him."

His grandfather's gaze burned with fury from the memory, but there was deep compassion in his eyes along with tears.

"Silver Shadow," Max said, calling his grandfather by his pack hunting name. "It was not your human side that was weak, but your wolf side that was strong. You did not steal my father from me; you kept me from being stolen by shame. You did not betray me, you protected me. The taint of a coward is worse in our world than the taint of a beast. You raised me without that horror. So, don't die yet. You have to live to see your great-grandchildren."

His grandfather nodded, and Max's muscles uncoiled. He had to run . . . run from his past, run from the hurt, run from the lies, run from it all. His wolf form shed his clothes and he was a moving shadow against an endless carpet of snow.

Somewhere near the border of Uzbekistan . . .

PILFERED ISLAMIC GARB hid their sunburned faces and weapons. Wild game and stolen water had sustained them. The goal was to push ever north, where the sunburned faces looked more like theirs, where they could blend in as possible Russians. From Russia they could get to the Ukraine, then to either Poland or Romania where some sort of safe house existed.

Woods pulled out a map and compass, his fingers blackened by filth and animal blood. Fisher kept his nervous gaze on the horizon in lookout. Thankfully they had made it away from the open desertlike environment that had little water and was hard to hide in. The coolness of the shadows around them from the foliage felt good and the underbrush was bursting with life. Local farmers also had goats that could be quietly picked off from their pens.

"We're living like dogs," Fisher muttered. "We stink, we're out here eating with our hands, slobbering down half-raw meat because a fire burning too long could alert border patrols." He rubbed the hair down on the back of his neck and closed his eyes. "I just want to know what we did wrong. That's the part I don't get. Why are they after us, Woodsy?"

"I don't know, but Doc has our backs. He said be cool and stay alive, so right now, that's the focus. We may be living like dogs, but we're living."

"The problem is, you should be living like wolves," a strange, growling voice said from the shadows.

Before they could lift a clip something sharp pierced their throats—then there was blackness.

SASHA LOOKED AT the porch of Max's grandfather's cabin and slowly climbed the steps. Fatigue clung to her like a worn-out lover. She was mentally spent, more so than physically, but her body registered the despair as one and the same.

As she'd expected, Doc was waiting for her, seated at the long knotty-pine dining room table slowly sipping a cup of tea with Silver Hawk. Both old men looked up at the same time, but seemed to be waiting for her to speak first.

"I'm going back down the mountain," she announced quietly. "Gotta get ready to report in on Monday morning at nine hundred hours."

"Do you have a plan?" Holland gently asked. "Anything I can help with?"

She shook her head. "Not yet . . . I'm sorta getting used to this new reality and making it up as I go along. But I'll have a plan by Monday. And don't worry, I'm not going to do anything stupid. The one thing I've figured out is that the people who did this to us had at least a twenty-five-year jump on us, maybe more. So whatever I do, it'll be strategic . . . not half-cocked and crazy." Her voice tightened as she looked at the somber faces before her. "When it's time for payback, they'll never see me coming."

Nodding at them both, she spun on her heels to leave. Silver Hawk stood.

"My grandson hasn't returned yet, but you should have an escort. We had words. His temporary disappearance has nothing to do with you."

"You can ride back with me, Sasha," Holland offered.

Sasha stopped walking, but didn't turn around. "Right now, I'm not real good company, and I don't think anybody or anything wants to screw with me. I know the shadows . . . a bit. I know where the safe house cabin is, where I left weapons stashed. I know where the snowmobile is and the truck. From there, I know my way home. Tell Hunter I said I'll catch him later."

With that she opened the door and didn't look back, immediately becoming a fleeting shadow.

LATE AFTERNOON SUN filtered through the trees as she made her way back to the safe house cabin on the outskirts of the pack's private land. So many emotions were competing for priority within her that she simply focused on her breath, the way her muscles felt as they expanded and contracted beneath her skin. Soon the burn came, the urge to be one with nature, to be a wild thing running and hunting and a part of the very fabric of the forest.

Clearing a fallen log with ease, she pushed her body, sending all the anger and pain of betrayal into the run, into the snow, into each footfall—Then the hair on her neck rose.

Something was chasing her. Something large.

Survival instinct changed her jogger's pace into a panic run. Moving swiftly over obstacles and cutting hard pivots, she could now hear many forms whipping through the underbrush at the speed of lightning. Treelines became a connected blur in a flat-out dash. Then she made the fatal mistake of trying to get a glimpse of what it was, glancing over her shoulder while still hurtling forward—her mind diverted from the wolf to the woman as she reflexively reached for a Glock nine-millimeter . . . but it wasn't on her hip. The gun was at the safe house. The momentary loss of focus made her lose her footing.

She came down hard with a muffled thud in a small clearing and immediately pushed herself up and jumped to her feet, although semidazed.

Ready for hand-to-hand combat against whatever and however many there were, she widened her stance, lowering her center of gravity, and listened with sharpened senses for the attackers to show themselves. Bear, cougar, wolves, frickin' wild boar, what was it? One or many? Panic was blocking her senses. All she was sure of was that the threat moved too damned fast.

Sasha's gaze darted between low-hanging branches and scanned the ground for anything she could use as a potential weapon. Shit. Nothing. Her nostrils flared, trying to pull in the scent to decipher it. But after a moment, that wasn't necessary. It became perfectly clear what it was.

Four lean wolves loped out of the underbrush, one coming from each cardinal point to hem her in. Each growling a low warning.

Sasha turned slowly, assessing each predator. A huge ivory wolf with golden eyes stalked her from behind. One the color of dense smoke with a barrel chest seemed the most aggressive and was baring its fangs as it carefully positioned itself with a furious, deep brown stare. An amber-hued wolf and one with the markings of a German shepherd covered her flanks.

An eerie sense of déjà vu threaded through her along

with a sense of violation. Wait a minute . . . Normal wolves didn't chase and hunt humans—that much she knew from bored nights at home clicking past cable channels. Uh-uh. It was still day and not a full moon, so werewolves were out. She was going back the way Hunter had taken her, hadn't messed with any animal's food sources, hadn't desecrated any territory . . . This was bullshit!

White-hot memories flashed in her mind. Being picked on at school. Country kid raised in the city; city kid moved to the country. Rich jocks trying to run a train on her under the bleachers. Date-rape drugs in her cola. Broken bones. Theirs, not hers. Girl betrayal. Wrong accent wherever you're from. They'd drugged her for the boys. Ain't got no momma or daddy. Orphaned brat. Gotta take your meds. Foster care don't care. Don't ask, don't tell how you were made. Who's your daddy? Rod is dead. Special Agent Baker feeds your fish Fred! Even Hunter knew some.

One moment she had been standing in a kickboxer's stance, then in the next moment she had shed her clothes and was on all fours growling. Instantly the smoke-colored predator rushed her, and with single-minded determination she met the attacker midair, going for the throat.

Angry barks and snarls from the other three wolves echoed in the back of her mind as razor-sharp claws tore at her sides. Yanking her head back, she'd avoided a sharp bite to her neck as they hit the ground in a hard roll. Snapping quickly, she got hold of an ear and raked the length of a torso. Her aim was basic, get to the belly and open that sucker up.

Ripping the ear off, using every bit of combat training, physical training, and all the rage in her, she pinned the aggressor down, sliced into its belly, and lunged in to tear out its throat—but a submission yelp gave her pause.

Even in her crazed state the pitch was so piercing that it offered the two seconds of hesitation needed for a volley of whimpers to follow.

But she wasn't budging off the downed wolf, her paws pressed hard on its chest. Fury split her throat with a howl and she launched angry barks low in the gray wolf's face that simply made the beaten creature close its eyes.

"All right! Enough!" a female voice yelled, much to Sasha's surprise.

She looked up from the wolf beneath her with a possessive growl. Three very attractive nude women each with hair the shades of the wolves that had just circled her stood in the clearing. The gray wolf beneath her transformed into a female body, dark hair wild, eyes frightened, ear missing and severely bleeding. Sasha looked at her harder and growled, not clear in the least how to change back—not sure that she wanted to before she'd finished the job.

Three mournful howls joined to echo through the clearing. The sound set Sasha's nerves on edge and only made her lower her head in an angry snarl. When the woman beneath her tried to move her hand to cover the bloody stump where her ear had been, Sasha's fangs clamped over her windpipe in a brutal warning: *move and you die*.

Slowly, calmly, a huge black wolf parted the brush. Sasha kept her eyes on him and could tell he was male right away. He was a head taller and much thicker than any of the others. She scented him in the air and then saw a glint of silver chain around his neck. Instant recognition made her pull back. Friend, not foe. Despite her rage, her tail wagged slowly.

His eyes held hers for a moment and she watched him change form, wishing like hell she knew how to do that.

"She's not backing off!" one of the women complained.

"She won, now our shadow sister must be healed!" another argued.

"That bitch tore off an ear—that's not part of the code!" the third challenged.

"I don't even know you!" Sasha shouted, suddenly back in her body. She stepped over the woman on the ground, pointing her finger as she railed, spittle flying she was so outraged. "I didn't do jack to you. You oughta be glad all she got was her ear ripped off—because if that mutt had come at me in human form, she might have gotten a Bowie knife shoved up her ass. Be clear—don't you ever come at me like that again! You don't know me! I didn't do anything to you. But since she started it, I finished it."

Max shrugged, his tone unfazed. "I don't know why you called me," he said, addressing the other women. "Rather than show her the courtesy of meeting her at the home of our pack elder, you decided to sneak around and challenge my . . ." He let the words trail off, sending his gaze toward Sasha. "My friend," he said, lifting his chin.

"Your *friend* and not your mate?" the amber-haired woman said, clearly aghast as she folded her arms over her impressive bosom and glanced at her shadow sisters.

"As I was saying . . . challenged my *friend* without my consent," Max said, not even breaking stride in his statement or addressing her question. "But I think the results are clear. *She's alpha female pack enforcer.* Shadow Falcon steps down. Any questions?" He looked around the disgruntled group. "Just for the record, Sasha's verbal threat was not adrenaline-inspired bravado. She's combat-ready, Special Forces trained . . . in case you ladies want to test her again, that's not a good idea. Shadow Falcon is really lucky that she's still breathing."

Unable to steady her frayed nerves, Sasha walked in a tight circle around the woman on the ground. Every hot flash of emotion that she'd suppressed for years was now a pinpoint migraine behind her eyes. She snatched up her clothes but her skin was still on fire, burning up. She was sweating hard, everything was wet, so wet and slippery . . . She looked down and felt dizzy. Blood was everywhere, much of it hers.

Sasha swallowed hard, watching as the woman on the ground rolled over, moaned, and her warrior sisters ran to her aid. She was gonna be sick. She could see flashes of white rib bone, a little raw flesh hanging out where there was once skin. Vanity and pain collided. She hadn't felt it before but she felt it now, and only pride was keeping her upright.

"Get me out of here," she said to Max, trying not to make it sound like a plea.

"No problem," he said calmly, giving her his elbow and careful to remain expressionless, as he helped her.

If she weren't in so much pain, she could have kissed him for that. He glanced at her from the corner of his eye and then glimpsed the closest shadow. The others couldn't see his expression, but it clearly asked if she could make it a few feet without limping. Sasha bit her lip and nodded, then threw her shoulders back and stiffly walked into a shadow on his arm.

The moment he had her cloaked within a shadow, she collapsed against his side, panting. Moving as fast as he could, he lifted her under her legs and beneath her shoulders, and cringed as she bit her lip to keep from crying out. Then he was pure motion.

Aware that every leap, every bound, every jostle, was pure agony for her, he zigzagged through the forest using the path with the fewest obstacles, which unfortunately was not the most direct route. By the time he got her to the cabin and stretched her out on the bed, she was nearly in shock and had lost a lot of blood.

Working fast, he pushed together the shredded skin on her left side, eliciting a deep moan of pain from her as she roused from semiconsciousness.

"I have to," he said quietly, beads of sweat forming on his brow. "I don't want it to scar, and if I don't bring it together and flatten it out as it knits, it'll leave raised keloids where the wound filled itself in."

She nodded, squeezed her eyes shut, and clutched the sheets as he brought both hands over her ribs and began pressing the skin together, pinching and pushing torn muscles and flesh back in its housing. Fat tears rolled down her face as she split her own lip from biting down, began panting, then gasped, and finally cried out in agony.

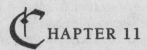

CHAPTER 11

THE SUN HAD long since set by the time Sasha roused. Max sat in a corner of the bedroom watching her intently and had only moved from the chair in the shadows to put on his clothes and boots. The runs, the fight with Fox Shadow, and Sasha's healing had drained him, but no matter how exhausted he was he refused to close his eyes until she awakened. Then he would feed her. She, more than he, needed to be replenished.

Blood from uncooked meat, hunted wild game laced with adrenaline, was what she required. Raw meat, with all the precious enzymes and proteins. Meat still practically twitching and warm was what her body needed to fully mend. But as he stared at Sasha's fitful sleep, he knew that while she was not in her wolf form the thought would probably make her hurl.

He sat forward in his chair with his fingers laced together supporting his chin, elbows on his knees, gaze intent. Even in the moonlight-washed darkness he could see the tender pink lines that tracked her sides from just near her breasts to the swell of her hips. Shadow Falcon was such a bitch. That had been totally unnecessary.

Sasha wasn't trying to vie for pack dominance. The only reason she was attacked was to drive her away, and if the females did it one by one, then by law, he couldn't intervene. Only if they'd jumped her and outnumbered her could he have evened the odds. Otherwise, his involvement would have stripped her of credibility before them . . . something else he knew they wanted. Yet she'd held her own like the champion she was.

Quiet pride filled him as he watched her sleep. Bloody, ragged, ripped up, but victorious—Sasha had walked out of her first dominance challenge an undisputed winner, and it would be a very long time before another challenger came for her. One more swipe and Shadow Falcon might have had a mortal gut wound . . . She was that far from entrails spilling onto the forest floor. It would also be a nasty healing. The amputated ear might require Western medicine by way of a good plastic surgeon. Shame, too, because Shadow Falcon was fine. Gorgeous on the outside, twisted on the inside, but that was Fox Shadow's choice. They were meant for each other.

However, he would have to clue Sasha in on the finer points of battle types. Battles for dominance within a pack usually needn't be so brutal. Those were different from territorial or defending attacks. It was assumed that once one showed the others who was boss, the defeated pack member was to remain alive to contribute to the group as a valued, unmaimed hunter. He'd have to tell Sasha that it was more like a regulated boxing match than a back-alley street fight where anything goes.

It was Shadow Falcon's misfortune to have gone after a she-shadow who had grown up rogue, outside a pack. What had the ladies expected? Sasha, clearly, had grown up fighting with no one to watch her back, no rules of engagement. If something or someone was coming for her, most likely her only option and baseline experience was ultimate force—deadly force and zero tolerance so the predator couldn't get back up.

Max smiled. She was beautiful in that state. He was just so sorry she'd been so badly injured, and the pain she'd suffered still made him ache. But he was glad she did what she did, for her sake, not his. This way, no matter what, her name would carry on the wind. The worldwide pack network would hear of a new, legitimate alpha female warrior. She would have to be given courtesy passage and safe lodging, if she were stranded. Whether she was his mate or not, she'd established herself among her own, on her own. Maybe for the first time in her life she'd know that different wasn't bad, or evil . . . that she was beautiful just the way the Great Spirit had made her, no matter the circumstances of her conception.

He watched her stir, thinking about everything probably harder than he should. Deeply philosophical streams of consciousness flowed within him as she groaned sleepily and awakened.

They were opposites and yet shared so much. He was a rogue within a pack; she was a rogue outside of the pack. She worried about her genesis, her conception, how she came to be, which made her different; he worried about the other end of that continuum, namely the circumstances under which he was born and, therefore, how he'd probably die. She was pure, sexy, silver shadow blur in motion; he was midnight, the very darkness itself. They both distrusted authority, but both were bound by it. Both had male elders who loved them dearly but had betrayed sacred trusts. Both had suffered isolation so vast the tundra couldn't compare . . . loneliness that echoed inside their bodies until they ached. And both were shadow wolves.

He heard his name rasped and was at the side of the bed, squatting down, in seconds. "Easy . . . the wounds will be tender, but they're healing nicely. Let me get you some water, don't sit up. Lie back."

Her body relaxed against the blood-encrusted blankets again and he went into the kitchen to get her some bottled water. He didn't have the heart to move her to clean her up until the redness and swelling went down. He couldn't cover her and risk having the sheet knit right into the wound—extracting it would have been torture.

"Here, baby," he murmured, returning to her side and opening the cap. He brought the bottle to her parched, cracked lips, gently lifting her head, and watched her drink so quickly that water ran down the sides of her mouth. "Easy, easy."

A coughing fit consumed her. "Ow . . ." She moaned and dropped back against the pillows as the fit abated. "Double ow."

"It's gonna hurt for a while, unless you eat," he said, stroking her tousled hair back off her forehead.

"I can't. The last thing I want right now is food—morphine would be good, though."

"Drugs would compromise the healing. However, it's coming along well." He brushed her forehead with a soft kiss. "The scars have flattened out and by tomorrow, at worst in a few days, the pigment will normalize."

"I don't have a few days," she said in a disgusted tone, closing her eyes. "I've got to report in. If they see this crap they might hot me right on the base."

Max nodded. "I know. That's why you *must* eat."

"All right," she said with a heavy breath. "What do you have that's easy on the stomach? Scrambled eggs, something I can . . ." Her voice trailed off. "Why are you looking at me with those big, puppy-dog eyes that say 'baby, you're really not gonna like this'? Is it some nasty shaman brew?"

"Sasha . . . baby—"

"I already don't like the sound of this."

"Fresh kill."

She just stared at him.

He rose. "I'll be back shortly."

"Oh, no, no, no," she said, struggling to sit up.

"Don't, you'll open up your wounds!"

She eased herself back down, but her discomfort did not stop her argument.

"First of all, you could have said something more . . . I don't know—eased me into it. You could have said 'venison,' or 'rabbit'—not 'fresh kill' like you'll be chasing behind a semi for road pizza."

He fought a smile and lost. "We are not scavengers. I assure you, I'll bring it down, not a semi."

"Oh, that makes me feel better," she said sarcastically. "You're going to bring a dead deer. God, I want to wake up and be back in my bed in Colorado Springs."

"I'll skin it, fillet it, and otherwise prepare it outside."

"Oh . . . thank you."

He chuckled as he turned to leave and glanced back at her, taking in her pale complexion.

"Let me ask you something," she said, her voice filled with attitude. "Why are you getting such a kick out of the fact that I fought her? I didn't do it for you, you know."

"I didn't think you had," he said, shocked. "You fought her for yourself."

Sasha hesitated. "Yeah . . . that's right."

"If you hadn't let her know you were not to be challenged, she would have made your life in this pack a living hell."

Sasha sighed. "Reminds me of the good old days of grade school, junior high, and high school." Sasha rolled her gaze up toward the ceiling.

He leaned against the bedroom door frame and struggled to get the amusement out of his tone before he spoke again. "I battled Fox Shadow for dominance earlier today, so she probably wanted to put you in your place. Essentially, make it known that while I still ruled the males of the pack, you wouldn't get a position of title without earning it. Today you earned it."

"I see."

"I'm going to go get dinner. When I get back, I'll fill you in on some of the nuances of life in the pack. Some of it doesn't make sense to me, either, but has been done since time immemorial."

"If I eat a little bit of whatever you catch, will my wounds stop hurting so much?"

"Yes . . . I promise."

"All right," she said, closing her eyes and gingerly putting her forearm over them. "Then hurry back."

SHE WAS DISGUSTING even to herself when he came back in the bedroom with a TV tray and a plate. Blood caked her hair, her nails, crusted the bed, and a shiver finally consumed her as the scent of fresh deer blood assaulted her nose.

Max set a tray down on the dresser and came to the bed with a bowl of water and a hot towel.

"Your nail beds are going to be really, really tender for a little while, because you might have hit bone when you opened Falcon up." He set the bowl down beside her and eased her hand into the water.

Sasha clenched her teeth.

He just held her hand steady and gently wiped between her fingers. Then he began to wipe the blood away from the rest of her body.

"I'll feed you and then try to get you in the tub . . . we'll get your hair washed. After you eat and heal a little more, all right?"

"Okay, okay," she said in short bursts, squeezing her eyes shut as she sat back. "Good thing I kicked her ass."

"Good thing you kicked it good, too."

"Yeah. I'm da woman." Sasha chuckled and then cringed. "Ow."

He brushed her forehead with a kiss and offered her a warm smile. "You are most certainly da woman."

"All right, I can do this." She peeped open one eye as he moved the bowl to a nightstand and returned with a tray.

"Ohhh . . . Hunter . . . wow . . ." She wanted to cry, it was so sweet what he'd done, given the way he could have presented the meal.

He'd cleaned up before coming back to her, too. That earned him big points. Just seeing the trouble he'd gone to made her smile. Hunter had served the meal as though they were at a posh restaurant and had carefully laid paper-thin slices of venison in a fan on a porcelain plate, put a wine glass beside it filled with cool spring water, and had added a tall water glass filled with pussy willow stems as flowers.

"Thank you," she said quietly, wanting to touch his face, but her fingers were too sore and it hurt to lift her arms.

"You're welcome . . . and I'm really sorry, more than you can know, that you got so badly hurt."

She watched him cut her meat on the plate. It was swimming in blood.

"Yeah, well, wasn't your fault—had to establish my dominance and pee on my tree, I suppose." She smiled as he brought a warm, dripping piece of meat to her mouth. Making jokes was not helping. She closed her eyes quickly and accepted the small piece he'd cut, and swallowed it whole. "Okay, okay, I can do this."

Max picked a small piece up with his fingers and

plopped it in his mouth as she squinted, making a gruesome face. "Steak tartar," he said with a shrug. "Rare filet
mignon. Sushi. It's really not that bad."

She nodded, but her facial expression remained uncon-
vinced. "It's just that I know where it came from," she
whispered, as though someone else could hear. "And it's
still warm."

"If I told you I heated it up in the oven, would that
make you feel better?" He smiled at her and shook his
head while chewing and then swiped another piece of
meat off her plate to pop in his mouth.

"Yes! Totally." She chuckled, painfully.

"Aw . . . c'mon," he said, taking another piece from
her plate. He opened his mouth, placed the fresh venison
on his tongue, and then closed his eyes. "Imagine you're
in a really, really nice restaurant. Allow the flavor of it to
just roll over your tongue and to hit your sinuses right off
your palate. Take your time, separate out all the flavor
nuances . . . Sasha, it's really good."

She couldn't believe it but the man had made saliva
build in her mouth, and just watching his mouth . . . those
lush, sensuous lips work . . . as his voice had bottomed
out to a low rumble . . . And the way his eyes rolled in
slow ecstasy beneath his lids. Damn. If she wasn't so beat
up, he would have made her want to jump his bones.

"Try it with less resistance," he said, picking up a
piece with his fingers and bringing it to her mouth.

Slowly, carefully, she accepted the morsel from him,
pulling his fingers past her lips, and then closed her eyes.
This time she allowed the meat to roll over her tongue and
the flavors to filter through her senses. It was so good, she
moaned.

He quickly fed her another piece, then more as she
licked his fingers and began feeding him in return.
Strangely, after just a few bites, her nail beds were no

longer sore, and she could even feel the tenderness in her side wounds ebbing.

She ate until the plate was empty. He went out and came back with more and she ate that too, her body mending itself rapidly.

Exquisite pain and restraint shone in his eyes as she finished what he'd brought her and sat back against the headboard breathing heavily. He gently kissed her sides where she'd been raked. Her hand absently stroked his hair.

"I'm going to bring you something that you're going to have to trust me on . . . it will make you better faster than what you just had."

She stared at him. His voice had definitely bottomed out and he had a lot more than five o'clock shadow beginning to cover his jaw. His hair had lengthened about two inches while they were eating, and he was hard enough to drive a railroad tie.

"Please don't tell me anything really scary, Max."

"No, no, no, nothing sick. But if you want the scars to knit quickly, organ meat is—"

"Organ meat?" she asked weakly.

He stood and raked his hair. "Heart, liver—"

Sasha squeezed her eyes shut. "You just had to ruin the moment, didn't you?"

"You've got to heal from the inside out, and the pigment has to come all the way back." He turned and left the room, calling over his shoulder, "Presentation is everything."

HE HADN'T LIED. She couldn't tell what part of the animal the next plate had come from, and with him feeding her what looked like gourmet samples off his long, sexy fingers . . . sometimes offering her a bit with a delicious kiss . . . whatever it was, was gone in no time.

"I'm going to draw you a lukewarm bath, clear water, no soap to sting . . . just to hydrate your skin, get the muck off, and make you feel better."

She almost said "I love you," jokingly, but something told her that he wouldn't think it was funny at all. "Thank you," she said instead.

He cupped her cheek, kissed her slowly, and then looked down at her wounds. "You don't have to thank me . . . I love doing for you, Sasha. How do you feel?"

Her fingers played over the tender, new skin that wasn't as sore as it had been and soon realized that she could lift her arms, sit up a bit, and even slowly bring her feet over the edge of the bed without yelping. "Much better . . . thank you, Max."

"You are a very stubborn woman. I said you don't have to thank me."

She stopped him from standing with the gentle press of her hand on his arm. "Yes I do," she said quietly. "Because I don't take it for granted that someone will do for me. I've never had that. It's new . . . and it's very, very nice. I love it, in fact."

He nodded and gave her his hand, and then cupped her elbow to help her stand. They both left it at that as they met in the middle of the verbal compromise, deciding without words to say the things that they loved, rather than being more specific. It just seemed less scary that way for two wolves.

She watched him putter after he'd deposited her on the closed toilet seat, readying the tub, testing the water temperature, and suddenly realized that she hadn't gone all day. Her foot bouncing, the sound of water running in the tub made her close her eyes.

"You okay?"

Too embarrassed, she just nodded.

"Sasha, what's—"

"Um, I really need to . . ." She nodded toward the toilet.

"Ah," Max said and walked out of the bathroom.

After she finished, she flushed and dragged herself over to the sink to wash her hands, leaning on it for support. As much as she'd just found every tender spot on herself again, she had to laugh.

"I guess that would have made it official," she called out, to let him know he could return. "Peeing in earshot makes you boyfriend and girlfriend."

He laughed hard. "So if I'm in the bathroom with you we're officially married?"

She laughed with him and sat down carefully on the now closed toilet seat.

"You ready to get wet?"

She looked at him and arched an eyebrow.

"Your mind is in the gutter."

A half-smile tugged at her cheek. "Hey, I'm just observant—I'm naked, you're taking off a bloody T-shirt. Pecs look great, abs are killin' me. Soooo . . ."

He smiled broadly. "You feeling that much better?"

Her shoulders sagged. "No . . . I'm just talking trash to preserve my dignity."

His eyes became slightly forlorn. "You are not making this easy."

"What?" She grinned as he came to help her into the tub.

"This is the last night I get to have you to myself . . . before you go back to them." There was no smile in his voice. The tone was sober and wistful.

"You act like I'm not coming back." She looked at him, no more teasing in her voice, as he helped her into the water.

"It's just that if they double-cross you . . . hurt you in any way . . . try to chain you in a lab, or . . ." He began to gently sponge her shoulders. "I'll lose my mind. I promise you they'll have to put me down."

"I'm coming back—I won't let them get me," she promised him quietly, touching his face. Water made the velvety covering on his jaw glisten as her eyes searched his. "I will come back . . . because the thought of them putting you down hard is something my soul couldn't withstand."

He closed his eyes and covered her hand for a moment. "Then we need a plan." He opened his eyes and looked at her hard. "You need to know what you're going to say to them when you go back . . . how you're going to play it, how you're going to make it so we can communicate and work in unison right under their noses without a problem."

"Yeah. I know."

They fell silent as his steady, consistent touch sponged clean water through her hair, over her shoulders, and down her breasts. The steadiness of it, the calm reassurance of it, made her relax and lean back and close her eyes.

"You're my contact," she murmured. "You are a tracker-shaman. They employ shamans and others with psychic abilities, so they'll buy it."

"All right," he said, pouring water down her bent legs. "So I found a disturbance in the Rocky Mountain chain here—which is why you came . . . you heard me talking in a bar, asking questions at the Road Hawg earlier that night. After what you learned about Rod, you had to be sure there were no more like him around. You found me, we went to a diner, and you investigated further. I said come up to see some tracks and abnormal wolf patterns that flow up and over the Canadian border. It goes all the way up into the Cassiar Mountains, up near Yukon Territory."

"Also why Doc was up here. Great minds thinking alike, we bumped into each other. You want to protect the few scattered Ute tribe members that are here and not in Utah . . . so you were willing to work with me, be my guide. But I had to get back to report in, plus a storm was coming." Her voice became quiet. "Then Doc told me what happened to the squad . . . and I was more determined than ever to hunt down anything that might have escaped and close a dimensional distortion, and make sure nobody is smuggling virally infected DNA."

She was glad that he had allowed the silence and the light, trickling sound of water to speak volumes for a while. So much had happened in such a short span of time that Rod's death, the deaths of the other squad members, and Woods and Fisher being on the run still didn't seem real. Until there was actual closure, it would remain a floating, airy thing that she couldn't wrap her mind around. Just like all the things Doc had told her. He'd said them plain enough, but it was so new, so unbelievable, that she had to remind herself that things had changed. And yet Hunter had helped her devise a plan that was close enough to the truth that she could pass a lie detector test, even get past the in-house psychics. That was genius.

"I'm going to try to get them to let me run point on finding genetic smuggling operations." She sucked in a huge breath. "I'm going to say that a source put a bug in my ear. A little birdie told me that the North Korean thing was only the tip of the iceberg."

Max's hands kept working, untangling her hair, and then he bent over to let the dirty, blood-darkened water out of the tub and replenish it with clean water. "Canada, especially up in the Yukon and above, is the perfect trade post for Russia, China, Pakistan, and Europe. All a good smuggler has to do is bounce off the tip of Russia, hide their way through Alaska, and pick up a hot trail in the Yukon. Finding a person out there is like finding a needle in a haystack. Borders are weak; the temps for moving DNA are perfect. And every legend you've ever heard about the wolf originates in said climes. We don't understand it, but there's gotta be a reason."

"Okay," she said, nodding. "You're my outside contact, have seen one, and it's on the move. You're my shaman."

"I see dead people, lady," he murmured, brushing her ear with a kiss.

"Yeah, and the truth is out there."

They both laughed.

Sasha slid down deeper in the soothing water. "I'm telling them about genetic smugglers because I want to have a seemingly bona fide reason to be digging into genetic processes. Up till now, they put me on a target and told me to blow it up. That's what we did. Went in, hit the ground, and blew it up. But I need to find out—"

He let his hands slide down her shoulders until his arms were submerged up to the elbows and his chest grazed the back of her head. "There are things you can tell me later, or never at all . . . there are things that will take time for me to disclose, too. Let's work on phase one," he murmured against the crown of her wet hair. "Let's get you back out from that tomb they have in the ground—alive. Free. Hunting with me as my partner, and me as yours."

She covered his hands as they gently stroked her tender sides beneath the water. "I can pull that off, Hunter. I'm good."

His kiss against her wet scalp was more ardent but his touch remained soothing and gentle. "I have no doubts."

"I don't want there to be friction in your camp about me, though," she murmured, her fingers gently sliding with his, splaying her much smaller palm over the warm, now tingling surface of his hand. "Your grandfather said you two had had words. If I'm a—"

"That's one of those things for later . . ." His kiss against her cheek was fierce as he continued to kneel behind her and caress where she'd been hurt. "I can't have that conversation right now . . . but just know it didn't have anything to do with you. Old family wounds— things I found out that were ugly."

She turned her head to nuzzle his shoulder. "That I understand. It's why I was out running. I found out things that should have turned my hair white today. But we're survivors, I guess . . . We love the people who made some bad choices, and we opted to live."

His warm mouth found the crook of her neck. "That was their shit, not ours. We'll survive it."

His hands covered her belly beneath the water's rippling surface, and gentle, circling strokes made her lean her head back against his shoulder.

"I like the sound of 'we.' Never used to use the word much."

"I never did use that word before. Never had occasion to."

A slight shudder passed through her as his lips grazed her shoulder. His arms were so long, his reach so all-encompassing, that he was practically hugging the tub with her in it. The position he had her in made her feel like she was floating. Safe. Protected in a womb. His massive chest was at the very edge of her back, warming her neck and pillowing her head. A deep thudding heartbeat lulled her into lazy, spine-gelling relaxation.

Warm currents of soft breath pelted the crown of her wet hair. Thick biceps bracketed her upper arms, moving back and forth in a slow, metronome-like rhythm of peacefulness, huge hands sending healing sensation up and down her abdomen, over her hips, his reach long enough to caress her inner thighs.

Soon her body awakened on its own, even while she dozed, swelling, lifting ever so slightly at each pass of his wide-splayed touch, her breasts bobbing, nipples kissing the broken water's surface until they stung. Her tongue darted out to chase the ache his lack of attention caused, seeking his mouth that only caressed her cheek. Disappointed, her lips parted to sip quiet streams of air as her thighs slid open to rest on either side of the tub.

Submerged and ignored, her nether lips pouted, leaking their own wetness. He'd felt it when he grazed her . . . she knew it when his breath hitched along with hers. For a moment, he petted away the offense, making her moan, but then went back to his lazy strokes inside her thighs, over her belly, and up her arms.

On each pass now, she was straining to make contact with his mouth, which refused to stray from planting gentle kisses on her hair and shoulder and neck. Her mouth hungered for his so badly that it was becoming parched, in need of his lips and tongue to quench the burn. But her body was still too tender to turn and take what she wanted from him.

His hands enfolded hers, his fingers laced between hers, his voice a low rumble in her ear. "You'll feel better tomorrow after a good night's sleep. If I do more than this, you won't be able to report for duty."

She knew it was true, but damn him anyway. She kept her eyes closed, her head leaning back against him, and simply told him the truth. "I am in so much pain, though . . ."

He kissed her ear roughly and forced his words into it like slow, liquid heat. "Trust me, I know."

His fingers unfolded and untwined from hers to flatten his palms over the backs of her hands. Taking them up, he carefully dragged them up her belly beneath the water, until she quivered as they swept her torso, then he brought them to gently rub the underside of her breasts. She began to close her thighs; it was an impulse, it ached so badly between them. He shook his head no against her hair and she let them fall apart again and breathed through her mouth.

To let her know he'd heard her, his thumbs stretched beyond hers to trace half-moon circles at the very edge of her nipples till she arched. The moment she did, his hands guided hers to cover the place that hurt until her voice rushed out, echoing back to them from the tiles. Her grip tightened, increasing his labored breaths, as he nuzzled her cheek watching, and then guided her hands away to rest on her thighs.

The edge of the water now felt like a knife of pleasure as she lifted her nipples above it and then sank back down below it, allowing the water to lick her where he wouldn't. But a huge hand placed on the center of her chest drew a whimper.

"Mine," he murmured in her ear.

At this point she was ready to tell him whatever he wanted to hear. She lifted her nipples above the water's edge and fought not to close her thighs. "Yours."

When his hands slid over her breasts she closed her eyes so tightly pinpoints of light formed beneath her lids. The slow flicking that plucked the water as he thumbed each sensitive tip made her dig her nails into her thighs.

"Hunter, I—"

"Shsssh . . ." he soothed in her ear, leaving her breasts to explore her belly underwater. "I know it hurts."

His large, water-soaked hands rubbed a lazy pattern inside her thighs, brushing by the plump, silken thatch that was so engorged her lips parted on their own. Her breaths became short jags. Her hands now clutched his wrists, needing something to hold on to. She couldn't help it, her hips bounced up to meet his touch. The sound of water splashing added to the symphony of staccato breaths, low, quiet gasps, and two heartbeats out of control. Lifting higher on each pass, her mound broke the surface and the water licked her bud. Just as suddenly, her gasp released his voice and two thick, seeking fingers sank deep inside her.

She turned and held on to his bicep; injuries be damned, she was coming. She pressed her face against bulging muscle, her thighs closed and became a pulsing vise. His other arm was sure, his hold steady. The convulsion was swift; she nearly blacked out.

Eyes closed, half floating, curled in a fetal position, his hand wedged between her legs, and her fingers gripping his arm, she lay breathing hard with her mouth open for a moment, dazed. By degrees, as the climax contractions ebbed, her grip loosened and the muscles in her thighs went slack. Thankfully he caught her with his other arm or she might have drowned. The thought of drowning and his wondrous touch made a half-smile slowly appear while her eyes remained closed and she tried to steady her breath.

"You do have healing hands."

He brushed her mouth with a kiss. "How're your sides?"

"What sides? The ones that are all jellied and loose?"

"Yeah," he said, his voice deep and raw. "Those."

She opened her eyes and then kissed him slowly. "Wanna go to bed so I can show you?"

He shook his head no so avidly that she had to catch his chin to make him stop.

"Let me get you settled," he said on a heavy exhale. "You lie down for a couple of hours. This was just to help you really relax . . . endorphin rush, so there'd be no more pain, and—"

"You're babbling," she said calmly with a smile, holding his chin.

"I know. Let me get you settled and—"

"And you're repeating yourself."

He closed his eyes and visibly fought to speak slowly and succinctly. "Let me get you under the covers, warm, resting. I'll take away the bloodied blankets. I'll clean up while you rest. Then I'll take you home. You'll rest some more, and then you'll be fresh and healed to report for duty so they'll never be the wiser."

She held both sides of his face. "But *you* are in pain."

"Yes. I am in pain. But it will pass." He didn't even open his eyes and simply covered her hands where they lay against his cheeks.

"I have a remedy for pain."

He leaned his forehead against hers and shuddered quietly. "I'll be all right."

"It won't open up my wounds, I promise you." She kissed him gently, suggestively rubbing her hand up and down his bare chest and toying with the amulet he wore, then sucked his earlobe. "I'll even give you your choice of remedies." She flicked her tongue over his mouth and then lowered her hand to rest on his stomach. "Those are your two choices. How badly are you in pain?"

"Chronic," he said on a raspy swallow.

"If you come to bed with me, we can both sleep curled up together for a couple of hours afterward . . . my remedy is swift."

"It would have to be, right about now."

She smiled. "Good. I'm glad we don't have to fight about it."

CHAPTER 12

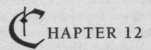

HE DIDN'T LIKE it, not one bit—letting her go, allowing her to be surrounded by the enemy, but it was her choice. It was her job. He hadn't really meant to put his tongue halfway down her throat when kissing her goodbye. Had to remember to hold her gently in the shadows when he'd delivered her back to her SUV in Ronnie's lot, although every cell in his body was shouting, *Mine*. If they hurt her, they'd die.

UP UNTIL NOW, walking up the steps to her own apartment, Sasha had thought she was a pretty tough cookie. But letting go of that man in the shadows was probably one of the hardest things she'd ever had to do. Never in her life had forty-eight hours been so crazy . . . so frickin' insane that she wanted to laugh and cry and howl at the moon.

Death, shadow dancing, wolf fights, revelations, and sex like, whoa. Healing, shape-shifting, life-altering truths.

Sasha trudged up the steps. She wasn't even fazed when Special Agent Baker opened the door in drag, wearing her curlers, scarf, and old-lady-robe getup. She just hoped that while she'd been in her apartment reinstalling surveillance devices that she'd fed Fred.

"Honey, are you all right? I was so worried . . ."

Sasha looked up blankly. It was no act. Her responses were normal. "My squad," she said sadly, not needing to pretend. "They didn't make it in Afghanistan."

Baker rushed down the steps doing the neighborly thing, and hugged her. Sasha allowed it. Hey, they were all military or a branch of Homeland Security. Special Agent Baker had a role to play, just like she did—but that didn't mean it didn't break her up to know that some of their own didn't make it. No matter what, she reasoned, they gave their lives for the cause. That deserved respect. Rod, Johnson, Gonzalez, Sherwin, all had served their country to the best of their ability. God rest their souls in peace. Her issue was with the brass. Special Agent Baker wasn't brass, she was a grunt, like herself. Just following orders. Part of the new Homeland Security team integration that put all branches under the same aegis.

Slowly but surely Sasha returned the hug.

"I went up into the mountains," Sasha said quietly, beginning the ruse. "I just needed a coupla days to get my head together."

AS SHE PULLED up to the base and flashed her ID, she wasn't really surprised when two MPs commandeered her Nitro, stripped her weapons, and provided her with a silent escort.

That was cool. They were following procedure to have her checked for contagion first. No hazmat suits required; what she had possibly contracted in the wild wasn't airborne. A scratch or a bite would require a blood exchange and the men gave her wide berth. Couldn't blame them. That also made sense.

Sasha kept her eyes straight ahead as they walked with her to their Jeep. The ride into the yawning cavern was tense and silent, and as their vehicle slipped into darkness she just hoped the very nervous men guarding her didn't get jumpy enough to accidentally blow her away.

Eyes forward in the elevator; the descent seemed endless. But her mind was focused on one thing: making sure she pulled off her shell game with the general. This would have to be the best game of poker she'd ever played, and she only hoped that Special Agent Baker had done her job reporting in, and done it well.

The MPs nodded toward a clear lab containment cell with fluorescent lights and a small boxlike cutout in one of the walls. Sasha sighed and stepped into the chamber as they shut and bolted the steel doors closed behind her.

Two feet worth of bulletproof, reinforced glass surrounded her, giving a slight fishbowl effect to the workspace beyond. Now she knew how Fred probably felt. She made a mental note to be nicer to him and maybe one day bring him a worm. Or even a girl fish.

A lab was on one side. Cameras were hidden within the isolation chamber, but she knew they were there. Had she had any modesty this would surely have killed it. Too bad the military was coed and more than half the personnel in the lab were guys.

She began to strip, knowing they had to be sure there was no sign of an attack bite. For a moment she hesitated, remembering the bitch fight she'd been in with Shadow Falcon. As she took off her fatigues, she became aware that a battle for dominance could have cost her her life.

As she pulled off her boots and yanked down her pants, suddenly she realized why Hunter was so panicked. She could be cut down like a dog that was thought to have rabies!

Turning slowly with her arms extended, she fought not

to double-check the places that had healed. All she could do was say a little prayer. When she saw Hunter again, she would seriously thank that man for making her eat raw venison.

"Is this okay, or do I have to lose the underwear?" she called out dryly. But her insides were jumping.

"Aw, *baby*. You look like a Victoria's Secret model, Trudeau, but you're gonna have to lose the bra and panties."

She smiled. Leave it to Winters to kick the bullshit. "Ha, ha, ha," she said flatly into a monitor, placing her hands on her hips. She squinted to see him better through the distorted glass. She could make out his boyish face, shock of brunette hair, and the way he wiggled his impish eyebrows at her. "In your dreams."

"Every last one of 'em," he said, laughing. "These decons are wreaking havoc with my water bill."

"Knock it off, Winters," McGill said with a smile in her voice. The heavyset blonde in her mid-forties ran the lab, and she pushed away from her desk to bring blood-drawing supplies to the cutout in the decontamination cell. "Some shaman you are. If you can't tell she hasn't been mauled while she's wearing that getup, then her stripping all the way down wouldn't do you much good anyway. Get a new set of contact lenses."

"Thank you, Clarissa," Sasha said with a wry smile. It was nice to have another female present who had her back. "Next time I'll wear cotton drawers so Winters has a better excuse."

"Well, our resident psychic should have known that I wait for these decontamination moments with you, Trudeau. I have fantasies about the tank, baby—one day it'll be me and you under glass."

"For that, Bradley would have to pull out his ancient spell books," Sasha said, laughing.

Joking around, even for a moment, was the MASH humor she needed to regain her balance. The rest of them needed it, too. Who wanted to be the one to make the call to have a friend and coworker put down? These decons were always tense.

When Bradley didn't answer, she squinted through the thick glass trying to see the expression of the lab team's dark arts expert, loving it when Winters could break his moody façade. The man was only about thirty-five but had the countenance of a British aristocrat which made him seem so much older. She could only see half of Bradley's face above his endless rows of satellite equipment. His brow was furrowed and his glasses had slid down his nose. His eyes seemed tired, like he'd been up all night tracking her on radar.

"How about it, Bradley," Sasha called out, needling him. "Do you have anything in those spooky books of yours, like saltpeter spells, that can cure a horny computer lab tech? Or can we just do away with these stupid decontaminations altogether? What do you say, guys? I'm gonna start wearing swimwear under my fatigues if you all don't stop gawking and hurry up to give me the all clear."

"Patience, patience, just turn around for me slowly so I can capture the body image . . . on my screensaver," Winters said, laughing.

"Ooooh, I will hurt you bad when I get out of here," Sasha said, chuckling.

Bradley finally smiled. "Don't knock the decons, Trudeau. Winters can't help it. I live for these moments, too. *Love* the black lace this time."

"Oh, so the guys are joining forces again, are they?" Sasha shook her head. "Can I get dressed?"

"I cannot believe you guys give her such a hard way to go. Don't worry, Trudeau. I'll slip something in their coffee that'll make both these lab rats behave."

"You ladies are so mean to guys locked in a lab eighteen hours a day. Can't even go looking for hotness on the Internet without—"

"Heads up, brass in pursuit. Corridor five and closing," Bradley announced. "Trudeau, you're clear. Get dressed."

Sasha snatched up her clothes and began yanking them on. She quickly thrust her arms through the cutout so Clarissa could draw her blood. By the time she was lacing up her boots, the entire chain of command for the project was there: General Donald Wilkerson, Colonel Matt Vlasco, Lieutenant Colonel Ralph Waters, Major John Adams, Project Leader and Geneticist Dr. Xavier Holland.

She watched the doctor's staff begin scurrying around after the exchange of appropriate salutes and greetings. She noted how Doc walked from monitor to monitor coolly, not regarding her, nodding, murmuring reassurances, looking into the microscopes, and then conferring. From what she could gather, Bradley's sat-comm screens had not confirmed anything alarming. Same deal with McGill's lab test monitors—if there was werewolf toxin present on any of Clarissa's instrumentation, the MPs in the room would already be moving toward her. Whatever Winters was showing them on his computer monitors didn't seem to make them bristle. The whole twenty-minute process of waiting and being watched through glass was worse than having a root canal.

Finally she was allowed to exit the chamber, and she stood at attention, her salute tight, waiting for permission to stand at ease. Eyes focused on a point on the wall, she listened for the instructions to move the meeting to the war room, and she followed the brass, listening to the echoes of boot footfalls from the two MPs beside her, and then took a position standing in the front of the room at attention as each member of the chain of command sat.

"At ease, Trudeau," the general said in a weary voice. "Where were you?"

"Permission to speak, sir," she said, her hands behind her back, shoulders thrust back, chin lifted.

"Permission granted," the general said, again sounding weary.

All eyes were on her, but none bored into her as intently as Doc's.

"I was on leave, sir. I looked for my squad brothers, who are also friends, sir. When I arrived at their apartments, something was wrong. I was worried, sir, given the nature of our missions. When I arrived at Captain Butler's apartment, sir . . . if I may speak candidly . . ."

"Yes, Lieutenant. We would appreciate candor."

Sasha nodded. "I was horrified, sir."

Senior officers murmured and quietly conferred.

"Continue, Lieutenant," the general said, sitting forward and making a tent with his fingers before his mouth.

"I panicked. I could see that Captain Butler took his meds, sir, or was trying to, but . . . there were spilled meds all over the floor. Carcasses. I feared that he might have gone after the squad, or worse, civilians. Something moved, may have been vermin, given the filth that was in there . . . the carnage. Then I saw him." She stopped briefly and sucked in a deep, steadying breath. "There was no option, sir. He was too far gone."

The general nodded. "Yes, we are aware," he said, his voice tinged with regret. "We found his body and are grateful that you did what you had to do given the personal nature of your relationship to Captain Butler . . . but you should have reported in after the incident."

"There was additional gunfire heard on . . . er, uh, reported by the local authorities," Major Adams said.

Sasha felt her face burn, but kept her eyes on a fixed spot on the wall beyond the brass. "Frankly, sirs, I panicked and opened up several rounds when I thought something else was in the apartment."

"And was there?" Xavier Holland asked.

"Sir, I realized I was in a residential zone, and to be sure I didn't hurt any civilians, I drove back out to the most isolated place I could—the empty lot of Ronnie's Road Hog Tavern. My thinking was that if whatever it was was still nearby, and had . . . Turned, then I should draw it away from a populated area and follow the protocols set up by the project if one of our viruses mutates, sir. I didn't know if it was one of our own, or a brand-new contagion source."

She stopped and drew a shaky breath. The brass at the table conferred. She was definitely not acting. Just remembering the apartment was enough. Remembering that Rod was dead, as well as several other men, made her chest constrict. Now came the delicate part, syncing up times and conversations for credibility so they'd buy her story.

"You did the right thing, removing the potential firefight from a highly concentrated civilian environment." Colonel Matt Vlasco looked at the other brass at the table, now speaking to them as though Sasha weren't in the room. "Given the highly personal mentor-protégée relationship between Captain Butler and Lieutenant Trudeau, I think it demonstrates an extreme level of clearheadedness for her to draw a potential predator away from a residential area."

She wanted to die.

"Thank you, sir." She wanted to die.

She wanted to die. They had eavesdropped on all their personal conversations. She wanted to die—wanted to kill.

"But we found your jacket, portions of your clothes, a destroyed cell phone, Lieutenant," Colonel Waters said.

"Yes. It looked like a Turn had taken place," Major Adams concluded.

"Sirs, permission to respond," Sasha said quickly, before more conjecture could occur.

"Permission granted," the general said.

"Thank you, sir."

Sasha stared at the general's four-star braid for a moment, willing herself to remain detached from emotion and to stay focused. Doc was so silent now, and his eyes held such a deadly warning glare that she couldn't look at him. To do so would make her leap across the table and go for the general's throat. General Donald Wilkerson had set all this insanity in motion, now he dared to want a quick and easy solution? *Bastard.*

"I called Dr. Xavier Holland," Sasha said, her voice firm and clear. "My first thought was that if Captain Butler had been AWOL and out of control, or if any other members of the squad had been injured, Dr. Holland would be the only one able to control a viral outbreak. He had the correct medicines, if a Turn had not fully occurred in those surviving men. I couldn't be sure that it had, because I had no physical evidence—no bodies. But when I contacted the doctor briefly, he was already up in the mountains starting his leave, sirs. His cell phone went out in the middle of our conversation, and frankly, I was in such a state of frustration I hit mine on the dashboard and flung it out of the window."

Major Adams chuckled and guffawed. "I've wanted to do that several times myself just from cell phone dropout, Lieutenant."

"But your clothes, Lieutenant," Colonel Vlasco said in a clipped tone, bringing the meeting back to the inquisition it was.

"A source stepped out of the shadows, sir. He surprised me when I went to retrieve my phone, and we did brief hand-to-hand combat, whereby my boots were damaged, my pants, and the collar of my jacket, from the fight.

However, I was able to subdue him with a pump shotgun, sir. Then he was ready to talk."

Sasha's gaze held the colonel's. "He turned out to be a bounty hunter from up in Ute Indian country. He said that there had been livestock attacks and they had been watching Captain Butler's apartment because of animal raids off their lands that they'd tracked back to his place. He saw me come out of the apartment, wanted to ask questions, but heard gunfire and laid low until I parked in the open lot."

Her eyes went to the general. "If one of our men, or more, had gone into the private Ute lands in the mountains . . . They could potentially spread the virus to residents who would be hard to find in the vast wilderness. All it would have taken was one. Then it occurred to me that Dr. Holland coincidentally said he'd gone there on vacation prior to a big storm, and my thinking was, sir, that perhaps the doctor also was going up there to eyeball the situation. He has a relationship with the native peoples, so I decided to head for where Dr. Holland might have gone. The guide seemed legit, his story made sense, and I needed him to lead me to where the livestock mutilations had occurred. It was also my intention to protect the doctor at all costs. He is the project's only link to finding a cure to wipe out this scourge, and he could himself have been imperiled in a wilderness situation. Suffice to say, I was working during leave, sirs."

"Good move, Trudeau. Good move," the general said, sitting back and lacing his fingers over his hefty stomach.

"I accepted the offer to accompany this guide and was armed. At no time was I at risk, and knew to look for signs of a mauling. I met up with the doctor there, and learned that the pack . . ." She drew a deep breath. Even now it was hard to say out loud. "That the pack had perished in Afghanistan on mission. Therefore, I terminated the search for the pack and with the doctor checked any and all tribal members for signs of viral infection—and found none."

"Excellent, Trudeau. The circumstances were initially a bit sketchy," the general said, looking around the table as though he'd had confidence in her all along. "But we knew you had been well trained for any and all circumstances."

"Thank you, sir," she said blankly, without looking at any of them.

"May I submit a request, sir?"

The murmurs in the room fell silent.

"Permission granted," the general said.

"May I attend the memorial service for my squad, sir—even though I am on duty? That was my only family. And now they are all dead."

It was so quiet in the room that only the whispering hum of electronic equipment could be heard.

"Absolutely, Lieutenant," the general said, his voice somber. "It was a great loss."

Sasha nodded and swallowed hard; she couldn't help it. "Yes, sir. It was." She lifted her chin higher. "Thank you, sir."

They seemed to be waiting, not sure what to say. She'd answered all their questions; she needed a moment to be sure that when she spoke her voice wouldn't waver.

"Sirs, may I make a suggestion?" This time she looked at them directly.

Each man at the table leaned forward, craning his neck to hear what she might say.

"Yes, Lieutenant," the general said, an expression in his eyes that seemed like compassion—an expression coming from him that she didn't understand.

"Sir . . . this scourge was the reason my entire pack, my family, was killed in action." She stepped closer to the large, oval mahogany table, noting that Xavier Holland was so tense he seemed brittle enough to crack. "Let me go after them," she said, her voice dipping to a venomous level. "Let me hunt down and wipe this disease-carrying animal off the face of the planet and chase it back into the demon doors it comes out of."

She stepped back and clasped her hands behind her, nearly trembling with unspent rage. "Sirs," she said, her gaze raking them. "I learned much from the indigenous peoples in the mountains. They have been dealing with this monster for centuries. There's a door in their ranges, it crosses over into the Canadian Yukon Territory. The bounty hunter source said they've been trying to sabotage black market efforts, because transactions up there feed labs in hot spots around the world. I should also add, sirs, that he's a shaman."

The general was on his feet. "You have a lead to where these things breed, maybe hide, where other nations not in the allied network can acquire a beast and therefore DNA from one?"

"Yes, sir. I have a lead. I do not have a location. The Ute scout will not deal with authorities outright. I was only allowed in because, frankly, I'm female, and while monitoring Butler's place, he'd heard me put down a virally infected man. The Ute are very wary of any government show of force, citing broken treaties in the past. But they want this gone as much as we do. They also don't want to see any nation, terrorists or otherwise, unleashing this menace on human populations—so they agreed to take me as far as they had gotten in their very underfunded search."

"We could cut this bull off at the pass, General," Colonel Vlasco said, his voice urgent as he gazed up at the now pacing general. "Rather than send Trudeau on missions like the one in North Korea—where we heard they got one of those monsters to experiment on after the fact, we could shut down the source of the samples."

"That's true, sir," Major Adams concurred. "Up to this point, all of us, anybody in this paranormal business, have been relying on random sightings, then having to spend endless resources and hours tracking the one or two we learn of to get to it before the other nations can capture it."

"Not to mention the collateral damage," Lieutenant Colonel Waters said. "By the time we find one, how many people have died? We've even had to go behind Butler's bar fights to be sure there was no . . . How many people have to be . . ."

Sasha blanched; revulsion made her dig her nails more deeply into her palms until she could feel small half-moon crescents forming in the heel of her hand. But she didn't blink.

"If we can find out where these various dimensional tears are, or demon doors as the indigenous clans call them," Dr. Holland said, speaking calmly and firmly, "then perhaps we can better understand how they come out, and how to block those portals with barriers—as well as shut down any black market attempts to broker dirty DNA."

"Make it happen. Special task force. Give Trudeau what she needs," the general said, heading for the door. "And, Xavier . . . See that she gets to go to the memorial service we'll have on base. That's the least we can do."

THE BASE WAS their family—dysfunctional, political, no different than anyone's family, really. It was all they knew. There were no civilians in attendance. It was cold outside, the flag was at half-mast, and the wind was whipping against her cheeks like a bitter slap in the face.

Mrs. Baker pretended to be one, though . . . a civilian,

which was cool. Sasha wondered who to give the flags to. What happened to the memories of men who had no one to look after them, to care for them once they were gone?

Suddenly she realized that VFW posts, veteran's memorial organizations, vet biker groups, and others who went around attending funerals made a great deal of sense. They would remember and she'd bring pictures of her squad to the keepers of the vaults, and she would have a good beer and a good cry and tell them about a valiant squad of young guys who died way before their time. She'd never understood why that was important until now. Before she'd always been invincible; so had they.

Taps left an eerie hole in her soul, like the baleful mourning howl of a lone wolf.

Yukon Territory, Canada . . .

TWO BODIES WRAPPED in furs and tied with ropes dropped onto the sleds. Dogs yipped and barked, ready to get on their way. Money changed hands between men. Thick gloves went back on huge male fists. Wintry blasts coated black eyelashes and eyebrows with snowflakes.

"When they wake up, they'll be scared shitless, so keep the ropes on 'em."

"SHE'S STABLE, JUST like I told you she would be," Dr. Holland said to the general. "Everything she's done is rational, exactly what any thinking person with her training would have done." He walked back and forth in the empty war room, his eyes locked with the general's. "For the past two days you've been testing her, and if she's going to get out of here to convene with her contact before he bolts, she has to get out of here ahead of the storm."

The general rubbed his palms over his face and sat down at the head of the table. "Xavier, for once you might be right."

At a loss, Dr. Holland just stared at the man.

"I never thought I'd see the day when we'd have such a breakthrough, but from all the reports and everything you've shown me, it seems that her DNA has adapted somehow to this demon wolf virus." He looked up at the doctor, his voice calm, his voice filled with regret. "I know you never approved of my methods, Xavier . . . but those young men who got sacrificed for science didn't die in vain. They'll help millions, possibly, if there's ever an outbreak. Understanding the key to Sasha's blood may very well be the answer."

The doctor looked off toward the monitors that surrounded the room but held his peace.

"It is madness, Xavier. What else could this be?"

The two stared at each other for a long time and the general finally shook his head.

"We can put a man on the moon, unravel the wonders of physical science, but we've entered this new millennium to find there are indeed dungeons and dragons, witches and trolls, warlocks and wizards, goddamned werewolves and vampires . . . I don't sleep at night, anymore, Xavier. Do you?"

Xavier Holland returned his gaze to the general and answered him honestly for the first time in years. "No, sir. I don't."

BOREDOM WAS HER watchword. Sleep was next to impossible. She stared at her dress uniform that she'd worn to the funeral as it hung neatly from a hanger on the back of a medical station door.

An MP knocked once, opened the door, and stood before

her without expression. "They are processing you out, Lieutenant. Dr. Holland has your orders and your release papers. As soon as he has all the paperwork signed, I will be your escort to the lot."

Just like that, he spun on his heel and stepped out.

"Hot damn!" Sasha whooped as the stone-faced MP left her room.

Sasha cleared her dorm bunk and began to hastily shove the few changes of clothes Doc had brought her into a duffel bag. Focus made her move swiftly; the protocol she and Hunter had established was simple: meet in the gym he'd told her about in Vancouver. It would be a good cover and he had a contact up there who could take them underground and off radar. She had to fly from Denver to Seattle, in surveillance-stripped clean clothes, then rent an SUV and head north—all before the storm. From there the storm would be their cover.

Not even the lab staff who'd become her friends could know where she was going . . . not this time, not yet. Not till they found out what was going on inside the chain of command. That was one of the key reasons she had to go underground with Hunter, but with the general thinking it was all his idea. Any glitches in communication had to seem technology related. But technology, as advanced as it was, happened to be the least of her worries.

Sasha flopped down on the bed with her bag next to her, swinging her legs like an impatient kid.

It was easy to beat equipment, fake it out; even the most sophisticated systems couldn't do what natural resources could. Therein lay the problem: as part of the paranormal unit, the Sirius Project had seers, shamans, and even those familiar with the dark arts as well as white magic. They had to.

Until now, the technology they had could only track the anomalies once they'd happened, once it was too late, once something had been loosed. But those with a sixth sense—they could give a heads-up warning, and the best of the best worked on the project . . . Even people with other technical skills, such as Winters, McGill, and Bradley, also had to have a little extra something to get into the unit. *They* were going to be a problem.

Her nerves coiled and uncoiled as she waited for Doc to show up and give her her walking papers. She tried to focus on what Hunter had said: in his underground shadow wolf society they'd have blockers, shamans just as strong as Winters and Clarissa on the psychic front, and keepers of the magic just as adept as Bradley, so they could cross their wires and throw them off the trail. All of it made her head hurt, the double-dealing and subterfuge. Yet all of it was necessary to keep sick men from thinking they could weaponize a demon, or worse, could mine one from an open dimensional portal. What was the general's sick plan? Hers and Hunter's plan was simple: make sure none of the crazy bastards could use it.

The sound of footsteps jerked Sasha's attention toward the door as she jumped to her feet. The doctor's easy smile greeted her as he came through the door.

"I know you're tired of waiting but your deployment orders were finally signed."

"Thank you, sir," Sasha said, beaming.

They both shared a look, and she knew he'd had to move mountains to make that happen quickly. They both also knew that in this environment, it would be foolish to say more.

"I want you to take care of yourself out there, Trudeau." Doc looked at her with such gentleness, even though his voice was gruff for the monitors. "I have something for you," he said, digging into the pocket of his white lab coat. "While I was up in Ute lands, an old shaman friend gave me this for you . . . he said it was his daughter's and he wanted you to have it to wear always—given all you did for his . . . people."

Dr. Holland tenderly grasped her palm when her mouth dropped open, and placed a small amber stone covered with etchings and framed in silver on a thick, handcrafted silver chain in the center of her hand. Immediately she knew whose it was and where it had come from. The honor was so great that the tight feeling returned to her chest.

There was nothing she could say in their present surroundings, so she let her eyes speak, and then went to her dear mentor and simply hugged him.

CHAPTER 13

IT HAD BEEN three very long days and even longer nights. On the second day, when he'd heard taps playing, it was all he could do to heed his grandfather's advice not to hunt the general down and tear out his esophagus. The look on Sasha's face alone tore at him. Then they'd escorted her back down into the labyrinth of tunnels that he couldn't chance being caught in. Not when they might be testing her, holding her captive, doing things to her that his wolf simply would not stand for.

However, as long as the doctor had sent periodic word that Sasha was safe and just being tested, he'd agreed with his grandfather's wait-and-see policy. Only blind faith had pried him away from his shadow post outside the base to go to Seattle and then make it to Vancouver before the storm. She'd only called his prepaid cell phone once from a prepaid one of her own, and then they'd ditched both phones. Only then could he get on a plane ahead of her and begin the hunt.

◆ ◆ ◆

"DOCTOR, DID YOU see this?" Clarissa said, walking over to the station where Xavier Holland had been going through reports.

The doctor looked up, his brows knitted, as he peered over half-lens Ben Franklin reading glasses. "What is it?"

Clarissa McGill quickly handed him a slide that was swabbed with a blood sample. Carefully lifting it from her gloved fingers, he rushed to a nearby microscope and studied the movement of the cells. Unable to believe his eyes, he increased the magnification and watched the fiercely aggressive activity on the slide. White blood cells had grown to twice the normal size, it seemed, to attack dark, oddly shaped black blood cells. The white cells surrounded them and the few normal red blood cells on the slide were slowly merging with the white cells, growing larger, to surround and absorb the antlike black cells.

"The contagion," Clarissa said, keeping her voice low so the others in the lab wouldn't hear. "It must have been dormant in her system—we didn't see it before."

"But look at how her immune system is fighting it," the doctor murmured, his eyes fixed on the slide. "It's making her stronger, her cells are carrying more oxygen, are more elastic. Red blood cells are not normally attack cells, but now, somehow, they are taking on the properties of white blood cells to absorb and conquer the contagion."

He drew away from the microscope. He'd only seen this once before, in a child, an infant that had been attacked. Not the blood, but the results—he'd been denied seeing any evidence of this under a microscope before. But they'd relentlessly tested Sasha while she was detained, and her blood had obviously remained normal for a three-day incubation before all hell broke loose under the surface of her skin. Amazing.

At first he'd thought it was a fluke, something that had

happened after he'd given the child, Max Hunter, an injection to stop the convulsions. Now he knew better. He began running to the high security area of the lab that required retina and fingerprint scans to open the vault. He had to know.

Clarissa was on his heels, and he wanted another doctor to witness, along with him, what could possibly be a vaccine breakthrough. It was a key that he and Lou Zang Chen had always hoped for. This wasn't a suppressant they had found; something in the shadow wolf blood actually built immunity. Silver Hawk would never allow him that much testing freedom, with good cause. But if something had changed in Sasha's blood, if something had been a catalyst to a dormant capacity for her body to heal itself . . .

His mind was on fire, his breaths short as he rushed into the vault. Loving Sasha the way he did, he wouldn't have dared introduce the virus in her just to see what might happen. That would have been reckless. But somehow, she had the virus in her system now. Silver Hawk had never allowed him to study Hunter . . . but they had Sasha's blood in the lab. Something about it was different. Never before had she had the werewolf cells tainting her blood . . .

Heart beating erratically, he walked through the cold room, Dr. McGill almost running to keep up with his long strides. This was impossible. Sasha had just been tested when she came back from North Korea. She had been with Rod prior to that, yet her blood was as it had always been . . . containing a slight anomaly, her shadow wolf secret buried deeply within her DNA chain.

He went to the section where blood samples from Rod Butler were housed and opened the flat panel.

"Doctor, get me a slide and put a fresh sample of Sasha Trudeau's blood on it," Xavier Holland commanded as he donned a pair of hazmat gloves, a mask, and goggles to extract a hypodermic sample of Rod Butler's blood from the tray marked INFECTED SAMPLES.

Rushing over to the microscope in the vault, he waited until Clarissa McGill stepped back and he was peering through the square, high-powered lenses before he added a drop of Rod Butler's tainted blood to Sasha's. But something was very, very wrong. Frantic now, he went to another microscope and quickly found a clean slide. He placed a drop of Rod's blood on it and peered into the microscope in horror, then tore away from it, pulling out sample after sample, repeating the process.

"Doctor, what's wrong?" she asked, alarmed.

Xavier Holland looked up from the microscope, sweat beading on his brow. "Get the general on the telephone. All the werewolf samples are gone. This is normal, untainted human blood."

SHE HATED WAITING, but waiting in airports *really* sucked, especially once all the food concessions closed. What sucked worse was waiting in an airport knowing a storm was coming, knowing that a delayed flight was possible but a canceled flight was probable . . . knowing she had somewhere to really, seriously be.

DOROTHY WILKERSON LET out a small grunt of disgust as she hoisted herself up from the living room sofa to get the telephone. Rarely did she have a chance to just sit and watch her favorite evening game shows and tonight, *Deal or No Deal* was on. Couldn't they just allow her poor husband to rest? Donald had worked nonstop for them for over forty years; at least they could occasionally let him have dinner with his wife. His career had stolen their dream of having children of their own; what more did they want from him?

She looked at the caller ID, which was blank, and

knew that it had to be the base. She picked up the telephone, and set her prim mouth hard. If the general didn't pick up on his private office phone, then obviously he didn't want to be bothered.

"Hello," she said curtly, prepared to shield her husband from any intrusion.

"Dot, this is Xavier. There's been an emergency in the lab. I need to speak to the general."

Her attitude immediately shifted from disdain to panic. She never knew the types of projects her husband had aegis over, but she knew Dr. Holland was revered and that he *never* called. There was something in the tone of his voice that made her begin to run through the house.

"Yes, yes, right away," she said after the second it took for her to recover her breath. Huffing through the house, she called out to her husband in a long, strident yell. "Donald!"

She was walking and talking to her husband out loud as she barged into his office. "Donald, there's some sort of—"

Her eyes couldn't make sense of what she was seeing. The phone fell away from her hand. His chest was gone. His face was gone. His throat was gone. But he was still sitting upright in his chair. Something had literally scooped the front of him out like he was an overripe melon and the red and white tangle of flesh and bones had been left as a gruesome pile on his desk. She backed away slowly, the scream struggling in her throat before it finally tore free.

SASHA SAID A little prayer of thanks. Hers was probably the last flight that would make it out before things really got nasty. The heaviest barrage of weather was still up above the Canadian border, but ice and rough headwinds were sweeping down from Seattle and they had to fly directly into it.

THE BASE WAS on full military lockdown. Everyone who worked with the project was a suspect. Xavier Holland sat before the investigators with Dr. McGill beside him.

"No. It couldn't have been Lieutenant Sasha Trudeau. She left earlier today headed toward Denver to catch a flight to go on a mission that would put her up near Seattle," Xavier Holland said emphatically.

The investigating agents looked at him, unmoved.

"You say you can't raise her by telephone," the older of the two agents said.

"There's a storm, she's either in flight or in an airport en route to her target," Holland argued.

"Mighty convenient," the other agent said.

"I want to speak to the colonel," Holland snapped. "This is bullshit. We can take this all the way to the Oval Office if you want to. The Secretary of the Army needs to be informed. This is a cabinet-level issue. What's more, you are not going to come in here and jeopardize decades of research and have inexperienced agents handling biohazardous materials that, yes, gentlemen, can kill you."

"One of your experiments get out of the cage, Doc? Were you all working on making another one like Butler?" The older of the two CIA agents looked at Holland hard, his semibalding scalp gleaming between combed-over brunette strands under the bright war room lights. He looked uncomfortable in his suit and adjusted himself repeatedly in it.

"You need Pentagon clearance for that kind of information," Holland said evenly. "But no. I would *never* make another one like Butler."

"This *is* a Pentagon-level emergency when a four-star general of U.S. Special Ops Command gets eaten to death in his own home by something very similar to what you weapons boys have been cooking up in your labs—no offense, ma'am," the younger blond agent said, glimpsing Clarissa McGill. He looked like he was fresh out of the academy, but clearly had to have skills and rank, or he wouldn't have been in charge of such a sensitive case. "We're all integrated under the same Homeland Security umbrella, so cut the elitist, jurisdictional crap. A man died here, word is you guys make or research the sort of thing that may have killed him, so if you guys—and ladies," he added as an afterthought, "know anything, tell us."

"*Doctor*," Clarissa McGill corrected, her gaze narrowed on both agents. "And I know for a fact that Sasha Trudeau wasn't a part of this. She is headed toward her mission destination—on *the general's* orders."

"Specifically, how do you know?" the lead agent scoffed. "What are you? Psychic, Doc?"

Clarissa McGill offered them a blank expression. "Yes. As a matter of fact, I am."

THE ROADS WERE getting bad. He'd been hanging out in the gym for hours waiting for Sasha to show. This was the only place that made sense to him. A bar would have too many humans. This old boxing dive was on the wrong side of town, only a few serious fitness buffs and athletes came here—guys tough as nails. Everybody else went to the more chichi gyms that served double lattes and fitness smoothies. If something were to get crazy, they needed to be in the warehouse district where there were plenty of shadows and few potential witnesses. *Damn . . . Sasha, baby, where are you?*

He'd been battling an uneasy feeling all day. Dexter, a shadow from the Canadian side, had told him things were heating up. There was a lot of activity rumbling behind the demon doors. Dexter didn't need to tell him that, he could feel it in his gut. His amulet was practically humming. But he hadn't seen Dexter yet. In fact, his contact for the gym hadn't shown, either. Where was Guillaume?

The thick scent of aging sweat hung in the air like a mildewed curtain. Hunter kept his peripheral vision sharp as he pumped iron, doing slow bicep curls with a short, fifty-pound dumbbell. Missing nothing, not even the mouse that hunted for protein-bar crumbs in the corner, he watched a few remaining stragglers spar with each other or work out solo against heavy bags.

Dim lights, long, looming shadows coming through the warehouse windows from the wharf; an icy blast of winter slicing through the humid gym funk each time someone entered or left kept him on guard. More people were leaving now. He was slowly beginning to regret picking this place. He'd wanted Sasha to be able to slip in somewhere remote, shadow littered, where no questions would be asked. Down here, nobody ever saw anything—even if a man got shot and dropped at one's feet. People either didn't give a shit or didn't give a shit. It was a good place to launch getting lost from, a good LKL, last known location. From here, one disappeared. But the fact that both his contacts, Dexter and Guillaume, had seemingly disappeared, and Sasha hadn't showed, made him wonder.

Max switched the dumbbell to his left hand and began the slow, burning curls. The shadows were long in the gym, but not long enough for him to have missed a flash, a split-second glimpse of something moving quickly toward him. He stood, spun out of the way, and the only reason he didn't immediately attack was that he had to be sure it wasn't a friend.

After two more attempts at an ambush, Dexter and Guillaume stepped out of the shadows wearing combat boots and long, black leather coats to conceal their heavy artillery. The few stragglers in the gym smiled sinister smiles and locked the doors, slowly revealing Uzis that had been hidden in gym bags. Max's grip tightened on the dumbbell. Dexter's dark brown hair was matted to his skull with sweat, his skin was pale, pupils dilated, and he looked twice the size he'd been when they'd last seen each other. Guillaume's long, platinum-blond ponytail was practically dreads and his pallor was so ashen he seemed closer to dead than alive—but his previously slight body was built as though he'd been competing in professional lifting competitions. And just like Dexter's eyes, Guillaume's normally crystal-blue eyes were bloodshot and dilated.

"What's going on, brothers? You don't look well." Max centered his weight, holding the dumbbell tighter, and now praying Sasha didn't find him tonight.

"We're fine. Good to see you, too, *mon frère*. Glad you came," Guillaume said, blotting the sweat from his face with his massive forearm. "Got a proposition for you."

"It's very, very cool," Dexter said, baring fangs as he spoke. "This shit is out of control. It feels so good, Max, like . . . I can't explain it."

"What did you do?" Max said carefully, watching the Uzi carriers in his peripheral vision as his shadow contacts, Dexter and Guillaume, began to circle. The armed men behind him had taken a stance, safeties off their weapons. Several Goth females he hadn't seen before entered the open room from the shadowed back office area of the warehouse, wearing pure leather and lace and carrying pump shotguns filled with silver shells. He could smell it. Max snarled.

"You've had this going for you all your life . . . this extra kick to the shadows, man," Guillaume said. "Why didn't you tell us it felt like this?"

"When did you get bitten?" Max asked, panicking. "How many attacked you?"

Dexter laughed and couldn't seem to stop. His voice was shrill and then kept getting deeper and rougher until his nose began to elongate and his fangs became curled and yellowed. "Don't be stupid!" he finally said. "You shoot up with it, man. It's like being on meth or crystal. You get the strength, the sex kick. It's just coming down that's a true bitch."

"Nasty side effect is it makes you crave human flesh but . . . that's in plentiful supply," Guillaume added with a shrug. "What's hard to get is clean shadow to bring you down before you can't control your shifts. The blood can't have any werewolf taint in it, or it'll just get you higher. You, my friend, are a pollutant, so don't worry. We don't need you to open up a vein. But the rest of the pack, their blood does what Mother Nature intended. Clean shadow blood goes in, heals you in a day or two like a stabilizer. Like taking a lude or a V after you've been high too long. That's where you come in. The pack trusts you, so you can get them to give up clean blood. Tell them whatever, and if it's coming from you, man, they'll believe you. Can't use another user, though. Once this shit is in your system, it's in it till you croak. We could make a mint with this product. It's *brand-new,* man. Who knew?"

Dexter was shivering but still seemed like he wanted in on the negotiations. "Let's put it this way, the humans had a stash of werewolf toxin that finally got out into the black market . . . it's damned easier to get it out of vials than off one of those motherfuckers."

"One of us always gets badly ripped up when trying to capture them alive," Guillaume said nonchalantly. "Recently, when we figured this awesome shit out, we tried getting a live one of our own. Results were ugly and the damned thing torched when our hunter crew had to blow it away or die. That's what's been happening to the different human factions who want one, too. The only way to drag one in alive is to figure out what human has the virus, and then grab him before the full moon. Gotta get the SOB before he Turns, get his blood just before he goes into transition while enough virus is pumping through him. But nobody but the American feds has really been able to figure out yet how to contain the damned thing once you catch it."

"That's what drives the price up," Dexter said, sniffing with a leering smile. "Supply and demand, brother."

"But God bless America, the humans had a live one in a lab, until they had to snuff him. Had an exhaustive supply of the good stuff, already packaged in vials. We heard you were seeing this chick that has pure shadow in her. Maybe between her and some of the other bitches that you could get to be donors, we could do a little business with the humans. Once they see there's another use for the product beyond making soldiers, somebody will wanna get paid. You know once a new drug is made, you can't keep it off the streets. Besides, they need another werewolf to run tests on. We can get them that, since we have virus now— in fact, seems every one of their nations wants one to play with. All we have to do is shoot up some Joe Schmoe, they lock him up, and he'll Turn on the next full moon. Shadows who want the product, can pay for the product—then pay for what they need to come down."

"You can buy your way out of being a beta, man," Dexter said, laughing. "Fuck an alpha challenge. With this shit in your veins—you're invincible."

"Here's the best part, though," Guillaume said with a sinister smile. "Not only will their nations pay, but we've got a contact real high up that found out it works on them, too." He looked both ways and his snarly smile widened to reveal yellowing teeth. "If the humans shoot up with a werewolf vial, they get like us. If they then take a hit of shadow blood, it brings 'em right back." He leaned in toward Max. "But it's a permanent condition. Once they go werewolf, they can't go back . . . have to keep taking the shadow hits—this is where we rule the free fucking world."

"I know you want in, man," Dexter said. "You're the only one who got bitten back in the day and have both wolf strains in you—you've always been rogue. You're like us. The three of us could hunt werewolves together, go through demon doors and bring them out alive. Normal shadows can't. Humans can't. Do you know how much one would bring on the open market? So, what do ya say? You in or out?"

Max stared at them for a moment, trying to decide which one to attack first.

Guillaume's gaze narrowed. "The choice is really rather simple, *mon ami*." He held up two massive fists. "On the one hand is world-dominating wealth and power, on the other hand is your certain demise. You can either work with us and make your lady help us with her inside-the-system connections . . . or we can just go find Silver Shadow and the rest of your pack that's still holding out for your decision. Be wise, think carefully. We can still make the downer product the hard way, with your asses in chains. You decide. But remember, these were the shadows who always ostracized you. Surely you're not going to protect a bunch of sons of bitches that made your life a living hell?" Guillaume shook his head as he lowered his hands and clasped them behind his back. "Tell me you're not that stupid."

"Who's your contact?" Max asked as calmly as possible. They obviously needed something else from him, or he wouldn't still be alive. It had to be his connection to Sasha and her ability to get in and out of the labs. Max measured his response, trying to probe for more information. "I like to know who I'm dealing with."

"Uh-uh, uuuhhhh . . ." Guillaume said, wagging his finger. "Cut us out, *non*. We cannot have that." He glanced at the human henchmen. "These gentlemen also need to get paid. They work for various government human interest groups who want to be sure their investments are protected. So, I cannot, *mon ami*—even though we go way back."

"Not to cut you out," Max said, backing up as they continued circling. "But to be sure we don't get screwed. Like, I don't want to find me and my lady chained to a lab table for the rest of our lives."

"Don't worry. A human who tried to back out of the deal got his face ripped off. We won't let you get screwed—but we won't be, either." Guillaume stared at Max hard and dropped his voice to a lethal whisper. "Now, for the last time, old friend, are you in or out?"

Footfalls yanked their attention in the same direction at the same time. Sasha! Unaware of the ambush, she broke through the barred door in a black leather blur, her black combat boots sounding as she landed hard, one hand on the floor to catch her balance.

"Get her! Take her down alive, what's in her veins is worth her weight in gold!" Guillaume shouted to the henchmen by the door.

Max whirled around before Guillaume could bring his attention back to him, and with the dumbbell in hand, he crashed it into Dexter's jaw. Guillaume transformed right before his eyes with Dexter, both ripping through their clothes to become huge, upright walking lycanthropes with extended demon claws, red glowing eyes, and distorted snouts. Sasha moved like greased lightning, going in and out of shadows, silver nine gleaming as she took a single, dead-aim shot each time, felling snarling predators by the exits with a bullet right between their eyes.

Spinning into the shadows, Max came out in flashes, wielding the dumbbell to crush skulls, break femurs, and drop Uzis before they got a shot off. But to his horror, Sasha rushed into the commotion, as panicked human henchmen began firing. Machine gunfire split the walls and shattered windows, spitting death in her direction. Enraged, half-transformed demons dashed after Max, chasing him into the shadows, but their deformed shapes never took to the shadows.

"Run!" Max shouted. "They can't cloak in the darkness!"

To give Sasha time to somersault away from a spray of Uzi bullets, Max hurled the short dumbbell, felling Guillaume temporarily. As Dexter fled, Max grabbed the long two-hundred-and-fifty-pound bench press weights by one end of the plate stack and swung it like a discus—releasing it to wipe out six human weapons bearers.

Sasha became liquid motion, heading into the shadows at breakneck speed. Max was right behind her. The demons were on the move, and they had to get them. Out in the frigid blast, he and Sasha hunted side by side. She ditched her spent nine-millimeter, threw him a partially spent Uzi, and kept one for herself. He sniffed the magazine. They glanced at each other and nodded. Silver.

As they stalked through the shadows for their fast-moving prey, they both seemed to know that this was only the tip of the iceberg. A slight scrape sounded above. They both looked up and fired. A huge compressor came hurtling down. Max pushed Sasha away and crashed through the wall. He heard her gunfire report and then heard the gun hit the ground. A large metal rail whizzed out of nowhere toward him and grazed his shoulder as he ducked. He headed toward Sasha, but a huge predator tackled him from above.

Zigzagging through the debris and warehouse shadows, Sasha had the dark-haired demon in her sights, if she could just get around him . . .

Cutting through the buildings, she tried to take a shortcut to head him off. She refused to lose him, had to bring the target down. Max exploded out of the side of a building with his hands gripped around the throat of the demon, its claws digging into his neck—she gave up pursuit of her target and was wolf.

Airborne, she came down on the back of the huge demon, savagely tearing into his neck. He screamed and released Max for a second as he tried to get Sasha off his back. In that brief moment when he stood, Max became all wolf, his massive jaws gouging out the demon's exposed underbelly.

Entrails everywhere, Sasha had the upper section of the beast, Max had the lower section of it, and they pulled in unison, severing the body. Max leaped over what was left and brutally tore the head from the body, exploding the creature into a bright spray of burning embers.

He nuzzled her quickly, eyes alert, she flanked him for a moment as they caught the scent of the one that got away and bounded in the direction of the fleeing demon. But as they leaped from shadow to shadow he began to skid to a halt to slow down as his amulet warmed, then began to burn.

It all happened in slow motion. He didn't have time to teach her to read the warning and she was leaping shadows too fast. He shifted into human form and tried to keep up with her wolf, yelling for her not to follow it into the shadow where it was headed. But she turned back to look at him in midair. Pure momentum did the rest as he yelled, "No!"

THIS WAS THE coldest, darkest shadow she'd ever encountered. It had no bottom, it seemed, because she just kept tumbling, falling faster and faster until her breath fled from her lungs. Then as the darkness abated to a dim twilight on the way down, fetid scents consumed her, turning her stomach.

Scorching heat replaced the freezing darkness and tore at her skin, collapsed her chest, and made each breath a hot wheeze. Smoke caused her eyes to water, and when she hit bottom, the sound of cracking, snapping objects made her think she'd broken every bone in her body. She couldn't breathe, much less pick up a scent in the horrible, foul air.

Dazed and badly bruised, she gasped for breath, trying to stand. But her wolf had retreated from the sheer uncertainty of it all and her human hands pushed against what felt like bones and gore. When her eyesight finally took it all in, she resisted a scream and stood quickly on a pile of rotting bodies.

Various stages of decay squished between her toes. The long silver amulet around her neck was glowing white-hot. Soon growls and barks filled the air with unmistakable howls of the hunt. She was under attack.

Spinning in a quick circle, she tried to detect any form of cover, but the shadow trees were all filled with eyes. Survival her objective, she dug her hands into the pile and drew out the longest, most jagged bones she could and armed herself with a weapon in each hand.

Something moved quickly and lunged. She ducked and came up beneath it with the sharp-edged bones and was showered with blood. Whatever it was, she got the best of it. Crouching, feral, she snarled as she keened her senses for the next attack. Something moved fast, was on one side of her, then the other. She spun and it came out to lunge for her throat and drew back. She speared it in the eye, a second of hesitation from the silver cost that particular beast.

Backing up quickly, she dug in the pile for another bone to replace the one that had just saved her life. But rather than come away with a weapon, something had her by the wrist and was yanking her down.

She would have swung a blade wild and cut off her own arm rather than go in the direction of the carnage to become a part of it. From some reservoir of strength she plunged her other hand down and stabbed as hard as she could—and fell back as she broke free. But multiple things landing and beginning to come out of the shadows told her that it would only be a matter of time. There were just too many of them. They all leered at her, walking upright on horribly half-bent hind legs, eyes gleaming, and fangs like yellowed, curved hooks dripping green-gray ooze. Their thick, matted fur was writhing with larvae. Surrounded, she clasped her amulet, looped it over her head, and held it out, brandishing it with one hand while wielding a thigh bone with the other.

The largest one came forward first, sniffed the air and smiled, then lunged. Sasha ducked, swung the amulet and caught him in the cheek, then lobbed a punch that sent blood splattering. The place where the amulet struck began to burn, and the beast howled, quickly becoming completely engulfed in flames. The others snarled and barked at her for a few moments, eyes narrowed, and drew nearer.

It was in their gleaming, evil gazes. They were weighing the odds. She might burn a few to death, but not all. If they rushed her, it was over.

They went airborne. Sasha swung the amulet, spinning in a circle. To her surprise, the ones on the front line burned in the air, raining cinders down on her as a ring of fire set up a protective wall. A loud crashing sound made her jump back and she saw Max push off the feeding pile and rush toward the fire bearing an Uzi. He extended his hand through the inferno toward her and she clasped it without thinking twice, pulling him into the protective ring. The moment he was inside, he opened up with silver shells, cutting a swath in the twilight darkness, causing a demon retreat and opening a path.

"Go!" he shouted, pulling her out of the safe ring.

She looped the amulet over her neck, running hard and

fast beside him. Sharp objects cut into her feet and soft gore made her refuse to look down. It was getting darker and darker. The encroaching cold was consuming, limb paralyzing.

"You have to call your wolf to get out of here," he shouted, breathing hard. "Don't think—feel. Do!"

In the next bound the gun fell away from his body and his forward-moving form transitioned into the beautiful, massive black wolf that he was inside. Only his amulet swung as he looked back at her with worried amber eyes. She ran to him and the fluid silver form came down on all fours to run hard and fast against the cold.

Heavy headwinds knocked them back as they entered a realm of complete darkness. Total trust was her only companion. She had to hear his breaths, follow his heartbeat, and trust his body heat as they flanked each other— scent was near impossible in the freezing, howling blackness. Then there was light. Gray twilight and asphalt. They were back at the warehouse district.

Max scented the ground and shook his head no.

She transitioned. "Damn!"

He transitioned beside her and punched a warehouse wall. "Son of a bitch!"

"I can't believe we lost one of 'em! Shit!" She walked in a circle, naked and shivering.

Max pulled her into a shadow. "We've got to find our clothes and get out of here."

She nodded and moved with him, limping slightly, the soles of her feet bleeding.

SHE HAD NEVER been big on being a thief, but sneaking into a vacant hotel room and getting a hot, soapy shower after where they'd been—hey. Having a fresh pair of clothes to put on and some gun shop ammo—definitely.

Wolf stealth was awesome, but she felt more at home now that she had twin nine-millimeters stashed under her vest, a couple of assault rifles in easy reach in the car they'd hotwired, and a beautiful, serrated-edge hunting blade that looked like something out of the movie *Psycho* tucked in her new boots. What could she say? Call her crazy, but after the shit she'd just seen, she was a weapons-carrying kinda girl. Only thing missing was some C-4.

Glad that Max's healing hands were enough and she didn't have to eat to close up the cuts and bruises, she thanked the Almighty. There was no question that she'd been sickened enough by what she'd seen to want to shut the doors to every hellhole realm.

Max seemed as disgusted as she was, if not more so. Shadows were involved. Now he understood where she was coming from; not that she had ever wanted him to feel this sense of betrayal. But it did open his perspective on things—betrayal was betrayal. Some humans and non-humans alike did things for selfish, personal gain. It made life suck for those individuals who were trying to live by some code called fair and moral. Her people, her government, had some shady dealings going on within its ranks and that made *her* ill.

They sat together in a bar where he knew some people, staring down into their Guinness stout. She felt badly that he couldn't trust a soul now, except his grandfather, Doc Holland, and her.

Sasha covered his hand, watching the disillusion glitter in his intense expression. "I know," she said. "I just have you, Doc, and Silver Hawk."

Max shook his head. "They were Shadow clan, Sasha . . . for thousands of years our mission, our honor, has been the same."

She nodded and squeezed his hand. "A four-star general was playing God, and we don't know why or how far up the food chain this bull goes on our end . . . There was some personal gain involved. Had to be."

Max lifted his head abruptly and stared at the television behind her. She spun in her chair.

"They killed him," Max said flatly. "Must have gone to his home, entered right through a window or vent shaft, and did him before he could draw his next breath. They said they'd ripped the face off a guy who didn't want to play their game anymore. How much you wanna bet that your general didn't have a heart attack like the media says?"

Sasha just closed her eyes and took a sip of her beer. "I would have liked to have asked him some hard questions. Damn! Guess it's between him and his maker now."

"You'll have to be very careful going home . . . there's going to be a witch hunt, or in our case, a wolf hunt."

"I know," she said quietly, setting her beer down with precision. "Storm is almost going full blast, give it another hour or so." She looked up at him and touched his face. "I'm going to call in from a pay phone using the code that connects me anywhere. I'll tell them what I know so far and will make contact through the special line in Holland's office that I know is recorded six ways from Sunday. That way, he won't be implicated in keeping vital intel from them—I'm reporting in to a trusted source that I'm supposed to stay in contact with because of my medical condition. Then I'll say I'm on the move because I'm being hunted, but I've made contact with my guide, you. Then it won't seem like I'm running or you're running . . . or like we were anywhere in the vicinity when the general, literally, lost his face."

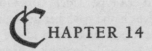

CHAPTER 14

SASHA STOOD WITH effort. Even though the wounds had healed, her body was tired, her heart heavy, muscles sore, and the beer was making her sleepy. She slowly made her way over to a pay phone, glancing at everyone, and trusting no one as she walked to the back of the establishment. Most of the customers had left because of the imminent storm, but something was raising the hair on her arms. She glanced at Max, who was engrossed in a heavy conversation on his newly stolen cell phone, but he also looked uneasy from where she stood watching him. A strange scent flitted by her nose as she connected the call and left Holland an urgent, detailed message. On guard, she kept glancing around. The scent of death was near; she just wasn't sure how close.

The second she hung up the telephone, a tall, fair, femininely handsome man stepped out of the shadows. His sudden presence made her start and then she composed herself. She was not in the mood to verbally joust with a vampire tonight. He seemed to know that and the fact that he was irking her also seemed to amuse him. Twisted. But she had to admit he had style, just like the vamp in Korea had, but not as much.

Giving this new vampire a quick appraisal as they both assessed each other, she noted his long sandy-brown hair that flowed over his shoulders like a shimmering wave of silk and the perfectly tailored faun-hued velvet jacket he wore. That helped her judge his undead age—definitely an eighteen-hundred-era-type. Thick, corn-silk lashes framed his wide hazel eyes as he gave her an appreciative, once-over-lightly gaze. He offered her a lovely smile from his full, cherub-pink lips and shook his hair back in that sensually arrogant way only prima donna vampires could.

"Well," he finally said, having preened to his satisfaction. "It seems the baron's assessment is correct. You are absolutely delicious."

"I don't know who you are. I don't know where you came from. But I'm having a really long night."

"And charming, too, I see." The vampire sniffed, leaning against the wall beside her, nonplussed.

"Can I help you? Like—"

"The question is, can I help *you*, *ma chérie*?" He placed a finger to his lips. "I could be your Deep Throat, *oui*?" he said with a droll little chuckle. "Geoff will positively die. Again."

Sasha frowned. She hated men who laughed at their own jokes, especially dead men who used double entendres.

"I think you gentlemen gossip too much. The baron was disappointed, I'm sure." She was out. The last thing she had time for was vampire mind games.

"Let me say this before your amour catches a whiff of me downwind. He's in such a primal state of mind, and I do not want to have to regenerate from a battle . . . not to mention that it's murder on my tailor." He pulled his perfect cuffs down and pushed away from the wall. "I have only agreed to help you because the baron lost a bet with me. It seems that although he is several hundred years older than I, and he used every power of persuasion on you, all he did was arouse you a tad . . . but not bed you, she-shadow."

Sasha stepped back and narrowed her gaze.

"Oh, please, we all know about the other variations on a theme. She-shadows are fantastically exotic to us because we cannot bite them in the throes . . . your blood is tainted with the silver wolf and it just makes us ghastly ill." He pressed his hand to his chest and made a face. "So, one must use extraordinary restraint when seducing one . . . which is also difficult, especially when you hard-transition in bed. Silver about the neck," he said, nodding at Sasha's amber charm. "Wards, amber, turquoise, it's a wonderful sport."

"Get to the part about why you would help me, anyway. The baron didn't screw me, so that means what, exactly?"

"So harsh a term, 'screw.' We're vampires . . . we luxuriate in the sensual arts. Nevertheless, the baron was intrigued by you, challenged, smitten . . . a tad obsessed."

"Be serious. After being dead for however long, with all the babes in history, you have got to give me a better reason than that."

He smiled and waved his graceful hand. "Touché. Fine. He helped you for the same reason I will. Our way of life is being challenged by this arms-race madness. As long as you couldn't really do much more than shoot each other, what did we care? Spilled blood was your folly and our feast. You, my dear, or your human counterparts, I should say, are part of our food chain. Once humans began the insanity of potentially obliterating each other in a nuclear holocaust, those of us, demons though we have been called, with special interest in unpolluted blood, had to become involved. Think of it as conservation. If you are dust and ash, soon we would be, also."

"Comforting thought." Sasha shook her head and folded her arms over her chest. "So, you monitor our nukes."

"Of course we do. We are much more intelligent. We

can't allow you to blow yourselves up." He sighed melodramatically. "You've become lemmings leaping over the edge of your own demise, now that you've discovered some of the nether regions of the apocalypse—otherwise known as demon doors . . . merely dimensional distortions caused by your own incessant warring. But like naughty children, you've opened the one with the snarling dogs. How quaint."

"And that's a problem for you, how?"

"You don't know?"

A hard frown creased her brow as she stared at him, very aware of his hypnotic power and his vast strength hidden by the graceful exterior. A monster was a monster. That's why she wasn't screwing the baron while getting intel in North Korea, no matter how tempting it had been. Shogun was another matter, but she shook the thought.

"Enlighten me," she said flatly.

"We have all night if you lose the big bad wolf . . . I could bring about a hundred and fifty years of practice to bear . . ."

Sasha snarled.

"I suppose not." He sighed and pulled a lace handkerchief from his sleeve and gently blotted his nose.

Switching tactics, Sasha let her shoulders relax. "All right, I'm just snarly because I'm frustrated." She watched the vampire perk up. "Knowledge, intel, that's what really gets me motivated to bargain."

"A game . . ." he said, delight and sensuality singeing his voice.

She looked over at Max, noting that his lip was beginning to curl.

"He has an awful temper, doesn't he?"

"Yeah, so let me just say, I'll negotiate. But I need to understand what's in this for you."

He smiled and studied his nails a bit. "We hate the werewolves. Infected, uninfected, ours is a long feud. I'm sure by now you know that vampires forget no slight. But these *wolves* . . . they compromise our way of life, poach our territories, and generally befoul the feeding grounds. We have enough willing humans to trade their souls for power, money, fantastic sex, regular blood feedings, and immortality—we don't need to do serial killings to eat people. That is soooo twelfth century." He sniffed into his hanky. "We understand that there are some nefarious forces that are about to try a very bizarre test, and we do not want this virus out among the general public any more than you." He leaned over and breathed in her fresh-showered scent. "Any human with that wolf virus in their blood is off limits for dinner. If it goes widespread, it will be just like the great potato famine for our species."

He pulled back and glanced at Max, who had stood up. "Now that I have given you something, later you can give me something . . . since fair exchange is no robbery."

"How far does it go—how wide, how high?"

He blew her a kiss as he disappeared. "Very high up, across many constituencies . . . people you wouldn't imagine, places you wouldn't imagine. Ta-ta."

Uneasy from what she'd learned, she walked back to the table where Max was standing. They both looked around and sat at the same time.

"Vampire source? Or pickup?"

"Both."

He nodded. "They always are."

"At least this guy wasn't hostile."

"Yeah," Max said, sipping his beer but not relaxing. "But we have to be careful, though. We don't know who's working both sides of the fence."

"True," she said, her voice clipped, and not liking his tone in the least. "I'm aware of that."

She watched the muscle in his jaw pulse for a moment before he downed his beer.

"Just make sure you are," he finally snapped, and called the bartender over.

"What's that supposed to mean?" she practically said through her teeth.

He accepted the beer from the bartender and set it down hard on the bar. "Mine."

"What?" She could *not* believe he was going there. "Oh, give me a break, man."

"I'm not sharing, under any circumstances, fuck that."

She tilted her head, suddenly feeling dangerous. "Let's get one thing straight. You don't own me. That whole 'mine-yours' thing was—"

"Said playing for keeps," he said with a snarl underlying his words.

"Be clear," she said, the lethal tone in her voice matching his. "I'm still a free agent. I will always be my own woman. I'm with you because it's my choice, not because I'm afraid of you—so if a little werewolf taint is making you act stupid, you'd better check that bullshit at the door."

His gaze narrowed on her. His eyes held a bizarre combination of outrage and hurt. Okay, maybe she had gone a little over the top by flinging the werewolf taint in his face, but he'd pushed her.

"I'm tainted, too, probably—from roughhousing with Rod. All right," she said after a strained pause. Fury lingered in the small space between them, and she used her words to cut through it, but she still wasn't taking his crap. "We just went through some unbelievable madness, so we're both hyped. Let's everybody calm down and get back on point."

Sasha sent her gaze toward the shelves behind the bar and picked up her beer to take a long, quenching sip. "I'll watch your back, you watch mine," Sasha said as she set her pilsner glass down and raked her fingers through her hair. Men. "The vamp said that they were monitoring everybody's activities, knew that special interests were trying to get the virus out into the general population— but the reason they were helping us was because it would affect their food chain if that happened. Now I owe the asshole."

"No you don't. You don't owe him jack. He was picking your brain and only got as much from you as you knew. That's why I hate those vampire SOBs. Slimy. If he told you a name, a chain of command, something you didn't know, then I'd say, yeah, you owe him. We've got solid leads—we know Guillaume and Dexter went rogue. Like they told me, somebody tore off the general's face, and stole Rod's tainted blood and replaced it—that means, like Holland told you earlier, there's an internal leak. Right now, we don't know who's the puppet master . . . but guaranteed, that vampire who approached you was gathering intel so they can do a hit. They're not big on Western due process." Max leaned forward and hunched over his beer, surly now.

She rubbed her palms down her face, hating to admit that his assessment was probably right. It was the jealous male thing that had made her check him. "I'm exhausted. That has to be it. I should have seen that clear as day."

"You're a free agent, you can see it or not. It's not my business, I suppose." He slid off his stool and stood.

She held his arm. "All right. Maybe I took it—"

"It's cool," he said, yanking away. He glanced at her hand. "No ring, no permanent bond. Fuck the shadow culture, right?"

She closed her eyes with a groan and dug her fingers into her hair as she leaned over her beer. "No. Just a battle-weary woman who is not used to being told what to do—and who will never get used to that . . . but who has honor." She glanced up at him. "I have more class than to screw some stray vampire for some intel, and the fact that you said something to me really pissed me off." She sat back and took an angry sip of her beer. "But you always gotta look at things from the side of the person doing the accusing." She glanced up at him. "Would you have done it if a stray vamp female sporting a pair of double-D jugs blew in your ear with some info? Should I have come up to you and said, down, boy—mine?"

He looked away, jaw pulsing, but she noticed he hadn't moved. "It's not like that . . . I—"

"I what!" She set her beer down hard, sloshing the dark brown fluid out of her glass. "Either you trust me as your partner—on every level—or you don't. Tell me right fucking now, or I'm out. I'm not going through this every time we have to—"

"Listen," he said, leaning forward to speak to her more privately. "What say we get lost until we get eight good hours of sleep? Eat. Replenish. We can't do a thing while we're both about to drop where we stand. Fatigue will make anyone edgy, all right? I'm sorry."

She looked at him hard and then looked away.

"I'm tired, you're tired . . . and I almost lost you behind a demon door—so, yeah, seeing you cozy up to one of the most dangerous breed of entities shook me for a minute. There. You satisfied?"

Sasha began fastening her leather bomber jacket without looking at him, but despite her resolve to remain pissed off, she felt that emotion slowly ebbing.

"I'm beat, need to go lie down, curl up somewhere warm and sleep off the adrenaline rush."

"You're seducing me," she said, unable to stifle a yawn.

"I was just on my cell with the home pack," he said in a weary tone as though sudden fatigue from their argument had drained the last of his energy. "I'll fill you in about what happened to the general on the way while we find somewhere to hole up for the night—somewhere nice. And you're safe. I swear all I can do is sleep."

WOODS WOKE UP and struggled against his binds, trying to sit up. Fisher coughed and then began bucking his body, fighting to get free.

"Whoa, whoa, easy, gentlemen," Crow Shadow said, a spill of black hair falling across his face in a curtain as he cut a piece of wild ram off the fire spit.

A large man stood slowly, thick and tall, his motions lumbering as he picked up two canteens. He poured some water into his mouth first to demonstrate it wasn't tainted.

"I'm going to cut you loose," Bear Shadow said calmly, flashing a huge hunting knife with a smile. "You can stretch, take a leak, eat, and drink. But if you run, you're dead men. You cannot give away our position. Understand?"

"What do you want from us?" Fisher said, drawing back from Bear Shadow's knife.

"Oh, Great Spirit—we don't want *that* from you." Bear Shadow shook his head.

Crow Shadow sighed. "You ought to have some appreciation. It's not like you woke up in Mexico in a tub of ice and cold water without kidneys or something. We're not body parts salesmen, we're not sexual predators, we're not bounty hunters for humans, and we're not werewolves. It's minus seventeen outside and we had a lot of people hand you off from country to country to get your asses here so Sasha can come claim you. So we *are* salvation. Any other immediate questions, gentlemen?"

XAVIER HOLLAND STEPPED out of his meeting with the colonel. Chaos reigned in NORAD. A five-star general from MacDill Air Force Base, Joint Strategic Command, was in teleconference with the Secretary of the Army, getting briefed and ready for a presentation that would hit the Oval Office.

His questions were quick stabs of words to his staff as he grabbed the reports chronicling the Sirius Project, Operation Dog Star. He looked at the monitors.

"Did anything come in from Lieutenant Trudeau yet?"

Winters shook his head, double-checking incoming lines in the doctor's office. "No, sir. Not yet."

EVEN THOUGH MAX was curled behind her and the bed was warm and soft, Sasha's mind kept worrying the problem like a dog worries a bone. Her eyes were closed, her body drawing in slow, steady breaths, but her mind was on fire, racing, zooming. It just wouldn't shut down. The riddles continued to knife at her mind until she could feel a piercing heat at her back and against her chest.

She slightly arched away from Max's chest, touching her amulet to bring it away from her skin and to get his away from her back. Where the amber had rested against her left a tingling sensation.

"You have to sleep and just let your mind ease, Sasha," he said groggily. "Or it will continue to send the amulet a beacon."

"How does it work, this beacon?" she asked quickly, suddenly wide awake.

"Only pack leaders and shamans have one of these," he said in a slow, rough voice, dozing between words. "Only the strongest alphas who lead a pack can make it through the demon doors to return . . . you saw how dangerous it was. And only shamans have them to commune with the dead or see the dead; others would not understand the whispers."

She sat up. "Your grandfather is a shaman, plus your

grandmother on your father's side was one from Haiti, right? This is so old, so valuable . . . if I'm not your mate, I should give it back."

He rolled over. "I do not want to talk about anyone on my father's side."

She noticed he avoided the "mate" comment again.

"Hey, we've got to use every resource at our disposal," she said, losing patience and sliding over his body to face him. "I've seen the power of these wards—it saved my life, and I'm honored to wear this amulet . . . especially since it came from your mother."

He stared up at her. "My grandfather said he would make you an amulet . . . I assumed it was new."

She touched the one on his chest. "No. That is not what Doc said."

"Then this is also his wife's, my grandmother, who then gave it to my mother . . . just as this is my grandfather's, who gave it to me when I became pack leader. He never relinquished it to my father." Max turned away and pushed up. "He was a beta male, I recently learned."

"It doesn't matter," she said, placing her hand on his shoulder. "You're not. I've seen you in action. What's more, your spirit is so good, Hunter." She pressed her cheek to his warm back, listening to his breathing, feeling the huge width of it expand and contract beneath her cheek. "Mine," she added quietly, trying to make up for the previous verbal stab, as she hugged him around the waist.

His hands covered hers slowly. "You sure?"

She nodded and kissed his back. "I'm sure." She released a sigh. "Why can't we just enjoy it without labeling it?"

"Definites are a part of the shadow culture. It's all I know. This is . . . new. Let me get used to it."

"Hunter, I care about you and have your back. I can't explain it, but the full Monte scares me. Still, a part of me says 'mine' each time we're together."

He let out a long, weary breath but said nothing for a moment. "Even with werewolf taint?"

She closed her eyes and hugged him tighter, cringing inside from having wounded him more deeply than she'd understood. "Yes . . . mine." She clasped his hand and placed another kiss along his shoulder blade. "Yours."

He leaned into the kiss with a cautious sigh, but didn't answer. However, the way his muscles relaxed told her that he finally believed her.

"Your grandfather gave you the stones of a mated pair that are very strong and go back in your pack for generations," she murmured against his skin. She could feel him relax even more as he turned and nodded, and then cupped her face with his huge, rough palm. "Show me."

"I never wanted to commune with the dead," he said quietly, taking her amulet up in his palms. He placed his in hers, facing her and sitting yogi style before her now.

She matched his sitting position and held his stone. He placed his free hand on her opposite shoulder, and again she matched his positioning.

"I was strong enough to hold my own behind a door, and I trusted you when you came for me," she said quietly. "Trust me now."

"The things of the shadow lands, Grandfather says, can be more damaging to the mind than what can happen to the body behind the wrong shadow door. I have never ventured there."

"Then I'll stay with you and you stay with me as we run," she said, squeezing the bulk of muscles at his shoulder. "This is where I'm strong, just as you were stronger and more prepared in the physical shadow we escaped from behind the demon door."

She waited, hoping he would have confidence in her. What she'd said was all she could think of to put him at ease. She didn't know it to be fact, just went on a hunch.

But the one thing she knew from all the training she'd received was that going into a battle with one's head screwed on tightly, being in a victory frame of mind, could decide an outcome. She was going for the win, even if she had to talk trash and posture a bluff.

Slowly, his shoulders relaxed and she watched his eyes begin to drink her in. She could literally feel his skin heat to an almost uncomfortable burn beneath her hand as beads of sweat began to form on his brow. Soon his entire body was sweat slicked. It was the most amazingly erotic thing to watch, the incremental transition that occurred right under her palm as the amulet heated up and glowed in her other hand.

His eyes held a faraway look in them, pupils opened so wide that only a thin rim of glowing amber remained of his irises. His breaths were slow and becoming ragged now and he intermittently licked his lips as though battling with some force within him that was stronger than his will.

"Call your wolf," he breathed out on a low murmur. "Call her just under your skin. Don't let her transform you physically, so you can stay in your human mind . . . but you want all the instincts of your wolf close at hand."

Easier said than done. Her wolf wasn't that easy to control, or at least she didn't have as much practice doing it as he obviously did. But she concentrated, determined, watching him and feeling a thick, desirous pull to him as her skin began to heat rapidly. It made her pant quickly and out of control, the sensations were so immediate. But she felt his grip tighten on her shoulder.

"Control your breathing. Don't let her run ahead of you."

She tried to steady her breaths and licked her dry lips. Aw, hell . . . her wolf was running, dragging her through mental shadows, awakening inner emotions, sending the intense need to be held through every cell—and the next thing she knew, she was gone.

Sasha looked back as her wolf peeled away from her human form as a silver gray mist. She could see her and Max still sitting on the bed yogi style, facing each other, but was fully aware of also being separate from that. Suddenly a warm breeze passed her, and a dark image of a male wolf slid by her, nuzzled her, and then bounded out the hotel window.

Instantly she followed him, but when her paws hit the ground, they were in a mist-filled, shadowy place with moss-covered earth. Deep forest in the late fall; the rich, musty scent of fertile soil and decaying leaves completing the cycle of life entered her nose. The dark shadow of wolf beside her began to trot to the edge of a clearing. He looked back once and then began to run.

Her body became a fast-moving blur. She was aware of running but then not. It was as though just being in the strange shadow land pulled her with a force all its own. She could feel his panic. Hunter was trying to reverse and stop their momentum as the ground became covered in snow and the wind became freezing daggers of pain. Snarling, fighting, struggling against the place they were hurtling toward, she called out in a baleful howl to let him know she was there with him, no matter what had panicked him.

He stopped fighting. They dropped to the snow. Hunter threw his head back and howled. It was the saddest, loneliest, most mournful call she'd ever heard. The desolate tone set her teeth on edge. His eyes glittered with unspent tears as a battle in the underbrush suddenly crashed through before them. A gorgeous silver she-wolf was locked in bloody battle with a werewolf. Badly lacerated, growing fatigued, the upright beast slammed her to the ground on the next lunge. Propelled by instinct, Sasha leaped at the attacker, trying to give the pregnant female a chance to withdraw. But the demon went right through her as though she weren't there, and as the she-shadow made one last attempt, her entire abdomen was gored.

Horrified, Sasha repeatedly attacked, not understanding why Hunter turned away, until the beast began eating. Winded, nauseated by what she saw, her eyes scanned the trees until they landed on a male shadow wolf that would not come out. Yet another werewolf leaped into the center of the carnage and both beasts snapped and growled at each other as they began to fight.

Awareness came in slow, painful increments. Instantly circling Hunter, she shielded him from seeing, blocked him with her body, and pushed him from this place. As she used the force of her wolf body to lean against his, she looked back to see a small struggling sack of flesh— then looked up into the sightline of a shotgun . . . the hunter had tears streaming down his face. The silver shell went through the center of her head, parting her hair, burning her scalp, and then she felt them moving again into the suction of the vortex.

They were in a lab; a man was strapped down to the table. He had on prison clothes. He was raging, screaming. Doctors and technicians were scurrying. She recognized Doc. He was younger, much younger. Two people looked familiar, she'd seen them in pictures—Sasha froze.

The thing on the table was in transition. She bared her teeth and barked, her wolf voice trying to send a warning as the restraints snapped. Hunter's huge black wolf tried to force her back to block her sight, but she had to know and fought him to see, then turned her head, howling . . . her mother, her father, all the men in the lab. It was pure slaughter.

She began running aimlessly, aware that Hunter was by her side. She just wanted to get to a place of peace, of calm. They were back in the moss-covered mist again. Sobs racked her body and soon her human hands covered her face as she sat on the warm ground facing Hunter. Tears had wet his face, also, and she reached out and wiped them away as he wiped hers.

"We had to come through the dark shadows to here . . . Only once you come back to your humanness can you ask the questions, Grandfather warned me. But many get lost in the wolf and cannot return."

She nodding, catching her breath. "I'm ready to ask the questions."

He held her face. "You didn't leave me . . . you even tried to fight my demons for me when it was futile," he whispered.

"How could I leave you to be trapped in that? It was terrible—no one should have to see . . . Oh, Hunter, I'm so sorry I brought you here. Forgive me."

She covered his hands with her own for a moment before he pulled her into a warm embrace.

"No . . . I needed to come here all my life. Forgive you? I should thank you." His arms held her tightly as he kissed the crown of her head. "I've never loved anyone like I do you."

For what seemed like a long while they sat in the shadows holding each other, recovering, allowing all the hurt to drain away with each calming breath. Soon their solace was broken as soft footfalls could be heard. They looked up at the same time, then quickly stood.

A beautiful Native American woman with luminous dark eyes and ebony hair dressed in traditional ceremonial clothes stepped out of the shadows. Her doeskin dress was intricately woven with silver and turquoise and amber beads. Eagle feathers and beads crowned her hair, and Sasha immediately felt Hunter pull away from her, yet hesitate.

"Go to her," Sasha murmured. "She has been waiting for you for a long time."

She felt a shudder of pain claim him as he walked forward and then stopped. The woman met him, walking the rest of the way, and slowly opened her arms and hugged him.

"My son . . ." she said quietly, closing her eyes. "You have given me peace." She pulled back and wiped his face. "I am so proud of what you have become. You have grown strong and noble. Ask anything of me and I will answer, I am your guide who has always been there for you."

Sasha turned away and hugged herself. The moment was too private, too intimate, and she felt she had no right to be there. As deep, booming male sobs echoed behind her, she moved deeper into the forest; she had to get away. His hurt was so personal that his dignity deserved space. As she cried for him, tears wet her face, and she walked for a while blindly, but stopped as she came upon the back porch of a home that seemed vastly out of place. A familiar woman came out and sat down on a wicker chair and beamed at Sasha and then waved. She was young and whole and excitement brimmed in her eyes as she stood and walked to the edge of the porch.

"Oh, please come home for just a little while, Sasha . . . look at you, baby. Look at who you are, I never knew."

All of a sudden she was running, bounding up the steps, falling into the embrace of a woman she'd never known. It was like looking at herself in the mirror, but with so many layers and textures that it was surreal.

A tender hand patted her back. Gentle guidance brought her into a house that slowly filled with more and more people, and without them having to tell her, she knew they were family.

"You've got people, baby," her mother said, kissing her face. "And we're all here to help you. Ask your questions."

SPENT, SHE MET Hunter in the clearing. He was sitting with his back to her as she approached. Her life made so much sense, now . . . her mother had been a seer from New Orleans, that's why she'd been in the lab that fateful day. She was more than military; Catherine Trudeau had come from a long line of women with special vision and had passed on that gift. New tears filled Sasha's eyes as she absorbed the depth of spiritual experience. Now she better understood why she had such an unfailing gut instinct and had been able to pull as much from her vampire contact as perhaps he had from her . . . as well as why she could so gloriously sync up to Hunter's inner vision.

She watched his proud, strong back and the way he calmly took in and released slow breaths. "Did you get your questions answered?" she murmured, speaking before she touched him, not wanting to startle him.

He nodded but didn't turn. "Did you?"

"Yeah . . . I know what we've gotta do when we go back."

Again he nodded. "As do I. Call your wolf."

THEY GASPED IN unison as they returned to their bodies. They were still facing one another, still sitting with one hand on a shoulder, the other clasping an amulet . . . though their eyes had aged with wisdom. She closed her heavy lids and felt his breath on her face and a gentle kiss on each eyelid. She returned the tender gesture as their embrace deepened. Healing touch soothed away harsh memories, selflessly offered pleasure as the antidote to residual pain.

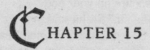

CHAPTER 15

THE STORM WAS raging outside when they stirred. They didn't even have to discuss it; they made quick work of getting dressed and gathering weapons.

"My spirit people died in the labs, down at NORAD, so they could see what happened there, just like yours died on Ute lands and saw the double-cross there. We need to go back."

"We need to go back with evidence, so we're not shot on sight." He pulled his fingers through his damp hair after shoving a nine-millimeter into a shoulder holster.

"Yeah. Damned vampire blocked and diverted the call to Doc—shoulda known when he showed up by the pay phone."

"Try again from here. We're long gone anyway, so who cares if they trace it? We're coming back in."

Sasha went to the phone and dialed the number and then protocol code to put her directly into the war room. "Put me on speaker. This is Lieutenant Trudeau calling in with vital intel."

"Sasha, where are you!" Xavier Holland said, his voice strained from lack of sleep and nerves.

"I'm up in Vancouver where I tracked a target. Who is in the briefing?"

"Colonel Vlasco, Lieutenant Colonel Waters, Major Adams, and General Griffin, of U.S. Special Ops Com, by teleconference. All at clearance levels. You may proceed, if you are secure on your end."

"Good, sir, I am, sir," Sasha said, pacing with the phone close to her ear. She glimpsed Hunter. Yeah, she was secure. "First I'd like to offer my condolences for the tragedy that befell General Wilkerson. But I have some things to tell you that no one is going to like."

"Proceed swiftly, Lieutenant," General Griffin barked over the telecom unit.

"Yes, sir," Sasha said, looking at Hunter across the room. "As you know, the general was interested in doing further experimentation with the werewolf virus. Initially, his goal was to weaponize it. However, as you know, the technology is just not there yet to ensure that the DNA would bond to the human spiral without incident. The project was bombing, lives were being lost, and the general had to salvage the investment."

Silence crackled on the line. That's when she knew she had 'em. How could she be lying when she was giving them intel that only those in the highest inner circles of brass would know? They were in "don't confirm it, don't deny it, and simply listen" mode.

"But it appears that in levels way above NORAD, sirs," she said, seizing the moment to press her point, "there was talk circulating about creating a vaccine, since the genetic-weapon use of it was so unstable. This is where General Wilkerson became imperiled."

"I don't understand—who could argue against the merits of that worldwide benefit? A vaccine that could be given to children, adults, to be sure that anyone who was attacked would never get this plague, would be—"

"An affront to the vampire food chain, Doctor," Sasha said, cutting off her mentor. "Vampires get sick if they drink werewolf-tainted blood. The more humans have it in their systems, the smaller their hunting grounds. If generations pass and our blood actually mutates to have a natural immunity to the werewolf scratch or bite, then vampires are screwed, to put it bluntly, sir. Those entities, apparently, take a long-term view—given the centuries they've been on the planet."

"That's phenomenal," the doctor murmured. "More than we'd hoped . . . A vaccine that could potentially stop both infections, or at least one virus, from the werewolves as well as attacks from vampires?"

"Yes, sir," Sasha said quickly.

"But how could they know our objectives and secret meetings?" General Griffin raged. "This was only discussed at the top cabinet levels!"

Sasha looked at Hunter and struggled to keep the sarcasm out of her voice. Old humans from the cold war era were so naïve. "I don't know, sir. They got intel from somewhere." To cover her tracks she gave up a dead source. "When I got here, my guide took me to a gym in a warehouse. If you check with Canadian authorities you'll learn there was a helluva gunfight, sir. That was me. We extracted the intel I just gave you from a half-transitioned subject before it was necessary to terminate him. It appears that he and his smugglers had been go-betweens for the vampires, had been promised immortality or something, and got infected. But once we subdued him, he led us to the vampire, who appeared out of thin air asking questions in a wharf bar."

With a nod, Hunter indicated there was no way that she could divulge it all. Firstly, the men sitting at the polished mahogany war room table at NORAD still weren't up on all things that went bump in the night. Those guys needed hard evidence, and she could prove her where-abouts by leading them to a destroyed wharf, which gave credibility—since there would be no werewolf body, or vampire bodies, if they caught any. Those things went up in cinders. One day she was going to have to set up en-tirely new protocols for evidence gathering, because the current human models simply didn't work. She was just glad that she'd never had to have that conversation with Doc. He was already up on the subject, had known of wolf differences long before she did.

If she told her commanding officers about the rogue shadow wolves, of their existence and their complicity in brokering contraband, the military would, in ignorance, move against the clans without distinction. It was best that their roles remained in the shadows. She also sup-posed the same was true of uninfected werewolves, but she wasn't about to admit that in front of Hunter.

"Then should we be concerned about mass Turnings in the Colorado Springs area?" Major Adams asked after a while, the strain of the silence on the line obviously wear-ing on him. "Since you've said there was a human who got infected and traveled clear up to Vancouver—that's a trail too large to contain. What's our exposure? A were-wolf already murdered the general. Are we at risk for a massive outbreak?"

"No, sir. Exposure is minimal, sir. We got the infected smuggler and put him down hard. A lot of his gang are also left on the site, sir. Primary contagion is contained."

She and Hunter shared a look. Dexter got away. She nodded, but things were already complicated enough.

"Police band scanners can put us on the trail of any un-usual deaths, and we can sweep hospitals for strange ani-mal attacks and do follow-up," Sasha said plainly, trying to give the brass some ease. "But I do need to hunt down those vials, however, because those could be brokered to unfriendly nations." She paused, letting them mull over that morsel of information. It would mean her freedom papers, her freedom to hunt, if they went for it. They had to trust her, and allow her to work with Hunter without intervention.

"At present," Sasha said, forcing as much authority into her tone as she could, "the vampires do not have the technology to trap, contain, and create the vaccine—hence they wanted the blood samples with werewolf toxin destroyed. The werewolves are not that organized yet and are not technologically adept. But somewhere along the way in the handoff, there was a double-cross and the vampires lost possession of the vials."

"Lieutenant, would you speculate, then, that is this when the creatures went to General Wilkerson to dissuade him from continuing with the Sirius Project vaccine?" General Griffin's voice was tight and gruff, but that he'd asked a question meant he was considering the plausibility of everything she'd said.

Choosing her words carefully, Sasha leaned against the wall. "A werewolf could have mutilated the general, given what the smuggler said was the method of torture—but only a vampire could have gotten into the lab, passed a retina scan, gotten into the vault, and come out with the vials of Rod Butler's blood. Not to mention that they're experts in handling blood. So finding a random human's blood to replace what was in the trays was no problem. They are also shrewd enough and strong enough to deliver the kind of wounds that killed the general. The giveaway is their stealth. Dorothy Wilkerson never heard her husband die. Werewolves are not that quiet, and once on a rampage, those creatures keep killing until the moon phases out. The moon wasn't full. Dorothy is still alive. Had an infected werewolf been in the house, she, too, would have been eaten."

"Then how in the hell did a goddamned vampire get into our labs!" General Griffin bellowed. "I thought we had all sorts of protocols against that!"

"We do, sir," Dr. Holland said. "We have every kind of charm, spell, ward, religious barrier set up. I don't know how that would have been possible."

Sasha pushed off the wall, her eyes steady on Hunter, who nodded slowly. The general's outburst confirmed he believed her line of reasoning.

"Human error," Sasha said flatly, making the line go silent again.

"Vampires are the most seductive of the paranormals. They can offer money, power, fame, *sex* . . ." she said, allowing her voice to drop to a vicious whisper on the last word of her statement. "If they want to take a human's mind and hypnotize him or her into certain behavior, they can. And all they need to cross all those wards and spells is *an invitation*. Anyone in the whole base complex could have been temporarily stunned, charmed, and let those mist-travelers into the tunnels. Once there, they could have lifted whatever they needed, including any of our technology. My sources are unorthodox, sirs, but I know these entities like the back of my hand, and my scout saved my life while we were under heavy fire at the wharf—so I trust him as a partner. The vampires could waltz right into the White House by blowing the mind of a security guard. We've just seen it cost a general his life. The situation is dire, sirs."

"Holy shit!" the colonel exclaimed. "How do we bar them? There has to be a way."

"We've gotta give Trudeau whatever resources she needs to get the job done and to lock our facilities down! I want those vials back. I don't care if her methods are unorthodox or if the woman howls at the moon! We cannot have this contagion and double agents running ram-

pant and killing our leadership. Gentlemen, redeploy resources so that the only soldier who has brought me answers can complete her mission."

No one spoke as the general's words reverberated
through the room. He was still breathing hard from his
impassioned outburst when he spoke again.

"Lieutenant," the general said, his tone questioning
now as it took on a quality like that of speaking to a peer.
"Please. Do you know of any way we can bar vampires
and werewolves from entry to our facilities, given the vast
vulnerability presented by possible human error?"

Sasha smiled and shrugged. "Sir, only one thing comes
to mind. A natural predator to all these entities with bad
blood . . . It can sense them on the premises . . . this very
noble creature called a shadow wolf . . ."

THE WIND HAD gone beyond howling; it was screaming
as the driving snow and ice lacerated their faces. Hunter
stepped into her, pressing his body to hers, parting her
thighs with his knee, his massive palm emitting sudden
heat at the small of her back, his fingers splayed wide
against her spine as he clutched her amulet in his other
hand and nodded for her to mirror his stance.

"See my grandfather's porch in your mind—match my
mind vision," he yelled above the screaming winds. "We
are one, same clan, life-mates, and must shadow travel on
the wind like the clans of old did to convene at summits.
Complete trust is required. Never let me go once we
enter—if you break the seal, I could lose you in there forever."

She squinted against the stinging snow to see his hair
majestically lifted by the winds. His dark frame towered
over her, snow catching in the five o'clock shadow that
covered his jawline and sticking to his long onyx lashes

and thick eyebrows. She could feel preternatural heat begin to waft from their amber charms. He brushed her forehead with a kiss. She held him tighter, grasping his leather bomber jacket in one fist. He nodded again, moving her away from the shelter of the building into the direct ferocity of the gale-force wind.

Snowflake shadows speckled the ground as he walked with her in an almost dance step, his legs between hers, spinning them around and following the direction of the wind, faster and faster until they almost fell. Then they suddenly entered a ground shadow at the edge of another building, and were gone.

That's when she felt it, the full velocity of the wind. That's when she screamed as she experienced what could only be described as her body exploding into a million snowflakes and moving with the unfathomable power of nature contained in the wind. Centrifugal force made it nearly impossible to breathe. She concentrated on Hunter's edict to keep him close, and she pressed her face against the warmth of his chest, tightened her legs around his, clenched her fists around leather and amber—if he let her go within this freezing black void, to forever move at this speed trapped between planes of existence, she would lose her mind.

Then, without warning, they were falling. It was as though someone had dropped the bottom out from under them and the force that had originally been thrusting them forward was sucking them down into a blackout-creating spiral. She landed hard and ungracefully on something solid. Him.

"Breathe," he said in a low, rumbling command. "Keep your eyes closed until the vertigo stops and breathe through your nose or you'll hurl."

He didn't have to tell her twice. The only thing halfway saving her stomach was that she'd done enough rounds of in-flight simulation training and other military-inspired, grueling tests to have some frame of reference. Still, this was no joke and not for the faint of heart. Maybe if she'd known what to expect—but sheesh!

After a moment, she slowly opened her eyes and blinked at the blurred landscape. Her skin felt hot and cold at the same time and everything beneath her leather jacket and pants felt like second skin. She pushed up from Hunter's huge frame and dragged her fingers through her hair, glad that it was snowing and cold outside. Finally giving in to the urge, she opened her mouth and drew in a deep breath, unable to gulp enough clean, normal air into her lungs.

"Take your time with that," he warned, placing one hand against her back and one against her chest. "It'll burn like—"

"Oh!" Panic consumed her; her lungs were on fire. Sasha doubled over gasping, but Hunter caught her and pressed hard with his hands.

"Through the nose!" he said firmly. "Or you'll be up-chucking blood."

She covered her mouth with a hand, drawing in huge, painful inhales through her nose, tears brimming from the pain.

"The compression from the speed collapses your lungs, damned near. Fill them up too fast and you'll burst blood vessels and capillaries." He blotted her nose with the edge of his sweater as it bled. "The old leaders would smoke peyote to help them transcend and transition into the shadow travel winds . . . so when they came out they were very relaxed and mellow for the meeting. We didn't have that luxury. The pain will pass in a minute. Then we'll stand."

She just leaned her forehead against his chest for a moment, wishing he'd at least given her a shot of tequila or something beforehand. Damn.

But true to his word, she could feel the burning sensation within her chest slowly ebbing, just like the roiling nausea had abated. The hot-cold sweats had ceased, too. Finally she had enough strength to look up at him. Half of her was really pissed off, the other half was grateful as hell he hadn't dropped her.

"The next time you have one of these cultural 'let's share' moments, I want a full debrief," she said, pulling away thoroughly peeved. "No more of this 'trust me, baby' crap. All right? That was insane."

He swallowed a smirk which made her ball up her fist.

"If I had explained all the hazards, you probably would have decided to wait out the storm and travel by conventional methods—through airports when they reopened for example—but by then, the trail would have been cold."

She wasn't going to dignify his comment by responding and refused to give him the satisfaction of being right. And rather than punch him in the eye, she gathered herself up on shaky hands and knees and began the perilous process of trying to stand, the entire time feeling like a newborn foal. When he got up first and extended his hand to her, she nearly bit it, not amused in the least that he drew it back as though she'd snapped at him. Well, maybe she had—but still.

"You have to admit that this was efficient," he said with too much mirth in his tone for her liking. "The old ones never had the benefit of modern inventions such as air travel . . . but those were perilous times and global clan treaties had to be approved during summits that brought together all the pack leaders."

"Yeah, yeah, yeah," she said, finally able to stand without holding on to the porch rail.

"Do you know what you just did?" he said, his voice free of teasing as he stared at her.

She hated that she didn't and could only stare back at him blankly.

"You mirrored me," he said quietly. "The first time I learned to do this, I watched my grandfather ride his horse into the wind and simply disappear. He told me he'd return to this porch and for me to meet him here and to bring his horse back. An hour later when I got home, he was sitting in his favorite rocker, smoking his pipe, his eyes closed, with the most sublime expression of peace on his face. I asked him if I could try it, and he said only when I can hold the image of where I want to go strongly enough to light my amber ward. It took me two more years of trying . . . to be able to still my mind enough to hone in on a destination—to light the amulet."

His tone was gentle and reverent as he neared her and touched her face with trembling fingers. "You looked at me with complete trust, saw this place *exactly* as I saw it, and took a leap of faith into a gale-force wind."

The expression on his face made her look away as the frigid air bit into her skin.

"The alpha leaders always traveled alone to the summits . . . I didn't know if one could share such a vision. I'd been told that one's mate was only to go into the winds of the shadow lands under extreme emergencies. That it was our kind's way of ensuring that the strongest of the gene pool made it out of a disastrous situation in union, as a pair. But I had no concept of how it would feel once—"

"Wait," she said, completely breaking the mood. "You mean to tell me you had never done this, didn't know if you could hold me in there, and—"

"All I needed to know was that I would have died trying."

She stared at him for a moment. "Why didn't you say so then?" What the hell could she say to that? Sudden heat flushed her face and a new level of appreciation for the man standing before her began to turn her knees to jelly. But there were bad shadows to chase, so she lifted her chin with a crisp, military nod. Besides, she would not be baited into a commitment to be his mate after knowing him for less than a damned week!

She spun on her heel and walked toward the front door of Silver Hawk's cabin.

"I'm feeling it, too. But I know what we have to do, first—so you can drop your guard. At ease, soldier."

She didn't turn around, but smiled in spite of herself. "Do you have a key to your grandfather's place?"

"Not necessary. He's not in there."

Hunter's comment made her turn and look at him. His expression had become all business, which drew that emotion to her fore, as well.

"This storm is a bad one, and knowing Grandfather, I'm sure he has sought refuge in the dens after a vision."

"We should go to him, then . . . make sure . . ."

Her words trailed off as Hunter shook his head and looked off into the distance.

"No. Check your weapons. Fox Shadow hates the dens; he's grown soft and used to living in the lap of luxury. He keeps a very well-appointed cabin about ten miles' hike from here that looks like a damned ski resort."

"No wonder he needed the cash." Sasha just shook her head as Hunter bounded off the porch, and then she picked up her pace to follow him.

THE RUN FELT exhilarating in the virgin snow. Hunter also hadn't lied. Fox Shadow's cabin looked more like a commercial lodge. Double-height, two-story, floor-to-ceiling windows, with the entire front of the A-frame structure made of glass. There were floating staircases, a wraparound deck, ivory leather furniture, track and canister lights illuminating expensive art, bearskin rugs, blazing fireplaces, and women every damned where.

But she wasn't hatin', just very aware, and she also knew each of the females in there probably was able to shift into a serious predator, judging by the way they fawned over Fox Shadow for a hit. Glimpsing Hunter from the corner of her eye, she watched his lip curl into a silent snarl.

"Punk bastard," Hunter muttered and spat on the ground as they watched Fox Shadow kiss the soft bend inside Shadow Falcon's arm and then replace his caress with a needle.

She didn't say a word, knowing somehow that the history between all these wolves went way back to some early-childhood slight that had never healed; she could practically smell it in the silent emotional fit Hunter was having, but she kept that knowledge to herself. There were much bigger concerns.

He silently slipped down and over the ridge and gave her the hand signals to come around the back. She double-checked her clips—two Glocks, one in each holster, two Berettas, one for each back pants pocket. A Bowie strapped to each boot. He had a handheld semi under the jacket, plus some crazy shit that she knew he hadn't put back on the store shelves as they "borrowed" some ammo.

The storm was in full swing, though, reducing visibility. The whipping winds moved the shadows at the treeline in erratic patterns, making it hard to stay concealed while on the move. Her focus like a laser, she made it across the wide clearing and into the shadows that flanked the house, staring up. The beta males had lost their ever-livin' minds!

Liquor was everywhere, nobody had on any clothes. But that didn't mean they weren't armed and extremely dangerous. And although she was supposed to be watching for an opportunity and waiting on Hunter's signal, there were just some things she didn't wanna see. If the shadow travel winds hadn't made her hurl, watching two she-shadows simultaneously give Fox Shadow head would surely do the trick.

A tap on her shoulder as she came out of a shadow almost made her fire as she spun to meet it. A familiar face caused her to hesitate. Adrenaline made her ears ring and cold sweat drench her skin.

"They went dark, and by rights we should put them behind the demon doors," Shogun said.

A tense moment stood between them. The last thing she needed now was jurisdictional conflict. The last thing she needed was very sexy, unfinished business to interrupt a critical hunt. He was dressed in a form-hugging, black thermal suit that fit him like second skin. She couldn't help but notice.

"But they're Shadows gone dark, not Weres," she said, wresting her mind back to her mission.

He nodded. "I know—but I needed an excuse to see you again. There was an unfortunate misunderstanding."

"I think I understood—"

"My *sister* is traditional. Prejudiced."

Sister? Still, what did it matter? "Listen, I—"

"Don't dismiss me out of hand, Sasha," he said quietly, his intense, almond-shaped eyes searching her face. "I came here, outside of my territory—and you know the risks of doing that—because in my mind it was worth it. My pack thinks I have lost my mind . . . perhaps that is true. Either way, meet me in New Orleans for the next summit when the UCE gathers . . . it's during the first full moon after Mardis Gras. Meet me."

"Why would I want to do that?" She looked at him, trying to keep her mental checks and balances, along with the very real threat he presented, in the forefront of her mind.

"There are important members you must meet there, and we feel unnatural movement beyond the demon doors headed toward that sector. If he won't educate you, I will," Shogun said, gesturing toward where Max had previously been.

She had to look away and she motioned with her chin toward the house. "This hunt is vital; I can't stop in the midst of it and even begin to address this. Not to mention, you're in shadow country, and a border breach could start a full-scale war."

"Believe me, I understand the dilemma. My goal is not war with the Shadows. I'm twenty men strong out here, and we have your backs." He reached out and touched her cheek briefly and then withdrew his hand. "I came to ensure that you'd never be infected. Anything you don't kill, or if you get in over your heads, we'll hunt with you. Tell your man we're not the enemy. We'll drag whatever is still kicking and screaming to the quarantine dens. Temporary truce for a common goal . . . a cease-fire for now."

He smiled a peaceful smile, snow battering his handsome face. "No matter what, I still want an alliance with you and anything more that you're comfortable with, Sasha . . . you're part of the prophecy. He doesn't own you. Remember that."

She watched him back away into the night and become invisible in the standing line of trees. It took her a moment to stop the warm shiver he'd sent through her.

HUNTER HAD MADE it up onto the deck. A scout of the perimeter proved that those inside were too far gone to even have sentries posted. They'd grown overconfident. Then again, with infected werewolf virus strumming through their veins, what did one expect? But as he drew nearer and looked more deeply into the house, a part of him seized. Mountain Shadow was with them? His closest friend and ally from years gone by? Hawk, too? Hunter glimpsed up at the moon, glad that it would be weeks before it waxed full again, yet completely morose to realize that his friends would never see another.

Leveling his semi at the glass, he stared at the pack one last time. Fox, Hawk, Rabbit, Mountain, with eight she-shadows, would be gone. As glass shattered and screams rent the air, he wondered if Bear Shadow and Crow Shadow had saved or eaten Sasha's men, Woods and Fisher, up in Canada. He didn't know and was at a place in his mind where right now he didn't care. All feeling had abandoned him as he walked forward squeezing off rounds.

SHE CAME THROUGH the glass at the back of the house in a hard roll and took cover. Shadow wolves were down, but several got up, transformed into quick-moving blurs of pure danger, and attacked. Hunter had gone to some insane place in his mind, dropped his weapon and transformed into a wolf—now was not the time! Four huge infected Shadow Wolf males snarled and lunged. With a double-fisted Glock nine-millimeter assault, she got two, aiming at their hearts through their spine as she blew their backs out midair.

He shouldn't have to waste his own, was the mantra in her head that kept her firing, kept her moving with no mercy. She remembered Rod as she held her weapons steady and kept firing without blinking. Demon-infected wolves had to die.

Coming down the steps, however, were several half-transitioned she-shadows with infected werewolf heads and fangs and gruesomely half-human upright bodies carrying pump shotguns. Hunter had taken a severe blow

to the back of head by way of a swung sofa from behind
and was lying sprawled and dazed. She got Rabbit with a
flung Bowie knife that he caught in his left eye as he
turned, and her Beretta did the rest. The two seconds that
Fox Shadow jerked his attention toward her was just long
enough for Hunter to jump up and get out of the way of a
pump shotgun blast.

"All of us," Fox Shadow shouted, "got what you always had, motherfucker! Even Mountain Shadow was
tired of taking second seat to your ass! He was a purebred, and should have been alpha to the pack, but you had
the unfair advantage—we just evened the score!"

Machine-gun spray lit the floor, splintering wood as
she ran across the gleaming oak and dove out the shattered windows. Hunter was on her tail; they had the same
objective—find the grenades in his jacket and blow the
house. Destroy the virus. But an anvil-sized fist came out
of the shadows, as they reached their destination at the
same time, and collided with Sasha's jaw.

She fell backward in what felt like slow motion. She
saw the one-eared Shadow Falcon go airborne, transitioning into full demon wolf as she hurtled forward. Hunter's
wolf pulled back, becoming his human form to snatch his
nine, level it at the same moment Sasha had lifted both
her arms, Berettas in her fists, she and Hunter squeezing
off rounds to both hit Falcon's back and chest.

Sasha's spine slammed the snow with a thud that
knocked the wind out of her, and she only had seconds to
roll out of the way of a dead, fast-moving carcass dripping gore. She was up on her feet in a flash, had a
grenade, pulled the pin, and hurled it toward the house.
The concussion from the blast knocked everyone back. A
loud rumbling in the distance made Hunter look at her
quickly. No words were necessary: avalanche.

But a deformed Fox Shadow lunged forward from

behind a tree, stronger than ever, more insane than he'd been before at the sight of his mate's lifeless form. Hunter held his ground, weaponless, naked, for what seemed like an eternity, as his pack brother rushed him. It took everything in her to let the battle finish the way she knew it had to—this was Hunter's kill. In a blur of fury, he'd grabbed the pump shotgun that lay near Falcon's limp body, lifted it, took dead aim, and pulled.

He never flinched as Fox Shadow's head exploded gore in his face, but simply stepped aside as his headless body hit the snow with a thud.

Yet there was no time to contemplate the vagaries of fate. She grabbed up Hunter's clothes in a bundle under her arm and reached out her hand.

"Run!" she shouted.

But he didn't move. He just looked at the destroyed house, his dead pack members who were transitioning back to human forms with glassy eyes. She understood where her man was; his entire squad, save for a few, had been wiped out. It was like losing one's entire family. But she didn't have time for the gentle touch. Survival was paramount.

"Show me the way to the dens!" she hollered over the roar of the snow bearing down on them.

He looked at her, blinked twice, got that faraway fatalistic look out of his eyes, and took her hand. This time, she wouldn't argue about the speed, his methods of transport, as long as they got an evac out of the hot zone.

They came to a tumbling landing in a very serene underground cave. A warming fire was built, she could smell food grilling, could hear it sizzling on the flames. A still pool that seemed like black glass was at the center of an animal-fur-strewn haven. The slightly pungent scent of tobacco smoke wafted past them and she and Hunter turned to greet it.

"Bathe, heal, eat, and attend to your spirits," Silver Hawk said, coming out of the shadows. "Now that I am satisfied you are alive, I can go deeper within, where the rock art comes alive and our history dances on the walls. When you come to my age and can sit still enough, you will see. But now is not the time. You must heal."

"I'm all right," Hunter muttered, wiping gore from his face and body as she clutched his clothes.

"The prophecies were harsh. Your spirit has been torn ragged, son," his grandfather said, and then with his pipe he pointed to a clean deerskin shirt, a pair of pants, and moccasins warming by the fire near a beautiful bead-adorned, doeskin dress and fur-lined moccasins. "Stay within the dens in the shadows with your mate until you can stand to look at yourself in the clear light of day." His aged eyes held Sasha's with a silent plea. "Heal him. I do not own such magic. Then let him heal you."

Before she could respond, the old man was gone.

She didn't speak, just took Hunter's hand and began walking toward the glistening pool. His body yielded, his strides long and fluid behind hers, no resistance within him, just a deep, resigned weariness that she could fully relate to. She stripped slowly and quietly and again took his hand. His face was crusted with blood but she cradled it in her hands nonetheless and kissed him slowly. Her silent prayer was that another warrior hadn't also been lost tonight . . . one that had traveled thousands of miles on a mission to possibly be crushed by the snow. But she could only care for them one at a time, and right now this one had fought hard and was in so much pain that she could feel it radiating from his skin. Right now was not the time to split hairs on what their relationship meant; it just was what it was at the moment.

"I've got your back," she whispered, then led him into the bath.

EPILOGUE

WITH A FULL moon approaching, and Hunter looking extra delicious, there was no need to out Winters—the kid couldn't help it if a vampire had come to him, looking like her, naked in his dreams, and got a bogus invitation into the lab. The kid was undoubtedly under duress when he caved.

Some things she and Hunter just never spoke of. She never said a word about the night they'd tracked Fox Shadow's traitorous ass down and made him disappear. Between them, the three rogue shadows—Fox, Dexter, and Guillaume—had been able to overpower the solo vampire coming out of NORAD with the vials; bitch of it was, Dexter got away, and some of the vials were still out there. At least Woodsy and Fisher had turned up in the Yukon alive and well, and Hunter still had two go-to guys left from the pack whom he could count on—Bear and Crow.

Speaking on an alliance proposal that was still niggling the back of her brain was out of the question at the moment, just like asking what a very intriguing stranger had meant about her being a part of the prophecy was for all intents and purposes taboo. Yet, there was so much to learn. New Orleans was definitely somewhere she had to go, but might not necessarily get into all the details why. A solid lead was a solid lead. She had to get her arms around the differences between vampire tunnels, shadow paths, demon doors, and really learn more about how regular werewolves functioned, plus supernatural politics in general. There were more species than she could have ever imagined, and way more than the government had to know about. Some contacts would always remain on a need-to-know basis. But an alliance with a Shogun werewarrior, in the spirit of detente, hmmmm. Yeah, some things were definitely better left unsaid.

The real crime was just how many Shadow Wolves had got turned on to the virus and got turned out . . . then had had to be terminated. Having to put down she-shadows gone were-demon had really messed with her man's mind. That would haunt Hunter for a long time; regular doses of primal female medicine seemed to be the only cure. Same deal with her—he had a way of taking the edge off that thing called raw pain. She'd have to make sure that she worked her schedule to be off base at the time of the next full moon. There was no sense in playing with C-4; what they had between them was always hot enough to blow.

Yeah . . . there were a lot of unanswered questions still plaguing her mind. Questions like where Shadow Wolves really came from, how demon doors opened, and how one could close them. She wanted to know which pack member she was directly related to, but needed to go on another spirit walk for that. It would take a while before she was ready to go there again. Then there was the nagging question of who had tipped off the vampires, and how far up the conspiracy went. Not to mention, where the hell that weasel Dexter was, and how much of the tainted product was still out on the street now.

The only good part of it was that the vampires wanted the samples destroyed as much as she did. Silver lining: she had a budget, very cool weapons, serious project authority, and the latitude afforded to Black Ops missions—as long as the job got done, the president and top generals didn't really wanna know. The bad part was that there was still a market for something that could turn a human berserk . . . drug market, weapons market, it really didn't matter. DIWs, demon-infected were-wolves, were a problem.

There'd always be a buyer for bad blood.

Turn the page for a sneak peek at L. A. Banks's next book in the Crimson Moon series

ITE THE BULLET

Coming soon from St. Martin's Paperbacks

AS SOON AS she was sure that Hunter was out of range, Sasha ransacked the backpacks until she found their amulets. He'd shoved them to the bottom, rolled in layers of clothes. The clasps had been broken. She took shallow sips of air, gently trailing her fingers over the tender spot at the nape of her neck and then up the back of her scalp to where a small knot had formed, trying to focus, trying to remember.

They had transformed on a shadow run. He'd picked up the trail of large game—a bull moose. It was too big; she'd tried to signal him. Hunter was larger than she'd remembered when he'd transformed again; two hands higher at the shoulders, larger jaw, barrel chest. His eyes held something in them that frightened her.

Sasha shoved the amulets back where she'd found them and began to pace inside the tent with her eyes squeezed shut. "Oh . . . God . . ." It was coming back in fits and starts, jags of horror that she wanted to forget.

He'd outstripped her on the run. The animal they hunted turned and lowered its mantle. hunter went up on his hind legs. Sasha opened her eyes and hugged herself with a start, breathing hard. He hadn't brought it down like a wolf. One powerful swipe from a forepaw had snapped a damned bull moose's neck!

How could she not remember? How could she not remember! *How could she not remember?* She tore around the tent looking for weapons, blood pressure spiking when she couldn't immediately find them.

Cupping the back of her head, she bolted out of the tent. Panic perspiration made everything she wore stick to her skin. Images of Hunter crouched over the carcass snarling as he devoured the animal's heart and liver brought her other hand over her mouth to keep from hurling. She could see it all clearly now—blue-black night, steam rising from fresh kill that had been opened and gutted. Oh, God, oh, God, when did she fall and hit her head?

Backing away . . .

She'd come to a skidding halt. Their eyes had met. She was so stunned that she'd changed back into her human form and stood. He did too, then cried out and yanked the chain from his neck . . . she'd spun to run, caught a low-hanging branch, and went down. Then she was inside the tent. His arm was anchored around her waist. She squeezed her eyes shut again, remembering his impassioned voice choking out a ragged apology behind her.

Hunter had purposely knocked her unconscious, and the reason why broke over her in horrifying clarity.

Hunter was infected.

She felt a scream of rage and grief build in her throat over the thought that something like this was happening. But she swallowed it. There would be time to grieve later.

Right now survival was imperative and she needed to find her gun.

Turn the page for a sneak peek at the next
Vampire Huntress Legend

The Shadows

BY L.A. BANKS

Coming July 2008
from St. Martin's Paperbacks

SURREAL CALM OVERTOOK her as she listened to Carlos. Rather than the sensation entering her, it oddly emanated from within her. She'd promised him that she would eat. Damali moved her hands by rote to appease him . . . stalling for time by picking up the paper bag, slowly opening it, taking out the plastic container, opening that with care and then allowing her meal to sit before her untouched as she listened intently to what her husband was saying. Something about the smell of the food now turned her stomach.

It was only when she saw him blink that she became aware that time had actually slowed down all around her. His lids slid closed as through a heavy curtain of onyx lashes had been dropped to thud one against the other. His voice was now like distant thunder—a rumble of unintelligible words, they were being spoken so slowly.

Background sounds thrust their way to the forefront of her senses. Her breaths and heartbeat, his breaths and heartbeat, were each so slow and so loud they created a collision inside her head. Even though she couldn't quite make out what he was saying, she gathered what she could from his private, urgent tone and then watched how he slowly leaned in close to her to speak.

Carlos's physical warmth suddenly felt as though she'd been wrapped in a blanket and then soon became a searing barrier like one would expect if one stood before an opened oven that had been left on broil for hours. She settled back from the uncomfortable body heat radiating off him, and as she did, the sound of her clothes rustling against the chair was jarring.

He swallowed hard, pausing mid-sentence, and she almost cringed from the change in decibel that had transitioned the low rumble of his voice to the mucous-thick sound of saliva coating his throat. Yet through all of it, she oddly knew what he was saying, not from the words, but the impressions that began to form behind her wide-opened eyes.

In a vision, Damali saw it. The poisonous vapor. The way it slid out of technology orifices and opened dark portals within houses, buildings, and within human minds. The airwaves were polluted. The gray-zone, the earth plane, was becoming denser, darker, more twisted and violent.

Shadow entities spilled over the very edges of Hell and into the psyches and spirits of the unaware, diving into the pools of light that are normally within each human being.

Damali sat transfixed as she watched how the demonic forces entered a living body and then swallowed up all the clean light within it, slowly corroding it until there was simply no living aura left. At the point of total eclipse, the person was no more. Gone was their will, along with every shred of humanity that had once defined them.

"Tell me your names," she whispered, horrified. This was so much worse than the plague of The Damned. It was such a quick transition, no incubation period. No abstinence of touch could keep a person safe. The airwaves were being infected exponentially, and even people in the most remote villages had radios and televisions in small general stores!

Carlos cocked his head to the side and asked her a question. She could tell by his worried expression that he was asking something important of her. But the reply that should have been hers was instead a shadow turning to her before it entered the body of a man on the streets. It smiled a sinister smile, bearing mangled, yellow teeth in a hollow black pit devoid of a face.

Her husband's voice drifted farther and farther away until she was spinning in a panicked daze within a crowded market, then she was on a crowded street. All around her people were being taken over. All around her chaos was simmering beneath the surface of human potential. An army was being raised right on the streets and right before her eyes. Vertigo claimed her as her vision jettisoned her from New York to Copenhagen, from Kenya to Milan. Remote islands, metropolises, it didn't matter, the invasions were unrelenting.

Arms outstretched, she ran toward a schoolyard and then skidded to a halt as high school students fell into darkness. She couldn't breathe. *Not the children.* Her gaze fell upon a middle school and she watched as dark entities swarmed the windows like locusts.

Damali covered her face and turned away. *Tell me this plague's name so we can send it back into the pit!* Within seconds she was in a hospital, her hands pressed flat against nursery glass, and she saw the shadows eerily slide into the nurses' bodies, but none touched the babies. Yet that provided no relief. One nurse simply smiled and turned off an incubator's oxygen.

"No!" Damali's voice escalated with her panic. She had to know what this entity was in order to fight it. Not vampire, not succubus, the team had never seen a manifestation like this. "Tell me its name!"

Suddenly every person on the streets everywhere she looked had a sinister companion, and they all smiled at her simultaneously and whispered back, "My name is legions."

"Damali. Damali!"

A tight grasp held her upper arms and she was mildly aware of being shaken. Time snapped back. She caught Carlos by his elbows, panting and covered with sweat.

"You all right? Damali, talk to me!"

"I saw it," she gasped. "It's already starting."

As soon as she'd made the statement, she shrugged out of Carlos's hold and covered her mouth and nose.

"Get that out of the house!" she demanded, jumping down from the stool and backing away from the counter, pointing at her untouched food.

"Oh, shit!" Carlos toppled his stool as he backed up quickly and stared at the larva teeming over the edge of the container.

The moment his silvery line of vision hit it, the entire platter exploded, sending disgusting, maggoty gore everywhere. Instantly shielded by a golden disc, the couple took refuge as they watched the wriggling mass rain down on the translucent surface to sizzle and disappear with a sulfuric stench. Everything the larva plopped down on made them fry and evaporate. Marlene's kitchen was well anointed, and Inez had undoubtedly backtracked through it and given it a second blessing.

No less than they'd expected, they immediately heard heavy footfalls and knew the team was headed into the kitchen in a call to arms. Carlos and Damali shared a glance.

"Inez is gonna have a cow," Damali said, dry heaving from the residual sulfur smell.

"After Marlene has a heart attack," Carlos muttered, checking twice before lowering the shield to be sure it had stopped raining maggots. "This happened in her kitchen." He looked at Damali. "You okay?"

"Yeah," she said, swallowing down the feeling of nausea and then stepping around his shield to assess the damage. "So I guess it's officially on now. Vacation is over."

Carlos nodded and set his jaw hard as fellow Guardians came to a halt at the kitchen's threshold.

"What the f—" Rider stopped mid-expletive as he spied Inez's mom and toddler, and he held out his arm to bar them from fully entering the kitchen. "Sulfur's so thick in here you'd think we'd entered a Hell hole."

"Jesus H. Christ," Berkfield muttered as his gaze scanned the black pock-marked kitchen cabinets, floor, counter, and appliances.

"I'll just be damned," Marlene's words seethed between her teeth as she entered the kitchen with Inez, both women placing their hands on their hips. Marlene's gaze narrowed as she surveyed the damage. "Up in *my* laboratory . . . where I do my sacred work?"

"Aw, hell to the no," Inez said, unable to curtail her rage as she walked across the smoldering floor and folded her arms over her ample breasts. "A breach in here, *my kitchen*, where I feed my family?"

"What happened?" Shabazz said, putting the safety on his Glock nine-millimeter. His long dreadlocks were static-charged with fury and the muscles in his toned arms, shoulders, and back kneaded like that of a stalking panther's as he walked deeper into the abused room.

Yonnie's and Carlos's eyes met.

"Were they looking for me?" Yonnie asked, making the group turn and stare at him. "'Cause if it's my time, I'll go out there and let them take me rather than bring this bull on the family, yo." He glanced at Valkyrie and lifted his chin. "Bound to happen sooner or later, so, if they're—"

"They'll always be looking for you, man," Carlos said in an angry rumble. "Just like they'll always be looking for me and everybody else on this team. We ain't sacrificing no family to appease the beast—got that, man?"

"Cool. Then, I'll take that as a no, this wasn't personal then," Yonnie said, sniffing the air and retracting his fangs.

"Oh, it was personal," Carlos assured him. "They personally want me, you, and everybody else on this team dead."